GALLIVANTER
EXPEDITION

I0769888

SAVING ANDIAMO

First edition. April 1, 2024.

ISBN: 979-8990210301

Written by Cassie A. H. Moore.

"But the real travelers are those who leave for leaving's sake;

Their hearts are light as balloons, they never diverge from the path of their fate and, without knowing why,

Always say, 'Let's go.'"

Charles Baudelaire

Saving Andiamo
Book One, *The Gallivanter Saga*
By Cassie A. H. Moore

PREFACE

SUMMONING MY STRENGTH, I carved out the last letter.

Wiping my wet hair off my forehead, I stepped back on legs that wobbled. My name, gouged into the stripped trunk of the tree, stared back at me.

At least now they would know who I was if they ever managed to find my body out here.

Slowly, I sank to my knees. My pants were streaked with dirt and sweat, filthy from stumbling through the jungle for hours. Mosquitoes swarmed around my face and neck, merciless as they landed on me. I was too tired to fight them.

I was too tired to stand.

The forest floor was damp, dark with dead leaves and sucking mud. Ants scurried around me as I gazed up at the name I had carved into the bark above my head.

Andiamo Gallivanter, 1923.

My name glistened in the sparse light that trickled down from the canopy high above me. I fought to stay upright, knowing that if I allowed myself to fall facedown on the ground, I might not possess the strength to stand up again.

Futility battered my exhausted brain. *"Give up,"* it whispered. *"There's no one coming to save you."*

I was alone.

This wasn't how I had expected to die. And less than a year out of boarding school. What had I done?

My breathing had become shallow and rapid. I tried licking my lips but I had no saliva. My tongue felt like a thick sock inside my mouth, a choking weight as I panted. My lips themselves had long since cracked open.

Though it was miserably hot out here in the humid jungle air, I had noticed earlier that I'd stopped sweating. My hair still hung stringy against my neck, but perspiration no longer dripped off my face or arms. My body was shutting down.

Narrowing my eyes, I concentrated on the bushes around me. I knew I had to stay alert, but I was battling constant dizziness and lack of energy.

"Just lay down for a moment," my body cried. *"Catch your breath and take a nap, just a few minutes, and you'll feel better."*

I fought the instinct, knowing it meant the end was imminent.

Death would not take Andiamo Gallivanter like this. I would die on my own two feet, straining to survive until the bitter end.

My whole life, the world had told me to settle down. I'd been chided to hold back my instincts, to give up and behave. That wasn't me, though. My adventure wasn't done. It couldn't be done. It might mean that this was my last chapter, but at least my story wouldn't be boring.

In spite of my exhaustion, I smirked. *"No, it certainly hadn't been boring,"* I thought.

Wheezing, I pushed myself up. *"Keep going,"* I told myself. My body couldn't go on much longer, especially in this heat.

I'd been lost for hours now, alone in a remote, unnamed jungle. With every step, my hope wavered.

"My team must be looking for me," I thought to myself. *"Andi, you're so stupid. How could you get yourself in a situation like this? And how on earth could you do this to the people you love? They'll never find you. It's impossible. I have to try to make it out of here and make my way back to the village. That's my only chance."*

I took my time, eyes scanning for animals and water sources. I stopped when I saw a bright green tree frog hopping away from me on a leaf. I peered at it, taking in its bulging eyes. I knew better than to reach out and try to touch it. The deadliest things in the forest were often the most colorful.

I listened as I continued walking, hoping to hear the faint gurgle of the river or the sound of people. I continued to call out in the wilderness, hoping someone might hear me.

"Hello? Is anyone out there? I'm lost. I need help. Bonjour? Aidez-moi!"

Mosquitoes attacked my face. My stomach growled with hunger, and I was still thirsty. But I kept putting one foot in front of the other, hoping each new step would bring me to a clearing where I'd be able to look out and see the fields beyond the jungle.

I yearned to sit down and rest for a moment. My feet ached from all the walking. My arms were sliced open and covered in bits of leaves. Twigs were tangled in my hair.

I hung my head and stared at my feet. *"Just give up and lay down,"* my brain whispered. *"You're never getting out of here."*

Was this even worth it? Was I already a walking dead woman?

I remembered back, unwillingly, to the last time I'd ever seen my father alive. He was so handsome in his uniform, a proud soldier heading off to the Great War. Little did we know he would be dead only a few weeks after he made it into the Western Front in France.

For the first time, I thought now about what must have gone through my father's brain in his final moments. Had he had time to look back on his life, like I was right now? Or had death been instant? Perhaps he hadn't even realized he was dying.

"To be surprised by death must be a blessing," I thought grimly.

I was overwhelmingly aware that I was dying.

Our family never knew exactly how my father had been killed. And now my sister and mother would never know exactly how I had died, either.

"How cruel," I thought to myself. *"How can my mother stand it? Both her husband and her firstborn dying alone, away from her, and she'll never have answers as to how either of their deaths happened?"*

"Don't give up now," a small voice inside of me argued back.

But how could I ever make it out of here?

"Stop it. You will."

Even if I do make it out, by some miracle, what about the rest of my crew? They've surely come into this jungle themselves to rescue me. What if they all died? The blame would be mine.

"You need to fight. It won't be easy. It will never be easy. But you need to save yourself, Andi."

"Let's go," I whispered, forcing myself to take another step. Then another. *"Keep going,"* my brain told my tired body.

I flashed back to the moment I'd introduced myself to Captain Gallivanter six months ago, as a gaggle of beautiful women surrounded him, flirting, asking about the open position on his traveling exploration team.

Not one of those girls would've wanted the job if they'd known that this was what the expedition would actually be like.

The last thought in my exhausted brain was the same question that had been echoing inside my head all day:

How had I ended up here, slowly dying alone in this remote jungle in Africa?

CHAPTER 1

"NO!" THEY SCREAMED, the fury of the group scaring the birds from the treetops.

I craned my neck and watched as the baseball soared overhead, over the creek, and into the thick brush across the banks.

"Joe, you moron!" yelled Roger, his face red with rage. "I told you already, that's my last ball!"

The wooden bat thumped to the ground as Joe squared off. "It's not my fault I hit a home run," he complained. "It's not like I planned for it to go that far!"

"Yeah, well, it's gone now," Roger growled, throwing up his hands in disgust. "My pops is going to kill me. He already said he's not buying me another, if I lose this one."

"We don't have another ball," Johnnie whined. "We'll have to do something else if we don't have a baseball anymore. Can't you go get it?"

"Across that water? Only if you have a death wish," Roger retorted. "The current's too fast. And it's flooded, besides."

The boys continued to bicker as I stood up, unnoticed. I'd seen exactly where the ball had gone. I wasn't afraid of getting wet.

I moved to the riverbank, slipping off my shiny black shoes and stockings and laying them on the shore. Hitching my skirt up with one hand, I waded into the bubbling stream.

The creek that wound past our school was normally shallow, a timid body of water. But the melting spring snow here in upper New York State had swollen the creek to triple its usual size. It threatened to overflow the riverbanks, a fast-moving, gurgling river that hurled branches downstream with impressive force.

Stepping into the cold water caused me to inhale sharply. I pulled my skirt up higher, but it was already getting soaked. The rocks under my bare feet were sharp and slippery. I pushed deeper into the stream, feeling the rush of water sucking at my legs.

The sound of the boys arguing was muffled by the roar of the water. Sticks swirled around me as I waded slowly, deeper, into the creek.

I reached the center, and the water was now up past my knees. It pulled at me with such force that I could barely stay upright.

For the first time, my courage ebbed. *"Should I go back?"* I asked myself, worried. *"What if this is too deep? What if I've gone too far and I get hurt out here?"*

As the water coursed around me and I wavered, finding it difficult to take another step, resolve gripped me. *"No, I can't go back now,"* I told myself grimly. *"I've made it this far already. I can only go forward."*

Shuffling my feet, I strained against the rush of powerful water against my slender body. Within a few more feet, I touched the shallow shore on the other side of the bank. I stumbled out, my entire skirt wet, and felt the rough sand.

Breathing hard, I headed into the woods. The trees above me groaned in the breeze, their canopy darkening the forest floor around me. My bare feet were now caked with dirt and pine needles as they carried me to the bushes where I'd seen the ball land.

I squatted, looking through the brush. There. The baseball was laying right where I knew it would be. I grabbed it, and stood up triumphantly.

With the ball gripped in one hand, I realized I wouldn't be able to hold my skirt up as high as I waded back across the water. My high collar was too tight to shove a baseball under it. I'd never thrown a baseball before, and I wasn't sure if I could clear the stream. Oh, well. I'd have to hold the ball in one hand, and my skirt in the other.

Without hesitation, I waded back into the freezing water.

This time, I knew to use my toes to grab at the slippery rocks underfoot. My wet skirt made it difficult to move. It felt like I was swaddled in blankets, trying to walk.

I took smaller steps, the water again sucking at me with ferocious strength. A little boy the next town over had drowned in the same creek, two springs ago.

As I reached the deepest part of the stream again, a large branch hurtled toward me, rushing along in the fast-moving stream. I winced, attempting to feint out of the way, but instead lost my balance. My right leg slipped out from under me and I lurched forward into water up to my waist.

Instinctively, I held the baseball high up over my head. My feet scrabbled against the slippery riverbed, trying to find a foothold. Now that half my body was submerged in the rushing water, my skirts heavy, it was even more difficult to move.

"Get moving!" I screamed at myself, desperately trying to get my feet under me. *"Let's go!"*

Abruptly, my left foot found a smooth base. I pushed hard and shot to my feet. I didn't bother with modesty now, yanking my soaked dress up so my knickers showed as I forged across the rest of the stream.

When my toes finally felt the soft squish of sand, and then cold mud, I let out the breath I hadn't realized I'd been holding.

I collapsed into the grass, catching my breath, letting the baseball fall to the ground. I frowned as I examined the bottom of my feet. I'd sliced my right foot open and it bled. I inhaled through my nose as I prodded it, seeing the blood ooze even as water continued to drip down my skirt and legs.

I squeezed out my dress and hurried to yank on my stockings and shoes, pulling them gently over the wound in my foot. I tried not to limp as I jogged back to the field, holding the baseball in one hand. I wasn't about to let the boys know that I was in pain.

"Hey!" I yelled as I neared the boys. "I got it!"

They stopped quibbling and turned in confusion. "What do you mean?" Joe stared at me. "Why are you all wet?"

"I went across the creek and got the ball!" I grinned, holding it out.

My classmates continued to stare. "Hold on," Roger said, putting his hand up. His eyebrows knit together, concerned. "You're telling me you went across that water and got the ball that we just hit over there?"

"Yes."

The boys exchanged glances as I stood there, dripping into the grass. I was taller than most of them already. Johnnie whistled. "Didn't a kid drown in that creek a few years ago, around this time of year?"

"Yeah," Roger said, his eyes flickering over my wet clothes.

After a long pause, I held out the baseball. "I think this belongs to you," I said, tossing it to Roger. He caught it, reflexively, but his eyes lingered on me.

"Thanks, Edi," he finally said, giving me a nod. "Boys, let's get back to our game."

He turned, and the rest of the boys gave me a curious look, then followed him back to the pitching mound.

"Hold on," I cried, stepping forward. "Can I play?"

The group froze, glancing at each other. Joe spoke up. "Baseball is for boys. Everyone knows that."

"Yeah, but I want to play," I protested. "I just got the ball back for you. It's only fair that you let me play now."

The boys looked at each other as Roger faced me. "You can play," he replied.

"I can?" My face lit up with excitement.

"Yeah, you can," Roger said. He lifted his hand and pointed, over to the clearing where the girls sat on a picnic blanket in a circle, talking. "You can play with them. Where you belong."

Without another word, the boys turned away and resumed their game.

CHAPTER 2

I TRUDGED HOME FROM school, bitterly reliving my humiliation at not being allowed to play baseball with my classmates after retrieving the ball in such a heroic way.

"Just because I'm a girl," I thought, my thin shoulders tense. *"Who cares if I'm a girl? I can play. I want to play."*

How ironic that I wasn't allowed to play baseball because I was a young woman, yet I was shouldering a man's load at home.

Just a few weeks ago, without my classmates realizing it, my life had turned upside down. My father, a Canadian by birth, had enlisted in the Canadian Expeditionary Force company, which was set to depart across the Atlantic toward France. They were proud to be among the first Canadians to join in the Great War. My father was thrilled to serve the country of his birth.

"Why you?" I'd cried, when he broke the news to us over dinner. "This stupid war isn't even on our soil! Why are you shipping out to help a bunch of strangers?"

"It's not a bunch of strangers, Edith," he sighed. "It's our fellow countrymen. They're struggling against a great evil, and it's my duty to step up and help. If you can do something, you should do it, don't you think?"

"Yes. But Dad, why does it have to be *you*?"

"They need every man to help, hon. It takes all of us."

I pushed my potatoes around on my plate, thinking. "Why not the women, then?"

"What do you mean, the women?"

"You said they need every man to help. But what about the women? Can't we help, too?"

He glanced at my mother. "That's not the way the world works, sweetheart. The girls are needed here, to keep their families running."

"But you just said it takes all of us." I scrunched my face. "If they need every man, couldn't they use women, too?"

He sighed, but my mother made a small sound of reproach. "It's a valid question, George," she insisted, her voice low. "Maybe you can help Edi understand why a woman's place is safe at home. You know, give her some fatherly advice? About her future?"

Even my young ears understood her unspoken message: *encourage your daughter to stay home and become a little more ladylike.*

"Yes," my father rubbed his face. "War is a dirty thing, girls. It's violent. Difficult. You have to march long days, carrying heavy rucksacks and weapons through the wilderness. You're forced to sleep in tents and ditches, sometimes under the rain, with bugs and rats and all sorts of nasty critters running around you."

"That's disgusting!" my little sister, Evelyn, exclaimed.

"It doesn't sound so bad," I shrugged. "You'd get used to it."

"It's not just that," my father continued, meeting my curious eyes. "It's also the same rations day after day, endless chores, using the bathroom out in the woods and fields. It's waking up and not having any idea where you'll be laying down to sleep that night. It's uncertainty. Sorrow. The loss of friends. Pushing your fears aside, facing down the demons in your own mind, and finding the will to survive, against all odds."

Evelyn and I stared at him. Her lower lip began to tremble, but my eyes were bright.

"Don't scare them, George." My mother's tone was tight. "That's enough. Who'd like some pie?"

"Me!" Evelyn howled, hopping to her feet and grabbing her empty plate. She hurried away as my mother rose, throwing a dirty look at my dad, and ducked into the kitchen for dessert.

"I hope you never have to experience anything like that in your life, Edi," my father said, leaning forward. "You'll grow up in a better world, because of the sacrifices that our soldiers are making right now. But let others deal with the war, honey. Living like that is no place for a little lady like you."

"But what if I want to?" I thought silently, looking into his dark eyes. *"What if that's exactly the kind of life I want to experience?"*

In no time, my father had been suited up and shipped out. Evelyn clung to my legs and sobbed as my father kissed us goodbye at the train station. My mother was so pale and quiet that I worried she might never laugh again. Watching the two of them wave goodbye to my father on the train filled me with resolve to take care of them.

With my father serving overseas, I took over the majority of his chores at our small farmhouse. Each day found me splitting wood for the fireplace, taking care of our horse and chickens, and repairing parts of the property.

I daydreamed about my father's time in France while I did chores, a small part of me jealous. He was knee-deep in action and adventure in far-off countries. He'd sailed over the ocean, listened to songs around the campfire, tried exotic foods, met new people.

I was stuck at home, practicing my cursive in my composition books, the only excitement in my routine being foxes getting into the chicken coop.

What I wouldn't give to visit France. How exciting it must be, even in the midst of war.

With sudden guilt, I thought of my family. My mother and Evelyn needed me here, to help. *"Get your head out of the clouds and get back to work,"* I chided myself. *"There's plenty to do around here without you dreaming about Europe."*

I reflected on the future I inevitably faced here, in New York. I'd finish school, marry a boy I'd probably grown up with, and likely settle into a house not far from my own. All my life, I'd be around the same people—the pharmacist, the butcher, the doctor, our priest, my classmates—and we'd grow old, here in Rochester, together.

The thought of that predictable future chilled my little heart.

CHAPTER 3

THE MORNING DAWNED clear and cold, an early snowfall creating a white haze across the fields outside our door.

I'd been up early with my dog, bringing feed to the horse and bundling firewood to stoke the fire. My mother fried eggs for breakfast while Evelyn slept in, tucked in a comforter upstairs.

I stomped my feet at the back porch and slid my boots off, pulling a chair near the fire to warm my feet and hands.

"You want a cup of coffee, sweetie?" my mother asked, as I shimmied out of my jacket and hung it on the back of my chair.

"Sure," I replied. My mother's habit of making coffee for my father hadn't skipped a beat when he left. She merely started giving it to me instead. I leaned down to hug Beau, who nuzzled against my face. His fur was cold. I shivered. Suddenly, Beau's ears perked up and he turned his head toward the front door.

I heard it too. Gravel grinding. Someone was driving up the road to our house in an automobile.

A sudden worry gripped me. Who here in rural Rochester could afford an automobile, besides the doctor? Hardly anyone I knew. Why would one be at our house?

It hit me. It must be an army official, coming with news of my father. We hadn't had a letter from him in weeks. My mother had been increasingly worried about it.

Beau sprinted to the door and my mother looked up from the eggs. Instantly, her face paled. "No," she choked, realizing what the sound of the car meant. She clung to the counter like she was about to keel over. "I'm not ready for this."

"This wasn't how my life was supposed to go," I thought feverishly. *"What if he's dead? He can't be. He was supposed to be here. He was supposed to take care of us. He can't be dead!"*

We listened together as the car parked, Beau whining as the door opened and slammed. Slow steps crunched through the gravel, and heavy boots echoed on the wooden porch. A knock on the door jarred my mother to action.

"Wait here," she whispered.

I couldn't have moved even if I had wanted to.

From my seat in front of the fire, I could hear the murmur of voices. A man, his deep voice sympathetic. My mother sobbing.

"Maybe he's wounded," I thought, holding onto a shred of hope. It hadn't dawned on me yet that the army wouldn't send officers out early on a Sunday morning to inform families about wounded soldiers. I sat motionless in my seat.

After a few minutes, I heard the front door close and the slow, labored steps of my mother as she walked back to the kitchen. Tears streamed down her face as she collapsed in a chair, cradling her head in her hands like a child.

I was petrified. I had never seen my mother so vulnerable. "Mama, what?"

She shook her head, tears flowing faster now. Unclasping her right hand, she dropped a letter on the table. I snatched it up.

"Dear Madam,

It is my painful duty to inform you that a report has this day been received from the War Office notifying the death of Lieutenant John Warren, No. 87497, which occurred in France, on the 10th of November, 1914, and I am to express to you the sympathy and regret of the Army Council at your loss. The cause of death was killed in action. If any articles of private property left by the deceased are found, they will be—"

I stopped reading.

The next thing I remember, I was laying in my bed upstairs, looking at the ceiling. I wasn't sure how I had gotten there, but I had a vague memory of crumpling onto the floor after reading the letter about my father's death.

The days that followed blurred together in a chaotic state of numbness. I alternated between comforting my mother and Evelyn, trying to do chores, and breaking down at the realization that I'd never see my father again.

Simple tasks, like walking into the barn for hay and catching sight of his old boots, or hauling a sled of wood I chopped using his ax, left me on my knees in the snow, sobbing.

Nighttime became a terror for me. As the lamps dimmed and the house settled into silence, my imagination invented every horrific moment of his death.

In my dreams, I saw my father gurgling blood, missing his legs and crawling through the dirt, dying in agony. I saw him gasping, clawing at his gas mask, unable to fend off the deadly mustard gas seeping through the trenches. I relived the horrific moment of impact as a bullet smashed through his skull, shattering bone and brain matter.

Each day, I woke up resolved to work myself to the bone in order to sleep more soundly at night, without being haunted by nightmares.

———◉———

OVER THE NEXT TWO YEARS, I gradually withdrew from everyone, even my mother and Evelyn. I'd rise before dawn and slip out of the house with Beau to take care of the animals, repair the barn, and fill the chinks in the house so the winter wind didn't blow through tiny spots that had cracked open during the summer heat.

Begrudgingly, I went to school but ignored my classmates. My father had entered the war and died before anyone else in our town even felt the implications of the Great War. They couldn't understand.

I'd grown taller, standing a full head higher than most of the boys in my class, but became lean in shouldering the stress and physical exertion of trying to care for our property.

In my loneliness, I invented things to do, to keep my mind from sliding back into pain. When my mother noticed that thick calluses had formed on my hands, she tried to force me to stay inside. While Evelyn helped her cook and knit, I read my father's adventure novels. I'd wait until her attention was on Evelyn to slip back outside to the mindless comfort of activity.

My latest project was stripping the old paint off the fence surrounding our fields. A relic of my grandfather's handiwork when he owned the farm, the fence was warped with age. Its white paint had faded to an ugly, crusted gray.

For weeks, I begged my mother to let me buy a few cans of paint, a wire brush, and some sandpaper so I could strip the paint down to the bare wood and repaint.

"Edi, don't you have something better to do?" my mother asked, shaking flour from her apron.

"Please, mom. It needs to get done."

"Can't you find someone to play with? Or something to go explore? Maybe Ruthie Williams would play with you."

"I don't want to see Ruthie." I shook my head. "It helps to work. Just let me do it."

She shook her head and turned away, but not before I noticed the tears that sprang to her eyes. We were all struggling to get used to a new way of life without my father around. The emotion came in waves. Sometimes we could talk about him, but other times an unexpected memory triggered sorrow.

I sat crosslegged in the fields after school every afternoon, sitting at the base of the fence posts. Blisters formed on my hands as I used the wire brush to scour the gray flakes off, then vigorously scrubbed with the sandpaper until the boards were smooth and bare. At this rate, it would take months to finish the job. Secretly, I was pleased about this. It gave me purpose in a purposeless existence. Grimly, I reveled in the hard work, covered in tiny particles of paint and bits of sandpaper.

That was precisely how my mother found me when she came out to get me for dinner and arrived upon my tired body passed out cold in the field.

"Edith!" she shrieked, waking me. "What happened?"

I opened my eyes, yawning. "I'm fine," I insisted, trying to sit up. "I'm just tired. Sorry, mama."

"Good Lord, Edi," she said, hauling me to my feet and dusting the paint flakes off me. "You can't go on this way, honey. You'll kill yourself."

"I'm fine," I repeated, stretching my arms. I winced as I held them over my head. She noticed.

"I'm not so sure about that," she replied, her forehead puckered with concern. "I haven't been sure how to talk to you about this, Edi, but I've been thinking about it for a while. I think maybe a change of scenery would help you get back on your feet. Get life back to normal. Well, a new normal. What do you think?"

"What do you mean?"

She searched my eyes. "Your aunt and I have been talking. Her neighbor attended a school, and has spoken very highly of the institution. Your aunt thinks it might be just what you need. She's willing to help sponsor your tuition, if you want to go there."

"What kind of school?"

"It's called Académie Sainte Thérèse de Lisieux."

"Where's that?" I frowned, trying to remember all the local schools. The name was foreign to me. "I don't think I've ever heard of it."

"You haven't. It's an all-girls school. A boarding school."

"Boarding school?" I repeated. How would she possibly be able to get along without my help? I kept our house running. She needed me.

"I'm going to level with you, sweetie," my mother said, crossing her thin arms across her chest as the wind gusted across the field, unfurling her brown hair across her shoulders. "You need a release from these heavy responsibilities. You've taken on the load of a fully grown man, and you're just a child. And I realize you don't sleep well anymore. I hear you get up early and go outside, you know."

I exhaled slowly, worried I was in trouble. Her face softened.

"You're stuck in a rut," she said gently. "You need to break out of this routine. You've pulled away from your friends, and from Evelyn, too. We need to find something to help you. And this might just be it."

"Can you get by, though?" I asked. "What would you do without me helping around here?"

My mother sighed. "Edi, I've let you help because *you* needed to help," she said, laying her hand on my arm. "I knew this was your outlet, your way to grieve him. I'll be just fine without you. We received that life insurance payout when your father passed. We'll have plenty to hire on someone to do the occasional odd job around the house. Evelyn and I can take care of the animals."

"Wait," I said, holding up my hands. "Where is this school?"

"Oh, yes," my mother smiled. "It's in France. Lyon, France."

"France?" I blinked. "But it's so far away!"

"I know. That's why I said this might be the perfect thing to break you out of your rut."

"I'm only eleven, though," I protested. "You'd trust me to live all the way across the ocean? In France?"

"I'd trust you to do just about anything, Edi," she answered. "You're strong. And smart. Is it what I pictured for you? For your future? No, not really. But we adjust to the world facing us."

She drew me into her arms, caressing my head. "Part of life is adjusting our sails to catch the wind, wherever we might be. And we don't always know exactly where that wind might take us. But a good sailor leans into the breeze and enjoys the ride as best she can, letting the waves and the wind chart her course."

As she held me, my spirits lifted. Just hearing about the possibility of boarding school in France was already restoring my soul. My face shone with excitement. My mother noticed.

"I think I have my answer," she smiled. "Let's go inside and write that application letter."

CHAPTER 4

MY ENTHUSIASM FOR ACADÉMIE Sainte Thérèse de Lisieux grew in the weeks ahead, as we worked to prepare for the mid-year move to my new school in France.

I was beside myself, dreaming about the chance to make new friends, learning without the worry of keeping our home going, and anticipating new nooks and crannies to explore.

"These girls sound so fancy," Evelyn cooed, staring at the welcome packet that Académie Sainte Thérèse de Lisieux had mailed to our home. "Edi, how are you going to fit in with all these high society girls? It says that the best families in Europe send their young ladies there."

I stooped over her shoulder and looked down at the tiny black and white photograph of a well-dressed group of girls. Their faces were unsmiling, their clothes expensive.

"I'll be fine," I insisted, willing myself to believe it.

"It says they have courses in needlepoint, watercolor, and social etiquette," Evelyn read. She looked up. "You can't do any of that."

"That's why I'll take classes in it."

Despite my eagerness, I was concerned about what my new classmates would think of me. After all the time I'd spent doing manual labor, I wasn't sure I'd fit in with the well-bred girls who attended Académie Sainte Thérèse de Lisieux. Did any of them have calluses on their hands?

My fears were allayed as I sighted the ship that was taking me across the Atlantic Ocean to boarding school. The steamer was departing from Boston and docking in La Rochelle, on the western side of France. It glinted in the bright sunlight when we glimpsed it, stepping off the train that had taken us in the day before I was set to depart.

I'd worked hard to convince my mother that I'd be fine traveling without her, in the company of two other families who were heading to visit their daughters in the same school. It was my first step into independence. My mother had already been concerned about hauling Evelyn out of school for the trip to Boston, and didn't want to make her miss weeks of class to accommodate the roundtrip schedule of the ship. I'd said my goodbyes to Evelyn at home, who was staying with my aunt until my mother returned.

"Plenty of girls travel on ocean liners by themselves, Mama," I had told her with a confidence I was faking. "I'll be fine. Trust me."

"I know, Edi," she frowned. "But you're my little girl. I worry about you."

"What could possibly go wrong?" I asked. "I'll have a room to myself, I'll eat my meals in the dining hall, and I'll sit up on the deck to enjoy the fresh air. It's not like I can go anywhere. I'll be around people the whole time. I'll get to know my new classmates' parents, too."

My mother hugged me, kissing my forehead. My voice muffled against her shirt, I added, "Besides, we both said a little adventure will be good for me."

She laughed. "A little adventure is good for everyone," she agreed.

⸻ ◉ ⸻

WE WERE UP EARLY THE next morning, ready for me to board the steamer. My mother was nervous, and I was, too. I had woken up before dawn, and laid in the hotel bed we were sharing, restless and worried. I heard my mother roll over and felt her small motions as she wiped away silent tears.

I couldn't verbalize it, but I was thankful my mother wasn't letting her own emotions stand in the way of my going away. I was sad, but too excited to let my mother's sorrow hold me back.

"She sure is a plucky mother," I thought to myself. In a short time, she'd lost her husband and was now losing her daughter. I wasn't sure I could handle it as gracefully as she did.

After breakfast, we headed down to the port. The area was crowded with families, businessmen, and sailors bringing trunks and loads of cargo up. It was loud, smelly, and dirty. Over the cawing of the seagulls, I could hear the scrape of barrels being rolled up the plank onto the deck above. Deckhands shouted at each other from different areas of the ship, while families hugged each other below. The ocean lapped at the boardwalk, sending a small mist of water up near where I'd set my suitcase.

I could hardly wait to get on board.

My mother hugged me tight as we looked up at the steamer, holding me for a beat longer than normal. "I love you, Mama," I whispered.

"I love you too, Edith," she whispered back.

I looked up at her, eyes big. I had suddenly been struck by the enormity of the moment. I was traveling halfway across the world. Without her. What if something happened to my mother and I wasn't around? What if this was the last time I ever saw her, or my sister? What if this was all wrong?

My mother sensed my panic and smoothed my hair. In a no-nonsense voice, she said, "Edith, you're a big girl. You're my smart girl. You are *ready* for this."

"What if I'm not?" I choked out, panic rising. "What if this is a mistake?"

"It's not a mistake. The only mistake would be for you to let fear write your story."

I felt like I couldn't breathe. What was I doing? Could I actually do this?

My mother knelt down on the grimy cobblestone street and looked me in the eyes. "Let me get one last good look at you," she said, searching my face. "One last look to remember my brave little adventurer. I love you, sweetie. I will always be your biggest supporter. I'll always be here, cheering you on."

A tear rolled down my cheek, warm and wet. I hugged her, lost for words.

"The world is waiting for you, my darling," she said as she peeled me off her, smiling through her own tears. "It's time for you to go and meet it, Edi."

As I waved goodbye to her from the deck above as the ship pulled away, my spirits lifted. The steamer was massive and promised lots of places to explore and people to talk to. I remained on deck long after most of my fellow travelers had gone to their rooms. The cold wind whipped my hair against my face as I stared out at the ocean, alive with rolling waves.

"This is the same view my father had, just weeks before he died," I thought. How ironic that I was heading to France to start a new life in the same place my father's life had ended.

What my new life might look like, I didn't know. But I was determined to make it better than the one I'd left behind.

CHAPTER 5

THE JOURNEY ACROSS the Atlantic took just under two weeks, and when we finally landed at the port in La Rochelle, I felt like a real adult.

With my classmates' parents—who were decidedly uninterested in me, leaving me to my own amusements—I boarded the train to Académie Sainte Thérèse de Lisieux, located in central France.

I stared out the windows as our train rolled through the countryside dotted with hills and colorful towns. Occasionally, we'd trundle through an area blackened with the remnants of war. Burned barns, overturned army vehicles, and shelled buildings gaped starkly against the surroundings. Every so often, we passed makeshift cemeteries, small wooden crosses atop little mounds of earth.

For the first time, I had a picture of what my father must have seen while he fought here. The beauty of the peaceful countryside was offset by crumbled buildings, bits of lumber and stone and scraps of metal laying in heaps everywhere.

I closed my eyes against that scene I had imagined so many times, blood pouring down out of my father's mouth and dripping onto the dirt where he labored for his last breath. Now that I was so close to where he had been killed in battle, it was more vivid.

I willed myself to instead concentrate on my new school.

Once I arrived at the train station in Lyon, it was a short walk through the town to the massive stone buildings that dominated the surrounding area.

Académie Sainte Thérèse de Lisieux sat at the top of a sprawling estate, neat gravel paths scissoring immaculate green hedges that bordered the three story buildings facing me. A large cathedral, with a tall stone spire soaring high above me, sat next to the biggest building. Leafy old trees filled the landscape, and the back and sides of the school appeared to be surrounded by thick forests with walking trails leading into the darkness. Meadows and fields fluttering with tall grass stretched as far as I could see.

I stood on the expansive lawn in front of a glistening marble fountain, uncertain where to go. My travel companions had already disappeared, talking amongst themselves.

"A place like this must have signs," I thought. I noticed a discreet sign placed strategically at the intersection of the walking paths. It listed the offices, chapel, church, stables, and dormitories in neat hand-lettered script.

I picked up my suitcase—the train porter was coming later with my trunk—and headed toward the offices. Pushing open a metal door, I stepped inside a carpeted reception area. A nun, dressed in severe black habit and veil, looked up from a wooden desk.

"Bonjour, mademoiselle," she said briskly, in French. "May I help you?"

"Yes, ma'am," I faltered, replying in English. "I'm a new student here. My name is Edith Warren."

She frowned slightly, switching to English. "You may call me Sister Marie, not ma'am. You are in France now, not America."

"How did you know I'm from America?"

"Your shoes, your posture, and your accent all tell me you are not from here," she replied. "But most of all, your height."

"My height?"

"Young ladies do not grow this tall in Europe, only in America. It is indecent."

I rolled my eyes involuntarily. "Mademoiselle, Mon Dieu!" the sister snapped, putting her hand over her heart. "How dare you roll your eyes at me!"

"I'm sorry, sister," I hastily apologized. "I forgot my manners. I've had a very long day of travel."

"Apparently. That is why you are here, to learn your manners and become a proper woman. One who holds her tongue and controls her eyeballs. And learns to speak French. We do not speak English here."

The sister had me fill out several forms, then handed me a class schedule, composition books and pencils, my stiff new uniforms, and a stack of school books. She hastily whipped through my schedule and the campus rules before asking if I had any questions, her tone making it clear that I should have none. "We'll telegram your mother to let her know you made it here," she said, standing up.

"This wasn't the adventure I was expecting," I thought.

The nun reluctantly carried my books for me as I hauled my suitcase up three flights of stairs, to the dormitories where the younger girls lived. As we climbed the sweeping staircase, the distant sound of girls laughing filled me with nervous excitement.

We walked down the hallway, through a large common room with a fire dancing in the grate. Ornate oil paintings filled the walls while overstuffed couches crowded the room. Wooden shelves held Bibles and hymnals. I hoped there was something else to read other than these two options.

"Do you have a library here?" I asked.

"Of course," the nun replied. "It's on the ground floor. Next to the dining hall. It is where many of the girls go to study."

I peered out the large floor length windows as we walked. The darkness of the woods was inviting. "Can you go outside to study, too?"

"Outside? To *study*?"

"Yeah."

"*Yes*, mademoiselle. We do not use American slang."

"I'm sorry," I uttered, then tried again. "So can you go study outside, on the grounds?"

She frowned. "I suppose one could, yes. But why would you want to be outside, when you can be inside? Or reading in front of the fire?"

I shrugged. What was the point of explaining my love of the outdoors to someone who would rather stay inside?

The sister led me down a hallway, passing dorm rooms as we walked. Inside, I saw multiple beds, desks, and plain wooden chairs. Books and clothing were scattered around, girls animatedly talking to each other.

We passed a room with two girls talking inside, and the sister slowed. "Which room is it, let me see," she glanced at a slip of paper in her hand. "Yes, this is it," she said, backing up and leading me to the door of the room we had just passed.

I stood in the doorway, uncertain. Both girls stopped talking and looked at me. The shorter one, a plump blonde girl with pink cheeks, smiled instantly. She was dressed like a human china doll, with a delicate lace dress and pearls around her neck.

"Hello, I'm Clara," she said cheerfully, speaking English.

"Hi, I'm Edi," I replied, relieved. "You speak English? Are you American?"

"They try to room people from the same country together," Clara nodded. "I'm from Chicago. Charlotte here is from Savannah."

Behind me, the nun nudged me forward by pressing the pile of books she was carrying into the small of my back. Haltingly, I stepped into the room and set my suitcase down.

The slender girl with dark hair and eyes stood, extended her hand. "Pleased to meet you. I'm Charlotte," she said shyly. "You better get used to speaking French in front of the sisters, even if you speak English to us."

"Nice to meet you both," I said. I turned to thank the nun but she had already pounced on a trio of girls in the hallway, scolding them in rapid-fire French.

I turned back to the room, feeling awkward. Three small beds sat on wooden bed frames, the other girls' trunks sitting at the foot of two of them already. Three identical nightstands and desks filled the rest of our space, two of them covered with books and papers. A large closet dominated one wall, already full of clothing. They were clearly settled in.

"How's the room?" I asked, trying to ignore the realization that I was already the outsider in this space. Charlotte and Clara looked at each other and giggled.

"What?" I asked, feeling like the butt of an untold joke.

"The room? It's terrible," Clara proclaimed as Charlotte continued to giggle.

"Why?"

They looked at each other, amused. "Sit down on something," Clara urged.

I crossed the room and sat down on my bed. The mattress barely moved as I settled my weight onto it. "We're supposed to sleep on that? It's as hard as the floor."

"Wait until you sit in the desk chairs," Charlotte added. "You'll learn the hard way, like we did. Welcome to Académie Sainte Thérèse de Lisieux, where nothing is comfortable."

I smiled, feeling better already. Maybe I'd have friends here, after all.

CHAPTER 6

CHARLOTTE'S PROMISE that Académie Sainte Thérèse de Lisieux wasn't comfortable echoed through my head frequently as I adjusted to life in a new school.

The culture was austere, rambunctious behavior repressed in the entire student body. Whether you were in your dorm room, the dining hall, or the common rooms, the nuns were strict and expected ladylike behavior and speech at all times.

I'd brought the bare minimum from home: several dresses and pairs of shoes, a felt hat, a thick jacket and gloves, a hairbrush and pins. A few other trinkets filled the bottom of my trunk, but among the few indulgences I had brought with me were my mother's Bible and my father's adventure novels.

My roommates, Charlotte and Clara, were kind but glued to each other's hips. We bonded over the mutual loss of all our fathers during the war, speculating that this was why the three of us had been roomed together.

Despite their losses, Clara and Charlotte both came from well-to-do European families, like the rest of my classmates. They were immaculately dressed, proper young ladies who sat up primly in their desks as we worked on our homework at night while I hitched up my skirt and propped my feet out the open window.

I was a good student, naturally inquisitive and curious to learn more in most subjects—save mathematics. I discovered I was a whiz at languages. I quickly became proficient in French, which was spoken by the teachers, as well as German, a fair amount of Spanish, and passable Italian.

My teachers, all Catholic nuns, were strict. I received no compassion from them, even as a new student.

"We have a prestigious reputation, Mademoiselle Warren," I heard from them, dozens of times. "You need to learn to fit in here. We are teaching you the essential skills you need to be a fine lady, to marry a rich man and live a lovely, pleasant life."

"What if I don't want to marry a rich man and have a pleasant life?" I complained to the headmistress once, as she held me back at the end of class and chided me for not sitting with my ankles crossed during the lesson.

She peered at me, nettled. "Every girl wants to marry a rich man and know her future is secure," she replied. "It's what society expects. What your family wants. What every little girl dreams about."

"But you didn't," I retorted.

She frowned at me, the scowl deepening the lines already etched in her forehead and around her mouth. "Do not be impertinent, Edith. It is unbecoming."

The biggest challenge I faced was my social life. As a new student, transferring in halfway through the year, I was pushed to the outside of girls' circles immediately. My roommates were already fast friends, and I was the odd one out. As much as I tried, I couldn't seem to penetrate any of the friend groups that had already been established by the time I arrived.

Clara occasionally took pity on me, inviting me to her lunch table and attempting to find topics of conversation our whole table could discuss. In just a few months, I'd experienced a lifetime's worth of conversations about the state of the weather.

"Good morning," I'd say to a quiet, well-behaved classmate.

"Good morning," she'd politely reply back. Typically, this came with a pointed look at my too-tall frame. Often, she'd exchange a withering glance with the girls next to her as they humored me.

"Some weather we're having today, isn't it?" I'd say, hoping she'd engage.

"Oh yes, it's very chilly today," she'd respond.

At that point, I lost track of what else I should say to merit a response. I'd give up, retreat into my own imagination, or a book, and ignore everyone around me. It was a routine that I already knew from home.

"Mademoiselle," our headmistress, the Madame, would say whenever she encountered me sitting alone. "You must *try* to fit in with the young ladies."

Within a few weeks, it was already clear that I didn't really fit in with anyone at Académie Sainte Thérèse de Lisieux.

To fill my time and escape from Madame's frown, I shifted my attention to nature, spending more time outdoors. This further isolated me from the well-bred ladies in our school, who had been raised to enjoy a bowl of fresh-cut flowers inside a vase rather than in a meadow.

Sometimes I'd run out to the front lawn in between classes, unlace my boots and yank off my stockings, tickling my feet with the thick grass. I'd shuffle through the manicured green hedges, balancing a stack of books under one arm with my boots flung over my shoulders. With the birds chirping overhead and the blue sky open above me, I felt free.

On more than one occasion, I lost track of time and tumbled headlong into the classroom several minutes late.

"You can't do this, Edi!" Clara would whisper frantically, as I panted and discreetly attempted to lace up my boots without a nun noticing. "You're going to get yourself in trouble! They hate when girls are improper!"

"Mademoiselle Warren," the sister would call, pulling open her drawer. With a pitying glance, Clara would stick out her lip as the sister would turn to reach for the wooden ruler on her desk and sharply rap my knuckles for my tardiness.

"Edith, you are no lady," the sisters proclaimed as they disciplined me.

As I walked away from the nuns' desks, rubbing the sting from my knuckles, the same thought continued to come to mind.

"You're right, sisters," I thought. *"I'm no lady. I don't know what I am, but I know I don't want to be that."*

CHAPTER 7

WITHOUT FRIENDS, I was left to read or wander the woods by myself in my copious spare time. After wandering by the school stables, hidden at the back of the campus, I impulsively decided to see if I could take riding lessons.

One crisp morning, I nicked an apple from the breakfast table, hiding it under my armpit as the nuns droned through their morning matins. We were required to go to the drafty cathedral every morning and evening for prayers.

I knelt on the cold floor, listening to their Latin recitations, daydreaming about taking a horse out of the barn and riding off into the countryside, never to return.

While Madame and the other girls headed to the last classes of the day, I detoured to the restroom. I shoved my books under the farthest stall from the door, then climbed up into the large stone arch that contained a thick glass window. I braced myself against the cold, rough rock, and gently pushed the window panel with one foot.

It creaked open and I scampered out.

"I'm so glad I'm not a lady," I breathed as I ran through the back hedges.

A lady wouldn't run. A lady wouldn't kick through a window to sneak out of the building. A lady wouldn't cut class. And most of all, a lady wouldn't get to have any fun.

My long legs carried me toward the old wooden stables as the scent of hay filled my lungs. I cleared the last tall column of greenery and rounded a blind corner.

I collided into someone.

The apple in my hand went flying and thumped hard into the ground as I awkwardly rolled, legs and limbs flying in a tangle through the grass. I sat up, not as dazed as I should have been after the hard collision, to see a teenage boy wobbling to his feet next to me.

"Holy cats!" he shouted in French, scrambling to help me up. "Mademoiselle, I am so very sorry!"

I rolled to my knees, straightening my skirt. To cover my embarrassment, I blurted out the first thing that came to my mind. "Is it bruised?"

The young man stared at my arms, confused. "I don't think so," he said, looking me over for injuries.

"No," I replied, feeling idiotic. "I meant the apple. Is the apple bruised?"

"Apple?"

Well, this couldn't get any worse, could it? I had a way with people. This was precisely why I didn't have friends. Instead of explaining, I crawled around on my knees, searching for the fallen apple. I discovered it, nestled in a bed of clover just out of reach. I grabbed it and held it up.

"Still looks good enough for horses?" I said, struggling to my feet.

"They'll eat just about anything," the boy grinned, standing up next to me. His French accent was unmistakable but he had switched to English. I was surprised at his fluency. "You're sure you're okay?"

"I'm fine," I said, dusting off my skirt. I was covered in bits of grass and clover. Holding out my hand, I offered it to the stranger. "I'm Edi Warren, by the way. You deserve to know who just about killed you."

"I'm Arnau Deschamps," he said, shaking my hand. He was tall and slender, with olive skin. Tiny freckles dusted his forehead and arms. Dark eyebrows emphasized his deep brown eyes, which smiled at me. He had riotous dark curls that caught in the breeze and lifted as the wind blew.

"Do you work here?"

"Oui, mademoiselle. I am a stablehand."

"I...I was headed there," I admitted, noticing Arnau's clothes. He wore simple, lightweight homespun clothes and leather riding boots, with a leather whip tucked into his back pocket. "Are you a local?"

"Yes," he said. "My family lives in the village. Where I go to school. My older brother worked here before me, but he got married a few years ago. The Madame liked him, and knew he was a hard worker. When I asked her about a job, she was happy to let another Deschamps boy work here in the stables."

While we chatted, Arnau and I had walked toward the barn. He motioned me inside, waving me to a paddock. "Come meet him. This one is Henri. My old boy. He's my favorite."

I reached up to touch his velvety nose. Henri's nostrils flickered. He stared at me, snorting warm air in a whoosh.

"He likes you," Arnau remarked, patting his neck.

"Only because he knows about this apple," I laughed, holding it out to him. Henri nickered in appreciation, crunching the apple with his big teeth. Drool and juice streamed down from his chin.

"Henri has a good read on people," Arnau smiled at me. "If he says he likes you, I like you, too."

"What exactly did Henri say?" I grinned back. Arnau's openness put me at ease. "Did he say he likes strange girls who bribe him with fruit?"

"That's exactly what he said," Arnau laughed, motioning me to another stall. "So, Edi, do you ride?"

I breathed in the tangy scent of warm horses, manure, hay, and dust. "I do, a little bit. I have a horse at home, but he's pretty old so he doesn't move a whole lot. I'd love to learn how to ride better. Do you know anyone who gives lessons?"

"I know a great teacher. He's serious. An expert. Many years of experience. And he's willing to give lessons. I can introduce you, if you want?"

"Oh, yes," I responded, a bit deflated. I'd been fishing to see if Arnau might be willing to teach me. But at least I'd see him at the stables while I had lessons with this other man.

Arnau dusted his hand off and offered it to me. "Hello, nice to meet you. I'm Arnau. I'll be your riding instructor, mademoiselle."

"You? But...really? How much will it cost?"

He tilted his chin. "Not much. Just agree to stop tackling me and I won't charge."

"I suppose I can agree to that," I laughed. "You better be a good teacher."

Arnau ushered me around the stables the rest of that first afternoon, introducing me to the horses and telling me about each of their personalities. He showed me where to fill their feed buckets and water troughs. Next, we went over how to saddle them up, check their hooves and teeth, and guide them around the paddock. I had a good working knowledge already, from life with my own horse back home. He was impressed.

"We can start riding lessons tomorrow since you already know the basics," Arnau glanced at me. "After school? Will that work? I get out in the afternoon and walk over from my home around the same time you're done with classes here, I think."

"It's a date," I grinned. "Tomorrow, the real fun begins. I just hope you're ready to put up with me every afternoon, from here on out."

"Oh, I don't think that'll be a problem," he replied lightly, his neck pink.

As we walked around the stalls, Arnau mused about which horse to put me on.

"You need someone who's patient," he said, thinking aloud. "You're clearly strong-willed, but you're uncertain about your riding abilities. Who can we give you?"

I stopped in front of a copper colored horse, who stared at me through long lashes. "What about this one?" I asked.

"Flic?" He reached out and stroked her neck. "She'd be good. I call her Flic. You know, the policeman—a copper. Because of her color. Yes, she might be the one for you."

That first gallop around the paddock with Flic was the beginning of Arnau and I becoming best friends. Bonding over a mutual love of horses and fondness of being outside in any weather, we spent nearly every afternoon together, rain or shine.

Arnau and I spent hours side-by-side in the stables, brushing the horses down, hauling tubs of water and buckets of oats and mucking the stalls with long metal rakes. We walked the horses around the corrals, often hopping on to trot them through the wooded paths that surrounded the school. Hours of outdoor activity resulted in me constantly running to evening mass with bits of hay in my hair, a flush from the cold still on my cheeks.

Sometimes it seemed Arnau, who despite his good looks was shy and reserved, understood me better than anyone else.

"Why don't you stay inside with the girls more often?" he asked me one afternoon, as we polished saddles together.

"I don't know what we'd possibly talk about."

"Horses?"

"No. The only girls who care about horses are the rich ones who had servants take care of them back home in their castles. So they don't even really know their horses."

"The girls came from castles? All of them?"

"Probably. They all act like it, anyway," I stood up, thrust my head in the air, and peered down my nose as I paced around, imitating my classmates. "Good day, sir, I am a princess displaced in this deplorable school, just waiting for my prince to come along and take me back to his castle, where I'll live happily ever after."

Arnau smiled. "Do you know why you don't get along with them?"

I sat down, causing bits of hay to flutter all over both of us. Truth be told, I wasn't all that interested to know why I stuck out like a sore thumb. It seemed like it'd been my reality as long as I could remember, even before I came to boarding school. "It doesn't matter."

"If it bothers you, it does."

"I don't care." I pulled the heavy saddle in front of me again. Did I care? Maybe a little. But I wasn't about to make myself vulnerable in front of him.

"What makes you different is the same thing that makes you special," Arnau forged ahead anyway. "Sure, the other girls may end up with their prince charming, but you'll end up with a life of adventure. You'll page through those adventures of your life someday when you're old and gray, and never have to wonder if you settled. Who else can say that? Will any of those other girls be able to say that?"

"I don't know," I smoothed my hand over the saddle pom. "Maybe my life will be predictable after all. Maybe I'm cursed to long for freedom the rest of my life, to want to run and crash recklessly through the woods and fields, but be cooped up in a stall most of the time, like Flic."

For a few moments, we polished in silence. Then Arnau paused and looked at me. "You've dared to be different already, Edi. That won't be your life."

"You don't know that."

"You're here in the stables right now instead of inside the dorms, right? Be you. There's nothing wrong with wanting to be real. It's not a crime to want to run free."

I looked down, hiding my eyes. In truth, I wasn't sure what I was doing. Or who I was. Or where I was going, or why I couldn't just be content while everyone else seemed to be doing just fine. Maybe I'd never actually be happy. Arnau could read me better than I realized to observe these things about me.

"Ma chère amie," he said softly, reaching his hand toward me. "My dear friend."

I tensed up. What was he doing?

A sudden thought about what it would be like to kiss him flitted through my mind. I pushed it away. *"You're as tall as him. You can't like a boy who stands shorter than you when you're in boots. How could he ever like you, anyway? You're a mess!"*

Arnau leaned over me, his arm brushing lightly over my arms. I involuntarily blushed. He flashed me a smile, grabbing the saddle brush on the other side of me.

"Besides, you could always talk about me with your classmates up there," he said carelessly, his grin wide. "I bet they say I'm cute, right?"

CHAPTER 8

AS THE YEAR PROGRESSED, I slowly found my stride.

I still didn't have many friends, but Arnau and the occasional conversation with Clara and Charlotte were enough for me. My daily routine became heading straight from class to the stables, and spending all day on Saturday at the barn. Arnau even built me a shelf over the horse tack to stow my books.

Classes continued most of the year, except for holidays and a brief summer break. Arnau and his family disappeared to the coast to visit relatives, and my daily visits to the barn continued but shortened.

It wasn't quite the same being at the barn without Arnau.

It wasn't practical for most American students to sail home for breaks, so our campus reduced to a small number who spent long summer days engaged in various carefree pursuits—swimming, dancing to the radio, playing tennis, and sketching wildflowers in the woods. Girls who didn't usually spend much time together united, forsaking old alliances for just a few weeks. I was invited in, temporarily, on the occasional trip into town.

Lyon was a quaint town with a beautiful main plaza that I loved visiting. I would lag behind the others who wandered into the small storefronts, gazing at the flowerpots, and whistle to myself.

Sometimes, I treated myself to a small café crème from a street vendor, then strolled through the winding streets and looked up at the ornate cathedrals and centuries-old buildings.

I chatted with the ladies at the pastry shop as I waited for them to make me a hot waffle drizzled with sweet chocolate sauce.

"Voilà la grande Américaine!" they'd exclaim when they saw me come in. "The giant American is here!"

I laughed it off, breathing in the warm, sugar-filled air. I could handle any amount of teasing, as long as they gave me an extra spoonful of chocolate on top of my waffle. They always did.

Those carefree days wandering through the ancient stone buildings, gazing up at lacy spires and worn medieval rooftops, watching the pigeons flutter in the stiff breeze, were some of the moments where I felt most at peace.

Here I was just a stranger, passing through crowds of locals who bartered in the street markets, listening to the hum of the city, rather than a fish out of water who didn't quite fit in with everyone else at school.

As I walked through the city, alone, I couldn't escape the constant questions that filled my mind.

"Is this my future? Will I wander the streets, by myself, in search of something I can't quite discern?" I thought. *"Will I only ever have myself, and an endless feeling of discontent, no matter what I do?"*

CHAPTER 9

THE NEXT FEW YEARS of boarding school unfolded, the rhythm of classes and mass and time at the barn blurred together.

The nuns kept us busy with schoolwork, on top of a growing array of ladylike activities that came easily to my genteel classmates. Most had grown up in high society, with lessons in curtsying and addressing royalty, drawing and watercolors, embroidery, and table manners already a part of their world.

Inwardly, I chafed when I imagined a future where the knowledge of using a full set of silverware came in handy.

"Salad fork here, dessert spoon there, then fish fork over here," Madame droned as we practiced setting an immaculate banquet table.

"Madame, couldn't you leave out the fish fork?" I asked, deliberately bating her ire.

"Heavens, why would you do that?"

"Well, I count seven different utensils here," I pointed to the table. "On top of that, we're setting three different goblets at each place setting."

"What exactly is your point?"

"Just that I think we could probably save the kitchen staff a lot of washing if we used the same fork for our salad, fish, and entrees instead of three different utensils. Plus, it would save the hostesses some time setting out a bunch of useless forks."

I received a sharp rap across the knee from Madame's ever-present walking cane.

"You must cultivate your gentle manners, my girls," urged Madame, ignoring my grimace. "If you do not already have a gentle manner, you must *create* one."

One such day, after a disappointing afternoon spent inside the atrium doing a step-by-step tiny watercolor scene of flowers, I felt like I might lose my mind. Clara sat next to me during class, and had offered unsolicited advice through the entire mindless session.

"Just a little lighter with the brush here," she leaned over my easel. "Be gentle with it, it's a delicate scene."

I was tired of everything being so delicate all the time. I was decidedly *not* delicate.

As soon as I could run back to my room and throw my art brushes into the closet and change outfits, I was practically running down to the stables. Arnau would be waiting for me.

Stepping outside, I breathed in the cool air and bent down to pick up a leaf that skidded across my feet. I crunched it in my fist and opened my hand, letting the wind catch the particles and scatter them through the air. I felt alive.

Strolling along down to the stables, I glimpsed Arnau pulling on his jacket against the cold. He waved when he saw me. "Andiamo!"

"Andiamo?" I repeated, playfully slugging him. I was aware that Madame would whack me again if she saw how forward I was being with a young man. "What's that supposed to mean? Are you calling me something dirty?"

"No, stupid," he grinned. He laughed and ducked under my arm to miss the second hit. "It's Italian."

"What's it mean?"

Arnau squeezed my arm. *"He's so very French,"* I thought, wrinkling my nose at his constant affection. He was always patting my arm and grabbing my hands.

"Wait here," he grinned. "I got you something. Let me go grab it."

I hugged my arms to my chest, feeling awkward. Arnau's family didn't have much money. He never complained, but all of the boys in his family had jobs and worked after school in order to help provide. He worked here, at the Académie Sainte Thérèse de Lisieux stables, often propping his lesson books up in the barn to look at while he raked the paddocks or filled troughs. His little brother would take over his job when he aged out someday.

Surely Arnau hadn't purchased something for me? I felt guilty at the thought. Any amount of money spent would be a sacrifice.

"It'll be the best gift you ever get," he teased as he rummaged through his bag. He straightened, hiding something under his jacket.

"Is it a dog? I would love an excuse to leave my room more often. Especially at night. Clara snores something fierce—"

He laughed. "It's not a dog." Advancing toward me, he stopped short. "Let's do this properly, Edi. Close your eyes."

"No."

"Be a good girl. Isn't that what you're learning at this fancy school?"

"Stop. Just show me already."

"No," he insisted. "Close your eyes."

"I face life with my eyes open."

"Edi. What a line."

"Stop playing games! Just give it to me already."

Arnau pulled a large book out of his jacket with a flourish, like a magician producing a rabbit from a hat. "Voila!" he exclaimed.

I snatched it out of his hands. "'Exploring The World, a Geographic and Cultural Guide'? What is this?"

"It's for you. I've looked at it in the window of the bookstore in town, every day for months, thinking of you. It's just what you need."

"A geography book?"

He grabbed it back. "Let me show you. Hold on."

I watched him, a curl of dark hair falling across his forehead. His eyes flitted across the words, until he found what he was looking for and smiled. He handed it back, cracked open to a back page with a lengthy chart. "Read."

"You're bossy today."

Arnau let out a roar of mock rage. "Mon Dieu! I've waited to give this to you for months, just read the book! Zut!"

"Jeesh. Okay."

My eyes followed his finger to a paragraph entitled, "Helpful Phrases In All Languages."

"What—"

"Read. Here."

I followed where he pointed. "*Andiamo, verb. Italian for 'let's go!' or 'here we go!'*"

I looked up, confused. "I don't understand. Am I missing something?"

"Edi, you're so dense sometimes," Arnau groaned. "This is why we're friends, I guess."

"Yeah, says the guy who bought me a book about strange words I'll never use?"

As soon as the words left my mouth I flushed, feeling bad. He'd just told me he spent months thinking of buying this book for me. No doubt he'd spent just as many months saving up the money to purchase it. And I was ungrateful? I swallowed hard. Finishing school hadn't taught me to avoid putting my foot in my mouth as often as I did.

Arnau ignored my outburst and poked me in the side, making me squirm. "Don't you see? This word describes you perfectly."

"What word?"

"Andiamo!"

My eyebrows knit together and I stared at him. "I'm sorry, I still don't get it."

"*Andiamo*. It's a word of action and energy. A word that wastes no time, and compels you to move. It drives you forward. You're just like this word, Edi. You're a girl of action and adventure. You push on. Always going. Moving relentlessly."

As Arnau beamed at me, I suddenly felt uncomfortable. He had hit the nail on the head—it did sound like me. Sometimes I wondered if he knew me better than I even knew myself.

"*What's wrong with you? Can't you just be happy in this moment?*" my brain said, as I stared back at Arnau, uncertain how to respond.

"Besides, it's Italian," Arnau added. "It's exotic. You know, the language of love and all."

"Huh," I replied. Rattling around my head was the emphasis he seemed to put on the word "love" just now. Was it my imagination?

"Andiamo," he repeated slowly. In his French accent, it sounded exotic.

"Andiamo," I said, pushing down my discomfort. A slow smile spread across my face. I liked it.

"I'm calling you that from now on. Andiamo. Andi, for short. *My* Andi."

"Why?"

"Because it fits you so much more than plain old Edi," he grinned. "Now, be a good girl and go read your book. Figure out where in the world you're going to be headed next, my Andiamo."

CHAPTER 10

FROM THAT MOMENT ON, if I wasn't outside with Arnau and the horses, my nose was stuck in that geography book.

I devoured it, spending late hours in the cramped and dark school library, systematically pulling out other books to learn about far-off countries all over the world. I recited foreign words I gleaned from this book, with no idea if I was pronouncing them correctly. In the cool, musty quiet of this big room, stuffed with leather-bound books and the stillness of the outside muffled through the velvet drapes covering the windows, I traveled the world—in my imagination.

Bedtime found me rereading my father's adventure novels, dug out from the bottom of my trunk. As I held them, remembering my father had loved these books, I felt close to him. I absorbed every detail, imagining myself a daring heroine alongside the men starring in each gripping tale.

I'd never admit it to anyone, but I felt more in common with those adventurers than a single person I knew at school. Even Arnau, who knew me better than anyone else.

From then on, Arnau referred to me exclusively as "his Andiamo." I shared tidbits of my geographic research with him. We talked about different places, what it would be like to see them, eat their foods, and hear people speak their languages in their home countries.

"Wouldn't you just love to go to these places?" I sighed, staring up from a photograph of the ruins of ancient Athens.

He shook his head. "Not really."

"Why not? I do. More than anything."

"This is my home. Why would I want to go anywhere else? It's enough to read about it and imagine. Travel's too much work."

"I don't want to just imagine. I want to go see it with my own two eyes," I replied, wistful.

"But aren't you happy here?" Arnau glanced at me out of the corner of his eyes.

"I am," I replied quickly, but an unconscious sigh escaped me. He noticed.

"You don't like France?" he paused, the bucket of oats in his hands. "You live here. You never even go back to New York. I thought—I don't know."

"What?"

He turned away from me, the back of his neck flushed. "I thought maybe you considered France your home now. That maybe you wanted to travel to a few places, but then come back here. Back to what you know."

I bit my lip. "I don't know where home is anymore," I confessed. "It's been so long since I've been to the States and—I never really felt right there. Like somehow, I didn't belong. And I'm used to school. But between the girls and the nuns, I just don't feel like I have anyone here."

"But you have me," Arnau replied softly, his back to me.

"I do."

"Is that not enough?"

"What do you mean?"

"Forget it." He busied himself with scooping more oats, his posture tense. "I'm just making conversation."

"Why are you so concerned about where I belong?"

"I'm not."

"It seems like it. Come on, Arnau. How can I answer this? I don't belong anywhere. Home is where you lay your head, I guess."

"So France *is* your home, then?"

"I guess," I shrugged, feeling exasperated. What was he getting at? Why did he care?

As Arnau scooped oats into the bucket, I stared at his broad back. His dark curls were long and his shoulders were strong. His olive complexion was dark, the result of all our shared hours in the sunshine. He was handsome, there was no doubt about it.

But Arnau was my best friend. "*And a friend is not your future,*" I told myself.

I resolved to suggest that we ride the horses more often and stay away from conversations like this one. It'd only get us both in trouble.

———— ◉ ————

RIDING BECAME MY ESCAPE, the only place I felt comfortable in my own skin.

Feeling the wind tangle my hair and blast against my face as we galloped through the open fields, or listening to the birds as we cantered slowly through the solemn forest was a healing balm for my restless soul.

It was a respite, the one place I could calm the thoughts that constantly tumbled through my head.

Increasingly, Arnau's words and friendly caresses confused me. It used to be safe to spend long hours in the barn together, brushing up against each other as we tended to the horses. Now it was safer to ride the horses, putting separation between us.

Arnau and I often raced our horses over the wide fields, yelling jokes and making fun of each other. We'd race at breakneck speed, then slow down to let the horses graze on clover, feeling the warm sunlight drench our skin. Sometimes he was busy cleaning the stables, and I trotted Flic out into the woods and trails on my own.

I felt perfectly at ease with the horses—more so than I did with the humans around me.

The horses didn't judge my height, or my messy mane of hair, or my too-wide mouth.

They didn't call me a freak because I preferred walking through the woods to sitting inside, gossiping with the other girls.

They weren't distant from me when my mind wandered, taking me to far-off places all over the world.

"Slow down!" Arnau laughed, as I raced him through the fields. "Let's let them graze so we can chat!"

"No," I replied, urging Flic faster. Instinctively, I avoided the conversation I wasn't sure I ever wanted to have with Arnau.

Now that I was seventeen, I was lanky and tall. I towered over everyone at my school, including the large French gardener who exclaimed, "Mon Dieu!" every time he glimpsed me. Years of working daily in the stables had chiseled my lean arms. I was stronger than I looked.

"Andiamo, you're an exceptional horsewoman," Arnau admitted one day, as we trotted back to the stables, our horses' mouths frothy from a hard run through the woods. "I don't think I've ever see anyone as good as you on a horse. Besides me, of course."

"Well, I guess your work with me is done, then," I teased.

"I hope not," he muttered under his breath. I heard him, and bolted off ahead of him, pretending I hadn't.

The nighttime hours between dinner and bedtime proved to be the most fruitful hours for misbehavior in our school. All the nuns retired to their own rooms, save Sister Fosette, who padded heavily through the halls only once, to give us the call for lights out. Girls gossiped, had fights, snuck out and hitchhiked into town to go to the movies, or shared forbidden cigarettes in these few hours of freedom.

Provided you were quiet enough to not awaken Sister Fosette, who usually snoozed in her rocking chair at the far end of the dormitories, you could get away with most anything.

Just not in my case.

That Tuesday evening unfolded like any other: long, dull, and filled with hours of tedium as I wrote an assigned essay. I sat in the common room, a pile of library books next to me, ink still wet on my essay. I was sour already, having only spent a short time outside at the stables that afternoon because of a rainstorm.

The rain pelted the windows as the girls inside lounged in various states of activity.

From across the room, I saw Clara come in with her own pile of books. I waved, signaling her over. We had the same essay assignment, and Clara was a faster reader than I was. Perhaps she'd give me some ideas.

As Clara headed toward me, a voice rang out loudly.

"Oh, Clara, what a cute dress you're wearing!"

Clara turned, and I followed her gaze to see an upperclassman, Emile, sitting in a chair in the corner.

Inwardly, I cringed. The whole school knew to avoid Emile, who hailed from one of the richest families in Europe and mercilessly bullied everyone in her path. A few weeks ago, she'd gone after a second-year student with acne across her cheeks. The little second-year had bawled as Emile asked her in front of a crowd if she had a disease or if it was just an awful diet that made her so ugly.

"Thanks, Emile," Clara replied, blushing as she tried to scoot through the room unnoticed. Clara was plump and despised being the center of attention, especially if it had to do with her body.

"It's darling, really," Emile cooed, unexpectedly standing and catching Clara by the shoulders. Clara froze as Emile held her at arm's length, studying her with a calculated coldness. The entire room watched.

"I mean, look at her, ladies!" Emile's voice rose as she forcefully spun Clara around. Clara struggled to hold onto her books. "Everyone, look at this dress!"

I stood up, unconsciously, as Emile started to smirk.

"I mean, just look at how this dress hides her fat, ugly hips," Emile continued, loudly. She grabbed the edge of Clara's skirt and lifted it up. Clara's underwear flashed, her chubby thighs on clear display.

"Emile!" I roared, surprised by the anger in my voice.

The room fell silent as several girls snickered. Clara was humiliated, her face bright red. The two books on top of her pile slipped to the floor, unnoticed.

"Shut up, Edith," spat Emile, still holding the skirt up. "I'm complimenting Clara. Look how well she hides that flabby jelly belly and those disgusting little legs."

I strode across the room and yanked Clara's dress out of Emile's grasp. "Leave her alone, Emile. You're nothing but a damn bully."

Eyes swimming with tears, Clara clung to my waist like a drowning child. Emile shrugged and bent over to pick up one of Clara's dropped books.

"Sorry, Clara," she said as she held it out. Clara refused to let go of my waist.

"Clara, I'm sorry," Emile purred, undeterred. "Don't you want to know what I'm sorry for?"

Clara shook her head as a tear slipped out and trailed down her crimson face. Emile took a step toward us and held the book up.

Suddenly, she reached out with her other hand and slapped Clara across the face. We both flinched in shock. The faint outline of Emile's hand appeared on Clara's pink cheek.

"*I'm sorry* you're so ugly that I have to slap some sense into you," Emile jeered. "What a waste of a person you are. You should thank me for knocking something into that fat brain of yours. At least if you had a brain, you might have one thing going for you in life."

I clawed Clara's hands off my waist as she started to cry in earnest. "Emile, you coward!" I shouted. "You pick on everyone around you, even though they've done nothing to you. Leave her alone."

Emile lifted her gaze to me, her face ugly. "Go to hell, Edith," she hissed. "Join your dead daddy there."

Without thinking, I swung my fist at her face. She squealed as I connected hard with her mouth. My hand came away wet with blood.

I had split Emile's lip open. Blood and saliva dribbled down her face and neck and she screamed, rushing down the hall to Sister Fosette.

"Edi, no," Clara whispered, both hands over her mouth. "She's going to tell Madame! You shouldn't have!"

All the years of work in the stables had made me stronger than I realized. Strong enough to hurt someone without trying. I knew, even then as the heat of battle ebbed away and Clara's tears dried, that I had gotten myself into serious trouble.

But inwardly, I was fiercely proud.

"I'm tired of trying to fit in," I thought to myself, grimly resolved. *"If I'm going to be different, darn it, I'm going to own it. I'm not going to back down anymore. Not to Emile, not to the rest of these girls, and not to the rest of the world."*

CHAPTER 11

IT WAS STILL DARK OUTSIDE when Sister Fosette tugged my sheets.

"Wake up, mademoiselle," she whispered. "Madame wants to meet with you first thing this morning."

I sat up. My night had been largely sleepless. I knew this was coming.

Carefully, I selected my most demure dress and pinned a brooch to my collar. I combed my hair and washed my face, then pulled on my only pair of stockings without runs and laced up my boots.

As I walked down the silent halls, the cavernous granite floors echoed with my footsteps. *"All alone,"* they seemed to say with every footfall. *"You're all alone on this one. This is how it'll always be, Edi. You'll always be all alone."*

I reached Madame's office. A fire burned in the hearth and cast long shadows across the walls. Madame had heard me coming, and watched me silently as I stood in the doorway, hands clasped in front of me. With a wave, she motioned me forward to sit. I perched on the chair in front of her desk.

As I adjusted myself, my long legs collided against her desk. She cringed. I tried to crumple my legs up under my chair and hunch down to fit in the seat. Immediately, I felt a sharp pain in my back.

"Sit up like a lady, Mademoiselle Warren," Madame frowned.

I bolted upright. My knees thudded again against the desk. I twisted sideways, splaying my legs out but sitting erect.

"Heavens above, Edith, push the chair back so you can sit up properly," groaned Madame.

I complied. Madame studied me.

"Mademoiselle, this is perhaps the first time I've seen you without the running commentary of your ridiculous opinions," she said briskly.

I looked down at my hands in my lap and responded in perfect French. "I'm trying to be ladylike, Madame."

"Oh, I think we both can agree that ship sailed long ago."

"What?"

"You don't care about being ladylike, do you?"

I felt anger stirring within me, but forced myself to be meek. "I'm sorry, Madame, I do care. I apologize for seeming like I don't."

Madame peered at me over her bifocals, the light from the fire reflecting in her lenses. She took a sip of tea. "I assume you know why you are here?"

I nodded.

Madame frowned. "According to Sister Aline, Emile spent the night in the infirmary. Her lip is split wide open and was bleeding for quite some time last night. She spent the evening icing her face to bring the swelling down."

Anger prickled me again. Emile had spent the last several years terrorizing nearly every girl at our school, even the girls she called her friends. She had gotten what she deserved. And I didn't feel guilty about it one bit. But in front of Madame, I needed to appear contrite and perplexed.

"Madame, I am so sorry," I exclaimed, hoping my face looked remorseful. "I truly did not mean to hurt Emile last night. It was a small disagreement. I hope I can patch things up with her."

Madame set her teacup down in the porcelain saucer with a soft clink. She leaned back. "Miss Warren, I give you permission to be frank. What really happened?"

I knew better than to be candid. When women tell you to be frank, they rarely mean it. And they always find a way to make you pay for your honesty later.

"I didn't mean to hurt her," I repeated. "I—things got out of hand. I hope I can make amends."

Madame got to her feet, her dark skirts brushing against the marble floor. "Mademoiselle Warren, do you think I am stupid?"

"No, Madame."

"Tell me the truth. Everything that happened."

I told her the whole story, plainly and truthfully. As I spoke, Madame paced behind her desk. Hands behind her back, she glanced at me. "Emile is a bully, yes?"

"Yes."

"And you stood up for Clara?"

"Yes."

"Why?"

I paused, not sure how to respond. After a moment, I said, "I guess I'm strong. Not everyone else is."

Madame studied me again. "So you feel it is your duty to protect?"

"Maybe."

Madame walked heavily back to her chair. "I see," she said as she sat. The wood groaned as she lowered herself into the seat. She pursed her lips and leaned her fingertips together. "Académie Sainte Thérèse de Lisieux is a prestigious institution. It is expensive, it is select, and it takes seriously its calling to mold the most well-bred women to become the best versions of themselves. We train up the finest young ladies to be productive members of society. To be educated, gentle wives and mothers, to manage their estates and servants with grace and dignity. To live comfortably and to grow old with dignity."

"Mademoiselle," she continued, staring at me. "When you hear those words, what do you feel?"

"I—I don't know."

"Yes, you do. Tell me."

"I...don't like them."

She smiled and leaned back. "That's because they aren't descriptive of you."

"Madame?"

"To be perfectly honest, Edith, you're a bit of a misfit."

"Tell me something I don't already know," I thought sourly. Either punish me for hitting Emile or let me go back to bed. I didn't need another reminder about how different I was. I saw that every day.

"I know it," Madame continued, "because I also am a bit of a misfit. A woman, running a school with dozens of staff, cooks, gardeners, keeping hundreds of girls in line? I *have* to be a misfit. I wouldn't be able to do this job without being an oddball myself. God knows you need to have a spine to do this kind of work."

I met her gaze squarely. *"A kindred spirit,"* I thought. But instead of smiling, Madame's face was cold.

"But understand me, Edith, as the headmistress of this institution, I'm bound to put my foot down even when I don't always want to," Madame said, her voice hard. "This incident with Emile—your flagrant, physical act of violence—has consequences."

"Consequences?" I repeated.

"I cannot allow a girl like you to remain here, damaging our reputation among other families. Especially not one who threatens the physical safety of someone like Emile. Someone whose family has contributed a sizable donation to this school, in order to help us achieve our educational goals with our students and staff."

I started to protest, but stopped. I could see the writing on the wall.

And strangely, I didn't care all that much. I had pictured myself remorseful, even tearful, begging for a second chance. Instead, I felt...nothing?

"You are being asked to leave here," Madame continued, nonplussed. "I will arrange with your mother to send you across France to attend Château de Fer, in Nice. We have an arrangement with them, a partnership for those students who don't fit in here but have come from overseas and must finish out the year in Europe."

She lifted her chin. "You will return to your room immediately and start packing your things. I can't keep you here one day longer than necessary, as I am not sure you can control your temper the next time you see someone who upsets you. Tomorrow, you will take the train to Nice. I've already arranged one of the sisters to get your ticket for you."

I crossed my arms over my chest, defiant.

She fixed her frown on me, staring through her glasses. "Edith, we cannot afford to have a fox constantly upsetting the henhouse. You'll find that your choice in life is to fall in line or continue to be a misfit. If you decide to be a misfit, you better find where exactly it is that you *do* fit in. Decent people won't accept you. So you'll have to find your own place, I suppose. Your own sort of people."

What was the point of finally realizing Madame was a kindred spirit? She was still kicking me out. Almost as if she was reading my mind, Madame softened.

"Young lady," she said in a gentler voice. "I hope you understand that my hands are tied. It's not that this is personal. I like you. I'm glad you stood up for your friend. But I have investors, families—people I cannot upset. Surely you're smart enough to understand that I need to put my feelings aside and do what's best for this school—and for me."

I found my voice. "I'd never do this to someone else. I'd make up my own mind to do what's right and I'd stick to it. Even if it upset some investors."

Madame peered at me. "Someday, you will have to make that same sort of decision. You'll find yourself choosing between your feelings and what's best for you. A smart woman knows the difference. A strong woman can actually *make* the choice."

Madame offered me her hand. I stood, uncertain, and shook it.

"Good luck, Edith. I think you'll be happy someday. It just won't be here."

CHAPTER 12

I WALKED SLOWLY BACK to my room after my conversation with Madame.

As I padded through the halls, still empty and only half-lit in the early morning, I choked up. Sure, I wasn't always happy here at Académie Sainte Thérèse de Lisieux, but it had been my home for a few years now. What if the next school was terrible and I hated it? What if I didn't make a single new friend in Nice? What if I had peaked here, and the rest of my future was just grim?

I was embarrassed that my mother would have to live with the shame of my expulsion. She loved me and had to know that I wouldn't hurt someone unless provoked, but she'd be angry.

"She's an ocean away, though," I thought. Disapproval is easier to ignore when all you have to do is toss a letter in the trash.

I reached my room, hoping Clara was still asleep and I could avoid telling her the bad news. As I creaked open the door, Clara stirred. "What are you doing?"

I slid off my shoes and crawled back into my unmade bed. "I didn't mean to wake you."

I clutched my pillows, laying still. *"This is my last morning in this bed,"* I thought. Who knew what tomorrow would bring?

On the other side of the room, Clara yawned. "Why are you dressed already?"

"I had to meet with Madame."

"Madame—no!" Clara shot up. "Because of last night? What did she say? Are you in trouble? What'd she say?"

"Yes."

"What? Which question are you answering? Edi, spit it out!"

"I'm being kicked out. She's sending me to Nice, to another boarding school there. She says I'm a threat to the students here."

Clara swore, flopping back into her bed.

"Clara!" I exclaimed. I'd never heard her use foul language as long as I'd known her.

"I'm not sorry," she spat, swearing again. "Couldn't you talk her out of it?"

"*I didn't even try,*" I thought to myself. Why didn't I try? I had no problem speaking my mind any other time. Why hadn't I defended myself? Was some small part of me actually relieved to be leaving?

I brushed my feelings aside. "I tried, but you know Madame. When she makes up her mind, there's no point to argue."

"Oh, Edi," Clara cried. "This is all my fault, isn't it?"

"No. You didn't beat someone up. I did."

"But you were defending me. So it is my fault. At least partly."

"Stop it. It's not. And you trying to assume guilt isn't going to help anything now."

A tear trickled down Clara's cheek. "I'm sorry. I can't believe this is happening to you. I feel terrible."

"No," I said, mustering up a faint smile. "Don't, Clara. Emile had it coming. If it hadn't been last night, it would've been later this week. Or next. Or a few weeks from now. I was bound to hit her sometime, right?"

"She really is awful," Clara agreed, tears still drifting down her pale cheeks. We laid in silence for a few moments. Finally, Clara broke the quiet. "What school are you going to?"

"I don't remember the name. It's in Nice somewhere."

"Oh. How far away is Nice?"

"I don't know."

"I could come visit you on holiday," she said.

"Yeah. True."

"And we'll still be able to write letters."

"Yes."

"Maybe we could bring a little group over to visit you some long weekend. You know, Charlotte and Arnau..."

My heart stopped for a moment. *Arnau.* Oh no. I hadn't even thought of him yet. How could I have not thought about him? He was my best friend.

Telling him this would be the most difficult thing I'd ever have to do, other than those horrible days I spent comforting my mother and sister after finding out about my father's death. He would be crushed.

I closed my eyes as my thoughts raced, erratic. I pictured Arnau's expression. Knowing I was cutting short any future I had dreamed of sharing with him as—what? His best friend? What exactly were we? If I hadn't punched Emile, what would my future with Arnau be? Would I someday be his girlfriend? Maybe—his wife? No. He was my best friend. Right?

I couldn't tell him. How could I face it?

Lost in my own misery, I barely heard Clara's soft comment. "What?" I opened my eyes.

"You'll be fine," she repeated, staring at me with a puckered forehead.

"Sure."

"You will," Clara insisted. "Of all the people I know who can take what life throws at them and turn it into something good, it's you, Edi."

"Right," I replied, feeling overwhelmed.

"Besides," Clara added with a small smile, "Nice will be a new adventure for you."

CHAPTER 13

MY EXPULSION MEANT I wasn't allowed to go to class but had to spend the day packing my possessions. The weight of telling Arnau that I was leaving pressed deeper into my soul with every hour. As classes ended in the afternoon, I trudged through the gardens to the stables.

I hadn't been brave enough to tell Arnau to his face that I was leaving. I didn't trust that I could control my words, or my conflicted emotions. One minute I felt like crying, and the next I felt hopeful, and still the next I was filled with regret. I was tempted to sprint back to Madame and beg for another chance, but my stubborn pride held me in check.

Instead, I begged Clara to run straight to the barn after class and bring him a short letter from me, explaining everything. I waited a respectable half hour, then slowly walked the path to the stable.

As I came around the corner, I saw Arnau outside the barn, his back to me, winding up a length of rope.

Why did I feel so guilty about saying goodbye to him?

"Andi," Arnau called over his shoulder, without turning around.

"How did you know it was me?"

"I know you better than anyone," he responded, slowly turning to face me. "I got your letter. From Clara."

The breeze caught his curls as he held my gaze. I couldn't read his expression. I wondered if he could read mine. We stood motionless, facing each other, for an eternity.

"So," he said quietly, his dark eyes searching mine. "This is it? The last time I see you?"

I nodded, my throat suddenly tight. Arnau tossed the rope over the fencepost and leaned up against the rough rails. The pose was so familiar to me that I caught my breath. I'd miss this. The familiarity. The routine. Arnau.

"Are you going to write to me every day?"

"Every day."

"That's quite a commitment," he jested, the lightness in his voice forced. "Writing to me every single day? That doesn't even sound like you. You're terrible at sending letters home to your mother, I know that."

"Well, maybe not every single day. But I'll write. Often."

I quietly cursed myself, frustrated with my tangled thoughts. A thousand different emotions were vying for my attention. Excitement, sadness, fear, guilt, sentimentality—I wasn't sure what to say. Or how to feel. This was our last moment together, probably forever, and I was screwing it up.

"Arnau, I'm sorry," I squeezed out, thankful my voice was steady.

"Sorry? For what?"

"I'm sorry I couldn't control myself," I blurted out, trying to hold back the dam that threatened to drown me if I let it. "I'm sorry that I ruined everything. That I'm being kicked out and forced to go to some stupid other school. I'm sorry I'm a failure. A freak. That everyone else here seems to hate me, or not get me, or not even care that I'm a human being with actual feelings."

"Don't be sorry."

I stomped my foot, suddenly angry. My life was being upended all over again. Wasn't it enough that my father died and threw our family into a never-ending somersault of adjustment? That I'd worked so hard to fit in to Académie Sainte Thérèse de Lisieux even though no one here really tried to get to know me? Now I had to adjust all over again, in a new place, away from the people I cared about?

Could nothing good ever happen to me? What if Arnau was the only truly good thing that *would* ever happen to me?

I hung my arms over the fence, feeling a chill through my heavy wool sweater. I felt defeated. Uncertain. Angry and sad.

Arnau joined me at the fence. "Don't be sorry," he repeated. "You're making your own path, Andi. There's nothing to be sorry about. It's unfortunate that it has to happen this way, but it's part of your journey, I guess."

I said nothing. His jacket brushed against my sleeve. "My Andiamo," he sighed. "Will you forget about me?"

I bit my lip to keep myself from screaming. To cover my emotions, I chose to jest.

"Yes, I'll forget all about you," I said lightly. "I'll forget about this whole school, all these years I've spent here. All the people, the faces, the classes—it'll just become a blank slate in my mind. A stretch of empty, wasted years."

I felt his gaze on me, searching. Uncomfortable with the examination, I turned to face him. I was as tall as him and couldn't avoid looking directly into his eyes.

Had I never noticed those tiny flecks of gold in them before now? Would this be the last memory I ever had of him, seeing the sadness etched in those warm brown eyes? Feeling awkward, I dropped my eyes, my face crimson.

Arnau suddenly grabbed my hand. "Edi, marry me. Please."

I stared at him. Was he serious?

"Arnau!"

"I mean it. Marry me."

"I'm seventeen!"

"And I'm eighteen. We're old enough to get married. Come on. Marry me."

"Why are you saying this?" I cried. "Why now? Why like this?"

He held my hand, both hands now clasped tightly over mine. "Because I would marry you. I understand you. We like each other. Why not get married?"

Conscious of his hands, warm against mine, I was at a loss for words. Marriage? A simple life, in France, with Arnau? Was that what I wanted? I had thought about it before, I couldn't lie. Imagined what it might be like to be married to him. What if I *did* want it, and I didn't even know it yet?

As I hesitated, Arnau abruptly dropped my hand. "That's your proof," he said, laughing bitterly as he took a step back.

"What?"

"That's your proof that you're ready for a new beginning. Another chapter in your life."

"I don't understand," I stumbled over my words. "Proof?"

"That look on your face. Your reaction when I asked you to marry me. That tells you everything you should know."

My cheeks flushed with embarrassment. "Arnau, what are you talking about? Did you—was that a real proposal?"

"It doesn't matter if it was. You'd never be happy settling down here with me."

"But I like you," I protested. "You're my best friend. I could be happy. We could be happy."

"You *could* be happy. But you wouldn't be."

"But how do you know that?"

He smiled, a sad smile, and reached out to my face. I thought he might kiss me, but instead he smoothed an errant lock of hair from my forehead.

"I know you, Edi," he replied. "I understand you. And I know you'd never be happy with a traditional life, with a marriage and kids and chores in the house and friends to gossip with on Sunday afternoons after church. You were created for something more, for a life of meaning. To go where others have never been. Hell, to show other girls that there's more to life than spending all your time and energy trying to find a husband."

With a sinking feeling, I knew he was right.

He started to speak again, but instead stopped himself. I stared at him, my forehead wrinkled. I didn't know what to say.

After a moment, he loosened the blue handkerchief he'd always casually tied around his neck in the summertime, protecting his skin from the sun.

I'd seen him use it in a million different ways in the years I'd known him. Sometimes he wet it to cool his face, other times to cover the horse's eyes when they were afraid, sometimes to dab a cut from a branch as we galloped through the woods. He busied himself undoing the knot, smoothing it out, then rolling it up. Unexpectedly, he motioned for me to hold out my arm.

I obliged. He held my arm gently for a moment, then wrapped the fabric around my arm, right above my elbow.

"What's this?"

"Oh, it's just a little token," he smiled. "You know how knights used to ride with a lady's colors? I assume you learned that up there in your fancy school."

"Are you saying I'm your knight?"

He laughed. "You are. My Andiamo, my knight in shining armor. You can wear it and think of me as you're off on your adventures."

"Well, that's hardly ladylike," I laughed shallowly. I didn't think I could bear this sorrow building inside of me. I couldn't let him see how much I was hurting. Had he really meant his proposal? What if I was making a mistake? Was I meant to stay here, with him, or meant to leave?

"It's time for you to find yourself, my love," he said, putting his arm across my shoulders. "You can't be afraid to live your own life. It'll work out. You'll be fine."

I hugged Arnau tight. "You'll be fine," he repeated as I buried my face in his shoulders.

"Will I?"

"Of course," he replied. "You're a force of nature. Unstoppable."

As he hugged me, Arnau buried his face in my hair. I felt the weight of his profound sorrow in this simple, intimate gesture. He'd never done it before.

And now he'd never do it again.

Or...would he?

"Goodbye, my Andiamo," Arnau breathed, his face still pressed against mine. "Say hello to your new adventures for me. It's time to go."

CHAPTER 14

"BAH!"

I spat as a series of newspaper clippings fluttered down over my face. It was my fault for opening my book as I laid on my back in my bed.

The only redeeming thing about the miserable six months I'd spent at this new boarding school in Nice was the amount of reading I'd done. The librarians knew me by name, no doubt taking pity on the tall, friendless girl who spent almost all of her free time in the quiet chamber of the library.

The people I met inside the covers of books kept the loneliness at bay. At least, that's the lie I willed myself to believe.

I'd tried to make friends. To start over with a clean slate. I'd attempted conversation with classmates, only to have them walk away while I was still talking. My teachers were just as cold, waving me off and muttering angrily in French as they grabbed their belongings and breezed away.

No one, including my new teachers, could see beyond the label that was affixed to me after being expelled from Académie Sainte Thérèse de Lisieux.

I was a pariah.

The only soul on campus who seemed to be willing to even meet my eyes was a plump, middle-aged librarian who wore thick glasses and heavy sweaters. In the last few weeks, we'd had several whispered conversations about the stories I'd enjoyed as I checked out new books.

"You read so many travel books," she remarked, writing down the titles on a slip of paper. "Why? Have you lived in all of these places?"

"No, ma'am. I just love the idea of traveling the world. Maybe someday I could visit another country or two."

"Ah, oui. A dream. That's good."

"Yes. But...it's just a dream."

She looked up, her eyes softening. "Maybe, mademoiselle. Maybe. But haven't you seen the news? That famous aviator, Amelia Earhart—she's seeing the world. Why not you, too, someday?"

I smiled. "I guess I need to read more about her. She is pretty remarkable."

The librarian pushed her glasses up with one finger. "I'll find you some articles. You will be inspired. You'll keep dreaming."

"Sure."

True to her word, since that conversation, the librarian had been snipping articles out of the local newspapers and saving them for me. It was amusing to see what she thought my interests were. Occasionally, she'd even underline a few lines, circle something, or write a little note on an article to draw my attention to it.

This morning, she'd slipped a few fresh articles into the book I checked out before class.

"I have some good ones today," she whispered as she carefully wrote down my name in her ledgers. "There's a short advertisement about a man. You'll see."

"A man?"

"A travel man. He goes all over. In his automobile."

"Oh, like a traveling salesman?"

The librarian pushed her glasses up. "No, no. Mon Dieu! Just read it."

After class, I tossed my books on my desk and flopped onto my bed. I'd been given a tiny room to myself, because no one wanted to room with a troublemaker who'd been expelled.

For a moment, I laid on my back, staring up at the ceiling.

I couldn't have imagined feeling as hopeless and friendless as I did. Even Arnau's and Clara's letters couldn't lessen the aching loneliness I felt. And how long would they even keep writing to me? Clara had promised to come visit, but Arnau couldn't afford that. They'd never make it here. Would I ever see them again?

I sighed. Loneliness felt like a physical weight, rendering me immobile.

With one arm, I pulled my new library book off the nightstand and opened it up. The newspaper articles fluttered around me, fragile and crinkling as they floated to a stop on my pillow. One by one, I flipped through them until I found the one about the travel man.

And *gracious*. Was he ever a travel man.

I read and reread the short article, staring at the photo of the handsome blonde man standing proudly in front of an automobile, a hat perched on his head.

"Captain Grant Gallivanter searches for travel companion," I read the caption underneath the photo. "Beauty, brains, and boots—a tour around the globe offered for a lucky young lady!"

As I kept rereading, I realized my life could be changing forever, in this very moment.

According to the brief article, Captain Gallivanter was searching for the perfect travel companion as he embarked on an around-the-world tour in a convoy of Model T Fords. He was part of a new organization, the Odysseus Society, promoting world peace and partnering with the League of Nations. His expedition was a race against another team, both trying to be the first to circle the world in their automobiles and win a million dollar prize.

I was hooked.

The article mentioned a rally to be held Saturday night in Nice, where Captain Gallivanter would be presenting about his upcoming expedition and sharing thrilling pictures and footage of previous travels. I frantically checked the date, and realized that it was only two days away.

Nothing could possibly deter me from making that rally, I resolved. I'd be there.

And I'd fight my way into being that lucky young woman...whatever it took.

CHAPTER 15

IT FELT LIKE AGES UNTIL Saturday finally came around.

I had pinned the article up on my wall and stared at it every night, considering how to best present myself to Captain Gallivanter. *"How can you make a stranger instantly like you?"* I wondered. *"Especially me. I'm not all that likable."*

On Saturday afternoon, I dressed carefully. Contrary to my usual tomboyish habits, I was eager to capture the essence of Captain Gallivanter's ideal young lady, the one with "beauty, brains, and boots." I decided to wear my most fashionable dress, and had even gone out and purchased a tube of red lipstick.

I stood at the mirror, staring at my reflection. I'd curled my dark hair and brushed it until it gleamed and fell around my shoulders. I twisted, staring at my blue dress, looking at the waistline hitting at my hips. The fabric shimmered, the hem of beads clacking with every move I made.

With a grimace, I applied the lipstick. I'd never worn it before. The chalky, waxy feel on my lips was repulsive. Nevertheless, I smiled in the mirror, tracing my lips, mimicking the other girls I'd seen as they excitedly prepared for dances and special events that I was never invited to attend.

I studied myself. A stranger looked back at me. I wiped the lipstick off.

"That looks more like me," I thought, staring at my bare lips with satisfaction. I knew I wouldn't be able to speak normally in that lipstick. I'd be too self-conscious about smearing it to get a word out. But doubt nagged me. The article specifically said the captain was looking for a beautiful girl.

I gritted my teeth and reapplied the red lipstick. *"Whatever it takes,"* I told myself. I just hoped I'd be able to speak normally through the layer of lipstick on my mouth. And not smudge it across my teeth.

"It's so much work to try to be beautiful," I groaned to myself.

I arrived downtown with plenty of time to spare, eager to be near the front of the crowd to better my chances of speaking to Captain Gallivanter.

As I walked down the wide street near the harbor, I looked out at the ocean. The breeze lifted my hair while the sun dappled the ancient cobblestones in front of me. The palms overhead rustled to match the heavy swish of my dress.

A small line was already forming at the town hall where the rally would be held. People stood shoulder to shoulder, chatting as seagulls crooned from their perch next to the sailboats bobbing in the harbor. I sidled up to the end of the line and smiled at the pink-cheeked young woman in front of me, who had turned her head to study me.

"My goodness!" she blurted out unceremoniously, craning her neck to look up at me. She caught herself, and smiled to cover her blunder. "My apologies. You're just very tall."

"It's fine," I laughed. "And am I? I've never noticed before."

"You're funny, too!"

"Thanks. I'm glad I've got a few things going for me." I stood behind her, awkwardly, hoping she wasn't the type of stranger one encountered who would start to talk your ear off when you just wanted to be alone with your thoughts.

Just my luck. She was.

"What brings you here?" she said, studying my outfit as I took in hers. She was wearing a red dress, lined at the neckline and hem with tiny crystals. Her cheeks must've had rouge on them—they were brilliantly pink—and she was wearing the exact shade of lipstick to match her dress. Her heels were shiny, her posture perfect.

"I'm here to listen to Captain Gallivanter's presentation about his expedition," I replied. I didn't want to show all my cards, in case she was hoping to apply for the job, too.

"Yes, isn't he wonderful? *So* good-looking and brave. I can't wait to hear him speak," she said with enthusiasm. "Did you hear he's looking for an assistant to travel the world with him? A *girl*?"

"I think maybe I did hear that was a possibility," I answered cautiously.

"Wouldn't it just be divine?" she sighed. "Think of sitting next to him. Talking and laughing. He's handsome. And so passionate. A go-getter. Just the kind of man I'd love to end up with, really."

"I suppose," I said, unwilling to pour out my heart to a stranger. She had no such qualms, apparently.

"I'd love to meet him and apply," she said brightly, but then frowned. "But honestly, I can't imagine going around all over with a man like that. You know."

"What?" I asked. I didn't know. I was watching her mouth move, wondering how she spoke through the bright lipstick she wore. Would it ever be something I got used to feeling on my mouth? I hated it.

"I mean, what kind of man is willing to travel all over the world with some beautiful young girl? It's not what people do. That's just *asking* for trouble."

"Maybe not every girl wants romance. Maybe the right girl just craves adventure."

"Sure, honey. You're quite the innocent, huh?"

"You're telling me you think it's impossible for a man and a woman to be friends?"

Blushing, she giggled. She shifted her weight on her spindly stilettos and her skirt swished. "Well, I suppose they could be *friends*—if that's what you want to call it."

I rolled my eyes. Was this what everyone thought? These notions hadn't even crossed my mind. Couldn't a girl want an honest whirl around the world without getting herself entangled in a relationship?

"Besides," continued the girl, sniffing. "No proper lady would ever go on a trip like this."

"Why not?"

She blinked. "Because no man will ever want to marry a girl who's lived with another man like this. I mean, imagine sharing every meal, driving together every day for hours, staring up at sunsets and stars together? And who knows what else could happen? The intimacy! What husband would ever want his wife to share that with someone else? Men aren't built like that, sweetie."

I was quietly flummoxed.

She had a good point. Would I be jeopardizing my future to go off on a trek like this? Would I ever meet a man who would understand that drive within me to see the world and resist settling down into the quiet life? Maybe not.

But then again, could I live with myself if I didn't at least try to take this opportunity?

I pursed my lips and impulsively made up my mind. Consequences could catch up with me later.

I had one mission now: I had to follow Captain Gallivanter wherever he was going.

The crowd eventually ambled into the building and settled into seats. I found the closest spot to the large wooden stage, calculating that taking the very end seat would enable me to jump up quickly after his speech and grab him to chat. I fidgeted in my seat, a bundle of nerves.

When the lights dimmed and the music swelled, the audience broke into applause. *"It's a full house in here,"* I thought, looking around with wonder. Captain Gallivanter certainly drew a crowd by reputation alone.

The curtains parted as Captain Gallivanter strode confidently to the middle of the stage. His boots clacked across the polished wood as he welcomed the crowd with a strong voice made captivating with just the slight hint of a foreign accent.

"He must come from nobility, with an accent like that," I thought, watching him. Blonde, tall and muscular, with bright blue eyes, a clean-shaven face and a clear complexion, it was easy to see why he was popular with the ladies.

He was younger than I expected, too.

He was wearing an official-looking uniform, consisting of crisp khaki pants, brown boots, and a heavy brown wool jacket. His slim waist was belted with a wide leather belt, cinched in tight. A cap perched jauntily on his head. Across one shoulder, he wore a cheetah skin draped artfully, as if to remind us that he was a mighty hunter. A large knife protruded from the top of his boots.

"Welcome, ladies and gentlemen!" he boomed as the crowd applauded. His voice was deep and masculine. Commanding. He was obviously a man used to being in charge.

He was a masterful storyteller, speaking with passion and conviction, punctuating his stories with pictures and soundless film he displayed on a large screen and smaller photographs his assistants passed around the audience. Excited hands scrabbled for the small black and white photos, murmuring as they viewed them.

By the time they got to me, they were bent at the edges but still thrilling. Exotic locations, people in strange outfits, and animals dotted his photographs.

The captain told us about the million dollar prize that he and his small crew were competing for, battling a larger Canadian crew out of Quebec. The teams were racing each other to see who could be the first to circumnavigate the world in their Model T Ford automobiles. The winners, as judged by the sponsoring Odysseus Society, got to split the million dollar prize money between themselves.

"It's a race of endurance, testing the human limits," Captain Gallivanter proclaimed. "It is not a competition for the faint of heart, or even the strong. It is a competition for the *strongest* of individuals. Those who reach the end of their own limits, and press on, unrelenting and unbowed."

I was smitten.

Not with Captain Gallivanter, but with the life he lived.

After a thunderous applause, Captain Gallivanter bowed and invited curious patrons up to speak with him, along with an open invitation for those "beautiful young ladies" who would be interested in applying to be his travel companion on his upcoming expedition around the world.

I bolted from my seat, but there was already a crowd around him by the time I got to the front of the auditorium.

I waited and overheard as dozens of excited people prattled on about their own travels, admiration for his club, and asked questions about his trip and automobiles. Several attractive young women were vying hard for his attention, and he deftly flattered them all as they hung around him, batting their eyelashes.

I'd have to do something different here. I stood no chance with these gorgeous vixens in my way. Confidence was my only hope.

"Captain Gallivanter!" I thundered, my voice clearly heard over the gaggle as I stood a head taller than most everyone in the area. "I'm your girl!"

His blue eyes met mine, and unconsciously ran up and down my body. He raised an eyebrow and replied, "My girl?"

"Yes. I'm the perfect girl to be your travel companion!"

He coolly studied my face, then shrugged. "I'm looking for a girl with good looks, a quick mind, and someone who can keep up with a rigorous schedule," he announced to the girls around him. "I'm open to all sorts of applications from you dolls!"

"Think quickly, Edith!" I told myself frantically. How could I stand out in this crowd? Suddenly, it hit me.

"Kapitän, ich bin die einzige das perfekte Fräulein, die Sie suchen!" I hollered in German. Everyone in the room stopped to stare at me, startled over the harsh and jarring words in a language that still made many people here uncomfortable.

Rapidly, I switched to French, repeating the same phrase, then Italian. "I can speak many languages. It'll be useful for you, as you travel!"

Captain Gallivanter laughed as he looked at me. "My, that's quite impressive, Miss—"

"Edith. Warren."

"Miss Warren." He smiled as he said my name.

"Edi will do."

Pushing forward through the crowd, Captain Gallivanter stepped toward me and offered his hand. The girls around him shot me dirty looks behind his back.

"How many languages do you speak in total, Miss Edi?"

"I'm fluent in French, German, Spanish, and Italian," I fibbed a bit. "I'm trying to learn Portuguese, too," I added, though I wasn't. I'd never heard it spoken, but I'd read about it in Arnau's geography book.

"Five languages. That's quite the party trick," he replied, his eyes still on my face.

"I'm also an excellent writer, and a quick study in managing a camera, and I have a head for mechanics. I'm stronger than most girls. I could learn to work on the automobiles."

He chuckled. "We'll leave the camera work and mechanics to the men, sweetheart, but I admire your style."

One of the girls closest to him stroked his arm, flirting aggressively, and tilted her head back to whisper something in his ear. He hid a grin. I flushed. "What?"

"She said—your height. That—ah, well. That you'd be a *giant* addition to the expedition."

A lifetime of being teased about my height had numbed me to comments, luckily.

"And you don't think that would work out to your benefit, Captain Gallivanter? It would," I replied coolly. "I'd be the talk of the town, everywhere you go. I'd guarantee that you'd have a crowd gathered—and everyone would be able to see me easily when I'm on stage. Or in a crowd, like this. I would command the room, everywhere I go."

He opened his mouth to respond, then closed it. He stared at me.

"You do have a point there," he replied thoughtfully.

Determined to take advantage of the moment, I continued to press my luck. "I'm also well-versed in different cultures already. I've been reading about other countries and tribes for years. I know geography and I'm good at recognizing animals and plants. I have a good sense of humor, and—"

"Okay, okay," he waved. "I get the picture. You think you're the perfect package."

"Yes. I am. For this."

The girls around him giggled and exchanged looks. I didn't care. I knew I had piqued his interest. He glanced around the girls, then looked at me again. "What do you say we chat a bit more over a drink tonight?"

"Sure."

"Fine. How about Le Chat Noir, down the street here, in an hour?"

"I'll be there. Thank you, Captain Gallivanter."

He tipped his hat at me and turned away, back to the attention of the girls. *"Thank goodness I'm not that shallow,"* I thought to myself as I walked away. I couldn't imagine throwing myself at a man, however exciting he might be. Or wanting to be with a man like that, who was stupid enough to fall for these girls' manipulations.

Still, the thrill of a private meeting with Captain Gallivanter was exciting. I bit my lip to hide my smile as I pushed through the crowd, toward the door.

One hour.

I had one hour to see if my life might change for good.

CHAPTER 16

I STRODE OUT OF THE building into the cool night air, excited and terrified at the same time.

I congratulated myself on cleverly getting his attention by speaking in multiple foreign languages. My confidence ebbed, however, when I remembered the way he looked at the gorgeous girls around him.

Having nothing to do for the next hour until I met with Captain Gallivanter, I wandered around the back of the building and found a spot on the crumbling brick seawall overlooking the bay.

Sailboats bobbed up and down in the incoming tide as sailors packed their ropes and baskets for the night.

The sun had already set over the horizon, and the moon and stars were just starting to shine in the velvety sky above. The tang of fresh fish grilling in the restaurant next door, mingled with the salty breeze of the ocean, made my stomach gurgle.

I stared at the water, wondering if I'd ever get the chance to sail on that ocean in search of adventure.

A few moments later, the door at the back of the theater clanged open. I turned to look and watched as Captain Gallivanter peered out, looking right and left, before quietly stepping through. His hat was pulled low over his face.

"Captain Gallivanter?" I called, confused. Where was the gaggle of doe-eyed beauties hanging on his every word?

"Ah, umm, ahem," he sputtered, then lit up when he saw me. "You!"

"What are you doing here?"

He rubbed his face, embarrassed. "I...was leaving."

"Through the back door?"

"Well...yes." He looked like a little boy who'd just been caught snooping in the present pile under the Christmas tree.

"Why?"

He shifted. "Sometimes the crowds are just too much. They drain me. All those people in there, asking me questions...the girls...it's like this everywhere I go. Every town. It's been like this for months."

"I'd think you would enjoy it, though? Aren't you a performer?"

He laughed regretfully. "I do. And I am. Sometimes. I mean, these people fund my expedition. Some of them might be future patrons who come along with me on trips. But I don't know, it probably doesn't make sense to you. It just gets old, being in the spotlight."

I stretched out my long legs and pointed to them. "Believe it or not, I think I know what you mean. Sometimes you'd like to just blend into the crowd instead of have the entire crowd stare at you."

He sat next to me on the ledge, taking off his hat. "Yeah, maybe you do get it, doll face."

"Why do you say that?" I blurted without thinking.

"What?"

"I'm not a doll." I felt the heat rise in my face. Here I was, putting my foot in my mouth again.

Instead of clamming up, Captain Gallivanter seemed to relax. His shoulders softened as he ran his hand through his hair. "I've never really thought about it before. I guess it's just part of my charm. Sweet talk and all. You ask a lot of questions."

"I know. And I don't think it's charm. I think it's savvy."

"Savvy?"

"Yes, I think you've calculated what exactly to say to people to get them to like you," I replied. "I think you've created a character that you play. You ingratiate yourself to people but this isn't really you. You keep your own feelings to yourself, but you'll do what it takes to get supporters. To rally people around you so you can tell them the story."

"Maybe."

"And even now, you're uncertain what to say because I've hit the nail on the head," I continued, perhaps too boldly. "I get it. I understand this whole act."

"Oh, you get it? How can you possibly get it? I've talked to you for a few minutes, that's all."

"I understand you," I replied, turning to gaze at the ocean again. The sky was almost completely dark, and the streetlights cast a warm glow over the buildings surrounding us. We were quiet for a few moments, absorbing the scene together. He broke the silence.

"Why do you say you get it?"

I chose my words carefully. "I'm the same way. An outsider, parading through life. Playing the part. I don't know where I belong. Or if anyone will ever really understand who I am. Or even if anyone will ever care to take the time to get to *know* who I am. But I'm still trying to figure out the character to play, too. How to get people to like me. The real me."

"Interesting." Captain Gallivanter's tone was warm. I looked up to meet his gaze. Something friendly twinkled in his expression as we locked eyes. Unexpectedly, he smiled. "You're quite a girl, you know."

"Thanks."

"So you're really interested in joining this expedition?"

"Yes!"

Captain Gallivanter grinned at my exclamation, holding up his hands. "I need to admit, Edith, that it's not going to be easy. It may be quite dangerous. We're planning to circumnavigate the globe, which means going through dozens and dozens of countries over the next few years. We'll have to fundraise our way at every stop, which means putting on a performance—just like the one you saw here tonight—and garnering support from strangers, all the time."

"I can do it. I want to do it."

He paused, studying me. "We don't always know where our next meal will be coming from. Or what it's going to be."

"That's fine by me. I don't need much."

"I've had nights where I've slept out on the ground in the bitter cold. And plenty of times where I endured terrible weather, rain and snow and fog, and had to battle my way through. And the natives in some countries? They're not always so happy to have visitors. I'd need someone who can do a dozen different jobs, on top of whatever else might come up while we're on the road—"

I interrupted him.

"So how do I sign up for the second interview?"

He reeled back, surprised. "You actually want to do this?"

"Yes! It sounds incredible!"

"But didn't you hear what I just told you?" he asked, watching my face. "It's not an easy venture."

"I understand. So when will you be having second interviews?"

"Um, ahem," he said, stalling. "About that..."

My heart sank. Oh no. He had someone else in mind and he didn't know how to tell me.

"Just tell me, please," I heard the heaviness in my own voice as I spoke. "If you already have the job filled, I'll be disappointed but I'd rather know now."

He hesitated, shifting his weight on the crumbling seawall. Below us, the water shimmered in the darkness. "Can I be honest?"

"I hope you always are."

"We haven't really had many applicants. Not any good ones, anyway. In fact, I'm a bit stunned that you're actually serious about doing it."

How could this be? I figured I'd have to fight my way through a sea of more beautiful, brilliant girls. "Why haven't you had more girls apply?"

He sighed. "I suppose it's just too unusual for most girls. Their parents don't want them to leave home, or they're hesitant to leave school or jobs, or their friends and family insist they shouldn't travel the world with a crew of men. I thought I'd have more people apply, but we haven't. A lot of girls have said they're interested—and they certainly let me believe that they want to be on the team with me—but when it really comes down to it, they back out."

I thought about it for a moment. Those were some good reasons not to do it. But it didn't sway my decision.

"So how do I sign up?"

"I appreciate your interest, Edi, but it's not that easy," he shook his head. "We have to work on getting you travel visas to all the different countries, and...hold on, how old are you, anyway?"

"Eighteen." I'd just had my birthday a few weeks ago. No one celebrated it, other than the cards I received from my mother and sister. I'd sat alone under a tree and read a book to mark the special occasion.

"Eighteen?" He stood up, dropping his hat off his lap onto the ground. "No. I'm sorry, Edi."

"I'm eighteen! That's old enough!"

"You're too young. You seem older than that. No, I can't possibly take a girl that young on a trip like this."

"Why not?"

"Why not? Because it's a difficult journey. It requires self-discipline, mental fortitude, and maturity," he sputtered, pacing in front of me. "Eighteen. That's young."

I stood up. I matched his height.

"Captain Gallivanter, look at me," I said. "I'm no child. I'm eighteen, yes, but I've spent a lifetime preparing for something like this. I've lived abroad for seven years now so I'm not only independent and self-sufficient, but I also know how to pack light. I've worked on a farm and in the stables, and I'm an exceptional horsewoman. I'm strong, I'm smart, and I've read more about other cultures than probably anyone else you know. And all of that is in addition to being fluent in several languages."

He stared at me, uncertain.

In desperation, fear of my chance slipping away, I tried my most direct appeal. "Captain, everything in my life has led me right to this opportunity, to this moment. I'm ready. I want it. Please. You'll never find anyone else who wants this more than me."

He sighed, and sat back down. The streetlights illuminated the creases around his eyes as he squinted, thinking. "I don't know. What would your parents say?"

"I have only my mother, Captain. My father's buried in France."

I looked down at my feet. Even several years later, it was painful to speak about him. His death had been a deep blow to my soul. I had bottled up my feelings, concentrating on my mother and sister, struggling to let anyone else know how much his death still hurt. I had always been highly conscious that I'd gone to school for seven years in the country where his body lay in an unmarked grave. Sometimes I wondered if I had ever walked near where he'd been killed, gasped his last painful breaths, blood-soaked on the battlefield.

"I'm sorry."

"It's okay."

"You think your mother would be fine with you leaving with my expedition? Really? Most mothers I've met haven't been too eager to let their little girls go off with a strange man, around the world, visiting remote villages full of people who can't speak English."

"I do. She's always encouraged me to live my own life. Besides, she shipped me off to boarding school here. She's already used to me living an ocean away. She knows I have a good head on my shoulders."

He glanced over at me, studying me. "You know, speaking of your head..."

"What?"

"Well," he hesitated, "This sounds shallow, but I want to lay all my cards on the table here."

"What?"

"I know this sounds stupid, but I have an image. I've thought a lot about it, planned this for a long time. We're adventurers, explorers, people of interest and mystery—"

"Yes?"

"I was really hoping to find a girl with a bob," he admitted. "You know, like those flappers in America are getting. They always end up getting talked about in the newspapers."

A flash of irritation rankled in me. *I spent all that time curling my hair today to look nice, and it turns out this guy doesn't even like my hair,* I thought. Men just didn't understand what we went through.

"Fine. I'll cut it."

"You will?" His tone was incredulous.

"Do you have scissors?"

"Scissors? What? No. Not on me."

I pointed at the Bowie knife in his boot. Captain Gallivanter slowly pulled it out, the light from the nearby streetlamp catching the blade in the darkness. I put out my hand, and he handed it to me, bewildered. I held the heavy knife in my hand and closed my fingers around the smooth hilt. It was warm from being pinned in his boot.

"This will do," I said, determined to prove my mettle.

With a swift motion, I yanked a chunk of my hair straight out in front of me and started hacking at it with the knife. A few sawing motions later, a long lock of my hair landed on the ground at my feet. I separated another chunk but before I could cut it, his hand locked around my wrist.

"Stop! That's enough!" he laughed as he held my wrist still. "Good Lord, you're a spitfire, you know that?"

"I told you I'd cut my hair. I'll do whatever it takes to prove that I'm your girl."

"I didn't think you'd actually do it!" he exclaimed, his blue eyes twinkling.

"Then why'd you hand me the knife?"

He just laughed harder. "I don't know if I should admit this, but that was just a test," he grinned. "I merely wanted to see how you'd comply with orders. You know, you'll be getting a lot of them from me over the next few years."

He stood up. "You're a rare one, Edi," he smiled, offering me his arm as he put his hat back on. "Let's go."

"Where are we going?" I said, shooting to my feet.

"We're going to find a proper hairdresser, someone who can fix this hack job you did. And then we're going to send a wire to your mother."

My spirits rose and I leapt to my feet, clutching his arm. "What are you saying, Captain?"

"I'm saying 'welcome to the Gallivanter Expedition,' Miss Edith," he grinned. "You're right. You're the perfect girl for the job."

CHAPTER 17

DOUBT CREPT IN AS I trudged back to school late that night.

Cap, as Captain Gallivanter told me he preferred to be called, had found a barber and persuaded him to cut the rest of my hair, even though his shop was long closed.

"She attempted it herself," he grinned, nodding at the chunk I'd sawed off. "We're hoping you can finish the job."

The barber groaned, muttering in French about the impetuous nature of young people.

As he carefully cut the rest of my hair into a daring bob, the scissors snipping in the silence as Cap stood against the counter, watching with his arms crossed, I felt a rush of pride.

I'd done it. I'd made it onto the Gallivanter Expedition.

The exhilaration of winning the coveted spot faded after Cap dropped me off at school, with the promise that he'd pick me up the next morning to meet the team and telegram my mother.

I stood at the front door of my dormitory and stopped, looking up at the imposing building, heavy with ivy. My heart sank as I thought about climbing the steps and walking down the long hallway to my solitary room.

Could I live up to the expectations facing me?

Captain Gallivanter had searched publicly all over the world for a beautiful, spunky, brilliant girl who could electrify the media and serve as an ambassador to thousands of foreigners.

Was I really the best person for the job?

On top of that, despite my assurances that my mother would be pleased with me leaving school to go on this whirlwind trip, I worried what she would actually think. I had discovered that

I'd be making a small salary while working on the expedition, so I decided that I would send most of it home to her. Maybe that would sweeten her opinion of me giving up on my education. After all, I only had a few months of school left.

No matter how many excuses I tried out to bolster my confidence, a small voice poked through my defenses with a steady refrain: *can you actually do this?*

I closed the doors quietly behind me, removing my jacket and shoes. Tiptoeing up the stairs, I heard nothing but the distant sounds of girls preparing for bed and the reassuring tick of the antique grandfather clock at the foot of the stairs.

Carrying my shoes and jacket, I walked silently down the hall. This was how a ghost must feel. Passing dozens of happy girls brushing their hair, applying face creams and washing their cheeks, giggling over private jokes and gossip, all while not being seen.

With every step I took, however, instead of feeling lonely, I felt growing resolve.

"I don't belong here," I said to myself. *"I never have. They've never given me a chance. They don't even know me."*

I passed more rooms, looking in on the girls inside who were oblivious to my glances.

"I can do this," I told myself, starting to believe it. *"Of anyone in the world, I can."*

Another room, another scene of girls living their lives without caring that I existed.

"I have nothing to lose," I realized as I walked. *"Nothing to keep me here. No home to miss. It's like I've already been preparing for this journey my entire life."*

Flashes of me sprawled out on my bed, poring over Arnau's geography book and my father's action stories, sprang to mind. Me exploring the woods and the city centers, alone. Splitting wood, mucking the horse paddocks, hauling heavy saddles: the work of a man, not a lady.

I had never been afraid to do a man's work, follow my own interests, or live an independent life. I wasn't about to let doubt stand in the way now.

I crossed by the last occupied room before glimpsing my dark and lonely room at the end of the hall. Inside their warmly lit room, a trio of girls sprawled out on the beds, snuggled up in blankets and sharing a private conversation.

They were happy. Meanwhile, the only joy I'd known in my own room was from the pages of books. The stories of other people, living their adventures.

The contrast was stark. They had each other, their inside jokes, their customs and inevitable futures. They shared the same hopes and dreams. They were mundane, predictable. That was fine for them.

It wasn't fine for me.

"I don't want an ordinary life," I said to myself. *"I choose to live an adventure. Even if I don't know what it'll be."*

I entered my room and stared at myself in the small mirror above my desk. In the darkness, a stranger with a bob looked back at me. In her eyes, I saw confidence.

I could do this.

It was time for me to go.

CHAPTER 18

THE NEXT FEW DAYS FLEW at dizzying speed.

Captain Gallivanter was waiting on the steps outside my school when I stepped outside in the morning, a telegram from my mother in his hands.

"Good morning," he said as I approached. "I believe your headmistress will need this notice of consent before you can depart."

Wordlessly, I took the telegram. "You've already talked to my mother?" I asked, incredulous. "What did she say?"

"She's surprised but not too surprised," he grinned. "We had a few back and forth transmissions. She told me to remind you to be safe and smart, and that she loves you dearly. She wants you to write and tell her the whole story. Oh, and she told me she'll kill me if anything happens to you."

"She did?"

He smiled. "Not in quite that exact wording, but close enough. Do you need me to help carry anything out? Or help you deal with the headmistress?"

I motioned to my suitcase, sitting on the top step. "I only have this. The school will ship my trunk home on the steamer at the end of the year. And no, I'll handle the headmistress. Give me a few minutes."

He nodded, picking up my suitcase. I turned and made my way to the office.

Privately, I had resolved to never step foot in school again, despite my promise to my mother that I would finish my education someday. When I reached the headmistress's office, my conversation was short and direct. I told her I was unenrolling, and my mother's note of consent would serve as my official permission for a leave of absence to do some traveling.

The headmistress didn't even look at the telegram before she signed my forms and filed them away in her cabinet.

I slipped out the doors of the school without even a goodbye glance. Captain Gallivanter was already in the car, waiting for me.

The Gallivanter Expedition logo gleamed up at me from the side of the Model T Ford, a gold-tipped globe that boldly proclaimed our team name. My breath caught as I realized that logo was mine now, too. I was a part of the Gallivanter team.

"That was fast," he remarked as he handed me a pair of thick goggles. He was wearing an identical pair, held to his head with a tight leather strap. He looked like an airplane pilot.

"It wasn't hard to say goodbye," I replied, holding up the goggles. "Will I have to wear these all the time?"

"Yes," he said, staring at me from under his own. "These windshields are plate glass. They'll slice us both up if we were to crash. Skin can regrow, but once you damage an eye, you're out of commission for good. So we wear them all the time. Even on short trips."

The tires crunched as he reversed on the gravel and pulled out, taking us toward the hotel where the rest of the team was staying. As he drove away, I stared out the window.

"This is all happening even faster than I ever dreamed. You sure don't waste any time, do you?"

"No. Efficiency is my favorite hobby," he replied. "We're on a tight schedule already. It's going to require you learning quite a lot in a short amount of time. I hope you're ready for that."

"I'm a quick learner," I replied, watching as he handled the automobile. I bit my lip as I watched him pump the pedals, managing all three as he shifted gears to navigate us through the city. "Will I learn how to drive one of these?"

"You will," he glanced my way. "Have you ever driven before?"

"I've never had the chance."

We arrived downtown to the Hôtel de la Mar, where Captain Gallivanter and the rest of the crew had been staying. He checked me in and asked the porter to take my belongings up to my room.

"Why don't you spend a bit of time writing to your mother and your friends and family, telling them the good news?" he suggested. "I have a lot of work to do today, and Chito and Bernard are running errands. You'll meet them soon enough, and it'll be pretty hectic once we get going here. Take the downtime now, while you have the chance. You won't have many opportunities to relax, in the upcoming days. Come down to the lobby when you're done and we'll go from there."

"Okay," I agreed.

Obediently, I went to my hotel room and flopped on the bed to write a letter to my mother. I explained the whole expedition in detail and how I had ended up being chosen as the lucky girl.

I peered at the long letter, then hastily scrabbled out an empty promise that I'd be able to finish school later, after this educational experience of a lifetime would foster a new joy for learning.

I sealed her letter, then penned short letters to Arnau and Clara and Evelyn, sharing the news and our itinerary. As I rolled off the bed and caught a glimpse of my face in the mirror, I smiled. My face glowed with excitement.

It was lunchtime when I wandered to the lobby to search for Captain Gallivanter. I spotted him in a quiet corner, hidden by potted palms and surrounded by a thick stack of papers sitting on several open maps.

An untouched cup of coffee balanced on the floor next to his boots. He was scribbling on a map, his left hand pinning an open book to his lap.

"Hold on," he smiled absently, finishing a note he'd been jotting. He marked his spot in the book and set it to the side. "Sorry," he said, inviting me to sit down across from him at the table. "It's a staggering amount of work to plan this tour. You have no idea."

"I'm glad you're doing it, Captain Gallivanter. I'd hate to be stuck with it."

He laughed, raking his hand through his blonde hair. He was handsome, I thought to myself. With his easy confidence and obvious intelligence, he put off the air of someone who could calmly face down a charging grizzly bear and wait until the last moment to shoot it dead.

"I told you already. Call me Cap," he said, crossing one leg over the other to get comfortable.

"Only if you call me Edi."

"Deal."

"We have a lot of work to do to catch you up with the expedition," he started, leaning forward. "Let me start with some quick background first."

"I'm all ears."

"Our team has been together a few weeks already. We came over from the United States together," Cap leaned back into his chair. "This concept for a worldwide trek started a few years ago, as the League of Nations formed after the Great War. It was suggested that different crews from different parts of the world consider engaging in a good-natured competition, something that would capture the attention of the public but also showcase how people in other cultures and countries lived their lives."

"Like a World's Fair exhibition?"

"Similar. The goal is to take pictures and film short clips from unique places, and show that footage to the folks back home. You know, to involve them in the journey. Make presentations, put out newspaper articles. Stuff like that. Break down prejudices."

He bent down and took a sip of his coffee, and then continued. "The lofty idea, of course, is that goodwill between different nations might prevent another catastrophic world war."

"That makes sense," I mused.

"The idea grew and a small committee formed a club. It became popular. Some bigwigs got involved in it, formed an organization called the Odysseus Society, and pushed it forward," Cap explained. "They set guidelines, publicized it, and invited interested teams to apply. We have a copy of the rules, but basically, the first team documented traveling through the most countries wins."

"That sounds easy enough."

"It's less about speed, though, and more about endurance. The goal is for our team to travel through more countries than anyone else. That means remaining on a careful schedule, staying healthy, and avoiding careless mistakes."

"Makes sense," I said.

Cap stretched. "Along the way, we're expected to document ourselves in these countries, network with local guides and any American ambassadors, and publicize our trip in local newspapers. That's how we'll keep track of the others, by the way. They're starting in Europe. We're starting in northern Africa, which is why southern France was our last fundraising stop before we drive the cars south next week."

"Why Africa?"

"It's the harder route. I'm hoping it will get us more attention in the newspapers. That increases our chances of sponsorship. And more popularity will endear us to the locals."

"How much time will this expedition take?" I asked curiously.

"Probably a few years," Cap smiled. "We're allowed to take as much time as we think we need. Automobile repairs are expected from everyone involved, so if we need to take a few months off at any point to get work done or stock up on supplies, that's allowable. In addition, we're allowed to take time off for family emergencies, if it's needed. Hopefully we won't have to."

"You talked about a prize at the end of this, right?"

"Yeah, that's the exciting part," Cap leaned forward. His enthusiasm was infectious. "As if the reward wasn't just in the opportunity to see the world. No, the committee determined that there should be a hefty prize at the end, in order to drum up excitement and keep the public's interest strong. They decided to make it a million dollar prize pot for the winning crew."

"A million dollars," I replied, dazzled. "Does the whole crew split it if they win?"

"They do," Cap replied. "That's the main reason why our crew got together and decided to stay as small as possible. All of us come from challenging financial situations. None of us came from families with money. We're all here, each on our own merit."

"How many other teams are we competing against?"

He smiled. "Just one. Our odds to win are good."

"What?" I shook my head in disbelief. "Why aren't there more teams? Who wouldn't want to see the world and get a chance to win that much money? That's a fortune!"

"I know. I feel the same way. Why wouldn't you do this? It's an incredible adventure," Cap replied, then nodded at the maps and books between us.

"There were a lot more teams, at first. Dozens and dozens. But in the years it took to assemble this crew and do the preparation, secure all the applications and visas, they all dropped out," Cap said. "We've been doing our own publication, plotting our route, and fundraising for so long. It's unbelievable how much work it's already been, and none of it fun. One by one, the field cleared out until it was just us and the Chinook Voyageurs."

"Who are they?"

"The Chinook Voyageurs hail from Quebec. They have a catchy motto, something about being the 'warming wind sweeping through the world to create a warmth between human hearts.' They're good," Cap absently bounced his leg. "It's a bunch of guys who grew up boating together on the St. Lawrence River. I guess a few of them even race ice canoes across the frozen river during winter. One of their crew is from big money, and is funding most of the trip."

"Do we have a fighting chance against them?" I asked. Having a Canadian father, I knew the reputation of Québécois men. They were fearless.

"They're bigger than us and better funded," Cap admitted. "They have several more automobiles and plenty of crewmen to rotate driving. But we're smarter and more adaptable. What's more, we're hungry for it."

Cap glanced at my face and winked. "And you—you're our secret weapon."

"I am?"

"We'll be the first expedition in history to have a woman with us."

No wonder Cap was so excited to bring me on the crew. I was his bragging rights. But was I the one he actually wanted? He'd clearly dreamed about this expedition for so long.

"Did you have other women apply for my position?" The question left my mouth before I could stop it.

"Well...no." Cap squirmed. "Lots of women were interested, at first. Some wrote to me after seeing advertisements in the papers. As you saw, a lot of them met with me after presentations. But once I provided the details about what they could expect, I heard crickets."

"So...I'm it."

"You're it."

I grinned. "You're lucky I hated boarding school so much. And that my mother trusts my judgment."

"Apparently it was meant to be," Cap smiled. "Fate brought us together. That, and a thirst for excitement, apparently."

CHAPTER 19

CAP AND I SPENT THE afternoon together, walking through our itinerary and trip guidelines. After a quick lunch, he drove me to a tailor to be measured for my uniform.

"We're on the move in just a few days," he reminded me, as the tailor measured me behind the curtain. "Normally, we'd have more time. I didn't really expect to pick you up this way. After all these months of looking for the right woman and striking out, I'd given up on finding one. I figured it'd just be the boys and me."

"Sorry to throw your plans for a loop," I called as the tailor stretched a measuring tape around my waist.

"No, I'm glad you did," Cap replied from the other side of the curtain. "It's just going to be a bit of a scramble, that's all. We're off to Spain after this, then straight across the ocean to northern Africa. I have to make sure you have everything you need."

As the tailor wrote up my measurements, Cap slipped him a hefty tip to ensure a rush order on my wardrobe.

"The whole team matches," he said, as we drove back to the hotel. "I designed the uniforms myself, after a careful study of what the optimal clothing for our travels would be. We want durable fabric, something that can withstand all the elements."

He glanced over at me. "And sorry, Edi. No skirts. You'll need a full range of motion and legs that are protected from mosquitoes and poisonous insects. You'll be living in pants from now on."

I pictured the look on my classmates' faces if they saw me wearing pants, and grinned.

As soon as my uniform was made, a messenger dropped off my new clothes. Cap ordered me to my hotel room straightaway, telling me to try them on and see how they fit, as we'd be wearing them together for a press conference at the end of the week.

Closing the door of my room, I unwrapped the heavy wrappers and pulled out each layer, one by one.

Inside, I discovered several khaki and white shirts with large metal buttons, and pants, along with a thick brown belt that gleamed with an expensive brass buckle. A leather vest, velvet soft on the inside but smooth and shiny on the outside, had several deep pockets sewn in around the outside and two small hidden pockets on the inside chest.

A series of tan undershirts, some short-sleeved and some long-sleeved, a few pairs of long khaki pants, scratchy brown wool socks, and a long, lightweight scarf lay folded inside. A wool peacoat with many pockets in a matching shade of tan completed the parcel.

Opening the heaviest box, I found a pair of stiff brown boots, shoelaces still tucked safely inside the lining. They smelled of expensive leather. Their whiff betrayed yet another reason why Cap had fundraised so hard: the entire crew had to be outfitted in materials that would withstand the extreme conditions of our long trip.

In a third package, marked boldly "do not crush" in French, I pulled away the delicate tissue paper to find a thick pair of goggles. The large lenses were edged in silver, and secured by a wide leather band as thick as my fist.

"Good gravy," I said aloud, realizing how much time these goggles would perch on my face. I pictured myself with permanent indentations around my eyes, like a raccoon.

Underneath the goggles rested the final pieces of my uniform. It was a leather cap that fit snugly over my head and ears, and a large khaki helmet with a small leather band encircling the brim.

I pulled the leather cap over my head first, feeling like a barnstormer. Cap had researched the optimal amount of clothing we needed, and the most utilitarian items he could find. The different types of clothing were best suited to carry us through heat, snow, rain, and bug-infested locations.

I had been drilled over and over again in the importance of packing light, restricted to a single small travel bag of personal items along with my uniform.

Dutifully, I tried on the shirts and shorts, then undressed and tried on the long-sleeved shirts and breeches. The pants ballooned comfortably at the waist, but tapered in at the knee.

"This is what I've been missing all this time, huh?" I thought. *"Maybe I'll never go back to wearing dresses."*

I sat down and pulled the wool socks over my pants, then slipped into the leather vest and buttoned it up. Carefully, I strung the belt through the large loops and cinched it.

Lacing the boots took some time, but it forced me to slow down and think.

I'd be living in this outfit for the next several months. Every morning, I'd get up and put this on.

I wondered if this was how my father had felt, dressing in his military uniform. The thought of my last view of him, standing tall in his khaki uniform at the train station, choked me up. What would he have thought if he could see me now? Would he be proud?

Or would he think this was utter foolishness?

Grabbing the goggles, I slipped them over my head and adjusted them so they were tight. I stood up and looked in the mirror.

I was looking at a stranger, but it was my reflection.

My newly shortened hair poked out underneath my cap. The khaki uniform and high brown boots accentuated my tall, lean frame.

I leaned forward to study myself, then stopped. I was missing something.

Impulsively, I crossed the room to my bed and reached under my pillow. The blue handkerchief Arnau had given me had been my private talisman, a precious item I slept with each evening.

Sometimes, when my loneliness overwhelmed me in the quiet hours of the night, I slipped my hand under my pillow and wrapped the handkerchief around my hand. It was silly, I knew, but it was my secret token. A reminder that someone had known me, cared for me. He never could have guessed how much that simple item had bolstered my spirits since he gave it to me.

I folded the handkerchief neatly and placed it in the breast pocket of my vest, right over my heart. The ends protruded slightly. Enough to remind me that it was guarding my heart at all times.

I stared at myself in the mirror, transfixed. I looked like an adult.

A *real* explorer.

Unconsciously, I traced my hands down over the pockets of my leather vest. I wondered what these pockets would be filled with, as I set out across the world. I looked down at my boots, glossed to such a shine that I could see my face, distorted, in the toe of each foot. I imagined these boots creased, crusted in dirt, as we traversed across sand dunes and mountain passes.

Slowly, a smile stole across my face. This was really happening. The adventure of my dreams was unfolding before my very eyes.

Edi was gone. In her place stood an explorer, ready for action.

CHAPTER 20

"COME MEET YOUR TEAMMATES, Edi," Cap tapped my hotel door. "We're meeting in my room, down the hall."

I finished packing my new clothes into a small satchel that contained a few toiletries, my hairbrush, my underwear and stockings, a pair of saddle shoes, a swimming costume, and a few other necessities. Regrettably, I threw my small tube of lipstick in, hoping I wouldn't have to use it often.

I fastened my bag and hurried to Cap's room. I knocked, and a large Hispanic man with a long dark beard and wild hair flung open the door.

"You must be Edith!" he exclaimed, a smile lighting up his face. "I've been looking forward to meeting you. I've already heard so much about you!"

"That's Chito Martinez," Cap said, looking up from the floor. He was surrounded by maps and journals full of neatly organized trip notes.

Chito looked intimidating, with his big frame and dark eyes and hair, but his friendly manner soon put me at ease. His primary responsibility, apart from driving, was to manage our supplies and food. "I love a good meal," he said, patting his stomach. "You won't starve with me around."

I laughed, as Cap stood up and pointed toward the other man in the room. "Bernard, come say hello," he said, nodding at me. "Meet your new teammate."

"Hello," Bernard said, not moving from his chair in the corner of the room. He was thin and slight, older than the others and quiet.

"Nice to meet you," I said, extending my hand. He abruptly jerked away, bolted up from his chair, and crossed the room to get away from me.

"Sorry, you'll get used to him," Cap said in a low voice. "He doesn't really like touching. But that's Bernard Harris. He's a whiz with mechanics, so he'll be the one who keeps our automobiles running."

Over the next few hours we sat together in our little team of four, Cap explained an organizational masterpiece. He had every conceivable detail of the next few months plotted to precision. Even money was laid out in neat stacks, labeled with the specific names of cities where he had planned for us to stop, refuel, and purchase fresh supplies.

I glanced over the different currencies, marveling at the array of colors and styles representing so many countries. Some bills were intricate and stylized, while some were small and thin with words and markings I couldn't read.

We planned to leave as soon as we could, aiming to make our first stops in Europe during the first month of the new year, 1923, to generate a buzz after holiday festivities had died down. Nice ended up being a good departure port for us, its wealthy citizens having given Cap a generous amount of the financial support needed to fund our expensive efforts.

Cap explained that we'd travel from Nice to Barcelona, and then travel along the Spanish coast to the Strait of Gibraltar, where we'd sail the automobiles into Morocco and then down through several African countries. We'd do a long leg through Africa, cutting across the continent until we reached Ethiopia and Yemen. After that, we'd either circle back through Western Europe to raise more funds, or head straight to India and China if we'd raised all the money we needed along the route, via ongoing donations and financial support.

"We need an exciting destination to explore first, to drum up interest from the public," Cap told us. "The African continent will do just that. The Chinook Voyageurs won't start with something so hard."

Cap sent me to work with Bernard, our mechanic, over the course of those remaining few days before we departed.

"I'm in charge of teaching you to drive these beauties," Bernard grumbled. "You better listen to me. You better not put a dent in them."

"I won't."

"Or a scratch."

"Noted, Bernard."

Bernard sighed, then motioned me inside. We stepped into the garage, the cool light from outside reflecting on the black hood of the three Gallivanter Expedition Model T Fords. Though Bernard didn't touch people, he lovingly ran his hands over the hood.

Over the next few days, Bernard patiently showed me every detail of the Model Ts. He drilled me in the most necessary tasks, like fixing a punctured tire, repairing the headlight, and maintaining the brakes, fluid lines, and gas canisters.

"To check the gasoline, the most important thing to keep track of, you'll lift up the seat like this," he said, lifting up the upholstered seat cushion in the front of the car. A large metal container lay on its side, and he unscrewed the small cap and set it on the ground.

"Use this to measure the gas," he said, pulling a long marked yardstick out and sticking it into the open hole.

"This has about, oh, ten gallons of gas or so in it," he said, pulling out the yardstick and checking the mark.

"How far can I go on that?" I asked, curiously.

"Pretty far, but you don't want to get stranded somewhere with an empty tank," he said. "You have to make sure you have a reserve can of gas in the trunk, just in case you need to stop and top it off while you're traveling."

Bernard also showed me how to change the oil, which was a more complicated task. It required me crawling under the car and fiddling with several tiny screws.

"If it drips out, just a drop or two, you know the oil level is about right," he said, watching as I carefully pried the top of the oil pan loose. Sure enough, oil dribbled down all over my face and neck.

"This is the messy part," Bernard said, looking at me as I lay on my back in the dirt, covered in oil droplets. "This is why girls don't like doing this kind of stuff."

"I don't mind it," I said, wiping the oil drips off my cheeks.

"Good," he replied, watching me closely. "I'm not going to do it for you while we're traveling."

"Why not? Aren't you the team mechanic?"

"Yeah. But you need to know how to do it yourself, in case something happens to me. Or you get separated from the group."

"What else do I need to know?"

"It's a four cylinder auto, with a horsepower of twenty."

"Horsepower?"

"Yes," Bernard said, patting the gleaming metal on the hood of the engine. The Ford was boxy and tall, the windshields two thick panes of glass, held in place with metal, that tilted to allow air to cool the automobile. "Think of it as being equal to the pulling strength of twenty horses."

"Oh. Wow."

I had to step up to the only door, located on the passenger's side of the car, in order to slide into the driver's seat. The seat itself was a long leather cushion, balanced on top of the metal ledge that held the gas tank.

Bernard showed me the fabric roofs and poles he'd packed, in case we needed to keep rain and snow off our heads. "We'll mostly drive with the top down, but we have this if we need it. That's the beauty of these Fords—we can modify them on our own."

"It's pretty clever," I admitted, watching as he showed me how to crank the tiny windshield wiper that perched right above my head on the driver's side.

"Right. The cars are the latest technology. Many people we encounter probably won't have seen one of these yet. So we need to be able to show them, teach them about the vehicle."

Though the cars had electric starts, he reminded me that the conditions might prevent us from using it. In case the engines got too cold to be warmed up by the kerosene lanterns we'd hang under them, we'd have to manually crank the Fords to life.

I slipped into the passenger's seat as Bernard climbed in the driver's seat, showing me the three metal pedals on the floor. They protruded out several inches, their ends disappearing under the bottom of the car.

"This is how you make this go," he said, pointing to the far right pedal. "Here's the brake. If you step on it, it stops. This middle pedal, that reverses the car—makes it go backwards. On the far left, this is the clutch."

"How do you use those?"

"You step on them with your foot, pressing down. Like you're stepping on a bug that you're trying to squish."

"I don't squish bugs. They don't bother me."

"You're an odd girl," he frowned. "Focus. You have a lot to learn."

"Sorry."

"Now, to use the clutch, you press your foot down—all the way to the bottom of the floor—with this left pedal. But you also have to use this handbrake," he said, pointing to a lever next to the door.

"Press this forward, like this, and you'll be in low gear. But if you press the handbrake and press all the way forward, you'll be in high gear, to go faster," he said, demonstrating.

"How fast can I go?"

"Oh, about forty miles in an hour. But we have work to do before you can drive. We're not done."

He showed me how to use a little metal bar, the throttle, on the steering wheel to adjust the speed of the auto. Pressing it down made it go faster, while slowly pulling it up slowed the Model T to an eventual engine idle. To turn it all on, I learned how to spark the engine using a different metal bar, the crank, sticking out awkwardly from the steering wheel.

But that wasn't all I needed to do, I discovered. I also had to turn the key on, activating the four coil boxes that connected to the four cylinders in the engine. I also had two choke buttons, one on the metal dashboard, and the other on the outside of the engine hood.

We slid out and Bernard showed me how to engage the crank to prime the engine in case we had to start it up in a cold place. "You have to warm it up so it can run smoothly," he said, demonstrating how he cranked the engine. "You try."

"How many times?"

"Maybe three or four times. But make sure you have the handbrake engaged, so the automobile doesn't roll over you as you turn the engine over," he cautioned.

I grimaced as I imagined the heavy Model T running me over. What a way to go.

"Riding horses is easier," I muttered.

"Horses? Bah," he grumbled, rolling his eyes. "Dealing with people is the hard part."

Initially overwhelmed by the amount I had to learn, I quickly progressed in knowledge and ability in handling the automobile.

Soon, I was driving around town with Bernard in the passenger seat, bracing himself nervously against the dash. Gradually, he settled in and relaxed as I grew more confident behind the wheel.

"You're not half bad, for a gi—a beginner," Bernard wisely stopped himself before finishing his thought.

Already, I was starting to click with the small team of men. I suppose they had imagined getting a stunning, elegant young woman with perfectly coiffed hair and expertly applied makeup, and were initially surprised to get me. But they seemed perfectly happy with me, drawing me into their routine and their jokes with ease.

I was so busy adjusting to the Gallivanters that I hadn't even realized that for the first time in a long time, I didn't feel lonely or out of place.

CHAPTER 21

BEFORE I KNEW IT, THE day of our long-awaited press release was upon us. Cap and Chito gave me a crash course in handling the press, sensing my apprehension.

"Be confident," Cap told me. "Don't think that you're better than anyone in the room, but assume everyone is dying to know what you've seen. Keep that little air of mystery—that detached 'you can't imagine what it was really like' attitude—but be friendly and approachable."

"And smile," Chito added. "Smile all the time. You're having the time of your life on this trip. Think of all the new things you'll see. And all the new foods you'll be trying."

"What do I do if they ask me personal questions?"

"Like what?"

"Oh, about my family, my background, you know."

"You can reply honestly," Cap said. "You don't have anything to hide, right?"

"No," I replied slowly, then hesitated. "I mean, I wasn't exactly popular in school, if I'm being truthful."

He laughed. "Neither was I."

"I was," Chito chuckled. "But *Bernard* definitely wasn't. That doesn't matter here."

"But won't people see right through me?"

"People will see what you show them, Edi," Cap replied. "Besides, where we're headed next says more about any of us than where we've been in the past."

"Are you always so wise?" I teased. "Does that come with the captain title?"

"I'm an old man," he winked. "It comes with the territory."

"Old!" I exclaimed, laughing. "You're young. How old are you?"

"I'm twenty-six."

"What does your family think about all of this, anyway?" I asked. I was dying to know. Cap never spoke about anyone or anything from his past. Did he have a girlfriend? A man like this must have women throwing themselves at him all the time.

He hesitated. "My family is in Poland."

"Don't you have a girlfriend? What does she think?"

"That's a subject for another time," Cap stood up. "Let's talk about your name, while I'm thinking about it."

I wrinkled my nose, frustrated. He must have a sweetheart and didn't want to tell me about her. Instead, I replied, "My name?"

"Yes. Our group is called the 'Gallivanter Expedition,' after my name, Captain Grant Gallivanter. Well, not my real name, but it captures what we're going for. But everyone on the team goes by it, for the duration of the trek. We're the Gallivanters."

"Wait. Grant Gallivanter isn't your real name?"

"Of course not," he smiled. "Don't you think that'd be a little too convenient for a world-traveling adventurer?"

"I thought maybe it was fate. Your name led you to this life."

"I wish," he laughed. "My real name is Walenty. Walenty Jankowski."

"Walenty?" I repeated. "That's unique."

"It's Polish. It means 'strong' and 'powerful.' And it's spelled with a 'w' though it sounds like a 'v.' It comes from the Latin word 'valeo'—you know, like Saint Valentine?"

"You've done a lot of research about your name, huh?" I teased. "I have no clue what my name means."

He grinned. "I do love to research. But you see why I changed it? It's a mouthful. For most Europeans and Americans, at least. Grant Gallivanter is much easier to say. And remember."

"So you're originally from Poland," I mused. "Are we ever going to go there on the expedition?"

"At some point."

"Are we going to see your family there? Will I get to learn all the secrets of the elusive Captain Gallivanter from them?"

"Edi," he groaned. "We need to talk about your name. Not my life."

"What's wrong with my name?"

"Well, for starters, your last name—your stage name—will need to be Gallivanter."

"But for me to have the same last name, as a girl...will people assume we're married?"

"In some places, it'll be better for people to assume we *are* married, Edi," he replied. "A lot of people aren't progressive like you or me. It's better for them to think we're husband and wife than to find out that we're traveling together as mere companions. We have to avoid any hint of impropriety on this expedition. It'll be an uphill battle, especially for you, a young lady traveling with men."

"Won't your girlfriend be upset, though, that I take the same last name as you?" I said, circling back to his personal life. I was still curious.

"Let me worry about that. You just worry about what your stage name is going to be. Your first name."

"Fine," I said. "Have any bright ideas?"

"I do, actually. How do you like Lady Gallivanter?"

Memories of the nuns telling me that I was no lady sprang to mind. "No, I hate it."

"What? Why?"

I debated if I should tell him about the cruelty of boarding school, but decided against it. *"Better to keep some things to myself,"* I mused. *"It's not like he's being completely open about his past with me, after all."* Aloud, I replied, "I just don't like it."

"I do, though," he frowned. "It's short, easy to pronounce. Recognizable. Captain and Lady Gallivanter. It's perfect."

"But it makes me sound like nobility, and I'm definitely not."

"It's just a stage name. It conjures up a certain image, a refinement—"

"Oh, I'm refined now?" I laughed. "You wouldn't be saying that if you saw how much oil I scraped out from under my nails this morning, after Bernard made me practice changing the oil on the Fords."

"Well, no," he grinned, shaking his head. "Of all the things I'd say about you, that's probably not one of the words I'd use."

"So don't call me Lady then. It's not me."

"Edi, we have to come up with something snappy. Something fresh. A name that conjures up the spirit of exploration, of a woman who traverses jungles and mountains, mingles with monkeys and natives. Your given name doesn't exactly do that. 'Edith' sounds nice and sensible."

"Yes, but not Lady. Anything else."

"What about Gal?"

"It seems a bit bland," I admitted.

"Pioneer Gallivanter?"

"Only if I'm carrying a pickax to head out West for the Gold Rush," I laughed.

"Fine, you come up with something," Cap smirked. "It's harder than you think."

"Challenge accepted," I said, drumming my fingers together. "What about Lassie?"

"Too Scottish," Cap replied. "It'll alienate the English crowds, anyway. They're a bit touchy about each other."

I searched my brain for a name. How would I describe myself? I wasn't like most girls. I loved being outdoors, wandering through the woods for hours, leaning under the big oaks on the lawn at school and staring up at the sky, working in the stables—

The stables jogged a memory. I remembered Arnau, the way he always called me his Andiamo. "It's Italian," he had said. "It's exotic. You know, the language of love and all."

I felt my face flush as I blurted out, "Andiamo!"

"Why are you blushing?" Cap asked, studying my face. "Why does that name cause this reaction?"

"I'm not blushing," I responded, feeling the heat crawl up my face even as I lied.

"You most certainly are," he laughed. "You're beet red. I've never seen you blush."

"Andiamo. Andi, for short," I repeated, attempting to distract him from my pink cheeks. "Andi Gallivanter. It sounds natural. And it's pretty close to Edi, so it'll be easy for me to use."

"Andiamo," he said slowly, trying it out. "What does it mean?"

"It's Italian. It means 'here we go!' It's a word of action. Let's go, driving forward. Andiamo."

Cap was still staring at me. "I don't understand your reaction," he frowned. "Is this some sort of romantic ode to a boyfriend or something? A pet name from a childhood sweetheart?"

Did I detect a bit of jealousy or was it my imagination? *He probably has a girlfriend,*" I reminded myself. I could feel my face getting warm again. The memory of Arnau's proposal and the look on his face when he said goodbye flooded my mind, unbidden. I pushed it down.

"I don't have a boyfriend," I retorted. "I just like the name. Andiamo. Andi. Andi Gallivanter."

"Andiamo," he repeated, then shook his head. "I don't know."

"I do. Andiamo Gallivanter. It's perfect."

"The press conference is tonight, Edi," he reminded me. "We have to come up with a name by then, and we haven't come up with anything better than Lady Gallivanter. I say we go with that. It's just a stage name, after all. It's good enough."

I crossed my arms. "But it's not *just* a name. The whole world will know me by this name, Cap. It should mean something. And matter to me."

"Let me think about it." Cap stood and checked his pocket watch. "We have a few hours before the press conference. We'll be suited up in our khakis and boots, and helmets, too. We have to look the part."

"I'll be ready," I promised.

Cap stood above me, studying my face. "You're going to be great, Edi. You're ready for this."

"I hope so."

"Oh, and wear that red lipstick," Cap mused. "You're on stage tonight, a performer. The world explorer, Lady Gallivanter. You're going to knock 'em dead."

CHAPTER 22

THAT EVENING, I DRESSED carefully in my ironed khaki uniform and curled my short bob into fashionable waves.

I checked my teeth and twirled in the mirror several times, hoping I looked presentable. Crossing the room to my travel bag, I dug for the tube of lipstick. "You again," I muttered.

Standing in front of the mirror, I applied the lipstick. I grimaced, then practiced smiling. It did catch the eye, however uncomfortable it felt.

It was starting to drizzle, so I popped my helmet on and jogged out the door of the hotel and headed toward the oversized balcony out back, where Cap was assembling a small mob of photographers and cameramen to publicize news of our expedition.

Cap was already there, Chito and Bernard leaning against the balcony behind him. As soon as his eyes landed on me, Cap waved me over. "Welcome, my dear! You look splendid, as always!"

I smothered a grin. Cap was already performing for the crowd, even though they were still busy setting up. *This* was the handsome, confident man I'd first seen on stage.

"Let's put you right here," he said, taking me by the arm and leading me to a white marble pillar bordered by palm trees. He stood back, taking in the scene.

"Yes, perfect contrast with the hair," he mused softly to himself. "I'll stand here, on the other side, and take the helmet off halfway through…"

"Cap?" I asked, anxiety gnawing at me as I looked at the cameras already pointed at my face.

"Yes?"

"What exactly do you want me to say?"

He grinned. "Let me do the talking. Just smile for the cameras. I'll ask you to introduce yourself and share what you're most excited about."

Chito and Bernard sidled up, and the cameramen lined up expectantly behind their cameras. "Everybody ready?" Cap called out.

"Yes, sir," came the chorus of responses.

I stood nervously in my spot, fussing with my hat. Cap noticed and leaned over to me, speaking softly into my ear, "Don't lock your knees, whatever you do. We can't have you passing out in front of the cameras."

"Okay."

"Confidence, Edi! Everyone watching wants to be *you!*"

"Yeah..."

"I chose you for a reason," Cap's warm breath tickled my ear. "Believe in yourself. I do."

I straightened and met his eyes with a broad smile. He winked at me. "That's my girl."

The cameras started whirring and clicking. Lights flashed brightly, blinding us. It felt surreal, even as the men smoked behind their whirring cameras and Cap smoothed his shirt.

Was this really happening to me?

Cap's booming voice interrupted my thoughts.

"Welcome, ladies and gentlemen!" he cried. "Prepare to be astonished! For the first time ever, this small group of adventurers will be going across the globe to mysterious lands, previously unseen by civilized eyes!"

Stepping forward, he continued. "The whole way, we'll be guided by our trusty Ford Model T automobiles, the latest in technological advancement. The primitive cultures we'll see will marvel at these modern inventions, these man-made machines shaping our world!"

I blinked, trying to keep a smile on my face though I was surprised by the force of Cap's charisma. Had he written this out in advance? He certainly had a way with words.

He turned to me, sweeping his hat off his head.

"Mesdames and messieurs, we are the Gallivanters. A team of professionals, united in a desire to explore and discover. And of course, you all want to know first about our newest team member," he beamed at me.

I smiled woodenly, hoping my lipstick wasn't smeared.

"I present to you the rarest of all women," Cap proclaimed. "Joining me along the way in this expedition across the globe is the stunning, the beautiful and brilliant lady of every man's dreams!"

I felt my confidence waver. It was awkward listening to Cap exaggerate my charms to the reporters. Good gravy, I certainly wasn't the woman of every man's dreams—I wasn't the woman of *any* man's dreams.

Cap gallantly swung his arm around my shoulder and pulled me close. We stood shoulder-to-shoulder. I didn't know if I should slink down a little to look shorter or stand tall. Was Cap the kind of man who was intimidated by a woman as lanky as him?

Cap solved the dilemma for me.

"The only thing greater than her stature is her thirst for adventure! Her call for exploration! Her desire to see things that no man has gazed upon before!"

He smiled at me, then gazed back at the cameras. "We're pleased to announce an intrepid adventurer, the inspiring young beauty joining us and risking everything to circumnavigate the world. Ladies and gentlemen, I present to you *Lady Gallivanter!*"

Instead of thunderous applause, I heard the gentle whirr of cameras rolling.

Cap squeezed my arm. "Tell us a bit about yourself, my dear!"

I smiled artificially, and stared directly into the sea of cameras, not sure what to focus on. "Um, well, I—I'm excited to be here," I faltered. This was harder than I expected, especially with no reaction from a crowd to encourage me.

Cap nodded encouragement, squeezing my shoulder. "She's a bit new to all of this, our delicate beauty," he interrupted.

Without warning, the memory of sitting with Cap in the hotel lobby flitted into my mind. *"We'll be the first expedition in history to have a woman with us,"* he had beamed. In that moment, it hit me. I was the first. I set the tone for everyone else coming behind me. And I'd be doing this—this performance—in front of cameras over and over again.

This was no time to be timid.

I pictured my gawky childish frame, hauling tree branches and cutting timber for the fire at home, blisters breaking open and oozing all over my hands. I saw myself standing on the deck, looking out at the ocean as I headed off on my own to boarding school for the first time. I remembered the feeling of punching Emile in the face, standing up for what was right even though it wasn't ladylike. I recalled the hundreds of times I'd galloped through the woods, hair streaming behind me, laughing with Arnau.

Who cared if I was ladylike? Strength and independence had carried me my whole life. It was time to show people that spirit.

I decided to match Cap's energy. I could act, too.

"I'd love to tell you a bit about myself, folks," I said, flashing a bright smile and stepping forward. "I grew up in New York, land of the free and home of the brave. I love my freedom, and there's nothing better than being in the great outdoors. I grew up in the country, splitting wood and mending fences and riding horses."

Out of the corner of my eye, I saw Cap's satisfied smile. Bolstered, I continued.

"I've spent the last several years as an independent young woman, attending boarding school here in France. I speak several languages, and have learned a whole lot about automobiles in the last few days. I'm thrilled to be headed out on this adventure with the Gallivanters. It's the journey of a lifetime, and I couldn't be more excited."

"The first expedition in history to have a woman," my brain whispered. *"I set the tone."*

Impulsively, I put my hands on my hips and raised my chin. "Oh, and the most important thing to know about me? My name. It's the name you'll never forget."

I grinned as wide as I could. "I'm Andiamo Gallivanter. Andiamo—here we go!"

I nodded at Cap that I was done.

"There you have it, folks." To his credit, Cap's smile didn't falter. He bowed in my direction. "The intrepid and gorgeous young explorer, Andiamo Gallivanter!"

Cap introduced Bernard and Chito, then gave a brief overview of our automobiles and itineraries. He ended by imploring fans to visit us—and send us their donations, if they felt so inclined to contribute to our worthy cause—as we presented in cities all over the world.

"Folks, if you want to journey along with us from the comfort of your own homes, we'll be having tour stops in cities across the globe," Cap crooned into the cameras. "Come and witness the majesty of our journey, the mystery of our adventure, and the peril of our travels."

He took his helmet off and held it to his heart, imploring.

"We can't do this alone, ladies and gentlemen. We need your support. Without you, this journey would be nothing. We do it all for the education and entertainment for the people right here, the people just like you. For just a small donation, we can continue our journey and ensure we have all the food and supplies we need."

I realized I had a lot to learn when it came to managing the press. I kept a smile on my face, but listened closely to how Cap expertly managed his speech.

"Without your help, we could find ourselves in a *dangerous* situation, without food or water, exposed to the elements," Cap proclaimed. "Your support ensures our health—nay, our success!"

He smiled, raked his hand through his blonde hair, and settled his helmet back on.

"And now, we bid adieu, as we must prepare for our long journey. Thank you all for attending, and remember to keep your eyes open, your loved ones close, and always be ready for adventure!"

With a quick bow, he saluted the cameras and strode away. He immediately started thanking each individual cameraman, clearly a master at working the crowd.

When the last of the cameramen and reporters packed up, Cap wandered back to me.

"Andiamo?" he asked, raising his eyebrows. "I'd already introduced you as Lady Gallivanter."

"Yes. I told you, the name matters to me. I want to be Andiamo."

"Apparently you have some special fondness for that name," he replied, a hint of irritation in his voice. The excitement of the press conference was wearing off for both of us. He took his helmet off and sighed while I felt a bit guilty. I imagined he was overwhelmed with the never-ending burden of planning the expedition. I didn't want to be a source of added stress for him.

"I'm sorry," I apologized. "But it's done and we don't have to debate it anymore. You chose me because I'm a straight shooter, right?"

"Right," he laughed ruefully. "That's part of your charm."

He rubbed his eyes and collapsed in a chair. "Gosh, it's exhausting to put on the old show on top of all this preparation. I've never been so tired, and we haven't even started yet."

I sat down next to him and looked over the balcony. The drizzle had stopped and the air was heavy and wet. The palm trees swayed in the breeze, droplets of rain shimmering on the fronds as they moved.

"Andiamo Gallivanter," Cap mused thoughtfully, head in his hand. "I suppose it works. I'll have to start using it now, all the time, to get used to it. It's exotic. It'll ingratiate us to the Italians, once we work our way across the globe. It's memorable. Crisp, snappy."

"Crisp and snappy sounds like me. The woman of every man's dreams, not so much, Cap," I laughed.

He grinned.

"It doesn't matter if you're the woman of every man's dreams, Andiamo Gallivanter. All that matters is that you're living *your* dreams."

CHAPTER 23

"I CAN'T BELIEVE THIS will delay us," Cap groaned. "I've put in months of work. We have a schedule. *Of course* the government would be the one snag."

As the late addition to the team, Cap had scrambled to secure the dozens of visas I needed to move freely within all the countries we'd be visiting. But now, just days before we were set to head out, my visas were stuck on hold.

Cap and I had visited the American ambassador's office so often that the receptionist recognized our faces even before we pushed our way into the building.

"I apologize, mademoiselle, we do not yet have the visas in order," she explained, over and over. Our frustration mounted.

"My expedition around the world has a set departure date," I pleaded. "I have to make it! I can't delay!"

"We're trying our best," the receptionist replied. "This process usually takes several months. We must contact each separate country's government office, explain your trip, and wait for their staff to fill out and mail the visas back. It just takes time."

"I know it does," Cap grumbled. "I've done just that for three teammates. Can't we hurry it along for one more?"

She shrugged.

Cap grew more desperate with each day that passed without my visas.

"It's important we leave on time, Andi," he told me. "We have a set schedule. We can't afford to lose time at the very beginning here. We're planning around winter snow, and closed roads and mountain passes. We can't delay."

"I know, Cap," I said, frustrated. "What can I do?"

"We could leave without her," Bernard suggested drily.

"Bernard," Cap warned as I crossed my arms.

"What?"

"We're a team, Bernard. We all go together."

"No," Bernard shook his head. "I mean we can take the Fords and go ahead of her. We have to get supplies at our first stop in Spain, anyway. It'll take a few days. She can wait here until she gets her visas and then meet us in Spain."

"She can't go alone," Cap shook his head. "It's not safe."

Before I could open my mouth, Bernard stood up. "We have three cars, Cap. It's going to take three of us to get them to Spain. We have no one to spare. She *has* to go alone."

I noticed Chito trying to catch Cap's eye. He was shaking his head.

Would they really leave me behind before we even got started? What if they decided it was just easier to cut me now? Were they having second thoughts about me?

Internally, panic and anger rose. I leapt to my feet. "I thought the whole point was that we were a team?"

"Of course we're a team," Cap said hastily. "But Bernard has a good point. We have to get to Spain by January. And once we get there, it's going to take several days to purchase all our food supplies, get the automobiles fully prepared, and get the cameras in good working order."

I bit my lip.

"Besides, I'm also considering getting a local guide to show us around Spain," Cap continued, glancing at me. "I have some leads but we still need to do a few interviews. If we can get the rest of us there and get a head start on that, you could just meet up with us in Barcelona."

"Do you not want me on this trip?" I asked, crossing my arms. I couldn't help myself from sounding angry.

"So feisty for someone so young," Cap replied. The amusement in his voice only made me madder.

"Cap, spit it out," I shot back. "Are you trying to stop me from going?"

"Do you honestly think that's what I'm doing?" Cap replied, smothering a smile. "I could think of a few other ways to tell you what I really think of you."

What was that supposed to mean? The thought of being left out put me right over the edge. I'd been over the moon about this expedition, and now it was falling apart before I even got to enjoy myself.

"Just tell me the truth!" I said sharply. "If you don't want me on the team, tell me now!"

Chito and Bernard stared at me, concern in their eyes. Swiftly, Cap stood up and grabbed me by the elbow. "Outside," he commanded. I let him steer me onto the balcony, where he closed the door behind us.

"What's wrong?"

"I don't want to talk to you," I retorted. "You don't even care if I'm on the team. You're ready to head out without me."

"Andi," he started, but I turned away. Angrily, I grabbed the edge of the balcony with both hands and gripped it, my knuckles turning white.

"Talk to me," he said, this time in a softer tone.

I shook my head, facing away from him. After this week of excitement, anticipating the expedition after so many years of being miserable, the thought of being left behind again—alone—crushed me.

"Please," Cap said, resting his hands on the railing next to me. "We're going to be living together on this team. We need to be open with each other. Just be honest with me."

I wheeled around. "Honest? You want *me* to be open?"

"Yes. It's you and me, Captain and Andiamo Gallivanter, going forward against the world. If we can't trust each other, who can we trust?"

"Oh, this is rich. Captain Gallivanter wants me to be open when he can't even be open about his own life."

"What's that supposed to mean?"

"You know what I mean."

"I don't," he replied, confused. "What are you talking about?"

I glared at him. "You've kept things from me. Your love life—look at you, I know you have one—your past—you wanting me on the team—*everything*. If you've changed your mind about me, just be man enough to admit it to me—"

"What? No," Cap interrupted. "I never said I want you off the team. Never. That's the last thing I want."

"You want to go on to Spain without me."

Cap ran his hand through his hair and exhaled in frustration. "You're wrong about that."

"You seemed all too eager to head off without me, and let me catch up at some point," I complained. "I didn't realize I was merely a shiny toy for the cameras, to get you some attention, and you'd leave me behind when you moved on."

Suddenly, Cap snaked his arm around my shoulders. "What are you doing?" I protested.

"Listen to me," he said, keeping his arm firmly in place. I wriggled around, but he only pulled me closer. "Stop fighting me and listen, you hard-headed fool."

Even in my outrage, I felt a small glimmer of pleasure as he held me.

"No, that's not why I'm here," I told myself, fighting the urge to relax into him. *"I'm not here for romance."*

"Are you ready to calm down and listen?" Cap asked. I glared at him, but his hip pressed against mine distracted me.

"Fine. What?"

He rested his arm around my shoulders and spoke softly. "I want you on this team. I *need* you on this trip with me, Andi. You're sensational. I promise you, I'm not trying to replace you. I'm not leaving you behind. I'm just trying to make sure we make our scheduled stops on time."

I didn't respond. He had said he needed me. What did that mean? He himself needed me, or the team needed me?

"You're stressed out," he continued. "That makes sense. It's a monumental shift, a totally new direction you're heading in. A few weeks ago, you didn't even know I existed. Now you're traveling around the world with me."

He was right, I realized.

"These emotions, these outbursts—it's all just a side effect of that apprehension we're all feeling," Cap said, his body warm against mine. "We'll be fine. We're all dealing with the same worries. I've felt this way, too. Just keep being open with me about it and we'll work through it together."

"Why won't *you* tell me anything?" I blurted. "You've evaded every question I've ever asked about your family. About a girlfriend. About everything."

I felt his body stiffen. He released his hand from around my shoulders. "What do you think you need to know?" he responded, his tone frosty.

I knew it. There was someone. A girlfriend, no doubt. The words tumbled out of my mouth before I could stop them.

"I'm to believe that you won't leave me behind when you're clearly leaving some poor girlfriend of yours behind? Doesn't she care?" I glared. I knew I was out of line but I couldn't stop myself. "Don't you care? Or is this what you do? You just leave people behind when you're tired of them?"

"My personal life isn't relevant to this expedition," Cap retorted.

"You just told me to be open with you. How hypocritical to ask someone else to be a straight shooter, when you yourself are not."

Cap turned away from me. I sensed his anger, though he said nothing in defense. I doubled down. "Don't you think I deserve to know? How am I supposed to work with you, eat every meal with you, maybe even sleep next to you on the road and not know anything about you?"

He sighed. "You don't want to hear my story. I'm not the man you probably assume I am."

"What's that supposed to mean?"

He hesitated, staring at the street below. Pedestrians mingled in the plaza below, happy to see each other. We were a contrast, high above their heads, standing uncomfortably next to each other.

"Fine," he replied, his voice low. "You want to know about me? You're right. There is someone. A woman. My fiancée."

"Fiancée?" I exclaimed. "You're engaged? Why haven't you told me about her? When are you getting married?"

For a long moment, he said nothing. Then he replied quietly, "We aren't."

I noticed pain in his face. "Sorry," I said, feeling foolish. "I didn't mean to pry."

"No, I understand your questions. You deserve to know me. I'm asking you to trust me, to put your life in my hands, so it's only fair," he said, staring at the street. "It's just...my life is...messy."

"You don't have to tell me."

"You're probably better off hearing it from me now," Cap exhaled. "You might as well find out about my checkered past at this point, before we're stranded in some godforsaken spot and it makes you want to leave."

"Checkered past? What do you mean?"

He sighed and his shoulders dipped. "Before this expedition, I was in prison."

Well, I certainly hadn't been expecting this. "When?"

"I was released nearly five years ago," he said, staring out at the ocean in the distance. I could see the horizon line reflected in his bright blue eyes.

"Why were you in prison?"

He stared hard at the view. "My fiancée put me there."

I could see he was miserable. "Well, now you have to explain *that,*" I replied lightly. "People don't usually throw their betrothed in lockdown."

His reply was slow. "I was born in Poland, though it wasn't Poland quite then—it was still the Kingdom of Prussia. My family was very poor. My father died when I was small, and my mother did her best to keep my brother and me going, but it was difficult."

Cap closed his eyes briefly.

"Honestly, my memories of my childhood are of being hungry—all the time, just so hungry. We'd walk by the bakery window in our town, and I would stare at the loaves of bread. Smell the baking cinnamon rolls. I told myself that someday, I'd be able to afford to eat like that. To provide for myself. To have a full belly for once."

Cap paused, and inhaled through his nose. "My older brother died when he was eighteen. Factory accident. I was sixteen. When he died, my mother struggled. I joined the Polish military, to help feed us. I lied about my age, and got in when I was just sixteen."

"Sixteen?" I exclaimed. "How on earth did you manage that?"

"We had my brother's papers," Cap admitted. "My mother was starving. She was unwell. I had to do something to help her. At that time, the military was in desperate need of soldiers. They had a handsome bonus for enlistment, in addition to a monthly stipend I could send home. I hated to lie, but I had no other choice. Not many other places there would hire a poor teenager, you know. I used my brother's birth certificate and papers, and was accepted without a second glance. I served for a year, but even I could tell my country was on the brink of war. I knew I had to get out, and soon, or I'd be cannon fodder in the front lines."

He glanced at me and continued slowly.

"My mother died while I was in the army," he said, his voice low. "Suddenly, I had no one. The few members of my extended family still alive were too poor to take me in. I was alone. After a year of military service, in early 1914, I took all my savings and headed to the United States of America. I got out of Poland just in time. Just a few months later, they were at war."

While I'd been learning to make biscuits and groaning about playing with the girls at recess, Cap had been toting around a rifle, fearing for his life. Our past couldn't have been more different.

Cap rubbed his face. "I'd made friends with a man who helped me get to New Orleans," he said. "This time, I used my real identification, not my brother's name. I wanted to do it right, to do it all honestly. If I was going to start over, with a new life, it had to be my life. I was only seventeen when I moved to America."

"You sailed across the ocean, alone, in search of a fresh start," I nodded. "I know something about what that's like."

He smiled ruefully. "America changed me. As soon as I got there, I wanted to belong. To be an American. How can I describe it?"

He thought for a moment. "America was freedom, after living in a part of the world that wasn't free. It was the place that would let me be anything I wanted."

Cap glanced at me. "After a childhood of nothing, what I wanted more than anything was to see everything. To travel. To me, that was the height of achievement. To experience different food, see monuments and art and jungles—the very thought was intoxicating."

I watched his face, seeing a new sort of strength in him that I didn't even realize he had.

"At age seventeen, I changed my name from Walenty to Grant, a name my American friends could pronounce. I used my soldier's pay to buy a small house, and I got a job as a construction worker," he added. "I even joined a church. I became an American citizen, too."

"Walenty."

He chuckled. "It's strange to hear someone use my real name now, after all these years," he admitted.

"Sorry."

"No, it's nice," he said. "In a way, it's comforting to come clean. To have you know me."

"So how exactly did your fiancée come into the story?"

"Ah, yeah," he smiled ruefully. "Milly."

"Milly?"

"Yes, Milly. I met her at a saloon one evening. The men hung out there after work. That's where I met Bernard, by the way. He was the best metalworker on our site, hands down. I knew he'd be a great mechanic for the Fords."

I pictured Bernard sitting in the darkest corner of the bar, flatly ignoring everyone around him. How had Cap possibly convinced him to join this expedition?

"Anyway, Milly was a singer—you know, one of those aspiring actress types—and she performed at the saloon some nights," Cap continued. "She crooned her way through that night's songs, staring at me the whole night. In between sets, she sat up at the bar and talked to me. Later that night, well—"

"I can fill in the blanks, Cap."

"No," he made a face. "Not *that*. I'm a gentleman. I meant that we fell for each other. That night was the start of a whirlwind relationship. Call it prewar jitters, or two people swept off their feet, but within a few weeks we decided to get married. We were young. I'd never before been in a relationship. Hell, I hardly had any friends, growing up. I was too busy surviving to think about romance. I didn't know any better. I didn't see the manipulation."

"Oh," I replied, scrunching my nose. He laughed.

"Ah, it's not so funny now to dredge up these memories after I've stuffed them down all these years," Cap said, rueful. "Milly assumed I was a rich and successful man. She set her sights on me and figured I'd be the one to lift her out of poverty and carry her all the way to Broadway, to life on the big stage. Problem was, I wasn't rich. I had saved most of my money from my time in the service, and put all of it into rebuilding my new life in America."

He was silent for a moment, reflecting.

"By the time I figured out how Milly used me, our relationship was already circling the drain. She was spending every night down at a different saloon or dinner club, trying to get famous. I'd come home from work, bone tired and body aching, and make dinner for us both. Sometimes she'd have a few bites before rushing off to perform. Most of the time, her plate sat in the oven, staying warm, while I ate by myself. She spent my paychecks as fast as I could cash them. New clothes, new shoes, new lipstick—she had to 'look the part of a real actress,' she told me dozens of times."

"We grew apart, pretty quickly. After a few months, I couldn't even remember what we'd ever loved about each other in the first place. Maybe it wasn't even love at all."

He sighed, then pressed on.

"Milly found herself a new man, someone who actually had money," he said, bitterness in his voice. "I saw them. Together. She intended to leave me, but she needed a reason. We'd been fighting. A lot. It was pretty tense between us. Right about then, the Great War was going on, and she decided to use that in her favor. She trotted right down to the war office and reported me as a German spy. Said I was hiding out, spying on the troops, reporting back to the Huns."

"That's insane! You're Polish, not German."

"Yeah, that's Milly," he replied. "She had a flair for the dramatic. Actresses, you know."

"What happened?"

He shook his head. "They arrested me. You remember how people were back then, thinking spies were hiding everywhere. She agreed to testify against me, to say she'd seen me spying and preparing reports to give to the Germans. My accent didn't help, even though it's so slight. Those American blokes couldn't tell a Polish accent from a German one, so no matter what I said to defend myself, my very speech sounded suspect to them."

"But how could she do that to you? Didn't she know you were from Poland? What you'd been through?"

"She never really knew me. You've known me for just a few weeks, Andi, and you already know me far better than she ever did."

"How long did you spend in prison?"

"About six months," he replied. "It was the worst six months of my life. I never want to be cooped up like that again."

"How did you get out?"

"It took them that long to set a trial date and bring me before a judge. The court appointed me a lawyer—a real sleazy guy, but at least he did his job—and when we arrived at the courthouse, Milly was nowhere to be seen," Cap rolled his eyes. "She'd skipped town, probably with her new boyfriend. Without a witness and with no hard proof, the judge let me go. My construction crew served as character witnesses, too. They backed me up."

We stood side by side, looking at the ocean. Behind us, I heard Chito and Bernard murmuring together in the room. It made sense why Cap was so eager to explore. Being confined in a cell for so many months would have been torture to this self-made man beside me.

"Anyway, that's my life in a nutshell," Cap said. "Heartbreak and hard time."

"Have you talked with Milly since planning this expedition?"

He grimaced. "She contacted me. A few months ago. When she saw my name in the newspapers."

"Of course."

"She wants to get back together. You know, now that I'm a big deal."

"You won't, though, right?" I asked, curious. Did he still have feelings for her?

"Never," he laughed hollowly. "Fool me once, shame on you. Fool me twice, shame on me."

"Do you think she's going to keep coming after you?"

He rubbed the blonde stubble on his chin. "Maybe. She's eager to reconnect with me, now that I'm appearing in international news. You know, it'd get her face out there, too. It'd help her career. Or whatever it is that she wants, anyway."

I made a face.

"It's ironic, really," he mused. "Milly wanted so badly to have the spotlight on her and here I am, in the world's spotlight right now."

"Do you like the spotlight?"

"That's a good question," Cap glanced at me. "I'm not sure I'd say I like it. Do I use it? Yes. Do I know how to work it? I've learned, over the years. But only because it's how this expedition can happen."

"You have to sell yourself to people?"

"Exactly. I perform. Play the part of the intrepid young explorer, captain of a courageous crew. That's how we raise the funds to do this. Clearly, I can't afford it. Neither can Chito or Bernard."

I hadn't realized how much Cap had been touched by tragedy and forged by challenge. Staring at him, I felt new respect for this man who'd endured pain and didn't let it make him bitter.

After a moment, he turned to me.

"That's the whole ugly truth," he said. "That's everything. You know it all now. You know who I am."

"It's not ugly," I replied. "Your life has been hard." I understood now why he was obsessed with this expedition. To him, it was everything he'd ever dreamed about—and he'd certainly needed dreams to carry him through some ugly realities.

"Yes," he said. "We all have our past. Maybe you can see now why I'm so ready to get on with this journey, to get moving. I've dreamed about this life for years. I've prepared for this expedition for ages. I'm passionate about exploration, seeing the world, learning, and meeting new people. Maybe, too, you can see why I'm so proud to represent our country on this global expedition. America let me become the man I always wanted to become."

"No kidding."

"And Andi," he added, staring at me. "I promise, I'm not kicking you off the crew. Knowing this, you can understand why I'm taking the risk to have you on this team, even though you're young. I know what I was capable of doing, even at a young age. I do need you. Your energy, and honesty, and womanly charm—"

I slugged him playfully. "I don't have womanly charm."

He laughed. "Well, I still want you."

I lowered my head and blushed, suddenly bashful. "I'm sorry, Cap."

"Why?"

"I'm sorry for my outburst earlier. You're right, I'm just nervous. I'm not some perfectly disciplined, well-behaved girl."

Cap grinned and nudged my shoulder with his. "That's good, Andi. A well-behaved girl would never survive this trip."

CHAPTER 24

AFTER CLEARING THE air, Cap and I decided to go ahead and send the expedition on to Spain without me.

He'd been working for months on a rigorous schedule for our team, booking hotels and making arrangements with dozens of ambassadors and local government officials. Waiting any longer for me would've knocked us off track, forcing Cap to redo all the work he'd already done.

I had just over a week to beg for my visas, then hustle to Barcelona and meet them. *"I'll do whatever it takes,"* I told myself, alternating between the desire to get violent with the ambassador's office or offer a bribe.

Bernard, Chito, and Cap let me come with them to the ship as they set sail without me. They drove the Fords up the ramp into the ship's hold, and I insisted on helping lug trunks of supplies and suitcases up the gangway. I walked carefully on the slippery metal ramp, marveling at the bustle of activity at the port.

People chattered all around me, while deckhands rushed from one place to another carrying bags and issuing orders. Crates were loaded, and smoke was billowing from the glossy black smokestack in anticipation of their departure.

After loading up Cap's cabin, the crew joined together to say goodbye to me.

We stood on the landing, talking, as we heard the cry from the bridge, "All set to depart in five minutes! Five minutes to departure!"

A tiny child next to us began crying, pressing his little face into his father's legs as his mother stood helplessly and watched. "I don't want to go, daddy!" he sobbed. "I'm scared! I don't want to leave you!" His father reached down, trying to soothe him, but the boy only clung tighter and cried.

Cap noticed and stepped over. He knelt down, and the little boy stared at his khaki uniform curiously. "Hi there," Cap said soothingly. "Are you headed out on this big boat?"

"Yes," the child hiccuped as fat tears rolled slowly down his cheeks.

"Are you a little bit worried about it?" Cap asked.

The boy looked up at his father, who smiled encouragingly, then looked back at Cap. "Yes."

"Well, let me tell you something, my friend. I've been on ships like this a lot. It's great fun."

"Really?"

"Really. And what's more, you'll have friends on board, too."

"I will?" the child asked, staring at Cap with wide eyes. "But I don't know anyone besides my mama."

"You'll know me. My name is Captain Gallivanter, and I'm going on this trip across the ocean with you. We're all going to Spain. After that, I'm going all across the world. I'm an explorer."

The little boy squirmed and stepped away from his father's legs. His parents exchanged smiles as he held out his hand solemnly to Cap. Cap grinned, reaching out to shake the little one.

"I'm Andrew," the boy said, his face still shining with tears. "Will you tell me about your trip?"

"Of course I will, Andrew," Cap promised. "We'll have lots of time to talk. You'll get to talk to my friends Chito and Bernard, too. We have lots of exciting stories we can share with you. But right now, be a brave little man and hug your father goodbye. You have a big adventure waiting for you."

The boy smiled. "I can't wait," he said, hugging his father's knees. His parents looked at Cap and mouthed their thank you silently, as he straightened and tipped his hat at them.

Cap rejoined our little team, straightening his uniform. "Well, gang, this is it. We won't see each other for a while."

Bernard interrupted. "I won't."

"What?" Cap said.

"I won't tell that little boy stories. I'm not talking to him."

I hid a smile. He was a master with the Fords, but had zero interest in people. He only seemed happy when he was tinkering around the cars, carrying his leather satchel of tools with him.

Chito abruptly enveloped me in a big hug, lifting me off my feet. I giggled as he spun me and my feet still knocked against the ground.

"Oof, I forgot you're so tall," Chito said, setting me back down. "I'll miss you, Andi. Be safe. We can't wait to see you on the other side."

I stepped in to hug Bernard, who quickly stepped back and shook his head. Instead, I offered my hand. He shook it, with his head down, and said nothing. I exchanged amused glances with Cap, who winked at me.

I embraced Cap, who held me tight against him. "Be careful," he said, his arms still wrapped around me snugly. "Don't change your mind and leave us high and dry. We'll have everything ready when you get there, and that's when the real fun will start. But we need you with us, okay? I need you. You're my partner."

"I won't change my mind," I promised, hugging him back. I could feel the muscles in his arms tense against me as we stood there.

A whistle blew and a cry went up from the crowd on land as people hugged, saying their last goodbyes. Men tossed their hats, kissing their wives. Families embraced. Businessmen and merchants shook hands, tipping their hats at each other. The crowd surged toward the gangway, lining the decks that faced the dock, waving at the people below.

"Goodbye, Andi! See you soon!" Chito and Cap cried, waving at me as they made their way into the crowd pushing up the ramp, Bernard walking silently next to them.

"Goodbye!" I called. I was sad that I wasn't going with them, but resolute that I'd get those necessary visas and join up with them as soon as possible.

"I can't wait," I thought, watching the ship start to pull away, the wake splashing water up forcefully against the docks where I stood. *"Everything's going to be different from now on."*

CHAPTER 25

I DETERMINED THAT THE best way to get my visas in hand would be to camp out in the ambassador's office until they got sick of me.

Sure enough, my plan worked.

After two days of me sitting in the ambassador's reception room, smiling brightly at the receptionist every time she made eye contact with me, the ambassador himself came out to figure out how to get rid of me.

"Ah, Miss Warren, how can we—*expedite*—your request?" he asked, peering over his spectacles at me.

I explained the situation, telling him about our trip and the crew waiting for me in Barcelona. "It's time sensitive, sir," I pleaded. "I can't have them leave without me, and they can't afford to wait for me much longer."

"Yes, well, let me see what I can do for you, my dear," he responded. "How old are you, anyway? You look so young to be going on such a grand adventure."

"I'm eighteen."

"Eighteen!" He exclaimed, pushing his glasses up to get a second look at me. "You're not much older than my son. I'd never let him go on a trip like this."

"Oh," I said, trying to remain polite. Cap was so good at dealing with people. I still had a lot to learn.

"Eighteen, my goodness," he said, studying me. "Dearie, can I ask something personal?"

"Yes, Mr. Ambassador?"

"Why do you want to go off on this journey, my dear?" he asked. "Don't you want to stay home, close to your family? Settle down with your sweetheart and start a little family of your own?"

"I don't have a sweetheart, sir. And it's only my mother and sister. My father was killed in the war. This trip allows me to take care of us, financially."

"Oh, I'm sorry," he said. Loss during the Great War had made us all averse to using flippant cliches. Perhaps the ambassador realized I was filling the role of provider for my family, even though I hadn't dreamed of shouldering this sort of responsibility until after my father had died.

"I really need those visas, sir."

"I understand," he said, shuffling back to the desk. "Let me see what I can do. Come back later this week, let's say two or three days from now, and we'll see what sort of progress we can make here."

I returned to the ambassador's office two days later, expecting to have to hurry him along again. To my surprise, he greeted me at the door and handed me a thick envelope. "They're all here!"

"All of them?"

"Visas to every country you requested, Miss Warren," he smiled broadly. "Even Andora. And Afghanistan."

"Oh, Mr. Ambassador! Thank you! This is fantastic!"

"You're very welcome," he replied. "You have quite the trip ahead of you, my dear. Go and make us Americans proud."

I walked out of his office feeling light as a feather.

Without Cap's expertise, I was learning on the fly. He'd spent the last couple of years meeting with hundreds of people, massaging the egos of major donors and rubbing shoulders with politicians and community leaders in order to ease doors open to make our expedition possible.

Cap was organized, methodical, and could turn on the charm when he wanted. He got things done. I was tall, awkward, and pretending to be more confident than I was. Yet now it was my turn to get things done.

With the visas in hand, I had to get to Spain as quickly as I could.

I hurried to the dock to talk with the booking agent for the boat that would transport me from Nice to Barcelona.

I crossed the busy street, waves lapping against the boardwalk and the fishermen dragging their cast nets into waiting boats in the harbor. Ahead, a small shack nestled between wooden barrels and crates. A hand painted sign sat propped up against the base of the building, proclaiming, "Book Your Next Sailing Trip Upon the Open Sea!"

I knocked on the clouded window. It opened a crack, and a grimy face peered out. Cigarette smoke curled out into the cold morning air, making tiny swirls above my head.

"Good morning, sir!" I beamed. "I'd like to buy a ticket to Barcelona."

"For when?" croaked the ticketing agent.

"As soon as possible. I believe there's a ship leaving tomorrow morning, at dawn?"

"Yeah. And no. Not that ship, lady," he growled.

"Why not?"

"It's full of soldiers. It ain't no place for a lady." He punctuated his words with a wet cough.

"Well, what about the next available ship?"

"Let me see," he scowled, flipping through a stack of schedules. "Next available ship leaving for Barcelona is on January seventeenth."

"That's weeks away! I need to go now!"

"Sorry, lady," he coughed. "Can't help you."

He started to shut the window. I shoved my hand in it to stop it from closing. I was getting mighty sick of people getting in the way of my great adventure.

"Listen, sir. I need to get on that boat tomorrow," I said. "I have the money, right here, and I can assure you, I'll be perfectly fine even if there are soldiers on the ship."

He hacked violently, and coughed something wet up into his hand. It glistened in the sunlight. He smeared it onto his pant leg and merely looked at me. I was growing desperate.

"Please. How can I convince you to sell me a ticket for tomorrow's trip?"

He took a drag on his cigarette and studied me.

"Please, sir. It's a life or death situation."

"Well," he said slowly, drawing out the words. "I suppose I could sell you a ticket. It ain't gonna be a nice trip, I warn you. Them army boys are wild. And they ain't seen a lady in a long time. It could be dangerous for you on that ship, missy."

"I can handle myself."

"I imagine so," he said, looking at me. "You're sure pretty tall." He took a long puff on his cigarette and exhaled. The cloud of smoke drifted right into my face. I resisted the urge to cover my nose and gag.

"What would Cap do?" I thought desperately. He always got what he wanted from people. I decided to turn on the charisma.

I drew myself up and widened my stance. "Sir, do you know who I am?"

"No."

"I'm Andiamo Gallivanter, co-star of the world-famous Gallivanter Expedition. The entire world is watching me, waiting to see what daring adventures I embark on. Into the jungles, the mountains, the wild places I head—but all this hinges on you."

He blinked. "Me?"

"Yes, sir. The entire crew is already at Barcelona, waiting for me. As soon as I arrive, we're heading off along the Spanish coast. But without me, the expedition cannot start. Do you want to be the reason that the world can't see our grand journey?"

"Well...no..." he replied, confused.

"I need to be on that boat tomorrow morning. All I need from you is for you to sell me a ticket—a single ticket—and I'll be on my way and out of your hair."

"A single ticket," he repeated, staring dumbly at me.

"One single ticket. And I'm gone for good."

He stared, sucking thoughtfully on his cigarette. The smoke curled around his head, wispy tendrils floating up and disappearing from sight. Finally, he nodded.

"Fine," he said, putting out his hand for the money. I swiftly dropped it in his hand.

"Thank you, sir. And the world thanks you, too."

"Whatever," he said, waving his hand to dismiss me. As he pulled his window shut, he added, "Be careful. It's a rough crowd gettin' on that ship tomorrow."

CHAPTER 26

ALL MY ITEMS ALREADY sent ahead with Cap and the crew, I had only a tiny suitcase to bring with me early the next morning as I boarded the ship for Barcelona.

The trip was only a few days long, so I wasn't concerned about my living quarters or creature comforts. I was too excited about our actual expedition to think much about the short trip from Nice to Spain.

I walked down the boardwalk and headed toward the ship. Sure enough, the French army was out in full force, young men of all shapes and sizes hauling crates of cargo and wheeling barrels up into the boat. As I approached the group, several of the soldiers straightened up and whistled.

"Regarde cette jolie fille! Tellement de choses que j'aimerais lui faire?" they nudged each other. "Look at that pretty girl! What I wouldn't like to do to her, huh?"

My years at French boarding school paid off as I snapped at them, using some of the choice crude French phrases every teenager learns first, when studying a new language.

"My mother would be horrified to know that her tuition payments had gone toward teaching me these words," I smirked to myself.

They whistled again, but this time it was a low whistle of admiration. They wisely buttoned their lips while their eyes followed me.

I gave my ticket to the agent at the dock, then headed up the plank to the main deck. A darkly tanned deckhand stood at the top, directing soldiers, and held up his hand as I approached. "Excuse me, mademoiselle, how can I help you?"

"I'm on this boat," I smiled. "I could use some help finding where my stateroom is."

"Oh, no, mademoiselle. There's been a terrible mistake. You cannot be on this ship. It's for men only."

"I already paid for a ticket."

"I'm sorry, mademoiselle. I will personally escort you down and get you a refund."

I straightened up and peered at him. I was a head taller than him. "No. I'm on this ship. I have to be in Barcelona by next week. There's absolutely nothing you can do to remove me from this boat, other than to tie me up and drag me off yourself. And I'll warn you now, I'll fight tooth and nail if you dare try to tie me up."

He stared at me, aghast.

"Besides," I continued, "Do I look like the kind of girl who can't handle myself?"

"No. But this ship is a modified ship, for the French poilu, the infantrymen. Didn't the ticketing agent tell you?"

I pictured the squat, dirty man smoking in his little wooden shack. No, he hadn't told me. In fact, he didn't strike me as the type that kept track of such pertinent details at all. I shook my head.

"The staterooms have all been converted into barracks. We have bunk beds, three high, multiple beds in each room. You see? This ship is for the men only. We have no space to have you take up an entire room for yourself, mademoiselle. The ship is fully booked."

I grimaced, but doubled down. I had no choice. "I understand, sir. But I have no other options. I have a crew waiting for me in Barcelona and this is the only ship headed out of Nice toward there in the next few weeks. I have to be on *this* boat. Even if it means sharing a room with a bunch of men."

The deckhand looked dubious. "Mademoiselle, I don't know how to say this. It—it could be very dangerous for you here. Alone, in a roomful of men, at night?"

"I know. But I'll be fine. I can take care of myself."

"I need you to understand, the captain and our crew—myself included—will not have the ability to rescue you if you need help."

"I'll be fine," I insisted.

The deckhand sighed and rubbed the back of his neck. "You understand the risk you're running here?"

"Yes," I nodded. "I promise you, I'm a tough girl. I'll handle myself."

"Fine. This is your problem now, mademoiselle," he said, throwing up his hands. "Just remember, I warned you."

He led me over to the stairwell and gave me directions to my room. With a final sigh, he watched me descend the grand steps to the lower level, where tiny rooms branched out from the narrow hallways. It was dim and crowded with men moving in and out, pressing up against each other and the walls as they filled the halls.

I tried not to gag. The air was thick with cigarette smoke, body odor, and the smells of leather and gunpowder—and that was just the smell of the troops. The ship itself stank horribly of disinfectant, dampness, and bilge water.

Two wiry young men grappled with each other, wrestling playfully, as I stood in the entrance of the hallway. A third man, smoking a cigarette, blew a stream of smoke and straightened up, sweeping his hat off his head.

"Hello, gorgeous!" he called loudly in French, then turned down the hall. "Check out this doll, gentlemen!"

Instantly, the hall erupted in lewd catcalls and whistles.

Head held high, I shoved my way through the crowd of men, suitcase held in front of me. *They're no different from my male classmates from grade school,"* I thought to myself, *"Except that they're even more immature."*

As I made my way down the hall, men jeering at me on either side, a dark-haired soldier grabbed me around the waist and pulled me in close. "Bonjour," he leered at me, his hot breath tickling my ear. "What room are you in? I'll keep you company tonight."

I slammed my elbow into his side and swung my bag at his knees in response. With a crude swear, he released me.

"A fighter," he smiled cruelly, showing a row of dirty teeth. "I like that in a girl."

"Come on, Marius, leave her alone," shouted a soldier from down the hall.

Marius frowned and stepped out of my path, but watched me as I made my way down the hall. I felt his stare as I turned my back and headed into my room.

"Was it going to be like this the whole trip?" I wondered, knocking on the door and tentatively trying it. It was unlocked, propped open. I pushed my way inside.

The room was empty, but had signs of men all around it. Helmets and rucksacks sat at the foot of each bed. The bunks themselves were simple iron cots, stacked three high, three sets crammed into the tiny room. A small bathroom with a tiny door and a foot-wide porthole, the sole source of light gleaming into the dark room, filled the rest of the space.

I looked around, searching for an empty cot. The topmost bunk of one tower was open, so I put my suitcase at the end of the bed and hefted myself up the ladder and laid down. Frowning, I shifted my weight to make myself more comfortable on the flimsy mattress. I could feel the iron support beams digging into my back through the thin cotton pad.

"It's only for a few days," I told myself, steeling my nerves. *"You can handle anything for a few days. Imagine what you'll be handling the next few months."*

I wiggled out of my khaki jacket and rolled it up, shoving it under my head. I figured I'd need to get some sleep now, because it might behoove me to stay awake during the night. I didn't want to end up with any unwelcome male visitors while I slept.

I must've dozed off, but awoke with a start as the door to my room crashed open. Several gregarious voices filled the room, and a flurry of jokes started as the soldiers started undressing, dropping shirts and pants onto the floor of our tiny cabin. A bottle of absinthe was passed around the room.

Embarrassed, I closed my eyes and turned toward the wall. As I rolled over, my dark hair caught the attention of the man sharing the bunk directly underneath mine.

"Hey!" he shouted with surprise. "We've got the girl in here!"

A series of exclamations filled the room. I heard telltale sounds of men retrieving their pants and pulling them back up. I stared at the wall, uncertain what to do.

Suddenly, my bunk shook and I felt a hand tapping my shoulder. "Mademoiselle?"

I rolled over and sat up, looking down at the round young face of a poilu. He barely looked older than me.

"Hi there," I replied.

The men stared at me, in various stages of undress. Mercifully, they all had their pants back on.

I took advantage of the momentary confusion and decided to channel my inner performer. Instinctively, I knew that I needed them to understand that I was an important figure—a famous, very public personality—one who'd be missed if something happened to me.

"Gentlemen, my name is Andiamo Gallivanter. I'm traveling with the world-famous Gallivanter Expedition, a journey taking us all around the world. I serve as the spokesperson, mechanic, cameraman and guide in my crew. Have any of you seen my pictures in the paper?"

Everyone shook their heads. Oh, great.

I continued. "If you haven't yet heard of me, I assure you, the whole world will know my name in a short time. We're embarking on a one-of-a-kind adventure, racing around the world, seeing all the most famous sites. You get the privilege of sharing this room with me this week, and someday you'll get to tell your grandkids that you roomed with the famous Andi Gallivanter one time, as a young man."

A few of the men laughed, muttering comments to each other under their breath.

A thin soldier, wearing the rankings of sergeant, stepped over to my bunk. "Mademoiselle, we need to talk," he said, removing his hat.

"Yes?"

"My name is Durant, sergeant first class. I'm in charge of the men, and I am quartered in this room, but—" he glanced around, looking at the men listening to us, and lowered his voice. "It's not safe for you to be here."

"I've been warned several times already, sergeant. Thank you."

"You don't understand, miss," he said evenly. "These men have been in the service for months. They've barely seen a woman that entire time. They're headed for leave, and don't always—ahem—*control* themselves well. They can be quite wild. Especially when they've been drinking. Which they will be, I promise you that."

"I'm not afraid."

"Maybe you should be," he replied, his voice low.

"I'll be fine," I repeated. I'd been having the same exchange with every man I'd encountered the last few weeks.

"I'm going to the ship's captain, then," he said, putting his hat back on his head and tugging it down. "This is no place for a young lady. You'd be safer somewhere else. Anywhere else."

He disappeared out the door, and the rest of the men watched me, whispering comments. They settled into their bunks, still swigging mouthfuls of the absinthe.

A short time later, the Sergeant Durant came back in. He looked irritated. As he walked in the door, he clicked his heels and called the men in the room to attention.

"Écoutez!" he called out loudly. "Listen up, everyone. I have just spoken with the captain about our situation here." He glanced over at me, and everyone's eyes followed him and stared up at me.

"The captain has informed me that despite my opinion, Miss Gallivanter here has paid for her ticket and has already been warned—several times—about the risks of traveling alone, as a woman, on this particular ship," the sergeant continued. "She has refused to heed their warnings and insists on rooming down here."

His tone changed. "Gentlemen, you will leave Miss Gallivanter alone. You will not speak to her and you will not touch her while she is on this ship. If you choose to ignore my orders and harass her, you'll deal with me. Am I clear?"

"Yes, sir," came the chorus of responses from around the room.

He crossed the room, boots echoing on the wooden floor, and approached the side of my bunk. "Mademoiselle, I will help you as best I can, I promise. But please know that I cannot be at your side as your protector at all times. I have duties to perform, so I'm cautioning you now to please be very careful. Some of these men—their blood runs hot."

"Thank you, sergeant," I replied. "I appreciate your kindness. And I'll be fine."

I laid back down, hoping nervously that I was right. *"This adventure isn't starting off quite the way I expected,"* I thought to myself, trying to keep my anxiety at bay.

CHAPTER 27

AS WE SAILED ACROSS the open sea that afternoon, black waves roiling against the ship, I stayed on the upper deck as long as I could.

I hoped the men might forget about me if I stayed out of their sight most of the day. I skipped lunch, but my stomach was gurgling loudly by that evening. I could smell the scent of beef stew coming up from the kitchen below me. I'd never been so hungry.

I heard the dinner bell clang, and watched men rush around me down to the dining hall. I was forgotten in the mad dash of grabbing food. I joined the long line of hungry men, picking up a metal tray alongside the rest of them, and waited in line for the cook to slop food on my plate.

As I stepped up to the counter, the portly chef didn't even bother to look up from the steaming vat of stew in front of him. He gave me a heaping ladle of beef stew, thick and hearty, a baked potato, and a small biscuit.

I grabbed a glass of beer—the only beverage I could see—and looked for an open seat in the crowded hall of men.

To my relief, I saw Sergeant Durant wave me over to his table. He appeared to be sitting with other sergeants.

I made my way over, winding my way through the thin aisles around the crowded tables, when suddenly a meaty hand grabbed my wrist. My tray nearly toppled over, and my beer sloshed over the side. I froze.

"How dare you?" I retorted, angry.

The large man attached to the wrist chuckled arrogantly. "Sit down with me, sweet cheeks," he said, tugging at my wrist. My glass of beer slid across the tray.

"Who do you think you are?" I growled, feeling the flush of anger redden my cheeks.

"Who do I think I am?" the man leered. "I'm Charles."

"Well, *Charles*, let go of me."

He released my wrist but stood up, blocking my path. "I don't think you heard me, young lady."

"I heard you just fine. Move."

He took a step closer to me. I stood my ground.

"I'm Charles," he repeated, a dark look on his face. "As in, *Captain* Charles."

"Captain? Of this raggedy group of soldiers? Good for you. Now get the hell out of my way."

"I'm Captain," he grinned. "Captain of this ship."

I gulped, suddenly nervous. He had the power to kick me off the ship at the next port, or lock me up on board at his discretion. At sea, the captain of the ship was the ultimate authority. Everyone obeyed him.

"Captain," I replied, trying to hide my fear. "How nice to meet you."

"And you, Miss Gallivanter."

"You know my name?"

"Of course I do, Miss Gallivanter. This is my boat. I know everything that happens here. Including when a lone woman is traveling with a bunch of bawdy infantrymen aboard my ship."

"Oh."

"How are you doing so far, anyway?" he asked, sitting down and patting the seat next to him. "Why don't you sit right here next to me and we can talk about how to make you more...*comfortable*...on your journey?"

I remained standing. "Thank you, Captain, but I'm fine."

"Oh, come now, Miss Gallivanter," he said soothingly. "There are certain benefits to a friendship with the ship's captain."

"Thank you, sir, but I'm not interested."

He stared at me with a look that made the hair on the back of my neck tingle. I wanted nothing to do with him. Behind me, I heard Sergeant Durant's voice.

"Captain Charles," he said, approaching my side and saluting. "I promised Miss Gallivanter that I'd accompany her here for dinner, so please forgive me for stealing her away from you."

"Fine, fine," the captain glared at me.

Sergeant Durant took my elbow and steered me through the narrow aisle, leading me quickly to his table. He plopped down next to me and leaned in close. "Lean into me like you like me," he said, glancing over my shoulder.

"Why?"

"Because I want to make it seem that we're romantically involved."

"What?" My forehead puckered. "Why?"

"Because if he thinks we're together, he'll stop looking at you like you're a piece of chocolate cake he wants to devour," he said.

"Oh," I made a face of disgust. "Good Lord."

"Yes, He is good. Because He sent me into your life to protect you on this boat. Now, lean into my shoulder. Like this."

Sergeant Durant leaned in close, batting his eyes and fixing a dopey smile on his face. I laughed. "Is that the look of love?"

"It's the look of a man who has a younger sister about your age and feels protective," he replied, smiling back at me. "You must be seventeen or eighteen?"

"Yes, eighteen. You're good."

"You're much too young to be on a ship by yourself. Especially this ship," Sergeant Durant groaned. "Promise me you'll steer clear of that captain. He was much too interested in you today when I reported your situation to him. He was watching you while you were on the upper deck, too."

"He was?"

"Yes."

"How do you know?"

"Because I was watching him watching you."

I blushed involuntarily. "Oh," I replied, embarrassed. Would I ever feel comfortable anywhere? Would this feeling of being a woman in a man's world follow me forever?

Sergeant Durant misinterpreted my blush and smiled. "Don't worry, Miss. I have a sweetheart back home. Marie. She's the most wonderful woman on earth. Besides my mother and sister, I mean. I just want to make sure no harm comes to you while you're on this boat, that's all."

"Thank you for looking out for me, sergeant," I said, grateful.

"Of course. I could tell you were uncomfortable back there."

"Well, I appreciate your gallantry. You're my hero."

He laughed. "Sure. Just remember, not all of us men are pigs. Some of us are quite nice."

I had a brief flash of Arnau's face, his warm brown eyes and tanned arms. The look he gave me when he handed me that geography book. His laugh, as I raced him through the fields. He was a gentleman, too. "I know that," I replied.

He smiled and glanced over my shoulder. "The captain's leaving."

"Good. I'll try to avoid him the rest of the trip."

"That's probably best," Sergeant Durant agreed. "He'll likely take his meals in his private dining room after this first night. You should be clear, as long as you avoid him during the day on the upper deck."

"I didn't think I'd have to worry about the ship's own captain, I guess."

Durant took my finished tray and stood. "You're a pretty girl, Miss Gallivanter. You can't be too careful."

I blushed. "I'm not pretty."

"You are," Durant said, putting our trays in the soapy wash bins. "Which is exactly why I'm going to escort you back to your cabin. And you're going to stay there, safe and sound, the rest of the night."

"Thank you, sergeant."

He smiled and offered me his arm. "Let's go."

CHAPTER 28

I QUICKLY READIED FOR bed in the tiny bathroom in my cabin, grateful that Sergeant Durant had ordered all the men in my room out into the hall so I could have some privacy.

Uncertain what to wear to bed while lodging with so many men, I chose to wear my starchy white shirt and khaki pants. They were stiff and new, but modest. I kept my boots on, worried that I might need to get up in the middle of the night.

I climbed up into my top bunk, and knocked on the thin wall to indicate to the men that I was finished. A polite knock sounded at the door, and Sergeant Durant's voice called out, "Are we clear to come in, Miss Gallivanter?"

"Yes, thank you," I called out, shaping my jacket into a comfortable pillow under my neck. I was grateful for the kind consideration from my roommates.

The door banged open and the men piled in. They shared the bathroom amongst themselves, then settled into their bunks, gradually drifting off into contented snores. I laid awake, worry racing through my brain. The uncomfortable realization that I'd be the only girl, traveling alongside a bunch of men for the next several months, was just now dawning on me. I hadn't even thought about what sort of pajamas I could sensibly wear in front of the crew while on the expedition. What was I doing?

As I tossed and turned in my bunk, I listened to the sound of the water spraying the ship underneath our window. A light rain was hitting our little porthole, soothing me with its rhythmic melody. *"This is just the very beginning of my trip,"* I thought to myself in wonder. *"I haven't even actually started the hard part."*

The thought was daunting. Could I handle it?

Suddenly, I heard the sound of the door quietly scraping open. Squinting in the darkness, I could just make out a tall form peeking into the room.

Dark hair. Thin. High cheekbones. It was Marius, sneaking into our cabin.

My breath caught in my throat. I laid completely still, flat on my back.

"Maybe he's just checking on something," I thought irrationally. *"Maybe he got lost and can't remember which room is his."*

Marius stood silently in the door, the pale light from the hallway streaming in behind him. He looked around the room, so quiet I couldn't even hear his breathing amidst all the snores coming from the other men.

"He's looking for me," I realized, terrified.

Slowly, Marius glided across the floor toward my bunk, apparently shoeless to avoid making noise. As he came closer, I was horrified to see that he was only wearing a pair of undershorts.

He reached my bunk, holding his breath, and started to slowly climb up the thin metal ladder at the foot of the bed.

I waited, steeling myself for what I knew I'd have to do.

Quietly, he reached the top of the ladder and prepared to climb into my bed. I waited until his torso appeared right over my feet, and then kicked his face as hard as I could. My heavy boots crashed hard against his nose and mouth.

"Merde!" he screamed, howling in shock at he crashed violently off the bunk.

"Thank God I'm wearing these boots," I thought as I listened to the startled melee of voices shouting and bodies moving on the floor below me. I peeked over the edge and saw several of the men pinning Marius down, angrily, on the floor.

Someone lit a lamp, and the warm glow illuminated the chaotic scene in our cabin.

Marius was still howling in rage, his bare chest heaving with anger and his mouth a bloody mess. One of the soldiers sat squarely on his chest, trying to keep two others from pummeling his face. Yet another soldier held his legs down as he squirmed, and two others had his arms pinned, spread eagle, on the floor.

Other men from nearby rooms had come running at the ruckus, and our doorway was crowded with soldiers trying to see what was going on. Several voices yelled all at the same time, and I caught snatches of furious swearing, men screaming at Marius.

"You tried to attack an innocent girl in the middle of the night? What's wrong with you?"

"How do you call yourself a man?"

"You'll pay for this!"

"Take him to the captain and lock him up!"

Several men dragged Marius to his feet, and I caught a clear view of his face. Had I kicked his front teeth out? It appeared so.

They dragged him violently out of the room and into the hallway, cursing him the whole way. The remaining few men in my room immediately turned to me, concern on their faces.

The soldier who bunked below me reached me first. "Mademoiselle, are you okay? Did he hurt you?"

Another man pushed in next to him. "We are so very sorry," he babbled.

"I'm fine," I replied, sitting up.

Their faces peered up at me, a mixture of surprise and worry. Several of them had messy hair. A few had blood on their shirts from their struggle with Marius. Sergeant Durant pushed the others aside and grabbed my hand tightly. His grip was fierce.

"Mon Dieu," he exclaimed. "Miss Gallivanter, are you hurt?"

"I'm fine," I repeated, trying to convince myself it was true. I knew I was close to crying, and I bit my lip to keep myself steady. I couldn't show weakness. Not now.

The sergeant rapidly issued orders without dragging his eyes from my face.

"Joseph, go with the men and make sure the captain knows what happened here. Denis, Chastain, inform our colonel what Marius did. Let him know the girl is fine, but Marius should be locked up until we reach shore, pending his dishonorable discharge. Albert, go get me a rag so I can clean the blood off the floor."

He scanned my body and added, "And another rag to clean the blood off Miss Gallivanter's boot."

I tried to smile. "I had to break in these boots somehow, right?"

Sergeant Durant frowned. "You're in shock, mademoiselle."

His words sobered me. It could have been much worse for me. What if I hadn't been laying awake? What if I had been in a room all by myself, instead of a room full of men who sprang to action?

The soldier cleaning the floor interrupted my racing thoughts.

"Sergeant," he called, "I have some teeth here. What should I do with them?"

"Toss them in the chamber pot," the sergeant scowled darkly. "Let him eat soup for the rest of his life, for all I care."

I didn't feel remotely bad for Marius, but curiosity got the better of me. "Did someone else hit him in the mouth, or did I do that?" I asked the room.

The men shook their heads. "I hit him, alright, but it wasn't in the mouth," said one dark-haired soldier, angry. "I hit him somewhere else where he's sure to remember not to try something like this again."

"Oh. So...." I frowned. "You're telling me I just kicked a man's teeth out?"

Unexpectedly, the room erupted in laughter. A few of the men clapped and whistled, but unlike their earlier whistles, these were low whistles of admiration. I sensed a newfound respect from the men.

"Nice job, Andiamo," winked one of the men, slapping me on the knee. "You'll be just fine out there," said another soldier, grinning at me.

The sergeant turned to the men. "Finish cleaning and we'll head back to bed," he said. "I'll take the first shift keeping watch on the door here. Lucas, you'll take second shift, and Vincent, third shift tonight. We'll take turns the rest of the week."

Looking back at me, Sergeant Durant patted my hand. "We'll keep you safe, Miss Gallivanter. This won't happen again. Not on my watch."

"It's fine, really," I replied. "I can handle myself."

"She's right, Durant," called one of the soldiers. "Nobody's going to mess with her now, not after they see what she did to Marius's face."

The sergeant looked doubtful. "I don't know. We should have someone stay up."

I protested. "No, you all need your sleep. I'll be fine, I promise. I've still got my boots on."

They all laughed, even the sergeant. "If you're sure," he smiled.

"I'm sure. Thank you, *all* of you."

"We'll spread the word, don't you worry," laughed one of the other soldiers. "We'll make sure every man on this ship knows not to mess with Andiamo Gallivanter, because she can cave his face in with one kick."

CHAPTER 29

TRUE TO THEIR PROMISE, the soldiers spread the news of the overnight attack far and wide. When I entered the dining hall the next morning for breakfast, the entire room stood to their feet and clapped for me. Embarrassed, I grabbed my tray and hunkered down next to Sergeant Durant.

"This is humiliating," I complained to him.

"What, that every man here respects what you did?" he responded. "They're proud of you. It's not easy to be the only woman in a man's world."

"It wasn't that big a deal," I said, cheeks pink as I poked my biscuit.

"Yes, it was," he replied. "You protected yourself from a dangerous person, all by yourself. That took courage. Clear thinking."

"I guess."

"Marius is locked up for the rest of the trip," Sergeant Durant continued. "He won't bother you again. No one will. We're all watching out for you now. Count us all as allies."

"Thank you," I said, feeling better.

The rest of the trip was smooth sailing. We had beautiful weather and calm seas, and the catcalling and harassment from the soldiers stopped completely. I managed to pass the time with the boys, playing cards and chatting. Their admiration was evident, and several found private moments to confess their respect for me being a "darn plucky lady," as one soldier proclaimed.

I especially enjoyed the company of Sergeant Durant and a few of the other men from my cabin, who had gallantly come to my rescue in that first night. When we landed at our port in Spain, I was slightly sad to be leaving my newfound friends.

Sergeant Durant and I hugged each other tight after walking down the plank onto dry land together. "Au revoir, Sergeant," I smiled. "Let's stay in touch."

"Of course. I'll follow your adventures across the world," he said. "I know you can handle yourself."

I waved as we pulled apart, picking up my suitcase.

"One more thing," the sergeant called, as he walked away. "Keep those boots on, Miss Gallivanter. And never forget what you can do with them."

⸺●⸺

AS I LEFT THE HARBOR, I asked for directions to El Hotel Antigua, the hotel that Cap had written that he and the crew would be staying at as they waited for me to join them.

Carrying my suitcase, I whistled as I passed through the vibrant market in downtown Barcelona.

Women in colorful shawls and dresses, rich with embroidery and ribbon, smiled and waved at me as I passed. Men in large felt hats nodded, offering me glimpses of juicy melons, bright red tomatoes, shiny peppers, and crates of exotic spices. Flower stalls were crammed with stacks of carnations, roses, and lilies wafting their delicate perfume as I cut through the narrow stalls. The smell of sweet dough frying mingled with the spicy scent of meat made me hungry.

I reached the street scrawled on Cap's note and glimpsed a pink inn with white wooden lattices and ornate metal gates soaring above a pristine lawn.

Our three Model T automobiles—each neatly hand painted with the name "Gallivanter Expedition, United States"—were lined up in front of the hotel. A small crowd stood in front of the cars, studying them.

Cutting through the lawn, I entered the lobby. Marble floors clacked sedately under my boots as I approached the reception desk. A short man, wearing a suit with a red carnation in the front pocket, smiled aggressively as I walked up.

"Hola, Señorita Gallivanter!" he cried, bowing behind the desk. "Welcome to our humble establishment."

"Hello," I replied, confused. "How do you know my name already?"

"Ah, Señorita, you're very famous already here in Barcelona!"

"I am? I just arrived, not even an hour ago."

"Si, I've seen your picture in our newspapers earlier this week. We keep a careful eye on our notable guests here at El Hotel Antigua."

"Oh," I said, feeling a spark of pride. I hadn't anticipated this sort of attention already, before the expedition even got going.

"Your amigos, the gentlemen, are expecting you today. They requested for me to inform you that you may put your suitcase in your room, freshen up, and join them on the back patio at your earliest convenience."

"Thank you," I blurted, grabbing my suitcase heading toward the patio. I had no interest in getting my beauty rest. I was too excited to see the Gallivanter crew again.

I walked through the open glass doors to the patio outside. Small tables full of hotel guests sipping coffee and chatting dotted the sunny pavement. Large ceramic planters boasted flowering bushes. I scanned the crowd, looking for Cap and the crew.

My spirits rose as I spotted them sitting together underneath a large arch of pink bougainvillea.

Chito saw me from across the courtyard and bolted to his feet. "Edi!"

"It's *Andi* now!" I heard Cap say, as the rest of the group stood up to greet me.

I ran into Chito's arms, dropping my suitcase on the ground. He picked me up in a hearty hug and whirled me around. My feet collided with the metal arch and we laughed as he set me down. "Our little star!" he exclaimed. "How was your trip over?"

"Fine," I replied, choosing to push the events of that first night into the back of my mind. I knew they'd feel guilty if they knew what I'd experienced on the ship. And the last thing I wanted was for these men to get overly protective of me before we even hit the road.

Bernard tipped his hat at me and sat back down. Cap smiled but quickly sat down, too, murmuring something to the young Hispanic man still sitting in his chair. I couldn't help but notice that he had remained seated while all the others rose to greet me.

"Andi, it's good to see you," Cap smiled as I sat down with the group. "I want to introduce you to the final member of our team, Paz De la Rosa."

"Nice to meet you, Paz."

Paz said nothing, but smugly grinned at me.

"Paz has been instrumental in preparing the automobiles here in Barcelona, as we waited for you, and we decided that he'd be a valuable addition to the expedition," Cap explained. "His knowledge will be helpful as we adjust to the first leg of our trip, getting used to our vehicles."

I studied Paz as Cap talked. He was slender and handsome, his crisp white shirt setting off the deep brown tint of his skin. His black hair was slicked back in a popular style, like a young Hollywood star, and his dark eyes studied me with barely concealed insolence. A faint smirk appeared on his face as he noticed my gaze.

"So. This is Andi?" Paz brushed an invisible thread off his leg. "You're not what I expected."

"What exactly did you expect?"

"Someone gorgeous," he smiled slyly.

"Gee, thanks."

"His father is super rich," Bernard announced. "That's why he's so rude."

"You think *I'm* the rude one?" Paz glared. "Did you just hear yourself?"

"What?" Bernard replied. "That's why you're here, aren't you? Because your dad is donating a bunch of—"

"Enough, Bernard," Cap snapped. He looked apologetically at Paz. "You'll get used to his humor."

"It wasn't humor," Bernard muttered.

"I feel good about this group," Cap swiftly cut him off. "We're ready to start the journey. Just a few more things to sort out, now that we're all together, and it'll be showtime."

"You speak English like an American, Paz," I said. "Are you from the States?"

"No. But my mother grew up in Ohio. She met my father during the Great War. She was a nurse in a field hospital. I've visited America several times with her," Paz replied. "I speak English flawlessly. I even know all your slang, from my American cousins."

"Interesting," I said, trying to be polite. I changed the subject. "What do we still need to do to prepare?"

Cap consulted his notebook. "We still have a few things to complete, but we were just discussing the possibility of leaving Monday. But now that we're all here together, I can finally reveal my pride and joy."

"Yes, we waited for you, Andi," Paz simpered. Across the table, Bernard rolled his eyes.

Cap stood up. "Let me go get it from my room," he grinned, disappearing. A few moments later, he reappeared with an odd suitcase-shaped object. Strange metal wires stuck out the top, and a large crank was fixed to one side. A small camera lens peeked out from one end.

"Here's the little piece of technology that's going to make us stand out," Cap boasted, setting it down on the table. "It's brand new. Hard to get one, actually."

"What is it?" Chito asked, as we all leaned in to examine the strange object.

"It's called a Kinamo camera. It's a tiny moving picture camera, housed in this case," Cap explained. "It's the latest thing being used by documentary filmmakers. The way the world captures images is changing, and we're going to be at the forefront of that change, my friends. The Chinooks don't have a movie camera with them."

"We're supposed to use this?" Bernard said, frowning as he picked it up. "It's pretty small. Not like any camera I've ever seen."

"Exactly," Cap grinned. "It's designed to be portable. We can take it all over the world with us and film the things we see. See this little spring? That's the motor. You crank it and the film rolls through."

Bernard picked it up, balancing it on one arm while he practiced cranking it. It made a slight whirring sound. I smiled. Cap was right: this could make us stars.

"Stupid toys," Bernard's voice interrupted my thoughts. Grumpily, he set the camera down. "For Pete's sake. Aren't the Fords enough for you people?"

CHAPTER 30

DINNER THAT NIGHT WAS served in the hotel's elaborate dining hall. We sat together at a large table, toasting each other with the bottle of champagne that Cap splurged on.

"To us!" cried Paz. "To the Gallivanter Expedition!"

Talk over dinner drifted from business to fun. We caught up on each other's families and inside jokes, teased each other as we tried paella. As waiters came to whisk away our plates, Cap leaned over and whispered, "Don't go up to your room yet. I want to talk with you."

One by one, the group headed upstairs to their rooms. I lingered with Cap in the lobby, waiting until Paz went up the grand staircase. Cap watched him as he walked upstairs, then abruptly pulled me into a hug.

"Whoa!"

"Sorry. I owed you a hug," Cap laughed. "I wanted to hug you earlier, but Paz—well, he requires some careful handling. I thought it best to present as professionals as he gets to know us. He's...particular about things."

"He's pretty pleased with himself," I muttered.

"He'll be a good addition to the team."

"And so will his daddy's donation, I'm sure," I thought sourly.

"Are you okay, Andi?"

"Yes."

Cap narrowed his eyes. "How was the trip over? Be honest."

"I told you, it was just fine."

"I worried about you the entire time we were apart, Andi," Cap replied. "I don't know what we were thinking. We never should've sent a beautiful young woman on a ship all by herself."

"I'm not beautiful."

"Don't be ridiculous," he responded. "Out with it. I can tell something happened and you don't want to talk about it. But I'm the leader of this crew. It's my name painted on those cars. I need to know what's going on with my team."

Haltingly, I told him about the encounter with the captain, the soldiers, and Marius. I tried to downplay the danger, but Cap's face got tighter as he listened. His body only relaxed when I recounted how I'd kicked Marius's teeth out.

"That's my girl!" he exclaimed. "You're a real trooper. Too bad we can't spin that into your stage story somehow. But it's too shocking to share with the public."

I smiled, then steered us to the conversation I wanted to have. "Cap, what's the deal with Paz?"

"What do you mean?"

"How long is he going to be with us?"

"Just on a short-term basis," Cap admitted, rubbing his chin. "I thought we could use him as we travel through Spain. You knew I wanted to get a guide. I want us to start well, and have local guides when we can. None of us know Spanish very well. He knows the culture. He can help us get around. He has connections."

"So he'll just be with us in Spain?"

"Most likely," he replied. "I suppose we might keep him on beyond that, but we'll see how the first few weeks go and then decide."

I thought about Paz being the only man who refused to stand up and greet me when I arrived. Maybe I was judging him too hastily. Perhaps he was just shy. Or it took him a while to feel comfortable with new people. I resolved to give him a second chance.

Cap yawned, checking his pocket watch. "You better get your beauty sleep, Miss Andiamo."

"What about you? Aren't you going to bed?"

"I will. I have a few more things I need to do. I'll go upstairs when I'm done."

I knew Cap would stay awake as long as he needed to, in order to prepare our team for the upcoming trip. "Goodnight, Cap," I called, heading upstairs. He nodded and waved, already heading to a lobby chair with a pile of papers under his arm.

Inside my room, I changed into a nightshirt and brushed my hair. I looked in the mirror as I brushed, my dark short bob framing my serious face. Was I beautiful, as Cap had said earlier?

"Stop caring so much what he thinks of you," I told myself. He was my boss on this trip, plain and simple. He had a complicated past. Besides, I was here for adventure. Not love.

I dug through my suitcase until I found Arnau's blue handkerchief. I folded it up carefully and tucked it under my pillow, thinking of him. It seemed like I'd already lived a lifetime since the last time I saw his face.

Unexpectedly, Cap's face replaced Arnau's in my mind. I pulled the covers up and drifted off to a dreamless sleep, exhausted after my long day.

CHAPTER 31

I WOKE UP TO BIRDS chirping outside my window. Rubbing the sleep from my eyes, I leaned out on the sill, drinking in the sunshine.

"Good morning, sleepy!" Chito called from the patio below. I smiled at the table of food sitting in front of him.

"I'll be right down," I called.

"Sure," he replied. "I'll order you some breakfast!"

I grinned as I got dressed. Chito certainly would make sure we didn't starve.

By the time I reached the patio, Cap and Paz were already at the table with Chito. While Cap and Chito greeted me, Paz said nothing but watched me over the top of his coffee cup.

"Today's our last press conference before we hit the road on Monday," Cap told us over breakfast. "One final media blitz to whip the public into an excited frenzy. And it'll be the first time that all of us, including Paz, are pictured together."

Bernard joined us on the patio, wiping oil off his hands with a rag. "I just took each of the cars for a quick rumble around the block," he told us, plopping down. "They're running beautifully."

"That reminds me of what I need Andi to do," Cap said, tapping his notebook. "Can you stand out by the Fords today and greet people?"

"What?"

"We all have duties before the press conference this afternoon," Cap explained. "Chito is headed to the market one last time. Bernard is picking up some tools, and Paz and I are writing some stories for various newspapers to have ready for local publications."

"And I have to stand by the cars?"

"It's not hard, Andiamo," Paz purred. "All you have to do is look pretty. Let the boys do the real work and just relax."

Irritated, I pushed my coffee away. "Can't I help with something else?"

"No, Andi," Cap replied, absently running his finger down his checklist. "Just stand there and talk to people about our expedition. It's good publicity. Wear your uniform."

I stalked upstairs to change into my Gallivanter Expedition outfit and walked out front to where our automobiles were parked. Their black hoods gleamed in the sunlight, the tiny American flags we'd affixed to the windows fluttering in the breeze. A few curious women were bent over, looking inside. They saw me and darted away.

I stewed as I broiled in the hot sun. *"Is this how it's going to be?"* I muttered to myself. Was I just here to draw attention? I thought of Arnau, laughing as he told me that I was his knight in shining armor.

Arnau didn't care that I was a girl. He never treated me like less.

But these men? Would they actually see me as an equal?

A group of older men wandered toward the cars. Speaking Spanish to each other, they nodded and tipped their hats. "Do you have any questions, sirs?" I asked in Spanish.

"What are you doing with these automobiles, señorita?" one of them spoke up.

I explained how we were departing on our around-the-world journey. The more I talked, the more impressed the men seemed to grow. As I spoke about the vehicles, a few of the men tittered.

"What?" I smiled.

"I don't believe it," one of the men grinned. "A young lady like you—they let you drive these? How much can you even know about cars?"

I opened my mouth to retort, but then pressed my lips together. Better to show than tell, I realized.

Waving them to the front of the Model Ts, I deftly popped open the engine. I propped the hood and pointed out the inner workings, reaching in to touch coils and hoses, explaining their functions as I talked. When we finished with the engine, I led them around back to show off the specially-made tires, abnormally thick to withstand the variable weather and terrain we were expected to encounter.

As I knelt down on the ground, hands gripping the tire to demonstrate the thickness of the tread, I heard Cap's voice. "Andi?"

I peered around the men to see Cap standing on the other side of the automobiles.

"Here!" I replied, wiping my hair out of my eyes with the back of my grimy hand.

One of the men whistled. "Señor," he said to Cap, shaking his hand, "You have one very impressive crew member on your team. Good luck to you."

The men thanked me and drifted away, chatting. I stood, uncertain where to wipe the smears of dark oil now streaking my hands. Belatedly, I remembered our press conference this afternoon. I should've thought of that before I was crawling around on my knees in the dirt just now, I realized. But I had been so wrapped up in proving my knowledge to the men that I hadn't thought about getting dirty.

Cap sighed and motioned for me to come closer. "Hold still," he said, pulling a hanky out of his pocket and wiping my forehead. "You smeared oil all over your face, Andi."

"Whoops."

"This wasn't really what I pictured you doing when I sent you out with the cars," Cap replied, noticing the wrinkles and dirt on my khaki pants. "I figured you'd attract the men with your good looks, not your knowledge of mechanics."

"You told me to get people excited about our expedition," I reminded him, snatching his hanky away to scrub my hands. "I can do more than just stand around and be your token girl, you know."

"We're just getting started, Andi," he replied, eyebrows raised. "Be patient. You'll have plenty of chances to prove your worth."

I bit my tongue. I couldn't start complaining before we even got on the road. I decided to pour out my frustrations to Arnau in a letter later that day.

The afternoon sun was hot, and sweat trickled down my back as I continued to chat with people who approached the automobiles. A few curious people took photos of me, standing next to the vehicles. When Cap came to urge me to freshen up before the press conference, I gladly escaped to the cool darkness of my room and a glass of water.

Inside my room, I stripped out of my sweaty clothes, down to my undergarments. I stretched out on the bed, grateful to lay down after standing in the street for so long, watching most people alternately gawk at me or detour around me to avoid talking.

I closed my eyes, trying to block out the worries that seemed to flood into my brain every time I had a spare minute to think.

Could I actually do this?

"There's no time for this," my brain said. I decided to write that letter to Arnau instead of giving in to self-doubt.

I scribbled quickly, intending to drop the letter in the lobby before I headed to the press conference. I smiled as I thought of Arnau. Even all these months later, he was still a faithful friend, consistently writing back and encouraging me.

"Arnau,

We're a few days away from officially departing on our expedition. I'm excited, but I've never been more terrified, either. It'll be an adventure, yes, but I'm afraid of what I might encounter. What if I'm making a massive mistake, going around the world? What if I get halfway around the globe, and want to come home? What—"

I heard a knock at my door and I laid my pen down. "Hold on!" I yelled, pulling on my pants and buttoning my white shirt up. I padded barefoot to the door.

"I thought you might be hungry," Chito greeted me, holding a plate of food. "You didn't get a chance to eat lunch today, did you?"

"No," I said gratefully, taking the plate. "Thank you." I sat down with the food. The plate was hot in my hand.

"How are you doing?" Chito asked, plopping down in the armchair next to my open window. He propped his feet up on the ottoman and sighed with contentment. "You got the best room of all of us, you know."

"I didn't know that."

"Cap wanted to make sure you were comfortable," he said, looking around. "He's worried that you'll be scared off by our group. Or that you might change your mind at the last minute and go home."

I squirmed, chewing a bite of meat. That was uncomfortably close to what I'd just been writing to Arnau.

"You've thought about going home, haven't you?"

I choked on my meat. "No," I lied.

"Yeah, you have," Chito said, crossing his arms across his broad chest. "I have, too."

"You have?"

"Sure," he replied. "Any sane person would have second—and third and fourth—doubts about this expedition. We have no idea what we're going to face, or how long it's even going to take. It takes a special kind of person to even go along with this harebrained scheme this far."

"Yeah," I said, feeling slightly mollified. It was helpful to hear Chito vocalize the feelings I'd kept stuffed inside my own brain.

"I mean, it's hard enough for me and I'm an old man who's lived," he continued, putting his hands behind his head and leaning back in my chair. "I can't imagine how you feel, as a young girl, just barely starting out in life. First time traveling this far away from home? And who knows what's going to happen out there? What kind of people we'll face, what situations we'll be walking into? This has got to be hardest on you, Andi. Harder than it is for any of the rest of us."

"I suppose." If Chito struggled with doubt, too, maybe I wasn't so crazy after all. Maybe this truly was a challenge.

Chito chuckled. "You just don't want to admit it, do you?"

"Admit what?"

"You're scared senseless. You're worried you're making a mistake, going on this expedition."

"Yeah, I am," I confided, relieved to have someone to talk to about my inner turmoil. "It's just the fear of the unknown. And of the ripple effects this will have in my life. What if this changes me? What if I can never be normal again? What if I can't just settle down after this expedition?"

Chito stroked his long beard. "You remind me of my niece. I haven't told you that before, have I?"

I shook my head. "What's she like?"

"She's fearless, a brave little thing. Like you. Not afraid to pick up a snake, or tussle with the boys at school. My Molly. Such a character."

"She does sound like me."

"And that's exactly why you have to go on this journey, Andi. For the girls like Molly. And the little girls just like you. They need someone to look up to. Someone who's strong and adventurous, someone who isn't afraid to live their own life. Hell, the little boys need it, too. We all could use a real live hero to admire, don't you think?"

"I'm no hero, Chito. I'm scared. A hero wouldn't be filled with such worry."

"Sure she would. You have a brain, don't you? Courage doesn't mean you turn off your mind and blindly stumble through life. It means you conquer your own doubts and keep moving forward, even *though* you're scared."

"So what's your Molly doing while you travel with us?"

Chito smiled wistfully. "She lives in California, with my sister. She's happy. Her letters are always full of their little pranks and games."

"What about you, anyway?" I asked, cutting another slice of meat. "Are you married? Do you have children?"

Chito paused, then looked up at the ceiling. "My wife is up there," he said, pointing toward the sky. "In heaven, with the angels."

"I'm so sorry."

"She died giving birth to our child. A little girl."

"Oh, Chito," I bit my lip. "That's awful."

"Yep," he said simply, staring up at the ceiling. "The baby didn't make it, either."

"I'm sorry."

"That's how I know I can handle anything on this trip," Chito replied softly, tugging on his beard. "I've already faced down the worst days of my life. I've lived through those days where I don't even have the strength to stand. This expedition? No matter how hard it could possibly be, it'll never come close to the hell I've been through already."

I poked at my food, not sure what to say.

"It takes a strong person to handle anything life throws at them, Andi," he continued, looking at me. "I already know you're one of those people. A strong person."

"I don't know, Chito. I'm just a girl. I don't know how strong I am."

"Gender doesn't have anything to do with your strength," he chided me gently. "Neither does age. What matters most is grit. And you've got that."

I nodded. I appreciated his simple kindness, encouraging me in my hour of self-doubt.

"Now, let's get changed for this press conference," he said, lumbering to his feet. "I've got to go make myself look cute," he quipped, winking at me.

"Me too," I sighed. Another afternoon of red lipstick.

It was time for Andiamo Gallivanter to make another grand appearance.

CHAPTER 32

OUR PRESS CONFERENCE was well attended, a massive group of men lined up to snap photographs of our crew.

Once again, Cap shared about the expedition and let us introduce ourselves. Paz positioned himself right next to Cap, lined up prominently in every shot, until Cap shifted me into that spot and asked Paz to move down.

"Of course," Paz replied, smiling through gritted teeth.

As we wrapped up the conference, several reporters asked to document our departure. Cap smiled.

"We plan to leave Monday morning, at dawn, and head down along the coast toward Tarragona," he replied. "We invite you gentleman here to the send-off, to catalogue what might be the most important journey you'll ever see come through Spain."

"Gracias!" Cap added, waving as they carried their cameras out.

With only one day left to prepare, we met early the next morning to go through our final pre-departure details. Cap drilled us on geography (in case we unexpectedly got separated), useful phrases (in case we encountered non-English speaking locals), and even basic survival skills if we found ourselves without food or water, or in need of medical attention.

With nothing left to do by the late afternoon, our supplies crated, and our bags packed and sitting at the doors of our hotel rooms, I suggested we go swim in the ocean near our hotel to enjoy the unseasonably warm day.

The crew seconded the idea with enthusiasm but Cap hesitated. "We're prepared," he said, scanning his checklist with a worried expression. "Right? We're prepared?"

"Yes, Cap," I said, tugging at his arm. "Let's blow off some steam. Come on."

We walked down to the beach, the late afternoon sun illuminating the sand and glistening off the waves. We borrowed towels from the hotel and kicked off our shoes. The ocean sparkled in front of us, the hot sun glittering on the waves that lapped at the shore.

I tugged at my ribbed jersey suit, its fashionable neckline lower than anything else I owned. I saw men glance at me as I waded into the water. I left my swim cap on the shore, opting instead to feel the cool water in my short hair.

Chito and Paz wrestled playfully in the water, sending waves splashing over the rest of us. Cap showed me how to squirt water out of my hand like a hose, while Bernard swam laps.

As the sun sank in the horizon, illuminating the sky in a vibrant pink and orange glow, Cap and I floated on our backs next to each other. "This is perfect," I teased. "I'm glad you came up with this great idea to take us to the beach."

He laughed and pushed my head underwater.

"Hey!" I spluttered as I emerged, laughing. He grabbed my shoulders and pretended to dunk me again. I resisted. He held me by both wrists, smiling. "You think you're so tough, don't you?" he teased.

Suddenly uncomfortable, I gave up fighting and stared up at him. Water droplets sparkled in his blonde hair and on his forehead. His bare shoulders showing above the water revealed his lean muscles.

Who was this man I was entrusting with my life? And why were my feelings toward him so strong?

I was struck with momentary panic. I'd only spent a few days with him, and I was ready to walk away from everyone and everything I knew to travel the world with him?

"What?" he noticed my face. He dropped my wrists. "Did you see something? A shark?"

"No," I said, staring at him.

"Andi, what?"

I stared at his face. One tiny strand of his wet hair was sticking to his forehead. Without thinking, I reached up and smoothed it back.

For a brief second, he smiled. Then he pushed my hand away. He took a step away from me, deeper into the water.

"Cap, aren't you scared?" I blurted. Somehow, I felt that hearing Cap admit his worries would help me sort through my own racing thoughts.

"Scared? Let me think about that." He stretched out his arms and floated, his head barely peeking out of the water. For several moments, he said nothing, just treading water and looking up at the sky. Suddenly, he spoke without looking at me.

"That's a complicated question," he mused, still floating. "Let's look at this logically. What are all the factors? What could go wrong?"

Even in worry, Cap was nothing if not disciplined.

"Fine," I replied. "Look at it logically. I'm listening."

He exhaled, still staring up at the sky. "I've spent years preparing for this expedition. I've sunk all of my own money into it. Mine plus a whole lot of other people's money, too. Researched. Organized. Fundraised. Planned. Recruited the right people. Created a whole persona. Brought in the press, the cameras."

"We're not even the only expedition doing this," he continued, his words coming quicker now. "The Chinook Voyageurs are attempting the same thing. And even if we do beat them—so what? So someone else comes along next year and goes even farther? So another crew can come in and wipe out our record by finishing the trip faster? Is this even worth the risk?"

I started to speak, but Cap beat me to it.

"On top of that, I'm responsible for the safety of everyone traveling with me," Cap continued, his voice tense. "I'm concerned. I've been concerned, all along. Every single day of this adventure, stretching back to the very first moment I put pen to paper and started to write out my plans for this expedition."

I floated next to him, feeling like a priest watching a man confess his sins. Cap's cool logic had failed him, and the jumble of worries he'd no doubt been keeping to himself tumbled out.

"What if my past comes back to haunt me? I'm worried that somehow, Milly will reappear in my life and find some way to ruin everything. That the world will find out I spent time in prison. I question that this isn't going to work out, that we'll get a few cities in and abandon the effort altogether. I'm concerned that the crew isn't going to get along, or is going to turn against me. Or that someone will decide it's not worth it and just leave."

Cap's chest heaved as he continued. "I wonder if I'm a good enough leader for us. There are men far more capable, more experienced than me, that should be doing this. What if I screw this up somehow?"

"Cap, stop," I said. I was becoming overwhelmed just by listening to the weight of Cap's burdens. He was right to be anxious—everything that was at stake was on his shoulders. Yet he was forging ahead anyway.

"And you," he groaned. "The team! What if you end up hurt? Or killed? Good God, I have other people's *lives* depending on me now. It's not just my folly anymore, it's all of you I've brought into this."

He stopped himself, chest heaving as he stared at the sky. It was changing to purple as the moon rose. When he spoke again, his self-control was back.

"We are going on an expedition, Andi. We're going to see the world. We'll face danger and trouble. I hope you know what you're getting into."

We floated together, letting the waves rock us. Chito and Paz splashed down the way, still enjoying the water. The sun was almost completely below the horizon now, and faint stars peeked out of the dark tapestry above our heads.

I thought about what Chito had shared, that Cap was afraid I'd back out. Did Cap worry that he'd scared me off in sharing all of this with me?

"Hey," I said to Cap, splashing him.

"Hey," he replied, glancing at me.

"I'm not one to let fear run over me," I said, my voice soft. "I've had a lot of these same thoughts. Probably the entire team has felt this way. Well, maybe not Bernard. Does he have feelings? Either way, we're here. Together. We'll get through this, together."

He said nothing in response, but I saw the hint of a smile on his face.

"We each *chose* to be here," I continued. "No one forced us. We choose this life. This trip."

I flicked water at him. "Are you hearing me, Cap?"

He sighed deeply. I couldn't tell if I'd convinced him, but I could see that the veins in his neck were still tense.

"Between the brains and knowledge of all the people on this team, we'll be fine," I assured him, trying to believe it myself. I was still nervous, but Cap knew how to sell this trip. Especially to me. Hadn't I begged him to go? Convinced him I wanted thrilling adventures?

"Think of all the work you've put in to prepare us," I continued. "We're knowledgeable on these countries we're headed into. We know first aid. Survival skills. You've researched meticulously, all these months. Our visas are in order. Our automobiles are tuned up. Think about all the press we've already gotten. We're famous and we haven't even started the trip yet. The eyes of the world are on us. No one's going to hurt celebrities."

Cap still said nothing. He closed his eyes as he floated.

"Look, we're all a little bit apprehensive, but we trust you. It just means we're ready to go," I reminded him.

"Yeah," he said quietly, eyes closed. "Thank you. It's going to be good. You know that, right? I have a good feeling."

I had a good feeling, too. Just being around Cap filled me with a warm sense of confidence.

Cap opened his eyes and looked at me, his expression unreadable. I met his eyes. We floated in the darkness, moonlight shimmering on the waves. The others were back on the beach, lighting a small fire with driftwood.

"We're ready," I repeated.

With a splash, Cap lifted his hand from the water and offered it to me. Uncertain, I took it.

"Listen to me, Andi. I'm only going to do this once."

"What?"

"We're shaking on it."

"On what?"

"On you sticking with me," Cap replied. "With this team. I need you, Andi. Remember that, no matter what happens. I need *you*. Don't back out on me. Don't leave."

"I'm right here. And I'll be by your side the entire way."

He squeezed my hand, then abruptly dropped it. "It's getting dark," he announced, clearing his throat. "We better get back in. This is when the sharks come out to hunt."

"It wouldn't do to get eaten before we even see Tarragona," I laughed. I was grateful the darkness hid my blush. It was nice to be wanted.

CHAPTER 33

I AWOKE WELL BEFORE dawn the next morning, nerves gnawing away at my courage.

"This is it," I said to myself a dozen times, laying in my hotel bed.

Unexpectedly, I thought back to a similar feeling I'd had as I laid in my bed that last morning at Académie Sainte Thérèse de Lisieux. I was overwhelmed and uncertain about my future then, too.

"So much has changed since that day," I thought. *"I feel like I've lived a whole lifetime since then. I look like a whole new person now. Would my old classmates even recognize me?"*

I prepared for the day, putting on the expedition uniform carefully. We'd be photographed this morning, no doubt, so I fixed my hair and applied my lipstick. As I finished, I stood in the bathroom, hands on either side of the sink, staring at my reflection.

Was I ready for this?

A knock sounded at my door. I opened it, and Cap stood there, fully uniformed, a bundle of papers and maps under his arm. "You okay?"

"Good morning to you, too," I replied.

A door opened down the hall, and Chito poked his head out. "Good morning, Gallivanters! Today's the day!"

We carried the remaining bags out of our rooms and loaded the Fords, convening in the lobby when we were done. My boots clacked against the marble floor, and I gazed at the ornate chandeliers glowing above my head and the velvet couches lining the lobby, realizing it might be some time before I saw comfort like this again. Cap checked out with the hotel staff and paid our bill while Chito offered pastries to the group.

"I'm not sure what kind of fruit this is," he said, studying the pastry he was gnawing. "Some sort of citrus. Want some?"

I shook my head. Butterflies filled my stomach.

"Is everyone ready?" Cap said, returning to our group.

"Any final words, Captain Gallivanter?" Paz asked.

Cap looked at our team and smiled. "This is it," he told us. "We've prepared for this moment for months. We've sacrificed, at the expense of our families and friends, to be here. This is a proud moment, team. Savor it. I'm glad each one of you is a part of this historic moment with me."

"You've prepared us well, Captain," Bernard said solemnly. "We're ready for this."

"Let's go see the world!" Chito shouted, pumping his fist in the air.

We pushed our way out through the front door of the lobby and headed to our automobiles. The morning air was cool, the sky starting to lighten.

A crowd of cameramen already waited at the cars. As soon as they saw us, lightbulbs flashed. Excited voices from the crowd of onlookers clamored for our attention. Someone started clapping and the entire crowd joined in.

"Thank you," Cap smiled at the reporters as we filled in next to him. "Your enthusiastic support and your good wishes will speed us along our travels, as we head out this day to travel around the world in our trusty Ford Model T automobiles, designed for optimal comfort and reliability—the ideal motor vehicle."

Chito and I exchanged amused glances. There it was. I'd heard Cap's speeches enough times now to catch the subtle endorsements he worked in to thank various sponsors and patrons. In this case,

Mr. Ford was sure to be watching the start of our journey, and Cap was giving him a nod.

"What we'll face, we do not yet know," Cap continued. "But whatever we encounter, the warmth of this moment—your cheerful faces, your support, your love for us—it will be a fire within our weary souls, warming us even on the darkest nights."

What a contrast his words were to the actual emotions he'd wrestled with just last night, I mused. I realized that I respected him more, knowing the worries and wounds that he carried but the strength that he possessed to press forward in spite of them.

"And now, ladies and gentlemen, the beautiful Miss Andiamo Gallivanter would like to share her feelings as we prepare to embark on the adventure of a lifetime."

Cap smiled at me as the crowd clapped. All eyes turned toward me, anticipation shining on their faces.

"You're ready," I told myself. *"You're Andiamo Gallivanter. Make history."*

I smiled wide and stepped forward. "Folks, Andiamo Gallivanter here, answering the call of duty. Adventure came knocking at my door, and I pitched right into it without hesitation. At the side of my trusty crew—and the excellent preparation of our dedicated and fearless leader, Captain Grant Gallivanter—I'm ready for the journey of a lifetime, the chance to change history books forever."

Holding one hand over my heart, I smiled. "I thank you for your support, my dear friends," I said, "I urge you to continue following our expedition as we navigate through the valleys and mountains, civilized and uncivilized cities of the world. We're the Gallivanters, and we are ready for adventure."

Cap was the first to clap. The crowd joined him, and the cameras panned the rest of the crew, getting close up shots of each of us.

"It's time," Cap announced, pulling his hat down tight and taking his driving goggles out of his coat pocket. "Are you all ready?"

"Yes, sir," we said in unison.

"Gallivanters, let's start them up!"

We had already decided that it was important for the cameras to capture both of us, the male and female faces of the expedition, each driving first.

"Especially you," Cap had said to me a few days ago as we planned our exit. "We want to show how capable you are. That even though you're a woman, you can drive the automobile all by yourself around the world. You have to be driving alone, without anyone next to you, or they won't believe it's possible for a girl to do it."

We walked to our Fords. Chito and Bernard climbed into the rear automobile, while Cap and Paz got the lead car and I climbed into the middle car.

I sat down, tugging my leather cap over my hair and tucking my dark strands firmly beneath the fabric. Over the top, I pulled on my driving goggles. I tugged them into position, then pulled the leather driving gloves over both hands.

When I had finished suiting up, I hung my arm out the window and waved at the crowd. They cheered. Cap looked us over from his car and I waved to him. He grinned, his eyes obscured by the goggles, and waved back.

"Let's go!" I heard Chito shout from the third automobile. He slapped the metal door energetically, like he was beating a drum.

"Don't you dare do that to my car," Bernard snapped.

Cap turned his key and his Ford rumbled loudly to life. The crowd roared their approval.

I turned my key and fiddled with the crank and handbrake. I knew what I was doing, but with the eyes of so many watching me, I was petrified that I would screw up somehow.

To my relief, the engine shuddered on. *"Thank God,"* I breathed. Cap had been right: every camera was on me, their bright flashes making stars in my vision.

Bernard was driving, with Chito in the passenger seat next to him. Paz waved to the crowd from Cap's car. "¡Adiós mis amigos! ¡Deséennos suerte!" he hollered. "Goodbye, my friends! Wish us luck!"

Cap pulled smoothly into the street, and I followed closely behind. Bernard trundled behind me. We waved goodbye, driving slowly down the cobblestone street.

Conscious of the crowds watching, I concentrated on managing the automobile. I heard voices in the crowd calling out to me, and I smiled as I sat upright. In front of me, Cap was waving, turning from side to side to smile and call out to people.

We rumbled down the narrow streets of Barcelona, our convoy close together. As we moved away from our hotel, the crowds disappeared and I stared out my front window at the scenes of everyday life in this Spanish town.

Women hung laundry on lines hanging outside their homes. A shopkeeper swept the porch in front of his store, pausing curiously as he saw us tootle past. Children squatted together, playing with marbles. Out of the spotlight, I started to relax. *"This is it,"* I thought to myself, a smile stealing across my face. *"We're really going."*

Weeks of preparation. Days of learning about my vehicle, packing and organizing items. Listening to Cap's exhaustive information about dozens of countries. Talking to my teammates and gleaning wisdom from books.

It was a surreal moment. I had the odd sensation that my future was finally unfolding, and that I was highly aware of the exact instant it was starting. Someday when I was old, I could look back on this moment and know this was when everything changed.

I breathed deeply, concentrated on the feeling of the warm wind flapping my short tufts of hair around, under my cap. The sensation of the heavy aviator goggles pushed tight against my face. The rhythmic bounce of the automobile, crunching along the street.

Hopefully, this moment would mark the moment that everything in my life changed for the better.

Our plan was to drive to Tarragona, which would only take a few hours. At that point, we'd stop and check over the cars. Their first hours on the road would be telling, in terms of what we could expect out of them for the rest of the journey. After that, we would have lunch before departing through a string of small towns along the coast.

We eventually reached the outskirts of Barcelona and pulled slowly through country villages. Fields filled our view, with hills softly blurring into distant mountains, their bases descending into a blue haze of thick trees.

As we rolled through these small towns, villagers stopped what they were doing and stared at us as we rolled through. On more than one occasion, a horse and buggy blocked the road, and we had to slow down to accommodate the pace of the horse.

I waved at people as we drove. I noticed that although Cap was the lead Ford, people's gaze often lingered on me, in the second car. Most folks had never seen a woman driving an automobile.

After a few hours, we neared a larger town. Cap held up his arm and gestured for us to stop. We reduced our speed and wove deftly through crisscrossing alleys into the center of Tarragona. Flags decorated many of the windows, while flower pots perched on nearly every stoop. Reaching an open block in what appeared to be the town's center, we pulled to a stop, lining our autos up in a row.

I turned my vehicle off and slid from the driver's seat, stretching my legs. Paz grinned as he hopped out of the car in front of me. "Welcome to Tarragona!" he boasted. "This is one of the towns where my family has an estate. Beautiful, right?"

"Aren't we supposed to have crowds waiting to greet us?" Bernard asked.

Cap put his hands on his hips, looking around. "Maybe they didn't hear us roll in?"

"Or maybe they're having lunch and a nice siesta," Chito chimed. "We could do the same?"

Cap ignored him. Chito was always hungry.

"I put press releases out to every local paper along the Spanish coast. They've been running for two weeks," Cap sighed. "They should know all about us at this point. We should've had people here. I don't know what to say."

We stood in a small cluster, looking up and down the streets. Townspeople went about their business, barely glancing at us. Cap cleared his throat. "It's still early in the day," he said. "Chito's right, perhaps people are lingering over a meal. Maybe we'll get our crowds later, after lunch."

"Good. That gives us a break, too," Chito grinned. "Let's eat."

CHAPTER 34

UNFORTUNATELY, THE crowds didn't appear after lunch.

We sat idly next to our vehicles for an hour, waiting to see if fans would show up, but we had no luck. After the adoring crowds in Barcelona, we were disappointed.

"Let's get moving," Paz groaned, after a drunk man in dirty clothes wandered up and tried to climb into Cap's car to sleep.

"Fine," Cap agreed, forcing cheerfulness. "It'll pick up. We just hit Tarragona at the wrong time of day, that's all."

We climbed in and continued along the coast. The ocean sparkled in the distance, the sun hot on our faces. Thick dust kicked up in my face, and I wrapped a scarf over my mouth and nose to breathe. Still, I was struck at what felt like the most beautiful scene I'd ever seen in my life, as I watched our little convoy trek across the countryside.

We reached another town just after the sun slipped below the mountains, and gas lanterns flickered in the streets. We pulled into a spot downtown and lined up our Fords, and I shook my scarf as I climbed out.

Bernard was already on his knees, checking underneath the vehicles, grumbling about the dirt. Cap walked over to us, holding a pile of papers. I looked at the top page, and caught the words "Day One" scrawled across the header.

"Good gravy," I thought to myself. *"This is only the first day, and look how much work has gone into that."* I didn't envy his job.

Cap laughed as he looked at us. "You guys look about as bad as I feel," he said, removing his goggles. A thick layer of red dust perfectly lined where his goggles and cap had protected his face.

"I could use a bath," Chito said, rubbing his dusty beard.

"And a stiff drink," Paz added.

"Sure, but I think at least one of us should stay out here with the Fords, in case anyone stops by to ask about us," Cap replied. "The rest of us can head into the hotel and relax. We'll eat dinner together tonight. I can stay out here for now."

"I'll stay too," I chimed.

"Thanks, Andi," he replied. "That'd be great. We'll catch up with everyone else in a bit."

I noticed Chito and Bernard exchange looks, then shrug. Paz didn't need to be told twice. He had already grabbed his bag and was headed into the hotel.

I leaned against Cap's car and stretched my legs. "Feels good to be out from that driver's seat," I groaned.

"What do you think so far?" Cap asked, peeling off his jacket and shaking the dust. "Is it the adventure you expected?"

"It's hard work."

"You're doing fine," he said, taking off his hat. His hair was mashed down and sweaty. "It'll take time for our bodies to get used to driving this many hours. But it'll only get easier from here."

"Easier?" I teased. "You mean, it'll get easier when we head into the uncharted territories? Into the jungle?"

"I meant easier to handle the *autos,*" Cap laughed, then sighed. "Now that we're alone, I need to apologize."

"Apologize? For what?"

"I was a fool last night at the beach," he replied. "I shouldn't have said all those things to you. I had no right to burden you with my private thoughts. I'm sorry."

"It's fine," I shrugged. "We were all jittery. Just because you're in charge of this expedition, it doesn't mean you're beyond worry. It's a natural emotion to have."

"I know," he said slowly, looking at me. "It's just…I don't know. You draw out these deep feelings from me. I just—"

"What are you guys talking about?" Chito's voice interrupted us. He carried two glasses in his hands as he approached, offering them to us. I felt my cheeks grow pink.

"Nothing," Cap replied, running his hand through his hair. "Did you two know that this area is famous for its olives?"

"Olives," Chito sighed, absently rubbing his stomach. "I'm starving. Say, Cap, can we chat a minute? Andi, why don't you head inside and relax?"

I hesitated, but Chito added, "I need to talk privately, Cap."

I grabbed my bag and carried my drink into the hotel, the porter ushering me to my room. Cracking open the small bathroom door, I grimaced at my reflection. Dirt caked my body and my hair was reddish-brown with grime. I had goggle lines on my face and my uniform was dusty.

I certainly wouldn't be winning points in the beauty category on this trip. I took a quick bath and scrubbed my hair and face. The bathwater turned brown with dirt. With my hair still damp, I put on a simple white shirt and a pair of khaki pants and headed to the lobby. I wondered idly what Chito had to discuss with Cap.

Cap sat in the lobby, still covered in dirt, writing furiously in a journal as he kept one finger on a map for reference. Bernard reclined next to him in an overstuffed chair.

"Hey Andi," Bernard called as I appeared. Cap glanced up and looked back down at his map. On it, he had penciled a path for us through several countries, circling towns and starring the places we'd be stopping to resupply.

"Hi guys," I sat next to Cap. "Everything good?"

"Yes."

"Everything good with Chito?"

Cap pressed his lips together. "That's his business."

I sat back, watching Cap. Something was bothering him. And it must've been something Chito told him. "Oh," I replied, still curious. "Are you sure?"

Cap ignored me and continued writing. I glanced at Bernard, who shrugged. I tried again. "Cap, we're a team. If something is wrong, let us know."

"Andiamo," Cap looked up at me, a warning tone in his voice. "Stop."

Surprised by his coldness, I slouched in my chair. Just an hour ago, he'd been chummy and chatty. Why, he'd let his guard down and opened up to me at the beach. What had changed? Realization suddenly dawned on me. Was it me? Was my crew unhappy with me somehow? Had I done something wrong?

I scooted my chair closer to Cap and kept my voice low. "Cap, is there something I should know? Did I screw up?"

"Stop!" Cap snapped, slamming his pencil down in frustration. Bernard jumped. "I think you're forgetting your place, Andi. *I* am the captain. *I* am in charge. *I* don't answer to you."

"Sorry, I just—"

"Why don't you run along like a good little girl and find something else to do?" Cap interrupted me, his jaw clenched.

"A good little girl?" I repeated, aghast. Cap said nothing but continued writing. "Fine," I replied, standing. If he was going to be rude, I wasn't going to stick around for it.

I stalked from the lobby, my anger growing with every step. After the deep conversations we'd shared, I felt like we were confidants of sorts. Apparently not. I didn't know where this attitude was coming from and I didn't want to admit just how much it hurt to be chided by Cap.

I lingered in my room until dinner, writing letters to my mother and sister and starting one for Arnau. I figured that Cap would loosen up after a good meal and a few drinks, but he was the first to excuse himself from the table that night. Citing the need to be up early the next morning, he hastily congratulated us on finishing our first day of travel and bid us good night.

I lingered at the table and listened as the rest of the crew exchanged tall tales from their childhoods, but I soon went up to bed, too. I tossed and turned for a long time, wondering exactly what had caused the drastic change in Cap's attitude.

"Surely time will heal this," I thought. *"We're on the road together for months, probably longer. He can't ignore me that whole time."*

CHAPTER 35

FOG BLANKETED THE PLAZA outside our hotel as we met to prepare for the next day's journey. I watched the steam rise on my coffee cup as Cap ran through our itinerary.

We'd skirt the Spanish coast as far as we could without stopping, and eventually board a small ship to take the Strait of Gibraltar to Morocco. From there, we'd head south through Africa. If all went according to plan, we'd then circle up through Europe and Turkey with a fresh stash of footage in order to fundraise more money from wealthy donors.

After our first leg, which had been plotted carefully, our exact destinations would depend on how much money we raised along the way. Due to the unpredictability of our journey, Cap had been forced to prepare for every possible scenario. He had an entire box of research he dragged everywhere.

"I'll be lead car again, with Andi following behind me, then the boys," Cap explained. "We'll stop for pictures and film if we see anything interesting, but it's important that we cover as much ground as possible over the next few days. That means no time to waste on chit-chat or gossip."

"What about flirting?" offered Paz, smiling devilishly. "Can we waste time on that?"

"No flirting, either," Cap replied, his ears going pink. "We have a schedule. It's going to be a busy few days."

I loaded my car, tucking my suitcase away, and pulled on my jacket and helmet. As the rest of the crew packed their Fords, I sidled up to Cap. I resolved to restore peace between us.

"Cap, is everything okay?"

"It's fine," he said brusquely, slamming the car door. "Get ready to go."

"I'm already ready."

"Then get in your car," he replied, his tone sharp. "We're leaving any minute."

I resisted the urge to stick my tongue out at him and trudged back to my car. I plopped in the driver's seat and pulled my goggles on, then slumped against the leather.

Paz leaned against my door, pulling his hood on. "What's wrong?"

"I don't know," I shrugged. "Cap's mad at me, I think. I don't know why."

Paz glanced over his shoulder and lowered his voice to a whisper. "What'd he say?"

How could I explain this without looking like a dumb kid whose feelings were hurt? And could I trust Paz? Well, Paz *was* a teammate. I could open up to him, right?

"He's just brushing me off. Calling me a little girl."

"Little girl?" Paz whistled. "You're crawling around on the ground, changing oil and hauling trunks in and out of the autos. I'd like to see a little girl do that."

"Yeah, really."

"Let's be honest, Andi," Paz leaned toward me, his voice low. "You're really the star of the expedition here. Without you, we're a group of men traveling across the world. Big deal. Lots of groups have tried that. But with you? A beautiful, charming young woman? No one's ever seen an expedition with a girl before. It's novel."

"I suppose."

He laughed. "You're not getting it. You're the *star*. Without you, we don't stand out. Cap knows that."

"You think so?"

"Of course. He's probably just jealous that you're going to get more attention than him."

I thought back to Cap's words. Was it jealousy that was making him so harsh with me? Maybe.

"What can I do?" I asked Paz.

"You can't do anything," he shrugged. "You're the most important person in this crew, though. Perhaps you need to put Cap in his place. Remind him of that—that he needs you. That he can't treat you like this."

Chito interrupted our conversation. "What are you two talking about over here?" he boomed, leaning over Paz's shoulder.

"Just talking about the day," Paz winked at me.

"Maybe I have an ally after all," I thought, feeling better. *"I guess Paz and I just got off on the wrong foot when we first met."*

Chito patted my head and slung his arm around Paz. "Let's go, sonny boy," he said, pulling him toward his car. "I'm feeling a bit peckish, so why don't you drive the first leg while I snack?"

As Paz climbed in with Chito, Bernard hopped in next to me, a sour look on his face.

"Hey, Bernard. We're driving together?"

"Cap told me to spend the day with you."

"He did, did he?" I mused, glancing at Cap. Had Cap seen me talking with Paz and wanted to separate us? Was he jealous of Paz showing attention to me?

"Yup," Bernard growled, crossing his arms. "Try not to run us off the road. And don't talk to me."

"You got it, pal," I retorted, feeling fresh irritation with Cap. Not only had he embarrassed me last night by calling me a little girl and then rebuffed my attempt to smooth things over, but now he was foisting crabby Bernard on me.

"Fine," I thought to myself, steamed. *"If this is how Cap is going to act, I'll be sure to make life difficult for him, too."*

We drove all day through the Spanish countryside, Bernard staring out the window without comment. Occasionally, he dozed off and awoke with a start when I hit a bump. "Jumpin' Jehoshaphat!" he hollered on one occasion, as I jerked the car through a deep rut. "Are you trying to kill us?"

As we parked in front of our hotel that evening, I jumped out as soon as the Ford stopped. "I'm going in," I announced, grabbing my suitcase and darting into the lobby. *"One should only be forced to deal with Bernard in short doses,"* I thought.

"I'm checking in for the Gallivanter Expedition," I said to the desk clerk.

"I see we have five rooms?" the man said, thumbing through his files. "Would you like to bring all the keys out to the gentlemen?"

"No. I'll just take mine, thank you."

He slid my key across the counter. "Here you go, señorita."

"Actually, I'll take a few of the other keys," I said, thinking rapidly. "I'll take all of them, just not the room key for Mr. Grant Gallivanter, thanks."

He slipped three more keys off the wall. "Enjoy your stay," he called as I left my suitcase sitting in the lobby and walked back out the front door.

"Got the keys!" I called, tossing them to Paz, then Bernard and Chito.

"Where's mine?" Cap asked.

"Sorry, it must've slipped my mind," I replied, already walking back to the lobby. "It's at the front desk. You can get it yourself."

Inside my room, I dropped my suitcase on the floor and kicked off my boots. A sheaf of paper and a pen sat on my nightstand. I grabbed them and trotted to the small desk in the corner, stopping to yank open the window as I sat down.

"Dear Arnau," I wrote, feeling a familiar well of emotion as I thought about him.

"Today's been a rough day, and I don't really know why. It seems that my crew captain has turned against me, and that will make for a very difficult journey ahead of us."

I paused, tapping my pen on my nose. Writing to Arnau was always such a bright spot in my routine, I realized. Should I pay attention to that feeling? Maybe there was more between us than I realized.

Unexpectedly, I felt a tug of regret. Did I actually love Arnau? Had I made a mistake in coming on this expedition? What if I should have said yes when he asked me to marry him all those months ago?

I wrote out what I was thinking, slowly forming each word.

"Maybe we should get married after all, Arnau," I scrawled. *"I could be happy being your wife. We could be happy together."*

I examined the words on the page. There. I'd actually written it. But even as I stared at it, I felt confused.

A quiet knock at the door interrupted me. *"It's probably Cap,"* I thought.

"What?"

"Can we talk?" Cap's voice floated to me from the other side of the door.

I stared at my letter to Arnau, seeing the words emblazoned across the white parchment. Cap didn't understand me. Paz was right: I was a publicity tool for him, nothing more. No one knew me like Arnau did. So why bother investing in a man who was going to treat me like a little kid?

"Andi?" Cap called.

"No," I replied. "Please leave me alone. I'm tired. I want to rest."

"Fine," I heard from the other side of the door.

As I heard his footsteps fall away, I tossed my pen onto the floor in frustration. *"Cap didn't even care enough to try harder than that,"* I thought angrily.

I crumpled my letter to Arnau up and threw it in the trash. I took out a fresh piece of paper and decided to write about the expedition but not my real feelings.

I wasn't going to let anyone get the upper hand on me anymore.

CHAPTER 36

I WOKE UP EARLY, MY stomach growling.

I'd skipped dinner altogether in an attempt to punish Cap over his bad behavior. I hadn't been too hungry, anyway, but now I was starving. I dressed quickly and headed to the dining hall.

Paz reclined at a table, sipping coffee. "Good morning," he said, pulling out a chair for me. "We missed you last night."

"Yeah, I was tired," I lied, sitting down.

"Tired? No," Paz studied my face. "You're mad. At Cap."

It was a statement, not a question. I realized Paz could easily read me.

"Yes, I'm mad," I replied, scanning the menu. I signaled the waiter and ordered. Paz waited until he'd delivered a steaming cup of coffee, then lifted his eyebrows.

"Are you going to say something to Cap?"

"What can I possibly say? He's in charge."

"Tell him you deserve respect. You're just as capable as anyone else on this crew. Don't let him boss you around."

I stirred a dollop of thick cream into my cup and said nothing.

"Come on," Paz wheedled. "He's controlling. Don't let him push you around. You're the star, not him."

"It's the 'Gallivanter Expedition', Paz. It's his name on the cars."

"So? Without you, it's a group of men. With you, it's something never before done. You'll be the first woman in history to circle the globe, Andi. He won't be the first *anything*."

We both jumped as Bernard sat down at the table. I bit my lip, worried that Bernard had overheard our conversation. Why was he so quiet?

"Hey, Bernard," I said, feigning cheerfulness. "How did you sleep?"

"Fine," he said, looking for the waiter. "I need coffee. Now."

Cap and Chito soon joined us and in Spanish, Paz ordered a pot of coffee for the table. Cap sat across from me and didn't bother to look at me. He spread a pile of papers out in front of him and alternated between taking sips of coffee and scanning his notes.

"I guess this is how it's going to be," I thought, watching Cap. *"We'll both avoid each other and pretend like everything is fine."*

Cap walked us through the day's journey, mentioning that he had scheduled a press conference in Murcia, the next big city on our route. "They'll be taking pictures," he said. "I know it's hard when we're driving all day, but make sure you're ready for the cameras. Button your uniform and clean the dirt off your face when we pull in. Andi, maybe slap on some of that lipstick for the cameras."

I bristled. "No."

He looked up from his itinerary and frowned. "I'm just asking everyone to look their best."

"I don't care. It's my face. I'll decide if I'm going to wear lipstick or not."

The whole table stared at both of us, mute. The tension was palpable.

"Fine," Cap sighed. "Do what you want."

"I will."

I waited until the waiter cleared the table, then stood up. "I'd like to stretch my legs before we take off today," I said, already breezing toward the lobby. "I'll be out by the automobiles when you're all ready."

Cap watched me go but didn't say a word.

Once we all packed up and hit the road to Murcia, we flew. This time, Paz was paired with Cap, and I drove by myself as Chito and

Bernard headed up the rear vehicle. Halfway through the morning, Chito honked the horn from behind me and motioned for us to pull off the road.

"Olives!" he yelled, pointing at the gnarled trees lining the road.

I grinned as Chito scrambled out of his car and plucked a shiny green olive off a branch, popping it in his mouth. He made a face and spat.

"Yuck," he groaned. "They're terrible."

Cap smothered a grin. "You can't eat raw olives, you know. They have to be cured."

"Another fact you've learned, I see," Chito smirked back, pulling two more olives off the tree. "Well, I may not be able to eat them, but I can certainly throw them."

Childlike laughter ensued as we climbed out of the Fords and grabbed for olives, playfully throwing them at each other and taking turns to see how far we could hurl them. For a moment, I forgot the tension with Cap.

"Let's switch up the seating this leg," Chito proclaimed, tossing the last of his olives at each of us as we dodged them and laughed. "I'll go with Andi, Paz and Bernard can drive together, and Cap can go solo."

We rearranged ourselves and Chito slipped in next to me, taking the wheel. "I figured you could use a friendly face today," he said as we pulled our goggles on. "You seemed a bit off last night. You didn't eat dinner."

"It was a difficult day," I admitted as the engine roared to life.

"We all have those," he replied, adjusting the mirror. "We're still getting used to each other, don't forget. It takes a while to settle in with new people and find your rhythm."

"I know."

"What can I do to put a smile back on those cheeks?"

I rolled my eyes. "Figure out why Cap suddenly hates me."

Chito said nothing but stroked his beard.

"I don't get it," I blurted, wanting to share my frustrations with Chito. I was tired of keeping things in. "One minute, he's confiding in me and telling me how he feels, and the next he's talking down to me. Calling me a little girl. We've barely even started, and already I'm not sure if I can put up with his attitude."

"Did he say something to you?" Chito glanced at me. "Did he say why his attitude changed?"

"No. He's said nothing. He just doesn't care."

"I don't think that's true."

"Well, I do," I said, staring out at the passing scenery. Trees bordered the road while brown and green hills swelled around us. Sunshine dappled down through the branches, illuminating the Fords as we drove.

"Tell me about you, Andi," Chito changed the subject. "Do you have a sweetheart back home who's missing you while you're here?"

"That's a bit of a long story."

"Enlighten me. We have a long drive ahead of us."

"I don't know where to begin," I hesitated. "I'm not even sure what it is, honestly. I wouldn't call him a sweetheart."

"Just tell me about him," Chito smiled. "What's his name?"

"Arnau."

"Ah, a Frenchie?"

I laughed. "Yes. We met in boarding school, in France."

"What's he like?"

I thought of the hours I'd spent with Arnau, racing horses through the woods and fields. Of our inside jokes and confessions. Of the times we spent confiding in each other as we mucked stalls, scrubbed the saddles, and stared up at the dust floating through the shafts of sunlight in the stable. "He's my best friend. He understands me like no one else."

"How long have you been together?"

"We're not really…together," I sighed. "We're best friends. But I think there's more. There could be more."

"More?"

I hesitated. I wasn't sure how much to share with Chito. We were still getting to know each other. But a memory of Arnau's brown eyes smiling up at me flashed through my mind and I blurted, "He asked me to marry him."

"He asked you to *marry* him?" Chito jerked the wheel as he stared at me. We skidded through a shoulder and rocks pinged against the bottom of the Ford. Paz beeped his horn at us.

"I didn't say yes. Obviously. Or I wouldn't be here."

"What do you mean, he asked you to marry him? You're too young, Andi. Jeepers."

"I told you. It's complicated."

"But you refused him?" Chito glanced at me. "Why?"

"Honestly, I'm not sure why I said no," I admitted. "I've struggled with some doubts that maybe I should have said yes. But I was leaving the school to go somewhere else, and I didn't want to tie myself down so young, and…"

"And you wanted this," he finished for me. "An adventure."

"Yes." I was relieved to be understood. "You get it."

"I was young once. I like to think I still am, on a good day." He patted his belly and winked. "I didn't always look like a big old bear of a man."

I laughed. "How did you know you wanted to marry your wife?"

"The million dollar question," he replied. "I don't know how to explain it. I just knew."

"But what did you know?"

"I just knew she was the one I wanted to spend my life with. The one person who I wanted by my side, no matter what I faced."

I leaned my arm out the side and let the wind rush against my open palm. How could I put what I wanted to know into words?

"Chito, how did you know that she was the one you wanted by your side? Was it because she understood you? Or where you came from? What exactly caused you to be sure?"

"Well, I don't know that I can pinpoint exactly how a person knows they've met the love of their life," Chito paused, scratching his nose. "Romance is a tricky thing. Sometimes it comes in the form of an old friend, and love blossoms slowly between two people. Other times, two people meet and sparks fly. It's an instant connection. But the person you spend your life with, well, you want them to know you. I mean, truly *know* you."

"Like understand where you've come from?"

"Not just that. They also have to understand where you're going. And be willing to go there with you."

I thought about what Chito was saying. If he was right about love blossoming slowly between old friends, was that what was happening between Arnau and me?

Unexpectedly, I remembered the thrill I'd felt when Cap confided in me. The way I had butterflies when he looked at me and smiled. Cap was the kind of person I wanted by my side as I faced this new, unknown next chapter in my life.

Or at least, he was before the last few days had ruined everything.

I pursed my lips at the thought of Cap. *"That's your answer, I suppose,"* I told myself sourly. *"Those days of Cap opening up to me are over. It's strictly professional now. Concentrate on the expedition, Andi."*

"You're too young to worry about marriage, anyway," Chito interrupted my thoughts. "You have plenty of time to have a whole army of boys come after you. You'll have your choice."

"I don't think so. And besides, lots of girls my age get married."

"So?"

"I don't want to be behind everyone else."

Chito chuckled. "Andi, I don't think you'll have to worry about being behind anyone else. You'll always be out in front, leading the pack."

CHAPTER 37

WE REACHED MURCIA AT dusk to find a single journalist waiting for us in the hotel lobby.

It was obvious that he'd been drinking at the bar, alone, for quite some time. His shirt was rumpled and spotted with spilled liquor, and he hiccuped when he introduced himself.

"Where's everyone else?" Cap asked, looking around. A man played piano in the corner, jazz music tinkling, but otherwise it was empty.

"It's just me," the reporter yawned. "The paper only sends out multiple people to cover the big stories."

"Well, we'll pose anyway," Cap replied. "After you're done with the photographs, we can talk about some notes for your article."

"There isn't going to be an article. Just the photo and a caption underneath."

I couldn't help feeling bad for Cap. I knew he spent hours writing press releases and laboriously researching local newspapers along our route, mailing letters to each office. Not having enough media attention would be a death knell to our expedition. Without it, we'd run out of funding.

"Go ahead and take the picture. I'll make sure you spell our names right in the caption," Cap said, rubbing his face.

The man snapped some photos, scribbled down our names, and hightailed out of the hotel on wobbling legs. As soon as he left, Cap collapsed into a chair. He looked exhausted.

"Should I put in an order for dinner?" Paz asked.

"Sure," Chito chimed. Cap didn't respond.

"I'll look for a menu," Paz strode across the lobby.

"Team, we need to figure this out," Cap leaned forward in his chair. "We need more coverage from the newspapers. We have to keep public interest high throughout our expedition. We'll need more financial support once we get through Africa, and though we'll no doubt have a lot more interesting stories to share after that leg of the journey, our success depends on our fame."

"What can we do?" I asked.

"I don't know," Cap sighed. "I thought having Paz with us would help, that he would be able to translate to the crowds for us. But there haven't been any crowds. Maybe we need another person on the crew—a hype man. Someone who follows us around and documents our every move. Someone with the sole focus of creating a frenzy with the media."

Chito frowned. "Can we afford another crew member?"

"It'd be tight," Cap shook his head. "I think we could do it for a few weeks. But if we don't get more publicity, we'll have to cut him, too."

"Shouldn't the automobiles themselves attract more attention?" Bernard asked.

"They're novel, but they're not pulling in the crowds we need," I said.

Paz rejoined us, menus in hand. Cap exhaled and leaned back. "Let's enjoy dinner and we'll figure this out later," he said. We all knew that was Cap's code for dropping the subject, because he was going to stay up all hours to work it out himself.

———◦———

THE NEXT MORNING, I bathed and padded down to breakfast in my socks and wet hair. Cap was sitting alone at the table, a stack of papers in front of him.

I froze. I couldn't face him alone. I decided to go back to my room and wait for the rest of the team to come down. I spun around and tried to walk away without being noticed.

"Good morning, Andi," Cap's voice rang out behind me.

I cursed my bad timing and turned around.

"Did you sleep well?" Cap asked, laying his notebook down.

"Yes."

"Good. Are you ready for another day of fun?"

"Sure," I said, crossing my arms in front of me.

"Do you want to sit down and have breakfast?" he asked. "I can order coffee for us."

"I'll do it myself," I replied.

"Sit down and relax, at least," he said, standing up to pull out a chair for me. "Here. Start the morning right."

"Fine," I replied, sitting. I purposely avoided his eyes. We sat in silence for a few moments as the waiter delivered coffee. As I sipped my mug, Cap sighed.

"Andi, I need to apologize," he said.

"For?"

"My comment yesterday," he said. "About you slapping on some lipstick for the cameras."

"Yeah."

"You're pretty without lipstick," Cap said. "Lipstick just shows up better on cameras. That's all I meant, I swear. You know what I meant, right? So much of our job is performing, playing the role in front of the cameras. We're selling ourselves to people. We know each other—who we really are—but they don't know us. Does this make sense?"

"Sure," I replied, crossing my arms again. How could he be so dense? Did he not realize that it wasn't just the lipstick comment, but his attitude over the last several days?

Cap sighed in frustration and went back to his papers. I snatched a local newspaper off another table and scanned it. There was no mention of us whatsoever.

"Listen, we have to work this out," Cap startled me. He slammed his notebook shut. "I've clearly offended you. And for that, I'm sorry."

"Okay."

"Andi, you may be tempted to think that I brought you onto this team just to get us some attention in the newspapers, but that's not it," Cap replied. "To me, you're not just a pretty face. It's not just about getting you in front of the cameras. You're on this team because you're the ideal person for the job. You're smart, you're capable, and you're hardworking. Believe me, I need you on this team. Please. I don't want to be at odds with you before we even get rolling."

His eyes were earnest. I softened.

"I just needed to know I'm valued," I said. "And when you do things like call me a little girl, it undercuts my value."

Cap groaned. "I'm sorry," he replied. "I never should have said that. I just—Chito—"

Just then, Bernard flopped down at the table. "Coffee," he said flatly, staring at my cup. "I can't function without it. Where is it?"

I stared at Cap, who flushed and looked back down at his notes. What had Chito said about me? Well, I'd ask later. At least things were back on track with Cap.

Paz and Chito soon joined us. They poured their coffee and leaned in. "We've been talking, and we think you should do it, Cap," Chito said. "Hire a hype man. Have his entire job be to see our adventures firsthand, write about us, build us up. Get everyone's attention."

"And it'll save you the effort of doing all that work yourself," Paz added. "You're wearing yourself out and we've barely started."

"That's true," Bernard nodded. "You're up later and awake earlier than the rest of us, every single day."

Cap rubbed his neck. "I don't know," he mused. "It'll be a drain on our finances. It's another mouth to feed."

"If we don't make a change, we may have one less mouth to feed anyway," Chito chided. "You're wasting away, Cap. Take some pressure off yourself. We need more help. And we need you healthy enough to be our captain."

Cap exhaled slowly. "Maybe. We could try it for a few weeks, at least. See what a real professional would do for our expedition."

Chito slapped him on the back. "That's the spirit. Come on, we're all in this together. A team, sink or swim."

He reached into the middle of the table, extending his hand. Paz joined him, and Bernard rolled his eyes but put his hand in, too.

"We're waiting on you two," Paz teased. Cap and I put our hands in, my hand on top of Cap's hand. His hand was warm and rough. I felt a little tingle as I rested my hand on his.

"Sink or swim," Chito repeated. "Here's to the Gallivanter Expedition. However long it lasts."

CHAPTER 38

WE QUICKLY WROTE OUT an advertisement for a hype man for the expedition.

"Wanted, a media relations aide to join a small crew for the adventure of a lifetime. The Gallivanter Expedition is traveling around the world in Fords and in need of expert documentation. Journalism background and camerawork experience needed, proficiency in multiple languages desired. Strong teamwork skills, adaptability and self-starter attitude are necessary. Serious inquiries only. Must be ready and willing to interview and depart immediately."

Cap added several hotels along the bottom, instructing applicants to leave their resumes at these stops along our route.

"Will this work?" I asked.

"It's how we got you, isn't it?" Bernard replied.

"We'll shake the trees and see who comes out," Chito grinned. "We always get a few nuts in every batch."

"We don't have time to deal with nuts, though," Cap said. "We'll go over the resumes and select only the strongest applicants. We can try to interview them in person, but we may have to hire someone quickly—maybe without meeting them first. We can't afford to slow our pace."

"Fingers crossed," Chito said. Paz kissed the chain around his neck and looked up to heaven.

Our expedition continued for a few more days, the process of unloading and loading the Fords each evening and morning becoming routine. Our team grew closer, swapping stories as we drove and dined together.

Despite our attempts to attract attention, only a few locals seemed interested in glancing at our automobiles. We forced cheerfulness, but the entire team was disappointed at the lack of people's interest in the Gallivanter Expedition.

As I entered the lobby one morning, I saw Cap talking to a short, portly man wearing an ugly fedora. He was wearing a fashionable pinstripe suit, punctuating his words with the walking cane he held.

I knew Cap's expressions well enough to observe that he was not a fan of this gentleman. *"Steer clear,"* I thought, attempting to sneak through the lobby without Cap noticing me.

"Andiamo!" Cap called. Drat. I forced a smile and joined them.

"Good morning, Captain," I replied. Cap's eyes crinkled in amusement as he caught the tone in my voice. He knew me well, too.

"Good morning," Cap replied. "I want to introduce you to someone. Andi, this is—"

"Allow me, please," the short man said, bowing deeply and lifting my hand to his mouth. "This must be the famous Miss Andiamo Gallivanter, the daring world explorer who is using her brilliant mind and beautiful soul to melt hearts all over the world?"

"Uh, yes," I said, raising my eyebrows at Cap over the man's head. He mouthed a silent scream as he shook his head. I tried not to laugh.

The man straightened up, but continued to hold my hand. "My name is Paolo Perez," he said, stroking my hand gently. His fingers were large and moist, and made me uncomfortable. I snatched my hand away.

If Paolo was rebuffed, he didn't show it. "Miss Andiamo, my dear, I must confess something," he drawled, looking me up and down. "You're stunning. Where on earth did you get that outfit?"

I looked down at my uniform and looked back at him. "We all have the same clothes," I said in confusion.

"Well, you certainly wear it well," Paolo gushed.

"Thank you," I replied, trying to be polite. I looked pointedly at Cap. "I was just heading out, I'm sorry. Nice to meet you."

"Oh, no you don't," Paolo grabbed my elbow. He only came up to my shoulder. "We're just getting to know each other, my dear."

Cap gently pulled Paolo off my elbow. "Paolo is going to help us out," he explained, guiding Paolo a few steps away from me.

"Yes, I'm so excited!" Paolo exclaimed. "I'm your new media relations aide! I even have my own camera to bring!"

Cap and I exchanged a glance that wordlessly communicated what we both knew. We were desperate and needed a hype man. We were running short on time. Paolo was our only choice. If the expedition wanted a future, it included this annoying man.

"Let's meet the whole team, shall we?" Paolo beamed, oblivious to our silent conversation. "Where's everyone else?"

I looked over his shoulder and saw Chito and Paz in the lobby. I pointed wordlessly. Might as well let them in on the suffering, too.

"Perfect!" Paolo said, trotting toward them. He whistled as he spun his cane.

I shook my head at Cap, who shrugged helplessly. "It's the best we can do!" he hissed into my ear, putting his arm around my shoulder as he guided me to the crew. "He's got some camera experience, at least, and has family in the newspaper business here. He could be helpful."

Paolo introduced himself to Paz and Chito, who politely listened as he rambled. None of us bothered to go get Bernard, because none of us wanted to risk having Bernard open his mouth around Paolo.

"I've analyzed your situation," Paolo boomed, shaking his head. "So terrible, this lack of media attention you're getting. Never fear, though. I have a solution."

"That's what we're paying you for," Paz grumbled. Cap shot him a look.

"You'll capture the attention of the world by intentionally taking some big risks," Paolo proclaimed. "You know, pose on the very edge of the cliff. Stand up and balance in the driver's seat while you race through the mountain roads. Things like that. It's sure to get you some publicity."

"I don't know if that's safe," Chito mused.

"Well, those are just preliminary ideas," Paolo responded, twirling his fedora in his hands. "What about this, then? We stage an accident..."

"How about we just talk about it as a team when we see an opportunity present itself?" Cap interrupted.

"Yes, of course," Paolo replied, pounding his cane on the ground. "Don't worry, my friends. I'll be sure to get you some attention. I'm an expert in this area."

"I hope so," Cap said. "Welcome to the Gallivanter team. Pack your bags, Mr. Perez. We leave here tomorrow at daybreak."

CHAPTER 39

RAIN POUNDED OUR FORDS the entire next day, slowing our vehicles to a crawl in some places as thick mud caked our tires.

Over and over, we had to climb out and scrape our tires clean when the weight of the cars caused them to sink into the ground. Every stop found me kneeling in the cold mud, my uniform soaked, the rain fogging my driving goggles. Even though I tried to wipe the mud off with a rag, dark dirt was caked under my fingernails and stained my sleeves and knees.

Cap drew the short straw and ended up with Paolo as his passenger. From behind their car, Paz and I watched the hype man's animated gestures and speculated about what he was discussing with Cap.

"I don't think he's stopped talking once," Paz observed.

The road wound us through the mountains, where we continued to hit soft patches of ground. Paz and I groaned as we got out to clean the tires again.

"Hold on, let me capture this!" Paolo sputtered, snatching the Kinamo camera from Cap's trunk. He deftly stepped around the muddy spots, filming us and jokingly narrating our actions. The sounds wouldn't be captured on film, which was lucky because Bernard regularly swore whenever he saw the camera on him.

"The beautiful Andiamo Gallivanter is here, cleaning the Ford with her bare hands. Even though she's a young woman, she's out here doing her part to keep the expedition moving forward. Andi, how do you feel at this very moment?"

He swooped the camera down into my face as I glanced up. The rain pelted me, tiny rivulets of water streaming down my neck. My hair stuck to my forehead. "It's very wet," I replied tiredly.

Paolo stood behind the camera and waved his chubby hand, motioning for me to do something impressive.

I wrinkled my nose and shrugged, feeling the beads of water rolling down my forehead. Paolo panned away from me, heading toward the other autos.

I finished scraping the wooden spokes of the wheels and stood up, trying to wipe my wet hair out of my eyes with my pinky, the only clean digit I had. My back ached from bending over repeatedly. Cap joined me, sloshing through the mud. "Here," he said, tossing me his rag. "You've got mud on your face."

"Thanks," I replied. "I've got mud everywhere. Do you have nine more of those?"

He laughed. "I'm going to go check the condition of the road in front of us here. It's getting soupy. We may need to take a break and let this rain stop before we go any farther."

Cap and Bernard walked together up the road and disappeared from sight. Still dabbing mud out of my ears, I joined Chito and Paz and leaned against the car. We watched while Paolo squatted to get a shot of the deep mud our Fords were sitting in, his stubby legs splayed as he tried to avoid getting mud on his suit.

"Bad news," Cap announced as he returned to the group. "There's a river over the road in front of us. It's all this rain. Looks like a flash flood."

"How deep is it?" asked Paz.

"Hard to tell," Bernard replied. "A few feet, maybe? But it's moving fast. It looks dangerous."

We huddled together as the rain continued to drench us, raising our voices to be heard above the downpour. "What do you want to do, Cap?" Chito asked, shielding his eyes.

"I'm not sure," Cap admitted. "Why don't we all go look at it and see what we think?"

We walked up the road together. The mud squelched underfoot, making a sucking sound every time we took a step. No wonder it was so hard to move the vehicles through this sludge, especially ones that were loaded with supplies.

I heard the rushing sound of water before I saw it. Coming around the bend, I saw a large stream cascading over the road. It appeared that the water was rushing down through a narrow mountain pass and pooling at the low point, which was where the road ribboned through. The water was dark, bubbling, and foamy. It looked ominous.

"We can't make it through that," Chito exclaimed. "Look how fast it's moving."

Bernard rubbed his chin. "It's not worth the risk to the Fords," he said. "Even if they could get through, it might reach the engines."

Paz shook water from his hair. "I vote we turn around. Find a hotel and turn in early. Try it again tomorrow."

"Can we even get to a hotel?" I asked, shuffling my feet in the mud. "It's taken forever just to get to this point. Maybe we're better off waiting."

"Well, we can camp out overnight if we need to," Cap replied, looking at the sky. "The rain will have to stop at some point. If we can't get through here, we'll have to backtrack and find another route."

"Hold on now," Paolo said, staring at the rushing water. "This is perfect."

"Sure, get a shot of this water," Cap replied, starting to walk away.

"Exactly," Paolo grinned. "But we're going to make it even more dramatic. We're going to send Andi out into it."

"What?" Chito exclaimed. "Are you crazy?"

"She can't go out in that," Cap shook his head. "It's too dangerous."

"Andi is capable of handling it," Paolo snorted, using the inside of his sleeve to wipe the camera he shielded under a blanket. "She's a strong young woman. She'll be fine."

"No way," Cap protested, staring at the water. It thundered in front of us, crashing down from the rocks onto the road. "It's too deep. And too fast. What if it sweeps her away?"

"It'll be a great shot, Captain," Paolo insisted. "Just imagine how it'll play out in the papers. And at your future presentations. Footage of the daring young beauty, Andiamo Gallivanter, intrepidly crossing a dangerous flooded river to press on in her journey around the world. It practically sells itself."

I bit my lip and looked at my teammates. He had a good point. It's what we had hired him to do—help us sell ourselves to the masses. And this was what Cap had brought *me* on to do—to garner interest from the public.

"I still don't like it," Chito crossed his arms.

"Neither do I," Bernard grumbled. "What's the point in risking her life for a stupid film?"

"What if we tie a rope around her waist, and one of us goes out first to anchor her?" Paz suggested. "Chito could go out ahead of her and weigh her down, so she doesn't get swept away."

"No, the shot has to be Andi. Alone. A sole woman, battling the raging river. You can't be in the shot with her."

In my mind, I'd traveled back to the long-ago moment when I forged the swollen stream outside our school and retrieved the baseball. A memory of Roger's face as he turned away, dismissively telling me to play with the girls, imbued me with sudden determination.

I could do this. I'd done it before. And this time, it was bound to earn me some real respect.

Paolo was right. It would surely get our team some attention. I imagined how it'd look for thousands of people to see me bravely battling this raging river. My mother and sister would be terrified, but proud of me. Arnau would see it, too, I'd bet.

I spoke up. "I'll do it."

"Andi, you can't," Cap shook his head. "It's too dangerous. You'll get hurt. You might drown."

"I'll be fine. I'm a good swimmer. I'm strong, like Paolo said."

"No. I can't let you do this," Cap wore a worried expression. "Your safety is worth far more than a good shot."

"If you're that worried, we can tie a rope around her waist and hold onto the end," Paolo interrupted. "We'll just let it droop in the water a bit, so it's not visible in the pictures. A little trick of the camera."

Cap fell silent, staring at me. Chito took up trying to reason with me. "Andi, even if you're a strong swimmer, you could get swept away. Easily. I've seen water like this knock a grown man off his feet. Don't do this."

I clenched my jaw. "I'll be fine."

Paz whooped. "That's our little star," he grinned at me. "I hope you're getting this, Paolo."

"The camera is already rolling," Paolo proclaimed, holding his camera up to his face. "Let's get a shot of that rope getting tied around your waist, Andi, and then you can head out into the water."

Chito and Cap stood next to each other, arms crossed.

"Don't do this," Chito repeated.

In response, I shrugged off my jacket and handed it to him. Looping the rope around my waist, I pulled hard to make a tight sailor's knot and removed my helmet and goggles, giving them to Cap.

"See? The rope's tight," I said, tugging on my waist. "I'll be fine."

With Paz holding the rope securely behind me, I walked toward the edge of the rushing river.

"Move a little to the left!" Paolo yelled behind me, over the roar of the water. "There. Right there. I'm filming now, so—go!"

I stepped gingerly into the water with my right foot and felt the force of the stream. It was more powerful than I'd anticipated.

"Keep going!" Paolo yelled. "Get out there!"

I stepped in with my left foot, struggling as the cold water soaked both boots. Determined to look good on camera, I took another step. Water was now up to my knees, and I struggled to stay upright.

"You can do this," I said to myself, through gritted teeth. I leaned forward and continued walking, barely able to move against the force of the water against my body. I could no longer hear anything but the mighty roar of the water.

Suddenly, I lurched forward and into deeper water. I was immersed up to my chest. I must've stepped into a dip in the road.

Instantly, I was swept off my feet and tumbled into the water.

Fear raced through me as my whole body submerged in the rushing stream. *"No, no, no!"* my brain screamed at me, but I couldn't stop myself from gulping water as I panicked.

I had no idea what was happening to me because I couldn't get back on my feet. I couldn't see anything but black, rushing water. The noise was deafening. Bits of branches and rocks were hitting me as I swirled underwater. I had no control over anything, not even my own body.

I was drowning. It was happening so fast.

"Dear God, I'm dying," I thought to myself, more terrified than I'd ever imagined feeling. *"It hurts. I'm not ready for this yet."*

Where was my team? Why hadn't they pulled me in yet?

My lungs burned as they filled with water.

I couldn't think clearly anymore. My brain was going fuzzy.

I saw Cap's face in my mind, then Arnau.

My sister.

My mother.

My father, gurgling on his own blood. Was this how it felt for him to die? My lungs burned painfully.

Mercifully, my mind went black and my body relaxed. *"Go to sleep now, Edith,"* was the last coherent thought in my dying brain.

I was gone.

CHAPTER 40

PAIN WRACKED MY BODY, unexpectedly. Through a distance, I could hear screams.

The next sensation I felt was rough slapping on my face. Voices screamed at me in terror, louder now. Unable to understand what was happening, my body wouldn't respond.

I felt a mouth over my own, blowing air down my throat. It hurt.

Involuntarily, I coughed. Water streamed out of my mouth and I gagged. Cracking open my eyes, I turned my head weakly and coughed up water. It hurt everywhere.

Cap's scared face was inches from mine. "Andi!" he screamed my name wildly. "Andi, please!"

He propped my head up. Confused, I couldn't speak. I closed my eyes and coughed again, hard. I had the vague sensation that I had just vomited my breakfast out all over my shirt. My eyes fluttered shut.

Again, I felt hands slapping my cheeks.

"Andi, wake up! Cough it out! Come on, wake up! Cough!"

I was hauled up into a sitting position and someone was cradling me in their arms. I heard the terror in Cap's voice as he yelled at me, his mouth right next to my ear.

"Wake up, Andi! Don't go. Wake up. *Please.*"

I couldn't talk. It hurt to open my eyes. Even so, I cracked them open and stared up into the blue eyes of Cap, hovering inches away from my own.

"Oh, thank God," he yelled, clutching me to his chest. "You're alive!"

His mouth covered mine in a passionate kiss.

"Stop it, Cap," Chito commanded, pushing his face away forcefully. "She needs to breathe."

Cap pulled his face away, but clutched me tightly against his chest. I laid in Cap's arms and searched weakly for his hand. I discovered he was already holding it when he squeezed my fingers.

My head lolled against him. I could barely control my own body. We laid in the mud, rain pouring down on our faces. The river thundered next to us as the whole team knelt in the mud, hovering worriedly around me.

"We thought you were lost," Chito exclaimed, tears welling up in his eyes. "How could we have let you do this?"

Cap rocked me in his arms like a small child. "Andi, good God," he whispered brokenly. I could feel his heart racing as he held me against his chest.

"What happened?" I croaked, alarmed at the raspy sound of my own voice. I coughed again.

"Get it all out, good girl," said Chito, pounding me on the back. "You got swept away in the river before we even knew what was happening. We tried to pull you back in right away, but the water was too powerful. It took three of us pulling to get you back to shore. We were afraid the rope was going to break."

"I'm so sorry," Paz cried, kneeling next to me. "I tried to pull you in. The water was just too strong."

I tipped my head back and tried to breathe. Taking in air felt like hot knives were scratching my throat.

"Are you hurt anywhere else?" Cap asked me, still holding me. His eyes ran over my body, worried.

I glanced down. I'd been cut with rocks and sticks as I tumbled along in the raging river, leaving scratches on my arms and chest. Blood pooled through the uniform of my left knee.

"I don't know," I rasped.

"We need to look," Cap said, gently pulling up my sleeves and checking my skin. "I'm sorry, Andi, I don't mean to embarrass you but we have to check for injuries."

I closed my eyes as he and Chito peeled up each pant leg and removed my boots. They worked together to pull off my shirt, leaving me shivering in my chemise, and gingerly prodded my stomach and back and arms. When they were finished, they carefully buttoned my shirt back up for me.

"You're sliced up pretty good in a few spots," Chito said, taking hold of my hand. "But you're going to be alright, kid."

"It hurts to breathe," I groaned.

"That's normal," Cap responded, his arms around me once again. I leaned back into him. "You swallowed a lot of water. It's going to take some time for your lungs to clear out."

He glanced down at me, then spoke to the crew. "We're going to need to keep her warm and limit her activity for a few days. We don't want her to catch pneumonia and get worse."

I hacked again, feeling sore all over.

"Thank you," I muttered, self-conscious over my weakened state.

"You should thank Cap most of all," Paz replied. "He saved your life. He was the one who had the sense to blow air into your lungs and bring you back."

"How did you know to do that?" Bernard asked curiously. "I've never heard of that before."

Cap propped me up a bit higher and fished out his handkerchief to wipe vomit from my shirt. He held me firmly.

"I read about it in a paper in Amsterdam one time," Cap responded slowly. "It's a newer technique there. Their theory was that forcing air into someone's lungs, even an unconscious person, can save lives. I didn't know if it would work. It just—it came to mind suddenly. I was desperate."

"And that kiss afterwards?" Paz asked. "Is that part of the theory, too?"

"Shut up, Paz," Bernard said shortly, as Chito glared at him. Cap said nothing, but continued to study my face.

"Can you stand up? We need to get you back to the car so you can rest more comfortably."

"I don't know," I replied, feeling fuzzy. "It's like I can't think straight."

"Oxygen depletion," Cap said, turning my wrist over and looking at the tips of my fingernails. "Your skin is turning pink again, so that's good. But you took in a lot of water and deprived your brain of oxygen, so it's going to take a while to get back to feeling yourself."

"Thank goodness you're a reader, Cap," Bernard muttered. "I guess all your research is coming in handy after all."

"We need to get her back to the cars," Chito said, standing up. "Let's go warm you up."

Cap and Chito gingerly hauled me to my feet. I wobbled, unsteady.

"What can I do to help?" Paolo asked, speaking for the first time. I sensed the apprehension in his voice, like he was afraid to draw attention to himself.

"I'll deal with you and your stupidity later," Cap replied, his voice hard. "That's the last time I listen to you. You almost killed her."

Cap and Chito supported me on either side as I hobbled to the automobiles, coaching me to move my battered body. "One foot in front of the other now, that's right. We need to get your blood moving and warm you up. Keep going."

With every step I took, I felt my brain starting to clear. By the time I reached the first Ford and the boys propped me inside, covering me with a blanket, my teeth were chattering from fear over how close a call I'd just had.

"Don't leave me," I whispered to Cap as he tucked the blanket around my feet.

"Never," he whispered back, resting his hand briefly on mine. His eyes fluttered closed for a brief second, his fingers wrapped around my hand unconsciously. Swiftly, he opened his eyes and straightened to give orders to the group.

"Paz, you're smaller than the rest of us. Squeeze in here next to Andi so you can keep an eye on her while I drive. We'll just find another place to stay, close to here, and regroup in the morning. Bernard, drive Andi's car. Chito, you can follow up in the rear with your car."

"What about me?" asked Paolo. "Where should I go?"

"You can go to hell," Cap said, slamming his door shut. "Take your damn camera with you."

CHAPTER 41

BACKTRACKING THROUGH the mountains, we trundled into a tiny town a few miles away. Chito dropped Paolo off at a nearby cafe as the rest of us descended on an old stone building, the only boarding house in town.

Paz spoke with the owner, who apologized that she only had two rooms available.

"That's fine," Cap said, as he propped me up in his strong grip. "Andi needs to rest. She can have the bed, and Chito and I can share the floor in her room and keep an eye on her."

The woman ushered us to our rooms, then returned shortly to mine with a pile of blankets, a bottle of some sort of dark alcohol, and a steaming bowl of soup.

"Gracias," Chito said, carrying the bowl to my bedside. "This smells good. I hope she has more of this for me."

I laughed, then wished I hadn't. My lungs still burned painfully, and I coughed again.

Cap unscrewed the lid of the bottle and took a whiff. "Holy smokes," he said. "This stuff is strong."

He poured out a small glass and carried it to me. "Drink," he said, putting it up to my lips. "Slowly. It'll warm you up."

"But I don't really drink alcohol," I protested weakly.

"Yeah, I don't really drink it either," he smiled humorlessly. "But today, we're both drinking."

He took a long pull and grimaced. Staring into the bottle, he steeled himself and took another long drink.

"Whoa, Captain," Chito said reprovingly. "Slow down."

"I want to forget this day," Cap muttered, staring at the bottle. "I wish I never would've listened to Paolo's stupid idea to send you out there. You almost died."

"I'm fine, Cap," I rasped, trying to prop myself up higher.

"Yeah, let's hope so." He took another swig. "You're not entirely out of the woods yet, Andi. You need to stay warm and rest. We need to make sure you don't get sick while you're recovering."

I closed my eyes and leaned my head back.

"Pneumonia could be fatal to her, in this condition," I overheard Cap murmur to Chito. "We may need to find a doctor in town if she doesn't bounce back quickly."

"I'll be fine, really," I said, eyes closed. "Stop worrying about me."

"Get some sleep. You need it."

I dozed off, waking as the setting sun peeked out from the clouds and blazed through the slats in the window. Squinting, I looked around. Cap was stretched out in a chair next to me, eyes closed, his legs resting on the foot of my bed. As I stirred, Cap's nose twitched in his sleep.

I lay still, studying him as he slept. His eyelashes were dark against his tan cheeks. I hadn't noticed until now that he was getting a dusting of freckles across his nose because we'd been out in the sun so much.

Oh, Cap. I didn't know where we stood after the accident today. The look on his face as I lay in his arms, soaking wet...that kiss...I hadn't imagined that, right?

Did it mean anything, or was it just the heat of the moment that caused him to react primally? The triumph of life over death?

Did I *want* it to mean something?

I laid in bed, looking at him silently. Suddenly, he stirred and his eyes opened. I closed my eyes and pretended to sleep. Cap softly swung his feet down off the bed, and leaned forward. I felt his hand gently touch my forehead, checking my temperature.

"Hey," I groaned, opening my eyes. "I'm fine."

For a moment, Cap's face leaned close to mine. Then he straightened up.

"How are you feeling?"

"I've been better."

Cap smoothed a strand of hair off my forehead, then abruptly sat down. "I think maybe we need to send a telegram to your mother. Just so she knows what happened. I don't think Paolo would dare write about this, but I don't want to risk her finding out about your near-death experience from the newspapers."

"I don't think we need to do that," I croaked. "It'll just make her worry."

"Do we need to send a telegram to anyone else?"

"Like who?"

"Oh, I don't know," Cap replied, his tone light. "Maybe to that gentleman of yours, in France?"

"How do you know I write to someone in France?"

"I see those letters you leave with the hotel clerks to mail for you," Cap stood up and reached for the bottle of alcohol. "Your family is living in America. Who are you writing to?"

"I went to school in France. I have friends there."

"Friends?"

"Yes," I muttered, subconsciously touching my throat. It hurt to talk.

"It's a man's name on the envelopes," Cap said, taking another swig from the bottle. "Is it a sweetheart?"

The door swung open as Chito stepped inside, carrying a tray of food. "Hey, kiddos, I'm back." He stopped short and stared at us. "What are you guys talking about?"

"We're just talking," Cap replied, running his hand through his hair. He set the bottle on the table and stood. "Now that you're here, Chito, I'm going to go check on the rest of the team."

As Cap closed the door, Chito carried the tray to my bedside and sat on the corner of my bed. He broke a chunk of soft bread off a loaf and handed it to me.

"Can I get you anything else?" Chito asked, a grin on his face. "I assume you're not in the mood for a glass of water."

I smiled and chewed the bread.

"How are you feeling?" Chito said, patting my leg.

"Why does everyone keep asking me that? I'm fine."

"We're just worried about you," Chito shook his head. "Especially Cap. He's taking it hard. He feels responsible."

"Cap saved my life," I replied slowly. "He shouldn't feel bad."

"You know it's not that simple, Andi. He's the captain of this team. He takes it seriously, as he should," Chito replied. "When he saw you today—when we dragged you back in—it was horrible. He was beside himself."

"I know," I said, blushing involuntarily as I remembered Cap's mouth on mine. "Chito, I don't know how to ask this, but I need to ask it."

Chito set down his fork and sighed. "I knew you'd want to talk to me about this."

"I'm sorry, but I need to talk to someone about it," I blurted. "Cap kissed me today, right?"

"And here I thought you were half-dead when that happened."

"I remembered *that,*" I said, thinking of the expression in Cap's eyes as he looked down at me, clutching me to his chest.

Chito's eyes found mine.

"Yes, he kissed you," he replied softly. "But he's the captain of our team. We're just starting this expedition. If you muddle this thing with romance—this trip that Cap has worked on for so long—it's not fair to him."

I picked at my bread.

"It's not fair to you, either," Chito continued. "You want to be here on your own merit, a member of this team who keeps up with the rest of us, not as the fair maiden hanging on the arm of the hero."

"I'm not hanging on anyone's arm," I muttered. "*He* kissed *me.* I didn't kiss him."

"And you think every man there didn't notice that?" Chito raised his eyebrows. "Andi, imagine the problems it would create if you tangled us all up in a messy relationship. We have enough to worry about without dealing with romantic tension. You can't. He can't. He knows that."

I frowned. "What do you mean, he knows that?"

"I've already had this conversation with Cap," Chito admitted. "That first day, after we arrived in Tarragona."

"What did you say?"

"I told him to stop flirting with you," Chito said. "I told him that his little crush on you was going to cause problems for all of us if he didn't get himself in check. And you got mad at him, Andi, because he backed off. Because I told him to."

I tossed my bread down, feeling frustrated. So Chito was the cause of my fight with Cap. I bit back the angry retort I wanted to toss back to him, realizing there was wisdom in his words. *"He's protective of me,"* I thought, staring at the hulking man sitting on my bed. *"He's protective of Cap, too. He doesn't want to see either one of us get hurt."*

Chito chewed on his food, watching me. I extended my hand for another slice of bread.

"Chito?" I said softly, tearing off a bite. "If you told Cap to back off, why'd he kiss me? In front of everyone?"

He shook his head, slicing a piece of meat. "A man can't always think with his head, especially when the person he cares about is in danger. Sometimes he thinks with his heart."

"What are you saying? That Cap loves me or something?"

"Oh, Andi," Chito sighed. "Why do you think he's drinking like that today? The man is nothing if not self-controlled."

"That's not an answer."

"And I'm not going to give you one," Chito replied. "All I'm going to say is that you'd do well to concentrate on being Andi the Explorer, not Andi the Lovestruck."

I considered his words and reached for a grape from his tray. Maybe he was right. Perhaps this was my gut check, to refocus on the expedition.

"If love finds me, it won't be like this," I resolved. *"I'll know it when I see it. And I'll embrace it—after living my own adventures."*

CHAPTER 42

OTHER THAN ALL THE cuts and burning sensation when I took a deep breath the next morning, it was almost like I hadn't drowned the day before.

Chito and Cap had slept on the floor in my room, but I surprised them by being the first one up and changed for the day.

"How are you feeling?" Cap asked, stretching on the floor.

"Better, thanks," I said, slowly flexing my knee and looking at the jagged wound through the hole in my pants. I'd have to repair the pants later. One of the boys must've washed the blood off my uniform as I slept, as it had been hung to dry in the tiny bathroom in our room when I stepped into it this morning.

"Can I get you anything?" Cap offered.

"No, I need to keep moving and stretch this knee," I replied. "I'm going out to the common room so you boys can use the bathroom."

I limped down the hallway to the common room, feeling winded after only a few dozen steps. We'd barely started the expedition and I was already banged up.

I nestled into a big chair and covered myself with a blanket. With the sun shining in on my bare toes, warming me, I closed my eyes and relaxed. I heard the distant sound of the boarding house owner singing softly in her kitchen.

"How simple her life must be," I thought. *"How domestic and predictable. She knows where she'll be, every single night of her life. I wonder what that's like."*

Did I desire a life like that? Living out the rest of my life in the same small house, in the same small village, around the same people every day—forever?

Was that what life with Arnau would be like?

"Andi?" Cap's voice interrupted my daydreams. "I made you some tea."

I opened my eyes. Cap stood next to my chair, holding a cup.

"I always drink coffee," I smiled. "Did you forget that?"

"She didn't have any coffee in the kitchen," Cap pulled a chair over to me and sat. "Trust me, I would've walked to the moon and back to bring you coffee today, if I could."

"Thanks. That seems like a lot of wasted effort, though. Unless the moon is part of our itinerary now?"

"Maybe it is."

I laughed and coughed. Cap winced.

"It's going to take time to heal completely," he said, reaching for my hand. "Let me see those cuts on your arms. Are they feeling better?"

I held out my arms to show him. He leaned forward to examine them, gently holding my hands in his as he turned my arms. "At least there's no debris in there," he said, shaking his head. "It's not infected. Gosh, it could've been a lot worse. I don't even want to think about it."

Did he hold my hand for a moment longer than necessary or was I imagining it? I thought back to his kiss and wondered. *"Stop it,"* my brain sputtered helplessly. *"You know what Chito said."* But I couldn't shake it out of my head.

The rest of the Gallivanters drifted down for breakfast, and Cap ran through the day's agenda.

"We need to get here," Cap said, pointing to the very southernmost tip of Spain. "We're nearly there. We're set to head into Morocco next, and we'll quickly move away from civilization once we get there. Our journey will start in earnest, once we leave Spain."

"Say goodbye to hotels," Bernard said.

"And coffee every morning," Chito added. "We'll have to conserve the supplies we have, to make sure we don't get too low at any point. We don't want to get stranded in the middle of the desert without any food or water."

"Right," Cap said, drawing a line down from our current location in rural southern Spain through a narrow pass heading toward Morocco. "Given the—what happened yesterday—we won't lose too much time, but we'll have to drive longer the next few days to make up for it and keep us on schedule."

"Then let's get going," I said. The entire team turned to look at me.

"Andi, you drowned yesterday," Paz said. "You can't just hop in an auto and drive for ten hours. You can barely walk. You won't be able to drive."

"I'm fine," I said, forcing a smile on my face. I didn't want to be responsible for slowing the group down, not after I'd already lost us a valuable day of travel time. We had more flexibility in the upcoming weeks, I knew, but not in these first few weeks. We had to make it through the mountain passes before the heavy snow hit.

The team exchanged glances. Bernard came to my defense.

"She'll go crazy just sitting here," he pointed out. "She seems to be doing okay, all things considered. What's the difference if she's sitting in bed or sitting in a Ford?"

"She can't drive," Chito shook his head. "Somebody needs to keep an eye on her."

"I'm the captain," Cap replied, staring at me. "It's my job to keep my team safe. Andi, you'll ride with me. And don't bother asking to drive anytime soon. It's not going to happen."

"Deal," I smiled. At least I wasn't holding us up for another day.

Within the hour, I was settled into the passenger side of Cap's lead automobile, my knee propped up on a blanket. Cap pulled his hat on and adjusted his goggles. He cranked the engine and the Ford rattled to life. "Let me know if you need to stop for any reason," he said over the clanking car. "We can take it as slow as you need us to today."

We rode along in comfortable silence for a while. Cap drummed his fingers against the steering wheel, and I hung my head out the window to feel the air rushing across my face. It was nice to be a passenger. I remembered the sensation of galloping my horse through the meadow with Arnau, feeling the wind tossing my hair.

Those days seemed so long ago.

Had I changed that much already?

I thought about Arnau, mentally promising myself that I'd write him a letter when we got to our lodging tonight. I wasn't sure how I'd explain what had happened yesterday, nor how he would take it. Would he be upset to hear that I'd almost died? Would he confess his love and demand that I come back to him once and for all? Would I want that?

Unbidden, my thoughts of Arnau were interrupted with thoughts of Cap. Of his touch, the concern in his eyes when he looked at me.

"How are you feeling?" Cap asked, breaking me out of my thoughts.

"I don't think I'd be winning any footraces today," I admitted. "I feel pretty beat up."

"Well, you still look good," Cap replied. His ears went pink as he looked back at the road.

We resumed our silence, my thoughts now turned to Cap. *"Stop thinking about him,"* I told myself. But he was funny. And sincere, a man of integrity. Committed. And passionate. Even in the moments when we fought, I couldn't deny that I felt attracted to him.

But what good was it to fall for Cap? Chito was right. We'd just started the expedition. If we dated and it didn't work out, it'd be a miserable experience for our small team.

Even as I tried to convince myself to stop thinking about him, I couldn't help but imagine what it would be like if it *did* work out. I'd walked away from the offer of a conventional life with Arnau. Would a lifetime with Cap always be filled with adventure?

My thoughts flitted to my mother. I owed her a letter, but I couldn't tell her much about this particular part of my journey. It'd do nothing but cause her to worry to hear that I'd nearly died.

Frowning, I realized that I hadn't received a letter from my mother or Evelyn, or even Arnau or Clara, since we started the expedition.

"Hey Cap," I said, interrupting our silence. "Why don't I get letters from my friends or family?"

"Oh, I thought you knew," Cap replied, glancing at me. "It's virtually impossible for people to stay in contact with us while we travel. We're in a different city every night. Sometimes we don't even know where we'll be staying until we roll into a town. It's hard to predict where we'll be, and without a fixed address to send mail to, it's just too difficult to communicate."

"But I've been sending letters to my mother and—and friends," I said, omitting Arnau's name at the last second. "Have they been getting my letters?"

"Yes. They have permanent addresses. The hotel clerks can drop them in the mail for us, and they'll get to your friends, no problem. It's just that they can't send letters back to us."

"But what if something happens while we're traveling? How can they get in touch with us?"

"They can follow our itinerary in the papers and figure out where to send us a telegram," Cap replied.

"And when is the last time we were featured in the papers, exactly?"

Cap frowned, staring at the road. "Well...that part isn't going as planned."

"So they don't know where we are, or how to get ahold of us," I said, suddenly feeling lonely. "We're basically cut off from the world. And everyone we love."

Cap looked at me out of the corner of his eye. His goggles concealed his expression.

"Yes," he said shortly. "We're isolated from everyone. That's why we have each other."

"So everyone I know is going about their lives, but I know nothing about it," I said, thinking aloud. "I might not even know if something happened. If my mother died. If my sister got sick."

Cap hesitated, then admitted it. "Right."

It was an odd thought, to realize that everyone else was living their lives, too, and I'd have no idea what they were experiencing until my own journey with the Gallivanter Expedition was complete. I prayed that my mother and Evelyn and Arnau and Clara would all be safe until I could find out what was happening to them.

"I guess we'll just have to hope that nothing major happens in anyone's lives while we're on this expedition," I frowned, trying to push my concern down.

"I'm sure it'll be fine, Andi," Cap replied. "We couldn't do anything about it, anyway. We can't control anyone's lives or what happens to them."

As we drove, the scenery changed. Gnarled trees and rocky hills gradually shifted into sandy canyons, with steep rocks rising around us. Every once in a while, Cap or I would point out an interesting sight to each other—a rock formation, or a small animal, or an interesting dwelling.

When we arrived at the small border town we had agreed to stop at, Cap pulled in under the shade of a small grove of trees. He stopped the engine and parked, then jumped out over the side of his car to come around to our one door. "Easy there," Cap cautioned, holding me steady as I climbed out. My knee was stiff and sore from being in one position for so long.

"It's hot here," I said, looking at the broiling sun.

"Just wait until we get into the desert. It can be this hot during the day, but freezing cold when the sun goes down."

Bernard joined us, Paz trailing behind him. Bernard had the pained look of someone who'd had his fill of conversation.

"Please tell me we're stopping to change passengers," Bernard rolled his eyes.

"We're eating lunch and seeing how Andi feels," Cap said. "How are you doing, anyway?"

"I feel pretty good," I said, lying. I felt lousy. My body ached, and I'd been coughing as we drove. Breathing hurt even more now. I hoped this was a normal recovery timeline for someone who'd nearly drowned, but I had no idea. All I knew was that I didn't want to delay our trip and I didn't want to worry my teammates.

"Let's trade drivers," Cap said, yawning. "I didn't sleep well last night. Too worried. I could use a quick nap."

"I'll drive you, if you're going to sleep," Bernard offered quickly. I smiled. Bernard hated small talk even more than me.

"I can drive Andi," Paz offered, flashing me a grin. "I can keep her entertained."

We ate a small lunch that we'd packed at the boarding house. We savored the crusty bread, cheese and olives, and curiously examined an odd-looking fruit our host had included in the basket.

"She called it a cherimoya, I think," Chito said, holding up the bright green, scaly fruit. "I'm not quite sure how to eat it. Paz, do you know?"

Paz examined it. "I'm not sure," he said. "It must be unique to southern Spain. I've never seen one of these before."

"Do we bite into it?" I asked, poking my fruit.

"You're sure this is edible, Chito?" Cap laughed. "That sweet old lady wouldn't have a reason to poison us, right?"

While we talked, Bernard had simply stabbed his fruit and cracked it open. The inside was white and juicy, filled with large seeds. Without warning, he popped a piece in his mouth. We watched as he chewed and swallowed without comment.

"What does it taste like?" Chito prodded.

"Good," Bernard replied, reaching for another piece.

"We gave the job of describing flavor to the one person on this crew who doesn't talk," Paz complained, slicing open his cherimoya. "Let's see. It tastes like...hm. Sweet and sour. Maybe a bit like berries and something else."

I cut open mine and scooped out the creamy, custard-like flesh. It tasted tangy, like a combination of bananas and strawberries, but it was more than that. It was complex. And delicious. I'd never had anything like it before.

"You know what this is," Chito said dreamily, finishing everyone else's cherimoyas. "It's the taste of adventure."

"And with that, I've lost what little respect I ever had for you," Bernard muttered. The rest of us laughed and stood up to get back into the Fords.

"Next stop is a brand new country!" Chito hollered as we climbed into our automobiles.

Paz cracked his knuckles and started up the engine. "I love driving these things," he remarked. "I don't get to drive as much as

I want. I'm always trading off with Chito or Bernard. Don't you enjoy driving?"

"Of course."

"Do you think you'd ever lead your own expedition?" Paz glanced at me.

"Huh?"

"You know, do your own thing," Paz said, gliding the car out onto the road. "Be the captain of a crew. Decide where to go."

"I've never had that thought," I answered honestly. I thought about the endless amount of preparation Cap had put in, schmoozing donors and researching countries and customs and plotting every detail. It sounded awful. It was the job no one coveted.

"You should consider it," Paz said, glancing behind him at Chito's vehicle. "I think you'd be even better than Cap at leading a team."

"I doubt that."

"Don't be so modest, Andi. How many times do I have to tell you that you're a star? You'd probably get way more attention on your own than just being on a crew with someone else in the lead."

"I don't know about that."

"Sure. A woman, leading a group of men? Now *that* would be headline news. That's what we need. We'd be sure to have the cameras clamoring for us then."

"Right," I replied, thinking. "But shouldn't leadership be more about ability? Not just because I'm a girl, but because I'm the right person for the job?"

"This isn't about leadership as much as it's about the spotlight," Paz said. "You'd get more attention being the one in charge, as a girl."

I felt uneasily that his logic might be right, but I didn't know that I could agree with it. Sure, I'd spent a lot of time in my life being told how women should act, but I couldn't help but feel that the best person for a role should get it—not just the person who got the most attention.

"Anyway, dream about it," Paz grinned at me. "I'd support you. Heck, I'd leave this expedition and join your crew, if you were in charge."

"Thanks," I said, uncomfortable. I'd just managed to sort things out with Cap. I wasn't eager to witness Cap and Paz get into it now.

"And they think girls create all the problems?" I thought, glancing at Paz. *"No, not girls. It's just people. People are the problem."*

CHAPTER 43

WE SOON ARRIVED TO the ferry that would carry us through the Strait of Gibraltar, from the tip of Spain to the northern coast of Africa.

The port was crowded, and we found ourselves hurried along with a diverse crowd of travelers, businessmen, merchants, and locals. The sounds of people calling out in different languages was thrilling. I drank it all in, reveling in the early hint of the exotic new chapter of travel we were about to start.

Just think—Africa. Why, I never knew a soul that had travelled there. And now I was minutes away from stepping foot in it myself.

The crystal waters served as a striking contrast to the sandstone ambers of the small port in Morocco where we eventually pulled in. After waiting to unload our cars and sign the required paperwork, dutifully presenting our passports and visas, we were finally free to pull off the ferry and out into the blowing sands of the desert-like climate.

As we followed the winding road through a small village and into the countryside, we came across a large wooden sign with strange script. "We'll stop here!" Cap yelled from the lead car.

Squinting at the sign, I wondered what language it was. I'd never seen anything like it.

"What is this?" I asked Cap, as he helped me out of the car. I winced as my sore muscles flexed in the hot sand.

"It's Arabic," he said, looking up at the sign. "It's used by most of the people we'll encounter in the next few weeks, as we travel through Africa. It's different from our writing, because they write and read from right to left."

"Like Hebrew?" I said, remembering a fact from Arnau's geography book.

He whistled in admiration. "My, Miss Gallivanter. Aren't you smart?"

"What does it say?"

"I'm not sure," he shielded his eyes in the bright sun. "I'd have to translate out of the book I have packed in the back, but I'm pretty sure it's telling us that we're on the right road. Welcome to Africa, everyone. This is where the real adventure begins."

We decided to capture footage of the team standing in front of the sign. We positioned ourselves around the wooden sign, smiling cheerfully as Paz cranked the camera.

"Why do I have to be behind the camera?" Paz complained. "Look at me. I should be in front of it."

"Sorry, you're too little to stand next to the rest of us," Bernard replied.

"No," Cap shook his head. "Because we originally picked you up as a guide, and we've kept you on. We've talked about this. You weren't a part of the publicized crew. We need you as a cameraman."

We smiled as the camera rolled, Paz capturing our waves and grins. As we packed up the camera, Cap huddled us up to talk.

"Team, there are a few things for us to know going into Morocco," Cap said. "Normally, I would've shared all of this already but the last few days have been...hectic. First of all, Morocco's been at war with the Spanish government for some time now. It's a colonial war, and from all that I've read, we shouldn't experience violence in the bigger cities. There's a small chance we may encounter some guerrilla troops out here in the countryside, so we want to move as quickly as we can into towns."

Chito and I exchanged looks. I hadn't realized we were entering a war zone. Cap had kept this information to himself until now.

"Paz, you're Spanish, so most of the people we'll encounter will hate you," Cap continued.

"No different from anywhere else," Bernard deadpanned.

"Hey now," Paz was offended. "I have friends. Unlike you."

"Focus, gentlemen," Cap said. "It's no time for jokes. Paz, you need to keep a low profile. It's lucky for us that you sound like an American. Go with that. Pretend that you're from Ohio, that you joined our expedition in America, like the rest of the crew. Whatever you do, don't speak Spanish."

Paz responded in Spanish. Cap glared at him.

"Andi, this is a culture that isn't especially friendly to young women," Cap continued, looking at me. "Most ladies wear a head covering or veil at all times, along with a large robe that covers their bodies. They're not permitted the same independence as men. You'll have certain buildings you can't go into, things you can't do. In this part of the world, women have little say. Men might speak to you more demeaningly than you're used to."

"Great," I groaned.

"Also, it's a very conservative culture, religiously and culturally," Cap continued, now avoiding my eyes. "They frown on unmarried men and women spending time together. If the hotel staff finds out that we're merely a crew, traveling together, they may deny us rooms. Or report us to the police."

"How are we going to get around that?" Chito asked.

Cap's ears went pink. He cleared his throat. "Andi and I are going to have to pretend to be married," he said. "We'll pretend to be on our honeymoon. We'll be a rich couple, traveling the world, drinking in the sights and sounds of new cultures. You three will act as our servants and chauffeurs."

We went silent for a moment, processing the implications. I tried to suppress the thrill that raced through my soul.

"I grew up having servants," Paz mused, breaking the silence. "Who ever would've guessed I'd have to pretend to be one?"

"Aw, can it," Bernard grumbled. "Cap, we'll do whatever you need us to do."

"So we need to act like we're in love?" I asked, wrinkling my nose.

"Shouldn't be too hard—" Paz grinned until Chito violently elbowed him. "Ow! Stop!"

"Yes," Cap said, ignoring Paz. "And it's only when we're in view of the public in an official capacity. When we check in at the hotel or if we meet city officials or religious leaders. Or if we run into the police."

"Got it, Captain," Chito said, pulling his hat back on. "Anything else we need to know before we roll into town?"

"Yeah, don't get shot," Cap replied, lending me his shoulder as I limped to the passenger side of his Ford. "Let's go, Gallivanters."

We climbed in together and started the automobile. "Sorry for surprising you with this information," Cap said, as the engine rumbled and we adjusted our goggles.

"What, the civil war we're going into, or the fact that we're pretending to be married?" I joked. "It's fine. We're adaptable. It's all part of the experience, right?"

"It's why I handpicked this particular crew. It is a trait you all share."

We continued on the road in a single file line, fine sand blowing across our windshield as we drove. The hot air was relentless, making me sweat under my thick jacket.

"I need to take this off," I said, pulling at it.

"Don't," Cap cautioned. "We're headed into a place where most women aren't allowed to show their wrists or ankles. You need to stay covered."

I frowned as sweat trickled down my back. I couldn't imagine living in an environment so hostile.

Small sandstone-colored houses and shacks started to crop up, their dark-skinned occupants staring at us as we rolled past. Several small children wearing long robes shrieked and waved as we went by, and ran after us yelling. "They're speaking Arabic," Cap remarked. "Your first time hearing it."

"It sounds like they're speaking music," I marveled. It was enchanting.

Dwellings and buildings began to merge into one continuous lump as we rolled closer to town. "It's showtime," Cap said, looking at me. "You better slide over next to me. I'll put my arm around you. We're pretending to be newlyweds, after all."

"Fine, but I'm drenched in sweat," I slid next to him. "You've been warned."

CHAPTER 44

WE DROVE SLOWLY AS we entered the crowded streets of the city.

People wearing turbans and long white robes, mostly men, swarmed around our cars as we drove in. The city was full of market stalls, strange fruits and vegetables, enticing loaves of bread and trinkets stacked high. The sides of many streets were a collection of crude awnings and tents. Everywhere we looked, people filled our vision. Small children darted in front of our autos.

The contrast in noise, having spent so much time driving through remote desert, was incredible. People called out to each other, argued in the streets, and sang as they walked.

I sniffed the rich smell of spices as we drove, inhaling sweet smoke and incense as we wound through the narrow paths crowded with pedestrians.

"What do you think so far?" Cap asked, looking around.

"It's incredible," I said, noticing the ornate metalwork framing many larger buildings. Windows and balconies were covered in intricate, lacy patterns, and mosaics colored walls and floors.

Cap motioned toward a small box on the floor. "Look in there for me," he said. "There's a detailed map of this city inside. I need it to navigate us to our hotel."

I fished it out and studied the map. Arabic words dotted the page, with tiny French names underneath. "Do they speak French here, too?"

"Yes. European countries have been battling over African ones for years. Here, the French came out on top. Why?"

"I'm fluent in French!" I exclaimed.

"Now you see why you were destined to be a Gallivanter," Cap teased. "I guess you'll be useful after all."

I guided us to our hotel, peering up at it as Cap parked our automobile out front. The building was beautiful and exotic, large metal lanterns hanging down from the ceilings everywhere I looked. Two doormen stood in matching uniforms, a red fez perched on each of their heads, watching us as we parked.

"Let's go, honey," Cap grinned as we slid from the car. He offered me his hand. "Our room is waiting for us."

We walked over to the rest of the crew. "Don't be offended, guys, but remember you're supposed to be our servants?" Cap asked. "That means you'll have to bring the luggage in, by yourselves. Andi and I are supposed to be wealthy tourists. Rich people don't carry their own bags."

"I do," Paz muttered, while Bernard shot him a look.

"Yes, master," Chito quipped. "We're here to serve you."

"We'll see you inside." Cap wrapped his arm around my waist and pulled me close. "Ready, Mrs. Gallivanter?"

"Ready," I said, trying not to blush. This was not what I'd expected out of the day.

The doorman greeted us and opened the lobby doors wide. Ornate tiles covered every inch of the floor, ceiling, and walls. Potted palms swayed in the corners of the room, and lights glimmered out in intricate patterns from dozens of hanging lanterns.

We stepped up to the reception desk, Cap's arm still snugly around my waist.

"Andi," Cap breathed into my ear, his warm breath tickling my neck.

"What?"

"Maybe leave this part out in your next letter to your boyfriend," he whispered. "He'd be mad."

"Don't make this weird," I whispered back. "We're just acting."

I concentrated on trying to ignore his arm around my waist.

The receptionist greeted Cap by coming around the counter. "Hello, sir," he said in heavily accented English, offering his hand and kissing him on the left and right cheek. "Welcome to our fine establishment." He stepped back, staring at me. I assumed he wasn't used to such tall women wearing pants.

"Thank you, sir. My wife and I are checking in. Captain and Mrs. Grant Gallivanter, from America."

"Ah, yes," the man beamed. "What brings you to our fair city, Captain Gallivanter?"

"We're on our honeymoon," Cap glanced at me and smiled. "My wife and I have always wanted to travel through Africa. With our servants, of course. We can't get along without them."

"Oh yes. Morocco is the most wonderful country on earth," the man replied, retrieving our keys. "We hope you will enjoy your visit here. Captain Gallivanter, we have many fine offerings here at the hotel for you. We have a lovely pool out back, very nice, and a cigar lounge for the gentlemen."

"A night relaxing in the pool sounds wonderful, darling," I said, playing along with Cap.

"No, I'm sorry ma'am," the man interrupted. "The pool is for gentlemen only. Not for women."

"Ah," I replied, feeling awkward. "What if I just dip my feet in?"

Cap squeezed my waist warningly. The man looked horrified. "No, Mrs. Gallivanter, absolutely not. No women are permitted in the pool area at all. Or in the hammam, the public steam rooms."

"Of course," I replied lightly. "I was just kidding. I know women can't have any fun."

I could see the mirth dancing in Cap's eyes as he looked at me.

"I will be sure to accompany my wife at all times, sir," Cap said to the receptionist. "We're delighted to explore your beautiful city."

"Yes, I can see you two are truly in love," the man smiled as he looked at us. "You are so evenly matched. Even in height. Enjoy your visit here, and let us know if there's anything we can do to make your stay more pleasant."

"My servants will be bringing our bags up to our room," Cap said over his shoulder as he guided me down the hall. As soon as we were out of sight, Cap dropped his arm from my waist.

"'Evenly matched, even in height'? That toad," he shook his head. "Let's check out the rooms. How are you feeling? You're still limping a bit."

"I'll live," I replied as Cap pushed open the door to our room. The room was vast, colorful tiles throughout the space. The balcony doors lay open, and the sounds from the street filled my ears. Fresh vases of flowers were placed on small metal tables throughout the room, and the bed was low. It looked like a mattress on the floor. The couches were the same. Jewel-colored floor cushions surrounded the couches.

"Not bad, not bad at all," Cap surveyed the space. "You can have the bed. I'll share the room with the men but I'll take some of these pillows to sleep on."

"Nonsense," I said, looking at the huge space. "You could fit the entire crew in here. There's plenty of space for both of us."

"We're not actually married, Andi," Cap said, looking uncomfortable. "I don't think we should sleep in a room alone together."

"Right. But you said it's important for them to think we're married. How will it look if you go sleep with your servants tonight? We're supposed to be on our honeymoon, after all."

"Well...I don't know. We shouldn't share a room, though."

I walked out to the balcony, noticing that all the balconies were close together. "Where's the rest of the team sleeping?"

He checked the key. "Right next door."

"So why don't you come into my room tonight, then climb over the balcony to get to the men's room and sleep there?"

He joined me on the balcony to look. "We're on the second story. It looks a bit dangerous."

"Fine. If you're too chicken to do it, I'll climb over and you'll have this room to yourself tonight."

"I don't know," he said, rubbing his chin.

Impulsively, I climbed onto the edge of the marble balcony. The broad railing was flat and wide, and I balanced easily on it. I jumped into the balcony next door without thinking. I landed hard on the marble floor as Cap hollered, "Andi!"

The jump jarred my knee, but I tried not to show the pain. I heard male voices sputtering at me from the street below. Apparently, they'd noticed my little stunt and didn't appreciate it, either.

Just then, the door to the men's room opened and Chito walked in, lugging an armful of bags.

"Oh, sorry, I thought this was our room," he said, retreating and closing the door.

"It is," I said to the empty room, rubbing my knee. "I'm just...checking it out."

"Holy smokes, Andi," Cap groaned from the opposing balcony. "You're going to be the death of me."

CHAPTER 45

WE RESTED FOR A FEW blissful days, soaking in the culture in Marrakesh.

Tempting scents I'd never smelled before filled the air as we pushed through crowded stalls of hanging lamps, meats, clothing, and religious artifacts. The streets were thronged with people who pressed up against each other, rushing by as we meandered. The sounds of strangers speaking different languages all around us was exciting, and the spicy foods we ate underscored the fact that we were a long way from home.

Laughing, we documented ourselves exploring the city. Cap fired off the best of our photographs to several newspaper contacts, including one of us smiling as a trained monkey scampered across our shoulders.

On our final morning in Marrakesh, we planned to meet for an early breakfast and hit the road. Cap usually squired me around the hotel to keep up our appearance as honeymooners, but he'd disappeared with his maps and notes in preparation for our departure. The hotel was unusually busy, I noticed as I descended the staircase.

As I reached about halfway down, a hubbub broke out in the lobby below me.

Men's voices excitedly chattered and I caught the words, "Andiamo Gallivanter!" as strangers pointed at me. Cameras started flashing, blinding me. I nearly missed the last step, shielding my eyes as I stood there, confused. How did all these people know me?

Cap and Chito appeared alongside me and each took an elbow. "Come along, Andi," Chito grinned. "Apparently we're famous now!"

"What?" I asked, bewildered. The men pressed in, vying for pictures as I squinted against the flashing cameras.

"Apparently, our good friend Paolo decided to write a thrilling account of your drowning," Cap explained, his voice low. "He sold it to a local paper, at first, but the bigger newspapers picked it up. It went worldwide. The story's appearing in nearly every paper in the world right now."

"Oh, no." I cringed, imagining how my family must have felt reading about my near death. It wasn't something I ever wanted to share with my mother.

"Well, that's not all bad," Cap rolled his eyes. "He painted me in a terrible light—the controlling dictator who is running an entire crew ragged and burning through money faster than a king—but I've already had several telegrams offering me wire transfers and financial support."

"So all this attention is paying off? Just like we hoped?"

"Yes," Chito answered before Cap could. "Look around. We're celebrities now. The entire world is going to know your name, Andi."

"It's great for us," Cap said, allowing a small smile. "We're already funded for the next leg of our trip and that's just from the telegrams early this morning. We'll be able to travel even farther, and for longer now. We're going to put our departure on hold and spend the rest of the day here, to do an impromptu media appearance. We'll take advantage of the public's interest and ride it all the way to the bank."

We spent the day entertaining journalists, photographers, and curious patrons who wanted to hear about our exploits firsthand.

"Tell us about drowning, Andi!" people begged me as they crept close to me, their cameras focused on my face. The repeated flashes of light made me blink as I shared about how I tumbled into the water and what went through my mind as I started to drown.

"My crew saved my life," I pointed out each time, nodding gratefully to my teammates. They took turns sharing about how they tried to pull me out. Cap downplayed his actions, simply sharing that he forced air into my lungs and helped me cough up water.

I thought back to the kiss he gave me, the terror in his voice, and how he cradled me against his chest. Those memories kept me awake at night, tossing and turning.

After every presentation, Cap cleverly praised the "generosity of strangers" as our sole lifeline on the Gallivanter Expedition. He mentioned that our funds were dwindling, and that every dollar that people donated could help us continue this groundbreaking adventure.

Transfixed by his words and open-mouthed over our thrilling story, it seemed like every person in the crowd opened their wallet and handed us money.

We gathered in the boys' hotel room that night, counting the thick stacks of cash and coins we'd accrued during the day.

"This is more money than I've ever seen in my entire life," Bernard said, wonder in his voice. "Did you know there was this much money in the world?"

"I feel like a banker," Cap laughed, stacking the piles neatly. We had so much money that we had been forced to go out and buy new suitcases to hold it all. "Not bad for a day of telling stories, right?"

Paz reveled in the attention, openly flirting with every girl who approached him. He was still in the lobby, we assumed, surrounded by beautiful women who were listening to every word he uttered.

"I'm a Spaniard," he grinned, as we told him we were going up to eat dinner in the privacy of our rooms. "I can't help but give attention to a gorgeous woman."

"Well, I can't help but give my attention to a good plate of food," Chito proclaimed. "I'm starving."

"Chito, you're obsessed with food," Paz complained. "Don't you think about anything else?"

"Food is his main love in life," I teased.

"And we can tell," Bernard added, poking his belly.

"Hey now," Chito squirmed. "What's wrong with loving a good meal? It brings me joy."

We continued pressing his buttons. "Other people have hobbies," Cap said, winking at me. "They don't spend all their time dreaming about cooking."

"Especially not men," Bernard sniffed.

"Who cares?" Chito growled, his voice suddenly sharp. "Listen, my family had nothing, growing up. We didn't have food to eat some nights. Those days when we had a meal on the table, well, those were the best days of my childhood. It was the only time my family actually got along and didn't fight. It was my happy place. And now, with my wife and baby girl gone—"

He choked up suddenly. "You guys are it now. My new family."

We sat quietly, sobered by the words from the one teammate of ours who was perpetually in a good mood. A smile rarely left Chito's face, but the sadness now was unmistakable.

"Sorry," Cap said, breaking the silence. "We were joking."

"It's fine," Chito replied, staring at his big hands. "We all have a backstory. A history."

"If we're a family," I said slowly, trying to lighten the mood, "Does that make me the annoying little kid of the family, because I'm the youngest?"

The team burst into laughter. Playfully, Chito tossed a floor pillow at me. "I don't think any of us would call you little, Andi. You're a head taller than Paz."

"Yeah," Bernard added. "And he's the annoying one, for sure."

CHAPTER 46

WE LEFT MARRAKESH WITH our suitcases stuffed full of money, happier than we'd ever been.

For the first time, our financial situation wasn't a source of stress. Cap wouldn't let us blow money frivolously, but he did allow us to grab some extra supplies before we motored out.

"Get another pair of pants, Andi, since you decided to destroy yours already," he teased. "Let's try to avoid ruining your uniform on this next leg of the journey."

Over the next few days, we traveled through Morocco, entering the barren landscape of the Saharan desert.

"It can be deadly here," Cap cautioned, as we pulled off to discuss our strategy. "I couldn't even manage to get a local guide to sign on to go with us. But we'll make it, I have no doubt."

"That's comforting," Paz muttered, wiping sweat from his face.

"I've charted the most efficient course through the desert, but the days will be long and hot," Cap continued. "We'll drive during the daylight, and camp out at night. It's critical that we conserve our supplies, especially the water. If we get delayed somehow—a damaged tire, a cracked gear—we don't want to put ourselves in a perilous situation."

As we took turns driving, I marveled at the desolate scenery. The flat sand stretched as far as I could see. Here and there, scraggly bushes peeked through the sand and small rocks, but there were no trees. Heat made the view shimmer as we gazed at the horizon, the constant wind creating ripple patterns in the sand.

Every once in a while, we glimpsed a pile of bleached bones as we drove. I wondered if they were from animals or humans.

Our days were long, so we broke the monotony by frequently stopping and rearranging drivers and passengers. We told each other jokes and riddles. We shared stories from our childhoods. Chito and Paz sang songs together.

Each night, we pulled over at sunset and set up camp in the middle of the sand. We hadn't seen a soul since we entered the Sahara. Out in this desolate country, a place where roads didn't even exist, we set up our sleeping rolls next to the Fords and laid down.

A small fire crackled as Chito prepared simple meals for us, using an array of different spices and ingredients to give us variety.

"I'm sorry, everyone," he apologized each time he served us a combination of rice and beans, canned or smoked meat, or hard cheese. "I can't do anything too creative right now, with us rationing the food so carefully."

"It's fine," we all promised. The extreme daytime heat tempered our appetites. We ate to keep our strength up, not because we felt hungry.

After dinner, we laid down and looked up at the stars, chatting with each other. The sky seemed bigger out here. So far away from city lights, the moon and stars were bright enough that we didn't need lanterns.

"What do all you think of this leg of the Gallivanter Expedition so far?" Cap asked one night, as we laid in our bed rolls.

"It's more work than I thought it would be," Paz admitted, his head resting on his hands. "All the packing and unpacking every day, refilling the gasoline and checking the oil and the engines all the time? It never ends."

"What do you think, Bernard?" Cap asked. Chito was already asleep, snoring away across from us.

"It's fine."

We chuckled softly. Bernard's brevity was endearing. Usually.

"What about you, Andi?" Cap asked, turning his head to look at me. "What's your opinion on the expedition?"

"It's the best thing that's ever happened to me." I met his gaze and smiled. "I wouldn't want to be anywhere else."

Cap smiled back and stared up at the sky, his grin still wide on his face.

"There's something else I want to know," Cap said, as we gazed at the stars. "I committed to this expedition years ago, wanting to educate people about each other. To see firsthand all the wonders in the world, and be able to share them with all those people who could never do what we do. I wanted to inspire them. I mean, look at Andi—think of all the little kids, little girls all over the world, who are reading about her. They're growing up marveling at what she's doing. Do you guys feel that way about this expedition?"

"That million dollar wager wasn't the motivation?" Bernard drawled. "I'm pretty sure winning a million bucks at the end of all of this would be my reason."

"I mean, that helps," Cap laughed.

"I couldn't wait to leave school," I confessed. "I hated it there. I've always craved adventure, and everyone else seemed content to learn about setting tables and doing needlework. As soon as I saw that newspaper ad, I couldn't think about anything else."

"Me too," Paz agreed. "I was dazzled by the possibilities. Traveling the world? Meeting beautiful women on every continent? Fame and fortune? It's almost too good to be true."

"Fame and fortune, and rice and beans," I laughed.

"Bernard?" Paz asked. "Why did you join?"

"Are you kidding me?" Bernard rolled over to sleep. "I couldn't afford one of these cars on my own. And you idiots are paying me to drive it around."

THE NEXT MORNING, THE relentless sun couldn't break through the dense, dark clouds that hung low on the harsh landscape. We woke up uneasy, and made our morning campfire in the dimness.

"I don't like the look of those clouds," Chito observed, stirring a pot of seasoned beans. "They look like they could mean trouble."

"What's the worst that could happen?" Paz asked, pulling on his jacket and yawning.

"A big storm and flash floods? A tornado?" Chito glanced up. "I don't know what storms they get in the Sahara."

"Do they get sandstorms?" I asked, running my fingers through my hair and watching particles of sand dance to the ground. Everything I touched was gritty.

"They call them 'haboobs' here." Cap looked up from his notes. "The African term for an intense dust storm. Nearly hurricane level winds, but full of sand. And yes, they're common. And dangerous. They can bury a man and his camel alive."

Quietly, we contemplated the prospect of bad weather as we ate our breakfast. Out here, we were battling the elements completely alone. We hadn't seen another sign of life since we left the city. No trees, no animals, and certainly no people. That itself was sobering, and the harsh desert weather we faced made it even more worrisome. We were already strictly rationing our food and water. What would we do if we faced a storm and lost those crucial staples?

In the distance, the clouds continued to darken.

"Are we hunkering down, or should we continue traveling?" Bernard asked, staring up at the sky.

Cap scratched his chin, his blonde stubble rasping against his hand. He hadn't shaved in weeks.

"I don't know," he admitted. "We're sitting ducks out here. The good thing is that there aren't any mountains or valleys near us, so we shouldn't get caught in a rockslide. But if we have rain, I don't know how a flash flood would affect us. And if we get hit with a haboob, we have no place to shelter."

"I say we continue on," Paz said. "Maybe the clouds will lift."

"I don't want to alarm anyone," Chito said slowly, "But we only have enough water left for two, maybe three days, at most."

"We've been rationing it," Paz exclaimed. "How do we have so little left?"

"It was only supposed to take a week or so to get across the desert from Morocco to Mauritania," he shrugged. "The Fords only have so much space. I packed three times what we'd need, just to be safe, but this trip through the Sahara has taken way longer than we expected."

"We have no choice, then," Cap said, pulling out his compass. "We have to keep moving."

We finished the rest of our breakfast in silence, uneasy about our situation. It didn't take long to pack up and get the Fords ready. As we pulled on our goggles, the wind picked up slightly.

As we drove, Cap using his compass to guide us in the right direction, I started to see smoke in the distance.

"What's that over there?" I asked Paz, who squinted at the horizon from the passenger seat.

"I can't tell," he replied. "It looks like a forest fire. It must be sand blowing off a hill."

We trundled on, our caravan driving single-file through the desert. A shimmer of heat rose from the road, making it difficult to tell exactly what was in front of us.

Paz and I continued to glance at the smoke. The back of my neck prickled for no apparent reason. *"We'll make it through,"* I told myself. *"We're a smart group of people. We have enough food and water. We'll make it."*

Despite our Fords steadily moving, the smoke inexplicably seemed to be drifting closer to us, rising high in the sky.

"It's sure an odd color for smoke," Paz observed. "It almost looks like the same color as the ground."

In front of us, Cap and Bernard abruptly screeched to a halt. "Get out!" Cap yelled, pushing Bernard out of the automobile and scrambling out behind him.

"What?" I called, confused.

"Get out!" Cap wrenched open our door, pulling Paz out.

"Why?"

"It's a sandstorm! It's coming right for us!"

I stared up at the giant cloud billowing above us. I froze.

Cap grabbed me by one leg and dragged me across the bench seat, pulling me from behind the wheel. As he yanked me out, I had an idea.

"Get the camera!" I yelled at Paz, who scrambled to get out of the way of my flailing legs. Cap had already darted away.

"No way," he said, pulling his helmet down tightly and adjusting his goggles. "I'm not digging that thing out. We're about to get hit!"

I pushed him aside and sprinted to the trunk. Luckily, Paz had been the last one using the camera, so it was in our vehicle. I opened the box where we carefully stored it, tore the wrappings off, and started cranking the handle.

"Andi, what are you doing?" Cap hollered, reemerging next to me. "This is dangerous!"

"This is also great footage, Cap," I kept rolling. "Let me film it!"

Overhead, what dim sunlight we'd had through the thick clouds was completely obscured as a huge cloud of sand billowed higher and higher in our field of vision.

I stepped out in front of the Fords and captured the moment, craning my neck high to pan all the way up the swelling cloud above us. I was thankful for my goggles, as the sand was already painfully stinging my face.

Cap hadn't left my side. He let me film for a few moments, then grabbed my elbow. "Hurry up!" he called, over the howling wind. "Our best chance for survival is to dig in and let it blow over us!"

The sky and sand now blended together in one dark, blurry brown mass. Cap and I bent against the force of the sudden gusts of wind that sent particles of sand blasting at us.

"Go," I heard Cap say, his hand on my back. We raced over to the Ford and knelt down, covering our heads with our hands. I cradled the camera in my lap, holding my jacket over the lens.

"Hold on to the car if the winds start to push you away!" Cap yelled, his words muffled in the wind. We could see each other, but barely. Sand swirled everywhere around us, blotting out the light. Every inch of my exposed skin hurt as I was pummeled with grit.

All at once, a pair of boots rushed by me.

"What?" I yelped, reaching for Cap. Opening my mouth to speak the single syllable filled my teeth with sand. I coughed and spat sand. I could hardly see Cap anymore, though he was still crouched next to me. My hand landed on his thigh.

"What?" he yelled over the deafening wind.

"Bernard!" I yelled back, pointing.

All I could see was a pair of lean legs running around the hood of our Ford. Squinting, I could make out the faint outline of Bernard, fighting the wind as he covered the engine with a large tarp. He struggled to hold it in place, using his body to pin the tarp down as he pulled a rope tight across it, using his teeth.

"Bernard! Stop!" Cap yelled, standing up from his crouch. "It's not safe!"

Bernard ignored him, darting by and heading to the next Ford behind us.

"He's going to hurt himself!" I cried, starting to stand, as Bernard disappeared from our view.

"Stay here!" Cap said, pushing me down forcefully. "Don't move!"

Cap crawled across the ground on his hands and knees, disappearing from vision after only a few feet. I crouched alone in the darkness, feeling my body buffeted by the strong wind and choking sand. Everything around me was blurry and shifting, like trying to see through a cloudy stream after footsteps stirred up the sediment at the bottom of the water.

After what seemed like an hour, I saw Cap's hand emerge from the darkness, touching the Ford as a guiding object. He crawled over on all fours and crouched next to me, shoulder-to-shoulder.

"He's okay!" he yelled, covering my forehead with his hand and yelling into my ear, his face inches from mine. "We just have to wait it out now! It can't last forever!"

We sat there, leaning against each other, for an eternity. Finally, the wind started to die down. Sand continued to swirl around us but the roaring wind lessened. A few minutes later, our bodies started to relax as the wind grew weaker.

"You okay?" Cap said, studying me. His beard was caked with sand.

"Yeah, are you?" I replied.

"Yes," he stood, shaking sand from his uniform. "I need to check on the others."

I stood up, stretching my legs. Reaching the back of the Ford, I put the camera back in its case, praying I hadn't damaged it in the storm.

Chito appeared next to me, slinging his arm around my shoulders. "Are you still alive?" he joked.

"I think so."

We walked back to join Bernard, Paz, and Cap. The wind died down eerily fast, and the sand settled back onto the ground, blowing around our ankles.

"What on earth were you thinking, Bernard?" I exclaimed. "What did you do to the cars?"

"I covered all the engines," he answered. "Sand getting in there, making its way into the lines, could've meant days, maybe weeks, of repairs. I didn't want us to get stranded out here."

"That was risky," Cap said reprovingly. "I know we had the tarps in the trunks, but things happened too fast for us to safely put them on. You could've been hurt. Better to come out alive and deal with a damaged auto than lose a life."

"I know, Cap," Bernard replied. "But the Fords are a part of our crew, too. They deserve respect. Some protection. My life isn't worth much, anyway."

"Don't be stupid," Cap replied. "Of course your life matters."

"Nah," Bernard shook his head. "I don't have much going for me. I'm not married. No kids. No friends. No career. I'm just a simple mechanic, and I don't mind it. People never made sense to me. Automobiles, they do. I'm happy when I'm working on the cars."

"You've got one thing wrong, though," Cap smiled, slugging Bernard on the arm.

"What's that?"

"The part about having no friends. That's a lie. You're looking at your friends."

Bernard opened his mouth to reply, then shut it. Gruffly, he rubbed his face before finally allowing himself a small smile.

"That may be true," he grinned. "You are my friends. All of you but Paz, anyway."

CHAPTER 47

"THIS WAS A HARD PLACE to get information on," Cap confessed as we took a break to refuel after we finished our Sahara run and crossed the border into Mauritania. A simple wooden sign, scrawled in French, had marked our entry into the new country.

"Why?" Paz asked, carelessly spinning a gold watch on a chain.

"Don't do that," Bernard snapped. "That looks expensive."

"It's *very* expensive," Paz smirked. "I could probably trade it for a car of my own. Maybe two. Of course, my father would never let me drive one of these around—he'd prefer his son to roll out in something nicer."

"Can you please focus on what I'm saying?" Cap held up his notes. "I do this so we know what to expect. It's important that you listen, so you know how to appropriately interact with the locals, as well as answer any questions the media might have for you."

"We're listening," I said, kicking Paz with my boot.

"Thank you," Cap said, shaking his head. "Mauritania is a huge country, and was colonized by the French only a few years ago. There's still a significant amount of conflict, I suspect. The slave trade is alive and well here, too. A few months ago, I sent inquiries to the American diplomat stationed here. He wrote back and asked to meet with us in person when we get into the country."

"Meet with us in person?" Chito tipped his head. "Why?"

"He suggested a guide for us, to help get us through the country. My guess is that he has someone in mind and wants us to meet him."

"That should be helpful," Paz grinned. "Look at me. I worked out for you."

"Right," Bernard groaned. "You're a real bonus."

We drove onward and soon arrived in the tiny village where the diplomat told us to meet him.

"It's mostly desert here. The majority of the population lives in the southernmost part of the country," Cap explained as we drove in. "The diplomat has his office here since this is the first stop for those coming in from the seaports. It's along a major trade route."

"You're sure this is this place?" I peered out. "There's nothing here."

Indeed, the city arose in the middle of the flat desert with a few putty-colored buildings. A small fort stood on one side of town, a large arch and spiked walls clearly the only actual structure in the entire area. A few dozen small buildings dotted the landscape, wooden beams and sails protruding from the fronts and casting shadows over the front yards, if they could be called that. There was no soil or grass, no trees, and no green plants of any kind that we could see.

"How do people live here?" Bernard questioned, as we eased the Fords to a stop. "Where do they get water? Or food?"

"They must have wells," Cap said. "I guess we'll have to get out and ask someone where the American office might be located?"

His question was answered by a booming voice shouting, "Welcome, Gallivanters!"

We turned to see a rotund man beaming at us from underneath the fort's archway. The ambassador grinned as we approached. "So glad to finally see you, my boy!" he exclaimed, clapping Cap on the back.

"I'm Harold Barrington, proud diplomatic representative for the United States of America to Mauritania. I've been at my post here for three years now, and it's a real hoot," he said, shaking our hands.

"Mr. Barrington—" Cap started, but the diplomat cut him off.

"Yes, it's a remote place here, but I sure get a whole lot more people passing through than you might imagine. Real interesting folks, too. Other diplomats and military men, international businessmen, all sorts of characters. We have a nice set up, a real nice little place here for you. It's a pleasure, yes sir, a real pleasure to finally meet you all."

Paz snuck me a look. I could tell he was trying not to laugh.

"Come on in," Mr. Barrington led us into the courtyard. "The boys will get all your belongings and bring them in."

I looked around. I hadn't noticed anyone else. Then I saw people emerge from the cool shadow of the awnings above.

"Yes, they're slaves," the diplomat explained, acknowledging the questions on the tip of all our tongues. "Of course, being an American, I can't condone it, you know. But it's part of the culture here, an accepted form of work. They came with the house, so to speak. So I use 'em when I can."

In French, he issued them a few orders. I understood that he was telling them to take our gear into our rooms and turn down the bedsheets for us. To one, he asked her to make a tray of tea and fetch his daughter.

I was taken aback as I watched the slaves hurry away to work. I couldn't imagine being forced to work for someone else the rest of my life.

"Never seen 'em before, huh?" the diplomat said, noticing my stare. "Slaves, I mean. Count yourself lucky, little lady, that it isn't normal for you. An ugly thing, slavery. But I can't dismiss them without causing problems."

"Thank you for your hospitality, Mr. Barrington," Cap said as we sat on wicker chairs under a wide sail overhead. "You mentioned in your letter that you had a guide in mind for us, as we travel through Mauritania?"

"Yes, I have the perfect person for you," the diplomat grinned. "They'll be here any minute."

The slave returned with a tray of hot tea, serving it to us on delicate saucers. I marveled that they had fine china in such a remote place. Being the diplomatic representative came with perks, apparently. I balanced my teacup in its saucer in one hand as I reached for a lump of sugar.

"Ah, Rosie, darling!" the diplomat announced. I looked up as I heard Paz involuntarily inhale.

The most stunning young woman I'd ever seen was walking across the courtyard. Her long blonde hair cascaded down her shoulders, and her face and body looked like they'd come to life from a Renaissance painting. Wearing an elegant dress covered with tiny embroidered sequins, she shimmered as she came to join us.

"My daughter," the diplomat said proudly, as she curtsied. "Rosie's a real beauty, isn't she?"

"Oh, she is," Paz agreed enthusiastically.

"Pleased to meet you," she drawled, her eyelashes lowered.

The men bumped into each other as they stood to greet her, teacups clattering in their hands. Paz reached her first.

"So nice to meet you, my dear."

Bernard shook her hand and sat without saying a word. Chito swiftly took over.

"I'm Chito. This is Andi—you're probably about the same age, you know—and Cap. Oh, sorry, *Captain* Gallivanter."

"Hello, Captain," Rosie blushed as she shook Cap's hand, dimples appearing in her porcelain cheeks. "I've been looking forward to meeting you for so long."

"Of course she has dimples," I thought grimly, sipping my tea to keep my tongue at bay. *"She's perfect in every way. And she knows it."*

I'd spent a lifetime avoiding the company of girls like this one. And here I was, in the most remote place I'd ever visited in my life, stuck with one. One who happened to be *very* interested in Cap.

"She's been here with me all along, you can't believe her ability to manage the staff," the diplomat gushed. "A real whiz at French. She paints and draws wonderfully, you should see her artwork. Honey, let's make sure to show them your art later."

"Of course, Papa," she smiled sweetly. "Andiamo, do you paint?"

"No."

"What about drawing? Or needlework?"

"Nope."

"Oh." Rosie turned her attention to Cap. "Captain, how long have you been in the travel business?"

I snorted reflexively, mid-sip of my tea. Cap frowned slightly as Chito kicked my foot. I was veering into Bernard-level bluntness.

"A few years now, I guess," Cap replied, glancing between the beaming diplomat and his daughter, who seemed to be edging closer to him on the couch. He cleared his throat.

"Mr. Barrington, I know we talked about the guide. When's a good time to discuss that?"

"Right now, my boy!" the diplomat exclaimed, standing. "Let's retire to my office, just the two of us boys, and talk it over. The ladies can stay here and entertain the rest of the gents."

Cap and Mr. Barrington left the room, Rosie watching Cap the whole way. When he left, she sighed quietly.

"So, Rosie, what do you do around here for fun?" Paz asked, leaning back in his chair.

"Oh, this and that," she replied. "It's pretty dull around here. I read quite a bit."

Never one to hold my tongue for long, I couldn't help myself from prodding her. "So what books have you read lately?"

"Oh, hmmm…" she stalled. "I can't recall."

"You're reading books all the time and can't remember a single title?"

Chito stood and dragged me up with him. "Let's get some fresh air, everyone," he said. "Rosie, can you show us around your home? It's…very nice here."

"Certainly," she gushed. She led us around her home, a converted fort that had been modernized and stuffed with fine European furniture and decorative trinkets. The rooms were large and comfortable, and we each had our own suite to stay in. After we toured the residence, Rosie led us down the single road that made up the city.

"I don't come down here much," she admitted, stepping daintily over potholes in her delicate heels. "But it's a lovely place, such wonderful people."

"I bet," I muttered. Life was usually kind to a beautiful girl.

When we arrived back to the courtyard where we'd taken our tea, Cap was again on the couch, waiting for us. I snagged the seat next to Cap, reclining into the couch, while Rosie sat in the chair I'd previously occupied, glaring at me.

"So when do we meet our guide?" Chito plopped down. "Is he coming here?"

"Well, good news about that," Cap replied, his forehead wrinkled. "You've already met the guide. It's Rosie."

Rosie dimpled at his words.

"What?" Bernard sputtered. "Why?"

"She speaks French fluently and she knows the culture here. She'll be a wonderful addition to our team."

"Do you have any experience driving automobiles, Rosie?" Chito asked, stroking his beard. "Any mechanical expertise?"

"No," she said, blushing. "I'm a fast learner, though."

"Have you traveled much through the country?"

"Not yet. But I can't wait to see it. I'm sure it'll be marvelous."

The diplomat cut in. "She's a gem, a real knockout. You'll see. She has a way with folks. Everyone just loves her."

"I'm sure they do," Chito agreed warmly, standing up. "Excuse us, Mr. Barrington. Can the crew step out and have a brief conversation? We'd like to make sure we prepare your daughter properly for what she'll be encountering with us."

"Certainly," he grinned, looking at his watch. "Rosie, darling, why don't you start packing your bags and we'll meet again at the banquet table at dinnertime?"

Once outside, Chito was the first to speak. "What are you thinking?" he cried, throwing his hands up in frustration. "She can't go with us! It'd be like bringing a little china doll along!"

"She has no useful purpose," Bernard cut in. "She speaks French, but so does Andi. She can't drive. She's never even been through the country."

"And she's bringing *bags*, Cap," I added. "Multiple bags. We don't have room for someone who's used to being waited on, hand and foot."

Cap threw his head back, exasperated. "She's coming with. Only as long as it takes to get through Mauritania. That's it."

"But Cap, be reasonable," Chito started, but Cap interrupted him.

"Stop. She's coming. Nothing any of you say will change my decision. I call the shots."

Cap strode away, clearly angry with us. "I'll be in my room until dinner," he called over his shoulder.

"What a joke," Bernard complained, shaking his head. "She has no place traveling with our team."

"Why is he bringing her, then?" I groaned. "We're all against it."

"Oh, Andi," Paz huffed. "You have eyes, right?"

"Yeah, so?"

"Use them," he snorted. "Just look at Rosie. Cap doesn't need logic. He doesn't need justification. He doesn't care about our opinions. He's attracted to her, plain and simple. And who wouldn't be?"

"So much for beauty, brains, and boots," I thought, remembering the advertisement Cap had placed that captured my attention so long ago. *"Apparently beauty is the only thing that really matters."*

CHAPTER 48

I LINGERED IN MY ROOM the next morning, not sure I could handle Rosie's blatant attempts to flirt with Cap and still enjoy my breakfast. Begrudgingly, I dressed in my uniform and traipsed to the dining room.

Inside, I found Bernard and Chito sipping coffee with Mr. Barrington. I joined them, and a dark-skinned woman dressed in long tan robes and a twisted turban served me a cup of coffee and a plate of fruit and bread.

"Where's everyone else?" I asked, taking a bite of bread.

"Cap went out to work on the Fords first thing," Chito responded. "Rosie wanted to help, so Paz took her out to show her the ropes."

"How nice," I said, pulling apart my bread with a vengeance.

"Tell me about yourself, Miss Andiamo," the diplomat boomed. "Where are you from? How did you end up here on this team?"

"I grew up in New York and went to school in France," I replied. "My mother's American and my father was Canadian."

"My, how interesting." He signaled for more coffee. "Tell me how you ended up on the Gallivanter crew, my dear. What a fascinating adventure it must be."

I shared briefly about my stint in boarding school after the Great War and how I found out about the expedition from Cap's newspaper ad, pinned in a book I was reading.

"Fascinating," the diplomat said, leaning on his elbow and staring at me. "What a stroke of luck."

"I'm not sure if it was luck or fate. I've enjoyed myself, though."

Cap and Rosie entered the room, laughing together. Paz trailed behind them, looking irritable. "Morning, Andi," he said, plunking down next to me.

"Ah, Rosie darling! And Captain Gallivanter! Take a seat, let's enjoy a nice cup of coffee together," the diplomat said, rising to pull out Rosie's chair for her. "Miss Andiamo was just telling me about herself."

"How nice," Rosie simpered, as she lifted her cup for coffee without even glancing at the servant waiting at her elbow. "I want to know all about you, Andiamo. You're such a unique woman. Let's start with the most important information: do you have a special young man somewhere, waiting for you?"

I stared at her. She was gorgeous today, wearing a light pink dress that brought out the color in her fair cheeks. A competitive spirit rose within me.

"I do, actually," I said, lifting my cup to my lips.

"Who?" Bernard replied, skeptical.

"Arnau," I replied. From the corner of my eye, I noticed Cap's sudden, sharp look at me.

"We've known each other forever," I added. "He lives in France."

"Tell us about this Arnau," Rosie said eagerly, leaning forward. "Is he handsome? What does he do?"

"Oh, he's very handsome. He's tall, with dark, curly hair and the most wonderful dark eyes," I replied, just to needle Cap. If he was going to throw himself at this stupid girl who was so different than me, I'd be sure to show him that he wasn't my type, either.

"So what does Arnau do?" Rosie asked, resting her chin on her hands.

"He works with horses," I replied, fibbing a bit. "He owns several. He manages a large stable. We used to ride together, through the woods, every day."

"How romantic. Is it serious?"

I took another sip, letting the whole room lean forward in anticipation. "It's very serious," I replied.

"I knew it," Rosie crowed. "You have the look of a woman in love."

"Sure. Of course." I stumbled over the words. "I'm in love."

"So are you going to marry him?" Rosie asked, clasping her hands together.

I'd backed myself into a corner now, hadn't I? I thought quickly.

"We've pledged our love to each other," I lied, alarmed by how easily the story slipped out. "We thought we were just too young to get married, so we decided to wait a while."

"*What?*" Cap exclaimed, his eyes wide as he stared at me.

"This is news to me," Paz said, looking around. "I haven't even heard you talk about this Arnau until now."

"I don't tell everyone about my personal life," I replied quickly. "I told Chito a while ago, that's all." I prayed Chito would back me up.

Thankfully, he nodded slowly, watching me. "She did tell me," he said. "Arnau proposed to her. Before she came along with us."

"He did?" Cap said, sounding angry. "You didn't tell any of us that!"

"I told you, I don't tell everyone about my personal life," I protested, blushing.

"That's kind of a big secret to keep to yourself," Paz said. "But good for you, I guess. Congratulations and what not."

Cap lifted his cup. "To the future bride," he said, his voice hard. "May you be happy together," he added, draining his cup and slamming it down on the table. Everyone at the table jumped, surprised by the sudden sound.

"I'm going to finish packing," he declared, pushing away his chair so hard it scratched against the floor. He stalked away from the group.

"Excellent idea," Rosie said brightly, hopping up from her chair. "I'll come help you."

I watched them go, realizing I'd just complicated my life with a stupid lie that was sure to bring me nothing but problems.

CHAPTER 49

WE DEPARTED ABOUT AN hour later, after lugging Rosie's suitcases into the Fords. She'd packed three of them, which didn't fit and had to be wedged in between the driver and passenger seats in each car. I said nothing, hoping someone else would complain.

Sure enough, Bernard didn't let me down. "You can't possibly be taking all of this," he groaned, hands on his hips.

"I packed light, like Cap told me," Rosie replied, eyes wide.

"How could you need more than one suitcase? You're only with us for a few weeks, at the most."

"Well, maybe you'll decide to keep me around. Permanently. Then I'll need all of this stuff."

I resisted the urge to put my head in my hands and scream. Cap thanked Mr. Barrington and shook his hand, then sidled up to me as Rosie said goodbye to her father.

"Let's have Rosie ride the first leg with you."

"Why me?"

"You can talk to her and get her acquainted with the expedition," Cap replied. "As the only woman on the crew, she'll need to learn from you how to fit in. How to manage things."

I bit my tongue. "Fine."

"Good," Cap said, buttoning up his jacket. "You can do some wedding planning while you drive, too. I already heard how she loves that kind of stuff."

He walked back to his Ford before I could reply.

As our cars rattled away, Rosie waved goodbye to her father until she couldn't see him anymore. "This is so exciting," she exclaimed, clasping her hands. "Don't you just want to die from the thrill of it?"

I flashed back to the sensation of my lungs filling with water, remembering how it felt to nearly die. "No," I said shortly.

"Tell me all about yourself," Rosie said, leaning forward. "I want to get to know the famous Andiamo Gallivanter."

"Well, for one, that isn't my real name."

"It isn't?"

"Nope. It's a stage name. My real name is Edith."

"Oh," she responded, thinking. "So Captain Gallivanter's name—"

"It's a stage name, too. His real name is Walenty."

Rosie blanched. I changed the subject. "Tell me about your life," I said. "What's it like to leave America and live in the middle of nowhere?"

Rosie had the same gift of gab her father had, I discovered. As she chirped away happily, I felt my defenses coming down. She wasn't so bad after all, I decided. If only she wasn't gunning so hard for Cap, we could even—maybe—be friends.

After telling me all about her life, Rosie peppered me with questions about Cap.

"What's he like? Where's he from? How did he plan the expedition?" She snuck a glance at me. "Does he have a sweetheart somewhere?"

I waved her off at the last question. "That's his business," I replied. "You'll have to ask him that."

Rosie sat back, her face glowing. "I'll find out," she promised. "Oh, those eyes of his. He's *so* handsome. And strong."

At her words, I felt my own cheeks turn red.

We stopped for a late lunch, out in a wide stretch of desert. Cap checked on us after climbing out of his Ford. "How are you doing, Rosie?"

"Oh, I'm swell," Rosie said, dimples showing. "It's just that I'm so warm out here. The sun is hot. I'm used to staying under the shade at daddy's house."

Cap frowned as he looked at her flimsy lace sleeves and chiffon dress.

"Why don't you wear some of Andi's clothes while we drive?" he suggested. "They're far more practical. You'll burn to a crisp without something covering your arms."

"Andi's clothes wouldn't possibly fit me," Rosie protested. "She's much bigger."

"So roll them up and cinch in the belt," Cap said. "Andi, can you help her out and get her some of your clothes?"

"Yes, sir," I replied, sarcastically.

"Thank you," Rosie flashed a smile at me. Turning to Cap, she lifted her long blonde hair off her neck and held it up. "Can you be a doll and undo this top clasp?" she purred.

I stalked to the back of the Ford, yanked my bag out, and threw it on the ground.

It was time to vent about the insufferable Rosie, or I'd explode with anger. And I knew exactly the person I was going to vent to.

Arnau was getting another letter.

CHAPTER 50

CHITO VOLUNTEERED TO drive Rosie after lunch, and she climbed into his car with a longing glance at Cap and Bernard, sliding into the lead vehicle.

Paz slipped into the driver's seat in my car. "Mind if I drive for a bit?"

"Only if you don't ask me a thousand questions about Cap," I rolled my eyes. "He's Rosie's favorite subject."

"What does she see in him?" Paz complained, guiding the Ford behind the lead car. "He's good looking, I suppose, but so am I. And I'm closer to her age. And wealthy."

"Paz, you have eyes, right? Use them," I spat, flinging back the same barb he'd hurled at me the day before. "Whose name is on all our cars? His."

"How ridiculous. Just because he's the leader."

I crossed my arms, staring out the window. After a few minutes of silence, Paz glanced at me.

"I keep telling you this, Andi, but I don't think you understand that I'm serious," he said. "I think you and I could go off on our own. Be the leaders of our own expedition. We know what it takes, and we have a lot more charisma than Cap."

"I don't know," I squirmed with guilt. "Cap's done a lot for us."

"So? He asks a lot of us, too. It's not like this is a luxury vacation."

"But this whole trip was his idea in the first place."

"First of all, Cap's certainly not the only person on earth to ever dream up a journey around the world. We could just as easily leave the Gallivanters and join the Chinook Voyageurs. They're doing the same thing as us, you know. Secondly, he's blown it. We didn't have crowds at all until the story of your drowning made us famous."

"Paz, you see how much work Cap puts into this trip, right? He's up first every morning and the last one to sleep. He's constantly poring over maps and books. This requires a massive level of organization and effort."

"How hard could it be?"

"I wouldn't want to do it," I shrugged. "It's a thankless job."

Paz thought for a moment. "Would you ever join the Chinook Voyageurs?"

"Our rivals?" I blinked. "No way."

"Why not?"

"I don't know," I said, perplexed. "They're our competition."

"We *made* them our competition. They're simply another team, going around the world. Just like we are."

"I don't know."

"You do know. You're thinking it's a good idea," he said, drumming his hand on his thigh. "Face it. They're funded better than us and they have more Fords. We're the underdogs here. They're better, bigger, and more professional. We see their articles in the paper, every time we stop in a new city."

"How can you say this?" I sputtered. He was making a lot of sense, I realized. But I didn't want to let my mind go there. I felt loyalty to this team. And to Cap.

Paz laughed bitterly. "Face the facts, Andi. Cap's already replaced you with another girl. Rosie is the new face of the Gallivanter Expedition. She'll be the one the cameras follow now, not you."

"But she's just temporary—our guide through Mauritania."

"Right," he said. "That's why Cap brought on a worthless guide, someone who has no helpful skills whatsoever? That's why he allowed her to bring three suitcases? That's why no one's bothered to ask what's going to happen to her, once we drive all the way to the south in this vast country? She's not going home, Andi. We're stuck with her."

I pursed my lips. Maybe Paz was right. Maybe Cap preferred a girl like Rosie over a girl like me. And what did it matter, anyway? I couldn't be with him.

I certainly didn't plan to go back to my lonely life at boarding school. Maybe I needed to be thinking about my next step, and where that might take me.

——◉——

OVER THE NEXT FEW DAYS, we scissored through the changing landscape in Mauritania.

Desert dunes gave way to rocky cliffs and small belts of vegetation. When we came across dwellings, we stopped and engaged with the locals, who came out of their small domiciles, smiling and waving at us. Occasionally, they pressed fruit and bottles of goat milk into our hands.

Cap held us to a fast pace, constantly rotating drivers and passengers. Every time Paz and I rode together, we grumbled about Cap and Rosie.

Doubling down on my lie about Arnau, I made an effort to write him more letters. I took advantage of free moments to scratch out notes to him, whether I leaned against the car or sat crosslegged around the campfire.

The tone of my letters had changed, somehow. I now poured my feelings out to Arnau in my letters, holding little back.

Something had shifted inside of me. With Cap's affection directed at Rosie, I wasn't sure what my future would be on the Gallivanter team. I wrote every doubt and frustration to Arnau, my safe port in the storm.

We set up our camp the same way we had as we cut through the Saharan desert, positioning our bed rolls around the campfire where Chito cooked for us. Rosie didn't complain about the food, but she insisted on sleeping on the bench in the Ford.

"I'm terrified of snakes," she called out through the darkness, as the rest of us laid on our backs, looking up at the stars.

"They're more terrified of you," Chito said. "We haven't even seen any snakes, the entire time we've traveled."

"It doesn't mean they aren't out there."

"Just let her be," Cap replied, wearily.

"Always defending her, aren't you, Cap?" Paz muttered.

Chito was the first to comment on my new behavior. "Have you suddenly become a writer?" he teased, watching me scribble away. "I don't remember you writing this much before."

"I've turned a new leaf," I said, not looking up.

"Are you writing to Arnau, your beloved?" Rosie cooed, plopping down on my bed roll.

"Yes," I said, watching for Cap's reaction. He had none.

"How precious," Rosie said, stroking my hair. "You should wear your hair up for your wedding. You have such a lovely neck."

Cap stood up. "Rosie, can you help me bring the silverware from the trunk?"

"Of course," she simpered, hopping up and walking away with him. My mood darkened. I kept writing.

"Hold on a minute," Bernard frowned. "How is Andi writing to this Arnau character? We're not getting any mail."

"Not right now," Paz said. "We did, when we were in the hotels."

"No," Bernard shook his head. "We got *telegrams* that day Andi's story was publicized. We haven't been getting any mail. How could anyone keep up with us? We're in a different place every night."

"We can still send letters to people," Chito said. "I've sent lots of letters to my sister and my niece, Molly. I just leave them with the front desk at the hotel. They mail them for us. Why, I have a bundle right here, ready for our next stop at a town."

"Right. But we're not *receiving* mail from anyone," Bernard pressed. "Arnau can't write back to Andi. Who knows what's going on in his life?"

I flushed. "So? We've pledged our affection to each other. It's a promise. Some people know how to keep promises. I don't need to hear from him every week to know he's being faithful."

"What if he's dead, though?" Bernard said. "You wouldn't even know yet."

"Bernard, stop," Chito groaned, stirring the bubbling pot over the fire. "He's not dead."

"He could be."

"He's not."

"We don't know about anyone else," Bernard insisted. "The world could be at war again. Everyone we know could've contracted an epidemic and died. We don't know anything, being isolated out here in the desert. It's been weeks since we were in a proper town with newspapers and electricity. Who knows what's happening out there?"

We fell silent. He was right. It was an alarming thought. We only had each other out here. It was if the rest of the world didn't exist for us.

Our dark musings were interrupted by Rosie and Cap returning with an armful of supplies. "This is so much fun!" Rosie squealed, handing me a spoon. "I just wish this silverware wasn't so spotty. It could use a good polish."

I noticed Cap and Chito exchange looks. I kept my head down and continued my letter to Arnau.

CHAPTER 51

THE DAYS OF ENDLESS travel through yet another desert tested our spirits.

They became a long blur of sand and steering wheels, a constant refrain of sweating through my clothes, sitting miserably in sticky wet all day as we drove, then shivering in those same clothes at night. Every article I wore felt crusty, made hard with dried sweat and sand.

We rose at daybreak, the black sky slowly softening with streaks of red and orange as the sun emerged. Stretching, we sat up and rubbed our eyes.

Chito sniffed the air. "It smells like rain."

I yawned. "Just what we need."

Cap laid on his stomach, a map unfolded across the sand in front of him. "We're only a few miles from a small village, I think," he said, tracing his finger down. "Let's try to get there before the rain starts. Hopefully they have a spot we can hunker down in to stay dry. I don't think I can stand sitting in soaking wet clothes the rest of the day."

We departed as soon as we packed and grabbed the dried jerky that Chito handed out, choosing to eat in the Fords to save time.

"I hope you're all up for a little race," Cap said, glancing at the darkening sky. "Last one to town gets soaked!"

Bumping along through the sand, we skirted along a series of large cliffs. The rocks soared directly overhead, the path taking us close to stunning sandstone plateaus layered with different colors of sediment. We soon arrived at a stand of small buildings, some hewn right into the cliffside. Several cows were tethered to small fences. Climbing out, we searched for people.

"Hello?" Rosie ventured, before anyone had time to shush her.

"Bonjour, mes amis!" A small boy stepped out from a dwelling, smiling up at us. His teeth were brilliantly white against his dark features.

"Bonjour," I knelt down, asking him in French what his name was.

"My name is Bewba," he responded to me, in French. "What are you doing here?"

I explained that we were on a travel expedition around the world, and in need of a place to shelter from the approaching storm. He nodded solemnly, his eyes big in his small face. "Come on inside," he offered, stretching out his arm. "I'm watching my brothers and cousins, but you can stay with us until the rain stops."

I translated for the group. With clouds rolling quickly now, we grabbed our gear and ducked into his home.

"What is he doing here all by himself? Where are his parents?" Chito asked. I translated into French, posing the question to Bewba.

"Everyone—all the men and women—they work in the copper mines during the day," Bewba explained. "They've been mining here for hundreds of years. I'm not old enough yet to work in the mines, so I'm in charge of watching the children."

"Won't that be a problem, if they're down in the mines and we have a rainstorm?" Cap said, frowning as it started to drizzle outside. "Will the mines fill with flood water?"

I translated for Bewba. He shook his head. "They have a watchman, who keeps an eye on the weather. They also have a stable structure, above ground, a place they stay in if the weather is bad."

"Let me ask him a question," Rosie said, squatting. "I speak French."

In garbled French, heavily accented by her southern drawl, she asked him how he liked school. Bewba shook his head and giggled. "She is very pretty, but her French is terrible," he told me.

Paz had a working knowledge of French and caught the joke.

"What?" Rosie said.

"He says your French is lousy," Paz replied. "He also said he doesn't like you, that you're a snob."

I hid a smile at the last part. Paz had tacked that one on all by himself.

Bewba introduced us to a gaggle of children in the home. They stared at us, shy at first, but soon were giggling and crawling all over us. The little girls kept touching our hair, braiding Rosie's long locks and my shorter hair into intricate twists. They shrieked with joy as Chito and Cap showed off their rifles. We filmed them as they danced for us and sang their native songs.

The rain drummed outside as we learned about life in rural Mauritania, warmed by the friendly openness of the children.

It was a challenging life, living in a small community in such a windswept, desolate place. Bewba explained how everyone he knew lived here, and how his family had mined a small copper mine for generations, selling their product to a traveling businessmen who came through with a team of horses and large wagons every few weeks.

"You're so far out here, away from civilization," Rosie said, as I translated for Bewba. "What happens if someone gets injured and you need a doctor?"

Bewba shrugged. "You heal up, or you die."

We passed the next few hours with Bewba and the kids, sharing our food with them and smiling at their cries of delight over the simple provisions they found novel, but when the rain finally stopped, Cap stood up.

"Bewba, we thank you for your hospitality and your company," he said while I translated. "It's time for us to go. We're on a tight schedule, and we've lost valuable time already, waiting for the rain to stop. We have to keep driving."

Bewba stood up and crossed over to Cap, shaking his head.

"You need to wait," he told us. "The cliffs here are always the most dangerous after the rain. Give them time to dry out. We've had many mudslides and rocks fall down, when the dunes get soggy like this. Sometimes we get bad floods and quicksand, too. It's not safe."

"We'll keep an eye out for mudslides," Cap assured him, pulling his goggles on. The rest of the crew stood up, saying goodbye and hugging the children.

I smiled at Bewba and offered him my hand. He grabbed my wrist. "Don't go," he said quietly. "Your captain doesn't understand how dangerous it is. People have been crushed. We lost a cow from a falling rock a few years ago."

"We've been through plenty of danger already," I reassured Bewba. "We can handle ourselves, I promise."

Our wheels slipped in the wet sand, struggling to get traction, as Rosie and Chito waved goodbye to the kids from the third car. Paz and I sat together in the second car, while Cap and Bernard navigated in front of us.

"Do you think we should've waited to take off?" Paz asked, watching Cap's wheels spin as the auto tried to get traction on the slushy ground. Grains of sand spat up from his wheels as we rumbled along.

"I don't know," I murmured, trying to keep the car moving forward. I could feel the resistance already. "Maybe Cap just wants to stay in a hotel tonight. He mentioned wanting to get to Kiffa."

We slogged over the wet sand for a few hours, stopping as we got stuck and had to dig our vehicles out. The landscape had turned mountainous, soaring peaks squeezing us into pathways just large enough for our Fords to drive through. Twice, we happened upon large rocks blocking the narrow path between canyons, and had to turn around and find a different route.

"I guess the kid was right," Cap muttered as we examined the second rock slide. "We're not far from Kiffa. It's the biggest city down here. It's sure to have a place to stay and some gasoline. We're almost there, team. Let's keep going."

Paz and I climbed back into our car.

"Imagine our next baths," Paz sighed. "It's been so long."

"I won't count on a bath just yet," I replied. "Now that we're reversing course again to go around this stupid rock slide, we're going to need to find a new route. It's going to delay us even more."

I tapped the steering wheel, waiting for Chito and Rosie to reverse and turn around so I could move my Ford. Slowly, I backed my car up and pulled forward through the imposing stone walls soaring on either side of us.

"I just want to lay in it for hours," Paz continued, still thinking about his bath. "Oh, warm water—"

Suddenly, a thunderous rumble jarred our senses. Horrified, I looked left and right, trying to discern where the sound was coming from.

"It's behind us!" Paz cried, pointing.

I slammed on the brake and turned just in time to see a massive chunk of the cliff give way and crash down onto the road right next to Cap's car. Rocks pummeled down onto the hood, buckling the metal and shattering the windshield.

I stared, helpless, watching the scene as if in slow motion. My heart stopped.

I saw Cap and Bernard's faces, shocked, as the Ford toppled over on its left side.

It lurched over sickeningly, metal crumpling and screeching as rocks continued to pour down. As the dust settled, the broken car wheels spun slowly, catching in the sunlight.

CHAPTER 52

"NO!" I SCREAMED, CLAMBERING over Paz and jumping out of the car without even turning it off.

I sprinted toward the wreckage as Paz screamed and slid to the driver's seat, struggling to stop our car. Behind me, I heard it crunch into Chito's Ford as both occupants cried out.

"Help!" I screamed at the others as I ran. I reached the automobile, its wheels still spinning in the air. I peered in the passenger door.

Bernard was dead.

Blood gushed down his face, and bits of glass were visibly stuck in his forehead. He sat limp, unmoving.

I screamed wordlessly, his face seared into my mind with horror.

I looked past him to Cap.

Cap was pinned on the overturned side of the vehicle. Rosie's suitcase lay on top of him, obscuring his face. I couldn't tell if he was alive or dead. But he certainly wasn't moving.

Paz reached my side and dropped to his knees in shock. "Dear God," he whispered, seeing Bernard's bloody face. He crossed himself.

Rosie pushed past him, toppling him to the sand. "Cap!" she screamed in my ear, clawing at me.

Chito pulled her away. "We need to get them out!" he yelled, tears streaming down his face. "Bernard—damn—Cap—is Cap alive?"

"I can't tell," I cried, climbing through the window across Bernard's lap to pull the suitcase off of Cap's face. Shards of broken glass sliced my hands and arms painfully as I wriggled in.

Suddenly, Bernard's eyes snapped open behind his goggles. I screamed, laying only inches from his face. His eyes were terrifyingly white against his blood-soaked face.

"Andi," he gasped. "The fuel lines!"

I feverishly remembered what Bernard had taught me about the Ford so many months ago, before we left France. The fuel lines were highly volatile to combustion, even in minor accidents. It was the biggest complaint people had against these automobiles. The newspapers were filled with grisly stories of people trapped and burned alive in their cars.

I knew instantly what he meant. Leave it to Bernard to tell us what could go wrong with the car, even as he lay dying.

"We've got to get them out!" I screamed at the others. "Bernard's still alive! But the fuel lines could be damaged. This whole thing might go up in flames!"

I felt rough hands grasp me around the waist and yank me out. My arms again scraped against the broken glass of the windows. I toppled into the sand, Chito still holding me. "Help me!" I screamed, scrambling to my feet.

Rosie had already clambered on top of the overturned car, balancing on the hood, and wrestled open the door. Chito and I pulled Bernard out, a tangle of heavy arms and legs falling all over as we struggled to drag him away from the wreckage.

Paz whimpered. "He's bleeding badly," he said, shaking. "He's not going to make it."

We ignored him, racing back to the vehicle. Cap still hadn't moved.

I feared the worst. The rocks had impacted his side of the car. It was a mangled mess of metal and broken wood, the entire frame of the Ford shattered to pieces.

Cap was a fighter. If he had breath in his body, he'd be struggling to get out right now. Why wasn't he moving?

"He can't be dead," I told myself, my heart in my throat. I felt bile rise.

Without hesitation, I shot through the open door, using my long legs to balance my feet on the edge of the door. Dangling, I shoved the suitcase off Cap's face.

He lay crumpled against the ground, deathly still. Blood covered his face and streamed from his blonde hair, dripping against the twisted doorframe underneath him.

"Cap!" I screamed in his face, hoping he'd wake up.

He didn't.

"Cap!" I heard Chito scream from outside the car. "Is he alive?"

"I don't know," I cried, searching for signs of movement. I couldn't tell. I slapped him, hard. Nothing.

"We need to get him out," Chito yelled. "Can you reach him?"

I tried to pull his arm toward me, but my hand slipped off. I looked down. I was covered in blood, my own wounds from the broken glass and metal now mingling with the blood from Bernard and Cap.

"Hold on," I yelled, using one hand to unclasp the belt around my waist. I hollered directions over my shoulder as I ripped the belt out of its loops, seeing that my hands were shaking.

"I need to loop something around him to pull him out, but I can't quite reach. Hold onto my legs, Chito, and lower me down!"

Fingers dug into my ankles and I abruptly lurched forward, toward Cap. I instinctively braced myself for impact against the metal dash, crunching down hard on my right wrist. I screamed in pain as lightning raced up my arm.

I didn't have time to nurse the injury, though. The car could catch on fire any second.

Using my left hand, I shoved the belt buckle between Cap's shoulders and the seat behind him, then caught the end, painfully, with my right hand. I winced and pulled the belt tight across his chest, under both of Cap's shoulders, and buckled the ends. I looped both of my arms under the belt, seeing blood ooze down from my shredded flesh and spatter onto Cap's face.

"Pull me out!" I screamed.

Chito bellowed from the other side of the car. "I can't, you're too heavy!"

I felt another set of hands grab my ankles, and heard Rosie shriek at Paz. "Get over here and help us!"

The three of them tugged and pulled, and together we managed to drag Cap up from the bottom of the car. Chito reached down with a strong arm and scrabbled for Cap. It took all four of us to drag him out.

We rushed to lay his limp and lifeless body next to Bernard. At least now if the car caught on fire, they wouldn't be in it.

Cap sprawled out on the sand, eyes closed. Rosie and I knelt over him, trying to find a pulse.

"He's breathing!" Chito yelled, his hand on his chest.

"Barely. It's shallow breathing," I cried, my ear to Cap's mouth. I could barely feel any breath. I touched Cap's left temple. Blood welled out of it alarmingly fast, tiny bits of glass still embedded in the wound. He had another deep gash on his thigh, which was pumping blood dangerously into the sand underneath him. It blackened as I watched.

"They need a doctor," Rosie exclaimed, picking glass out of Cap's forehead.

My brain recalled what Bewba had told us a few hours earlier, when we asked him about the presence of doctors in this remote desert. "You heal up, or you die," he had shrugged.

Swiftly, I dug through Cap's pockets, looking for his compass.

"What are you doing?" Chito asked, tears trickling through streaks of blood on his cheeks.

"We're going to get them to a doctor, in the closest town," I yelled, sprinting back to the overturned car. I rummaged around, pulling Cap's bag out. I tore it open and found the map laying on the very top.

"Here," I said, running back to the group and kneeling. My bloody fingerprints covered the map as I traced our route with my index finger. My hands were steady now, I noticed.

"We came from here," I frowned as I studied the map. "Cap said we were almost to Kiffa, which is down here. We're stuck in the canyon right about here—" I squinted and wiped blood out of my eyes.

"We're nearly to Kiffa," Chito finished, pressed into my shoulder.

"Right," I said. "Cap told us it was a big city, big enough for us to get gas and supplies there. They're sure to have a doctor."

"I'm not sure they'll live that long," Rosie cried, her blonde hair hanging in front of her face, matted with blood. "Cap's hardly breathing. He's passed out. And Bernard is cut up real bad, too."

"We have to try," I said. "Either that, or they die right here in front of us."

"Andi, you're hurt, too," Paz spoke up.

I looked at my sliced arms, slivers of glass protruding from the skin. Blood sprinkled the sand every time I moved.

Chito grabbed my hand. I winced in pain.

"Listen to me, Andi," he spoke urgently. "You're right. We need to get them to a doctor, in Kiffa. And you probably need a doctor, too. But the cars—we modified them, remember? They can't really hold more than three people. We're straining them, as it is. If we try to fit all of us in there—even just a fourth person—we'll risk overheating the engines. They'll shut down. We'll be stranded."

"I need to take them," I said, understanding what he was saying. "By myself."

"Right," Chito said. "You need a doctor, too. It's got to be you."

I nodded. I already knew it, I realized. His words just affirmed what I'd already decided.

"Let's get them in your car," I said, standing up and slipping my arms under Cap's side. Chito stood up and braced on the other side. Together, we carried Cap to the car.

"Slide him in next to you, in the middle," Chito said, grunting as Cap's limp body dragged in the sand. "He's in worse shape. He's going to need you to try to keep pressure on some of those cuts. The one on his leg looks like it hit an artery."

Rosie and Paz huffed behind us, carrying Bernard to the passenger's seat. Bernard's eyes were open, and he looked at me as I slid into the driver's seat and started the engine. "Good girl," he croaked, trying to smile.

Even his teeth had blood on them, I saw with horror.

"Hold on," I cried, suddenly remembering a scene from one of my father's adventure novels. I'd read it ages ago, a story about how a handsome knight had fashioned a tourniquet out of a piece of cloth to slow the bleeding and save his life after an encounter with a dragon.

I fished through my uniform pockets and pulled out my large blue handkerchief, the token of affection Arnau had bestowed on me.

Using my teeth, I ripped it in half to make it as long as I could. I quickly cinched it over the wound on Cap's left leg, above the deep gash in his thigh, pulling tight.

"I'm going," I yelled, pressing down on the pedals without hesitation. Sand skidded out behind me as we lurched forward.

I pushed the Ford as fast as it could go, the rock walls streaking by as I sped. Holding the map against Cap's injured leg with my damaged right hand, I glanced down at it as I drove.

Frantically, I tried to use one hand to shift and operate the choke and throttle levers on my steering wheel, keeping my right hand pressed into Cap's wounded thigh. Blood pooled behind the edge of the map as I pressed my hand tight against Cap's leg, willing his blood to stay inside his body.

I could feel the hot, slippery liquid pulsing out and soaking into the seat and the edge of my own pant legs.

If he died right now, I'd feel his life ebb away under my fingers.

I knew I was driving recklessly, but I didn't care.

"Don't let them die, don't let them die," I prayed out loud, repeatedly.

I knew in that moment that I loved Cap, and that I would do anything to save him.

It seemed like I drove for ages, glancing worriedly at Cap and Bernard as I roared down the road. Cap's face was white, and blood still seeped from his temple, his hair and shirt now soaked black with blood. If I looked closely, I could still see his chest rising faintly. He was hanging on.

Bernard's eyes fluttered open a few times. "Thank you," he managed to whisper at one point, before his eyes closed again.

I pushed against Cap's wound and pleaded with God to let them live.

"I'll be happy even if he marries Rosie," I told myself, tears streaming down my face. *"Just let Cap live. Let them both live."*

The sun started to set, washing us in a red glow that painted us deep crimson, with all the blood on our bodies. I fretted, wondering how I'd possibly navigate us in the dark without being able to see the map. Praying, I squinted and saw a faint glimmer of lights shining out across the sand.

"Dear Lord, I hope that's Kiffa," I said aloud, through a broken sob.

Bernard's eyes were open. "Me too," he rasped.

"Bernard! Are you okay?"

"I don't know," he wheezed. "I hope so."

Cap still hadn't said a word. I glanced at him. His face was dangerously pale. I wasn't sure how much blood the human body could lose and still survive. I rushed toward the lights, furiously honking the horn as I sped into town.

"Doctor! Doctor!" I screamed, blaring the horn. "I need a doctor right away!" I switched to French and bellowed. "J'ai besoin d'un médecin!"

I blazed past buildings, honking the horn and screaming at the top of my lungs. People rushed outside to watch me, wide-eyed.

"Je suis médecin!" I heard a male voice cry out, and I slammed on my brakes. Bernard and Cap lurched forward.

"You are a doctor?" I repeated in French, shouting into the darkness. "I have two men here, they were in an accident. They're bleeding badly. They need immediate help!"

"Yes, stop the car!" the voice yelled. A young black man with dark eyes appeared at Bernard's door. "Let me help," he cried, then turned to call out for assistance.

Voices babbled all around me in French as a dozen people in long white robes ripped open the passenger door. Dozens of hands reached for Bernard, pulling him out as he fell into their waiting arms, then reached inside for Cap.

I scrambled over the driver's side as they worked to pull Cap from the vehicle, frantic, and nearly fell flat on my face. Blood spattered the ground and the side of my Ford as two men and a woman pulled me toward a stretcher, but I refused.

"No," I shouted, straining to get back to Cap and Bernard. "Help my friends first! I'm fine!"

I watched as they pulled Cap from the car, his body sagging heavily. They laid him in a waiting stretcher and lifted him, rushing him inside. I followed alongside them, grasping Cap's limp hand as we walked into a large building.

Out of the blue, Cap's eyes opened behind his goggles. He must've been jarred awake as they dropped him in the stretcher.

"Cap!" I screamed, hot tears bubbling up. He looked at me and opened his lips.

"Need," he croaked, his eyes fluttering shut.

"What?" I cried, jogging next to him as they whisked him down the wide hallway.

I overheard the two men carrying him speaking rapidly in French. Unwillingly, I caught them say the words "massive head trauma," "bad bleeding," and "unlikely to survive."

Cap's lips moved as his eyes remained shut. "I need you," he whispered, then relaxed. His body went limp.

"Cap! Doctor, what happened? Did he just die?" I screamed.

One of the men bearing his stretcher reached down and held his fingers to his neck. He replied to me in French. "He's passed out, ma'am. Please, this is urgent. We need to work on him. His life hangs in the balance."

I stopped, letting them push past me and into another room. Confused, I turned around and stared. I was in a large building, carved from stone, but beds and medical equipment filled the rooms. Was this a hospital?

I looked for someone to ask. An older woman sat behind a desk, writing on a chart. "Excuse me," I said helplessly. "Where am I?"

She looked up at me and jumped. "You need a doctor, mademoiselle," she said, staring at my bloody arms and face.

"I know. But what is this place?"

"It's St. Jude's Catholic medical mission. We operate out of this building and serve the whole region."

"Maybe God heard my prayers after all," I thought feverishly. *"I drove here blindly, and stopped right in front of a hospital. What are the chances?"*

I swayed on my feet. The lady looked alarmed. "Let me call someone for you," she said, grabbing me by the shoulders and lowering me into her chair.

I nodded, and passed out cold.

CHAPTER 53

WHEN I FINALLY WOKE up, I was confused by the sound of French conversations happening around me. *"Am I at boarding school?"* I thought, searching my brain. I stared at the bandages on my arms.

Where was I?

A nurse saw me stir and approached my bedside. "Hello, dear," she said to me, her soft voice speaking French. "How are you feeling?"

I blinked, noticing that my right wrist was in a plaster cast. "What happened?"

"You had many cuts, dear," the nurse said, smoothing the hair off my forehead. "In some spots, you had shards of glass embedded in and under your skin. You earned yourself quite a lot of stitches. Your right wrist is fractured, and needs to heal."

"My friends," I blurted, the horrific accident coming back to me. "How are my friends?"

The nurse smoothed my pillow. "I'll have the doctor tell you that," she said, going to call him.

Cold fear gripped my heart like an iron vice. Why wouldn't she just tell me?

They must be dead.

I closed my eyes, tears seeping out at the corners. *"This was all for nothing,"* I thought, remembering the moment I first saw Cap standing on stage in France, sharing his daring adventures with the crowd.

How could such an energetic man be blotted from existence? How could the Gallivanter Expedition end in such terrible tragedy?

"Miss Gallivanter?" I heard a man's gentle voice. "I'm Dr. Mathieu."

I opened my eyes, tears oozing slowly down my face. "How do you know my name?"

"The whole world knows your name, miss. I recognized you immediately. You're famous. The newspapers wrote about your drowning accident."

"Oh, right. So the two men I came in with—"

"They're recovering."

"They are?" I cried, hope rising.

"Yes," he smiled. "Mr. Gallivanter lost a lot of blood. Head wounds are nasty bleeders. He had a deep laceration on his thigh, too. Almost nicked the artery. It was touch and go for a while. We had to do a transfusion on him. Luckily, we keep extra blood on hand here because of all the mining accidents."

"Cap's going to be fine?" I asked in disbelief. He'd been so pale and lifeless. I feared the worst.

"He has a severe concussion and might deal with some brain damage, at least temporarily. He had several lacerations that required stitches—many stitches—and some bruising in the ribs. He must've hit against something hard."

"Probably the steering wheel," I said, remembering the way the car lurched over.

"Yes, that would do it," the doctor said. "I figured it was an automobile accident, seeing as they were both covered in glass shards. Those things are death traps."

"How's Bernard doing?" I asked.

"He's comfortable," the doctor responded. "He also had some bruising and deep cuts. Stitches. He already asked the nurses to just leave him alone and let him rest."

I laughed, deeply relieved.

"You've been asleep for a long time," the doctor said, looking at his pocket watch. "Nearly ten hours. You must've been exhausted. But that's good, you need your rest. It'll take you all a few weeks to recover."

"Weeks?"

"Yes, *weeks*. Mr. Gallivanter especially needs strict medical supervision. He's not out of the woods yet. A severe concussion can cause all sorts of complications. And your wrist needs to heal up properly. We're a big facility, though, and we have plenty of rooms. In fact, your other teammates are sleeping in rooms on the other side of the building. They made it here shortly after you did, and we cleaned them up, too."

"Oh good," I said, feeling relieved. "We can all stay here together?"

"As long as you need to," he grinned. "You're a famous expedition. How could we kick you out in your time of need?"

I returned his smile.

"There's something else I wanted to tell you," Dr. Mathieu said, leaning close. "I asked the nurse to let me talk to you when you woke up, because I wanted to tell you in person."

"What?"

"I've been following your stories here and there, Miss Gallivanter. Ever since that story about you drowning. I want you to know how much I admire you."

"Me?"

"Yes. We're kindred spirits, I think. You see, I grew up in Montreal. I always wanted to be a doctor. People told me I'd never be able to study medicine, because I'm colored, the grandson of escaped slaves. That I'd never be able to get a job. But here I am, doing important work." He smiled down at me. "It's the people like us, breaking barriers, that are making this world better, one day at a time."

"You're from Montreal? My father was from there," I grinned. "No wonder it's so easy to speak French with you. You're French Canadian."

He laughed. "Who'd have ever thought that two Canadians would reunite in Africa, of all places?"

"How did you end up here?" I asked curiously, looking at him. He was professional, clearly knowledgable about medicine. It was hard to believe that anyone would have a problem with him being a doctor just because his skin color was darker than mine.

"Well, after medical school, I tried and tried to get a job. No one was willing to bring me on," he replied, holding his clipboard against his chest. "I was the best in my class, but no one bothered to look beyond my face."

"That's awful," I said. I knew something about unfair stereotypes myself.

"They'd interview me, but then make some excuse about 'not having the space right now' or 'needing to consider all the factors' but I never heard back," he continued. "A friend of mine worked as a secretary for a church, and told me they'd received telegrams requesting nurses and doctors here in Mauritania, at the Catholic mission. I jumped at the chance. Here, they don't see my skin color as a detriment—I blend right in. In fact, sometimes it's been an asset with the people here. I've never looked back."

A nurse stepped in and called for him. He stood up.

"Thank you, doctor," I said, grateful. "Thank you for everything. And for the encouraging words."

"You have a good head on your shoulders, miss," Dr. Mathieu replied. "You saved Mr. Gallivanter's life, there's no doubt about it."

"I did?"

"He would've bled out faster if you hadn't tied that tourniquet on. And he certainly would have bled to death if you would've waited any longer to get him here to the hospital. In his condition, every minute mattered. Now, try to get some rest."

He turned to go, then paused in the doorway. "Wasn't it Mr. Gallivanter who blew air into your lungs after you drowned?"

"Yes, why?"

"It just occurred to me how ironic that is," he smiled. "He saved your life when you drowned, and you just saved his. You've saved *each other's* lives. That doesn't happen every day. You certainly share something very special, indeed."

CHAPTER 54

CHITO WAS THE FIRST to come see me, tiptoeing to the door of my hospital room while I laid in bed.

"Andi!" he exclaimed, coming in to give me a hug. "You're awake!"

"You are too," I smiled. "Apparently we all slept long. Must be the comfortable hospital beds after all that sleeping on the ground."

I filled him in on what the doctor had told me about Bernard and Cap. Tears welled in his eyes as I recounted how Dr. Mathieu had explained how close a call they'd had.

"I thought they were goners," he admitted. "Especially Cap."

"They're going to be fine."

"Who knew we'd encounter so much danger, traveling the world in those spindly little Fords?" Chito smiled ruefully, tugging at his beard. "And here I thought it'd be a nice vacation."

Rosie and Paz soon joined us.

"They won't let us in to see Cap yet," Paz said. "They said he's still too fragile."

"What happened, after I left?" I asked.

"We managed to hoist the other Ford upright," Chito said. "We used ropes to create a pulley system, using the rocks. The driver's side was crushed. The force of the rocks hurling down must've knocked it off balance and tipped it over with Cap and Bernard still inside."

"Will it ever run again?"

"That's a question for Bernard, when he's feeling up to it," Chito replied. "We'll need a new windshield, new headlights, and we'll have to repair the doors and frame. But I think it'll still run. It's sitting out there, waiting for us."

"How'd you get here so fast?" I asked. "The doctors said you arrived shortly after I did."

"Oh, that was me," Rosie tossed her hair over her shoulder. "We piled into Chito's Ford and drove here. I navigated."

"Have you been here before?"

"No," she replied. "We drove around until we found a house. They gave us directions to Kiffa. When we got into town, I hung out the window as we drove through and asked people if they'd seen three bloody white people looking for a doctor. They led us here right away."

"Wow," I said, impressed with Rosie's cool head in the midst of chaos.

"I know," she responded, flashing me her dimples. "People will stop what they're doing and help me with anything."

Paz had been uncharacteristically quiet, but he finally spoke up. "How long do they expect recovery to take?"

"For me, a few weeks," I said, holding up my cast. "Bernard needs the same. Cap...he could take longer." I thought back to what the doctor said about Cap possibly having brain damage. None of us could see him yet, so we had no way to judge for ourselves how he was actually faring.

"So we're here for a few weeks, at the very least," Chito shrugged. "Let's consider it a well-earned break to rest up. The expedition rules allow for this very thing, so we're fine. And besides, in the span of the last few weeks, Andi almost drowned, we got stranded in a sandstorm, and Cap and Bernard were crushed by rocks. I think I'll be perfectly content to relax here for a while."

It took three more days for any of us to be allowed to see Cap. We begged for updates, but all we heard was that he was still in critical condition, too fragile for visitors.

To stave off worry, I passed the time by writing letters to Arnau, Clara, and my family. I churned out a letter every day for each of them, sending them off with the orderlies to mail from the hospital.

On the fourth morning, a nurse came into my room and told me that Mr. Gallivanter was awake and that the first thing he had done was ask about me.

"He's such a sweet man," the nurse sighed, batting her eyes. "Is it true that he really saved your life? I read the article."

"He did. How's he doing?"

"He's recovering slowly. As you know, he had a severe concussion and a staggering amount of blood loss. It can take days, even weeks, for a patient to normalize after such trauma."

"Can I see him?" I begged. "Please? I'm desperate."

"I don't see why not," she said thoughtfully. "He did ask about you. But this is our little secret. He's in the critical care unit, they're not supposed to have visitors in there. Especially not other patients."

She disappeared and returned with a wheelchair.

"Hop in," she whispered. "This way, no one will question your presence in Mr. Gallivanter's wing."

She wheeled me through the hospital. Entering a narrow hallway, she whisked me past several desks and into a quiet wing. As we rolled by, I noticed patients in the rooms here looked near death. Some had bandages over their entire heads, their whole bodies in casts. One room had a white sheet pulled up over a body.

"Lots of mining accidents here," the nurse said, answering my unasked question. "It's a dangerous occupation."

She checked the room numbers, then pushed me through the doorway and into Cap's room.

I nearly cried out when I saw Cap. He looked like a stranger.

He lay in a hospital bed, his shirt off. His chest bloomed black and purple with ugly bruises, cuts ribboning all over his neck and shoulders, face and arms. Several spots were covered in bandages, where he'd received stitches. The entire left side of his face was swollen and bruised, a thick white bandage wrapped around his head. A blanket covered his lap, but his leg stuck out, bare, a large wrap around his thigh.

I looked at his leg, feeling strange. I'd never seen Cap wearing so little clothing, but it wasn't that fact that made me feel awkward.

It was the memory of his hot blood bubbling out through my frantic fingers.

I relived it, staring at him. I felt the sensation of the slippery blood in my hands, me pressing down to stem the bleeding. The knowledge that this was the wound that nearly killed him. The feeling of his life pulsing away, under my touch. The realization that my hands, pushing into the wound, helped keep him alive.

What if I hadn't had that bandanna to tie the tourniquet onto his body?

What if it had taken five minutes longer to pull him from the wreckage?

My breath caught in my throat. I closed my eyes. The strength of my love for him overwhelmed me. I'd come so close to losing him forever. This expedition had nearly killed both of us. But the world couldn't lose a man like Cap. He was too rare.

"This is foolishness," I thought, hot tears prickling. *"This expedition. All of this. We've barely gotten started and Cap almost died. We can't keep going on like this. We can't continue. It's not worth it. What's it worth winning anything, in the end, if Cap loses his life?"*

The moment between us, as I felt his blood pouring out, had been strangely intimate. Something no one else could ever share. But we did. Is that how he'd felt after he rescued me from the water?

My feelings for him threatened to undo me. I suddenly felt dizzy, overcome with emotion.

"Andi?"

I opened my eyes. Cap's eyes were fluttering.

"Cap," I cried, bolting out of my wheelchair and coming to his side.

"Why are you in a wheelchair?" he whispered, his voice thin.

"I'm fine. The nurse had to sneak me in," I replied. "How are you feeling?"

He closed his eyes. I looked for a chair to pull over to his bedside. I noticed one behind me, and saw his uniform, bloody and torn, folded neatly inside a plastic bag on the seat. I pushed it off and pulled the chair over.

"Cap?" I said quietly, searching for his hand. I bit my lip as I realized his hands were bandaged. Instead, I rested my uninjured hand on his arm, my fingers barely touching his flesh.

I couldn't tell if he was asleep or if he'd fainted. Either way, his chest lifted and fell. I leaned back and watched him. His freckles stood out starkly against his pale skin. It must be the loss of blood, I thought.

I sat quietly, thinking about the journey that had led us to this point. Did I want to continue on? I didn't know. Was this a fool's errand? Some grand idea that sounded good on paper, but in reality was pointless and dangerous?

I watched Cap's even breathing, remembering how I couldn't see him breathing at all as he lay in the sand outside the wreckage of his car.

"No," I thought, looking at him. *"No journey, no amount of money or fame or notoriety, is worth this. It's not worth losing someone like Cap. Or Bernard or Chito or Paz, or even Rosie."*

Cap groaned and slowly opened his eyes. "You're still here," he whispered.

"Yes."

"Are you hurt badly?" Cap murmured, his head wobbling on the pillow as he strained to look at me.

"I have a fractured wrist and a few cuts, but I'll be fine," I said, holding up my cast so he could see. "You're the one I'm worried about."

He closed his eyes, wincing in pain, but opened them again to look at me. "The doctor saw you?" he asked. "The young one?"

I laughed. "Yes. He's from Canada, can you believe that?"

"He told me you saved my life."

I downplayed it. "Yeah, you're worth keeping around, I figured."

Cap's hand twitched. "Please," he said, pushing his bandaged hand toward me. Bewildered, I put my hand in his. His fingers, cocooned in fabric, closed around my hand.

"The timing is just never right for us," he rasped. "I don't know—"

A knock sounded at the door. It was the nurse. "Miss Gallivanter, time to go," she said sharply. "The doctors are starting their rounds any minute, and you don't want them to catch you here."

"Wait," Cap begged, his fingers still clenched around my hand. I was alarmed at how feeble his grip was. "I need to say something."

The nurse stepped out discreetly, but stood in the hallway. Cap noticed.

"I need to tell you, Andi," he said slowly, his voice weak. "Hiring you on was the best decision I've ever made. Ever."

"Thanks," I said, as the nurse tapped her watch in the hallway and motioned for me to get back in the wheelchair. I climbed in, and she immediately whipped into the room and wheeled me out.

The words we hadn't spoken hung heavy in the air.

If the nurse wouldn't have interrupted us, I would've told him what I needed to say, too. I was going to tell him that I couldn't do this anymore.

That I needed to leave the Gallivanter Expedition.

For his sake. To protect his life.

CHAPTER 55

AFTER A WEEK, THE NEWSPAPER reporters finally found us hiding out in the hospital.

We weren't sure how our story spread, but our dramatic entrance into town likely contributed. Reporters and cameramen showed up in droves, each wanting pictures and interviews and firsthand accounts of the journey and accident.

Remembering the money that poured in after my story broke, the team decided to hold a few press conferences. With Cap still recovering, we agreed not to tell him.

The reporters arranged me in all sorts of ridiculous poses that highlighted the cast on my wrist. *"The brave and beautiful Miss Andiamo Gallivanter survives yet another incredible adventure!"* was a popular tagline that appeared under many of the photos. They hinted that our story had attracted worldwide attention—that even directors in Hollywood were interested in making a moving picture about us.

The money cascaded in, and we carefully set it aside. We'd need it for hospital bills now.

When Rosie's father finally blustered into the lobby where we sat playing cards, he started yelling as soon as he saw us.

"Where's that yellow-bellied, putrid skunk of a man, Captain Gallivanter?" he hollered, looking around. "I have some words to say to him! We need to have a gentlemen's conversation, yes sir! How dare he think he can take my money and take my daughter and repay me like this? Why, my beautiful little princess was in danger with this raving lunatic all this time? How dare he!"

"Mr. Barrington, calm down," Chito exclaimed as Rosie went running to her father and embraced him. "What on earth are you talking about?"

"I've seen the papers, my boy, read 'em all!" He yelled, his face red with anger. "What kind of operation is this? Cap accepts my donation and agrees to show my baby girl a little adventure and then he almost kills her? It was just supposed to be a lark, not a life or death situation!"

"Hold on," Chito held up his hand. "We don't know anything about this. You made an agreement with Cap?"

"I sure did," the diplomat fumed. "I heard you were hard up for money. I funded the entire next leg of your journey, in exchange for Cap taking my Rosie along with you through Mauritania. She was supposed to have some fun, meet some new friends, maybe fall in love with—well, who cares," he stopped himself. "It's over. She's coming home with me. A little fun isn't worth losing her life."

Everything fell into place, the last puzzle piece landing neatly.

That's why Cap had allowed Rosie to come along as our guide, even though she had no helpful skills. That's why he'd given her so much attention, allowed her foibles like sleeping in the Fords and bringing multiple suitcases. He was being *paid* to bring her.

I shook my head, relief mingled with irritation. I was glad that Cap hadn't brought her along just because she was gorgeous, but I was frustrated that he hadn't told us the truth.

"Where's Captain Gallivanter hiding?" Mr. Barrington cried. "Tell him to get out here and face me. Or is he too much of a coward to do that?"

"He's in critical care," I said, rising to my feet. "He almost died. You can't see him, because *we* can't even see him right now."

"Oh," the diplomat said, looking at Rosie.

"And let me tell you something, sir," I said, trying hard to keep the edge out of my voice. "Cap held up his end of the bargain just fine. Rosie here had a great time, up until this accident. And it was an *accident*—it wasn't anyone's fault."

Mr. Barrington glared at me and tried to interrupt. I raised my voice.

"Calm down and thank your lucky stars that your daughter can walk out of here, with her head held high, knowing that she helped save two men's lives on this 'lark.' Maybe she's more capable than you realize," I retorted. "Maybe there's more to her than just having fun and meeting a nice man to marry."

"How dare you speak to me like that?" The diplomat's mouth fell open. "I sure hope that French fiancé of yours knows how you speak to men. He'll tame your tongue."

"Any man who cares to marry me will be able to withstand my words, sir." My voice was hard. "Otherwise, he's not really much of a man, is he?"

Paz whistled irreverently. I smiled.

"Rosie, say goodbye and get your suitcases," her father said, his face flushed. "We're going home. I'll be waiting outside."

Rosie danced around, hugging each of us.

"It's been so much fun, hasn't it?" she cooed, holding my face between her hands and squeezing. "What adventures we've shared! Will you write to me and tell me all about it? I'd just die to do what you're doing."

I felt guilty, thinking of the decision I'd made to step away from the expedition. Maybe she'd grow to be a suitable replacement. Cap clearly liked her, even if her father had bribed him to allow her on the team. Should I tell her?

Rosie interrupted my thoughts by embracing me. "You're so strong, Andi," she breathed, showing me her dimples. "I want to be just like you."

I made my way to my room after Rosie left, anxious to be alone. I was conflicted about how I should tell the others that I was leaving. I didn't even really know why I was leaving, or where I'd be going next.

Was this the right decision, to abandon the team?

Would Cap come to his senses and give up on the expedition, if I left?

Sitting down on my bed, I looked at the letter I'd started earlier. I'd kept up the habit of writing to Arnau every day for weeks now. I couldn't help but pour my heart out, especially in these last few days as Cap slowly recovered. It was like all the things I wanted to say to Cap instead poured out into the words I wrote to Arnau.

Maybe it was that simple. I'd go see Arnau after I left the Gallivanter Expedition.

"Perhaps that's the whole point of this," I thought. *"Maybe I had to go halfway around the world to be content enough to end up back where I first started, in France. With Arnau."*

With this new revelation, I smiled. I laid down, picked up my pen, and started writing.

"Arnau, I've made up my mind. I'm coming home to you."

CHAPTER 56

WE FIGURED THE PRESS would slow after a few days and we'd be left alone, but journalists continued to throng to the hospital to speak with us.

"Where are you headed next?" they asked, sniffing for future stories.

"You'll have to wait to find out," I waved them off, but inwardly cringed at my lie.

I hadn't told anyone that I was leaving. And frankly, I wasn't sure if Cap would recover enough to restart the expedition. Maybe he'd never be able to drive the Fords again. Maybe we were all headed nowhere next.

To our surprise, donations continued to flood in. They were usually addressed to the Gallivanter Expedition, but some people wrote to me personally and included money. I tucked a few bills away for my fare back to France, feeling guilty, but added the rest to the growing pile marked for the expedition.

Bernard and I recovered faster than Cap. Eventually, the nurses allowed us to peek in on him, but he was usually sleeping soundly when we looked in. I noticed that his skin was starting to return to a healthy pink color, his freckles less obvious.

After two long weeks, Cap was finally moved to another room, out of the critical care unit. The doctor cautioned us not to stress him, but allowed the four of us to crowd into his tiny hospital room.

"Look at that, the gang is back together again," Chito joked as Cap looked at us, smiling. "First time we've been in the same room at the same time in half a month."

"How do you feel?" I asked Cap, studying his body. His shirt was on, but I could still see the outline of bandages under the fabric. His leg was still prone and wrapped, but the bandage over his temple was smaller. Stitches peeked out from under the cloth.

"I want to say fine, but that'd be a lie," he sighed. "I'm having bad headaches. I get dizzy. I'm tired. Always tired."

"The doctor said it could take a while to recover," I said, remembering how he also cautioned me that Cap might have permanent brain damage. I had kept that to myself.

"Where's Rosie?" Cap asked us. We told him how the ambassador had stormed in and taken Rosie home.

"He also mentioned that he paid you to bring her with us, Cap," Chito said, his tone reproving. "Why didn't you tell us?"

"I don't know," Cap groaned. "It was such a mess. I'd written to the ambassador before Andi made us famous, before we had any money. I asked if there was anything we could do to earn some funds. I was prepared to do lectures, or even do manual labor. I didn't expect him to send his daughter with us. But I was backed into a corner. I'd already made the offer. I had to take Rosie with."

"Well, we're not going to need to worry about money anymore," I told Cap. "Possibly never again. Donations have been flooding in every day. We could tour the world in hot air balloons now, if we wanted to."

"Maybe we'll make it to the moon after all," Cap said, looking at me.

"Huh?" Paz frowned.

Cap's ears turned pink. "Never mind," he said quickly.

We lingered in Cap's room, happy to be together again as our team of five. But the longer we chatted, the heavier my feeling of guilt became. I couldn't bear the thought of leaving my friends here. But now that Cap was improving, it was time for me to plan my return trip to France.

"I'll meet you at dinner," I excused myself from the group, walking back to my room.

Entering my quiet room, I sat down on my bed. I noticed a stack of letters sitting on the bedside. An orderly must've dropped off the mail while I was out. I flipped through the stack, looking where letters were coming from. Idaho. Luxembourg. Miami. Rome.

I'd been getting stacks of fan mail now that we'd been in one place for so long, many of them notes from children who scrawled in wobbly letters that they loved following my journey around the world. One small girl had sent me a charming photograph of her dressed up in riding boots and her father's driving goggles and jacket. "I want to be just like you when I grow up," she'd written on the back.

I stopped flipping through the pile of letters as I recognized familiar handwriting. The return address listed Lyon, France.

Arnau.

I ripped the letter open and started reading. He had written to me in English, not his native French. His handwriting was bold and steady, just like him.

Oh, Arnau. So reliable and sincere. I smiled.

"My Andiamo,

I pray this letter finally reaches you. I've tried for months now to get in touch, but you've moved so quickly through cities that it's been impossible to catch you. I've written dozens and dozens of letters, but all have been returned to me. The papers here have carried articles about you, and today I finally found one that listed your hospital and address. I'm scribbling this out quickly, in the hopes that I can get it in the mail today. Forgive how short and direct it will be. I'm just trying to catch you, before you leave again.

You've written me so many letters that I could probably compile a book at this point. And I'll skip right to answering the questions you always ask: yes, I'm healthy. Nothing has happened and nothing is wrong. My family is all fine. The horses are doing well, and the school is just the same as it's always been.

Edith, you know me better than most anyone on earth. I know I can open up to you, but you know I don't always easily say what I'm thinking. I'm not direct like you. But I need to be direct right now, and I know it'll be painful for you. For that, I apologize deeply.

I wish I didn't have to tell you this way. But I do need to tell you.

I'm engaged. By the time you read this, I'll be married.

Sabine is a wonderful girl, and I know you'll love her. Her family lives down the road from mine, and we've been friends for a long time. After you left, we started talking more. In time, we fell in love. While you were out living your adventures, I embarked on an adventure of my own: I proposed to Sabine, and she accepted. Our families are thrilled. And we are, too. We can't wait to be married, even though we're young. We're moving into her family's home together, after the wedding.

Edi, I pray you never show this to anyone else because I'm going to be completely honest with you. You've poured out your heart to me for many months. I feel like I've become a sort of diary for you, a beacon as you struggled. So I'm going to pour out my heart to you, for once.

I realize that I'm to blame for this. I fear that I led you on when I proposed, that last day before you left for your new school. You had to know it would never work out between us. You'd never be happy with someone like me. You'd never be happy coming back to the same house, night after night, doing the same thing day after day.

I adore you, Edi. You know that.

But I proposed to you, knowing you'd say no, to show you what you really want. You'll never be happy where you are in the moment. You'll only be happy where you could be in the next.

Please know that after all this time, no matter how far you go, you'll still be my knight in shining armor. You're doing things I could never do. I admire that. I will always carry a special place for you in my heart.

You're no longer my Andiamo, but you will be someone else's Andiamo. I pray that you find that lucky man, and that he loves you for just who you are—as I do.

In admiration, Arnau."

I sat very still, the letter feeling like a heavy weight in my hand.

Arnau was married?

But—but—it was supposed to be me. Wasn't it?

CHAPTER 57

I HELD THE LETTER IN my hands, unmoving.

Slowly, hot tears trickled down my face. *"Stop crying,"* I told myself, the tears falling faster now. *"You're not someone who cries. You're someone who kicks the door open when it shuts in her face."*

But I couldn't control myself. I was humiliated.

All those years, riding almost every day with Arnau. Countless hours spent together in the stable. Letter after letter I'd sent him, where I'd bared my heart and soul. All for him to go and find someone else. I'd made myself an utter fool.

I dropped the letter to the ground.

I'd thrown away a relationship with Cap and had no chance at a relationship with Arnau. And now I was leaving the team. I had nothing. Nobody.

Just then, I heard a knock on my door. Paz peeked around the corner.

"Andi? What's wrong?"

I held my hand over my face, embarrassed to be discovered like this. All the feelings I'd kept bottled up for so long, about loving Cap and leaving the team, threatened to unravel me. But I couldn't confess this to anyone. Not even Paz.

Unwillingly, my eyes landed on the letter on the ground. Without warning, I broke down.

Paz swiftly crossed the room put his arm around my shoulder. "What's going on?"

"Arnau," I cried, hiding my face in my hands. I couldn't tell him the whole story. Better to let him believe my heart was broken over Arnau, rather than find out that it was breaking over the thought of leaving all of them and heading into the next chapter of my life alone.

"Your fiancé? I'm so sorry," Paz hugged me. "Did he die? Oh, Andi."

I cried even harder. "No!"

"But—is he hurt? Sick?"

"No," I choked out. "He's married!"

"Oh, that cad," Paz sniffed, holding me close. "He's been married this whole time, and stringing you along with promises of matrimony? What a jerk. You don't need that kind of man in your life."

"No," I protested, my face red with embarrassment, the tears raining down my cheeks. "No, he *just* got married. To a neighbor girl. They got engaged while we were away, and he hasn't been able to write to me until now to tell me. I just found out."

"Ah. And you've been writing to him all this time, thinking you'd end up together, not even knowing that he met someone else?"

"Exactly. I feel so dumb," I confessed, wiping my face. "What a waste."

"You're not dumb," Paz rubbed my back. "You're just not meant for him. You weren't meant to be together."

My tears slowed as my sadness was replaced by a new emotion. I felt doubt. I had planned to leave the Gallivanters, but now that I couldn't go to Arnau, where would I go?

I had turned him into my safety net, the predictable life that was supposed to be waiting for me when this whirlwind adventure was all over. Now, he was gone. What would I do?

I blew my nose, and Paz patted me on the head like a kitten. "I didn't even know you could cry."

"Very funny," I sniffed, dabbing at my eyes. "I just feel...stupid. I thought he was the one for me. But he's not. What if I never find someone to love, Paz? What if I never end up happy?"

"Oh, Andi. We just established that you're not dumb," Paz smiled ruefully. "You can't possibly be this dense."

"Dense?"

"Quit the act. Who did you risk your own life to save a few weeks ago, with no thought to your own safety? Who did you crawl through glass and break your wrist for? And don't you dare say Bernard. Nobody would go out of their way to save that crabby old sourpuss."

"I care about Bernard," I responded, deflecting. I knew where he was headed.

"Not like that you don't," he replied, giving me a hard look.

"I'm done with love!" I shook my head bitterly. "I'm done with everything. All anyone ever does is let you down and disappoint you and leave you feeling lonely. How can I tell Cap and Chito and Bernard about Arnau getting married? I'm an idiot. They'll laugh at me. I can't possibly show my face again, after they know. I've been a complete fool."

"You can't show *your* face? How do you think I feel?" Paz grimaced. "I can't bear to be around the group anymore. I froze up during that accident, Andi. I was worthless. I didn't even help pull them out of the Ford."

"Everything was happening so fast," I said, alarmed by the tone in Paz's voice. "You did what you could. They're fine now."

"No thanks to me," Paz said, his expression grim. "I've been wanting to tell you, Andi. I've been thinking about it for a long time. You said you're done with everything? Well, I am, too."

His voice cracked as he uttered, "I'm leaving the team."

"What?" I gasped. "Why?"

"I have my reasons," Paz said darkly. "You know we've talked about it."

"But—you're actually going to go through with it?"

"Yes."

"I thought we were just venting! Everyone gets stressed out. I mean, we spend every hour of the day together, day after day. We're bound to get on each other's nerves sometimes."

"True. But I've made up my mind. I've already wired a telegram to the Chinooks. I'm going to join up with them for their next leg, on a trial basis. They're happy to have me." He laughed bitterly. "Imagine that—a team actually *wanting* me."

"We want you, Paz! You're part of our crew!" Even as I said it, I felt the shame of guilt. How dare I judge Paz for doing the same thing I was going to do?

"Maybe you do. But the others? Cap? Bernard? They don't care," Paz shrugged. "It's better this way. And besides, the deed is already done. The Chinook Voyageurs are expecting me to meet them. They've made plans to get me from Kiffa to Europe. They already have the spare car and crew headed toward the coast, to come get me. Just think of that—they have a spare car! They have enough automobiles and extra crew to spare one for a few weeks, as they pick me up. Can you imagine that? We're down to only two cars now."

"You can't leave."

"Why do you think I've been so quiet these last few weeks? I don't want to be here anymore. No one wants me here, either."

"Don't say that."

"It's true."

"Paz, you won't actually do it."

He pursed his lips. "Wait and see, then."

"No. You won't. I know you. Who cares if you've made plans? Send another telegram. Tell them you changed your mind, that you want to stay."

Paz shook his head. "Stop, Andi. It's a done deal. I already signed the contract."

"Are you going to tell Cap?" I said, starting to feel angry. I didn't know if it was at Paz, or at my own hypocrisy. I was berating Paz while secretly planning to leave, too. "He deserves to know."

"He won't care."

"Yes, he will. How can you think that?"

Paz stood up abruptly, and swiftly kicked my bedside chair across the room. It clattered against the wall.

"I'll tell Cap, then," he growled. "I don't want to, though. And I *am* leaving."

Without another word, he stormed out of the room, slapping the wall as he walked out.

Would he actually go through with it? Maybe it was for the best that it was playing out this way, with both of us leaving. Surely Cap would halt this madness now. He couldn't possibly keep going with just a tiny crew of three. But still, it stung. We did care about Paz.

After all, that was why I was leaving, wasn't it? *Because* I cared.

But where would I go now? I couldn't go back to Arnau. And I'd never go back to boarding school. Should I go home? Back to my mother's house?

The thought of sleeping in my childhood bed, seeing my old classmates and neighbors, and sitting at the kitchen table again filled me with panic.

No, I decided. I'd outgrown my childhood home. I wasn't sure where I could go, but I resolved to tell Cap right away.

He needed to hear it from me, before I told anyone else. I wasn't going to be a coward and slink away, like Paz. I'd face it like a man.

Whatever his faults, Cap had been an excellent leader for our crew. No one could've done it better than him. He was armed to the teeth with plans and research for every single step. It wasn't his fault that things had gone off the rails like this. He had warned us from the beginning that Africa would be hard to travel through.

He deserved the simple respect of being told first, before the rest of the team.

CHAPTER 58

I WAITED A FEW HOURS, hoping Paz had gone in to talk to him, before I made my way quietly to Cap's hospital room to break the news of my departure.

I knocked lightly, in case he was sleeping. The room was dark.

"Come in," Cap called, his voice angry.

I stood in the doorway, uncertain. His foul mood was already evident. He lay on his back, blinking at the ceiling, fists clenched.

"I'll come back another time," I said, backing away.

"No. Sit down."

I sat gingerly on the chair next to his bed. "Did Paz talk to you?"

"He just left," Cap gritted his teeth.

"What did he tell you?"

"He told me the whole sorry story. How he can't bear to be around us anymore, now that he knows he let us down. How he's leaving the Gallivanters and joining the Chinooks. They're sending a car for him already."

He paused, and took a breath. "To hell with his pride!" he shouted, startling me. "Doesn't he know he belongs with us? We don't care about him letting us down, or whatever it is that he thinks."

"Oh."

"You already knew about this, didn't you?" Cap accused, turning his eyes to mine.

"Yes. He told me earlier."

"How nice," Cap said through a clenched jaw. "You conspired against me together. Listen, Andi, just because I'm still stuck in this damn hospital bed, you all think you can't tell me anything? This is *my* expedition. In *my* name. I'm still in charge here. I have a right to know what's going on. Stop keeping things from me."

"Tell him now," I thought desperately. *"Let him deal with the disappointment of losing two crew members all at once. It'll be better this way, in the long run. You know he can't continue this expedition. It's too dangerous for him."*

"Cap, I need to talk to you about something," I sighed.

"What now?"

"Paz isn't the only one leaving," I admitted. "I'm leaving, too."

"No," he interrupted, as I was still finishing my sentence.

"Yes, I am." Internally, I screamed at him, *"You don't understand, Cap! I'm doing this for you! To save your life! To stop you from getting yourself killed! I love you, how can you not see it?"*

"No," he repeated again, shaking his head. "You're a Gallivanter. You can't leave."

"I'm going to. I don't want to be here anymore. I don't want to be a Gallivanter."

Cap swore loudly. A nurse stepped in from the hall and chided us sharply. "This is a medical mission, you two. Language of that kind is not tolerated here."

"I'm sorry," Cap said, slamming his head back against his pillow as she walked out, then wincing.

"Don't do that," I cried. "You just had brain damage."

"I did?"

Hadn't the doctors told him? Maybe he just didn't remember. I knew memory loss was a common side effect of severe concussions.

"Yes, you did," I said, trying to distract him. "You must not remember much. You slept a lot the first few weeks. Your body was very weak."

"You're not leaving," Cap said, rubbing his neck in the familiar gesture I realized I hadn't seen in a long time. My heart lurched, unexpectedly. "I need to tell you something, too."

"What?"

"Look, I'm sorry about everything," he said, looking at me. "Bringing Rosie on and not telling you why, making everyone put up with her—"

"It's fine," I interrupted. "I get it. She's lovely. And that's all that really matters."

"What? That's ridiculous," Cap sputtered, glaring at me. "Why would you even say that?"

I rolled my eyes. "You can drop the charade now. Rosie is stunning. She's the ideal woman."

"Not to me, she isn't."

"Sure," I said, standing up and striding to the window, frustrated. I stared out at the cliffs outside, soaring high above the road. Those rocks had almost killed half our team.

Cap sighed behind me. "Andi, can you look at me?"

"No," I said, staring out the window.

"This isn't how I want to have this conversation," he said, then paused. Suddenly more calm, he said quietly, "You *have* to know what I'm trying to say here."

"What?" I whirled around, angry. My brain shouted, *"That's right, let him think you're mad. Let him think you're giving up. Anything but to let him know the truth."*

"Say it," I taunted. "You've never held back from me before. Oh, wait. You have. Too many times to count. I'm sick of it."

"Andi, my heart never belonged to Rosie. You know who it belongs to."

My heart swelled, but I pushed my feelings down.

"Right," I said, raising my voice. "And I'm supposed to believe you? If it's true, why didn't you tell me anything until now, when I just told you I'm going to leave the crew? You're just trying to keep me here. You're desperate. You don't want to lose your precious moneymaker. 'Andiamo Gallivanter, the girl who almost drowned.' It's a good headline, don't you think?"

"That's not it at all," Cap said, flushing. "You're so damn stubborn. You're not hearing me."

"Yeah, and you aren't stubborn?"

"I am. That's why I can put up with you."

"Gee, thanks."

Cap groaned in exasperation. "Listen to me. I'm tired of keeping this in. After the accident, I've laid here every day, thinking. I've just been too afraid to actually say it, but you need to hear this."

My heart leapt as he took a deep breath. "Andi, I love—"

I couldn't bear to hear it now, or I would never have the strength to leave.

"Stop," I said, storming out the door. "Save it for my replacement."

CHAPTER 59

I RUSHED BACK TO MY room and hurled myself into my bed.

I felt overwhelmed with emotion, and my first instinct was to reach over and write a letter to Arnau, to vent. I immediately remembered that he was married now.

I had no one anymore.

That was fine, right? Most of my life I'd gone it alone. *"But maybe you don't want to do it alone anymore,"* a small voice in my head said.

Kicking my shoes off, I hurled them across the room with a vengeance. I punched my pillow and shoved it under my head, closing my eyes to nap. I tried to clear my brain, but the words Cap and I had angrily tossed like grenades haunted me.

I intentionally skipped dinner that night, as the rest of the team dined without me. The next morning, I asked an orderly to bring breakfast to my room. "You're not going to the dining hall?" she asked.

"No, I'm staying here," I said, then added, "I'll take all my meals in here today, actually."

No one bothered me until mid-afternoon, when Chito came to see why I was avoiding everyone. "What's going on?" he asked, standing in my doorway. "We haven't seen you all day. Or last night. What's the deal?"

"I just need to be by myself right now," I said, turning on my side to face away from him.

"Can we talk about it?"

I felt guilty. Chito would be crushed that I was leaving the Gallivanter crew. I remember how he'd told me early on that I reminded him of his niece, Molly. He'd always treated me like I was the child he'd never had. How would he feel, knowing someone he viewed as a daughter was willingly walking out of his life?

"No. I want to be alone."

"Sure," Chito replied. "You know where to find me if you need me."

The next morning, I asked the orderly again to bring all my meals to my room. "Are you feeling well?" she said, crossing the room to lay her hand on my head. "Did you catch something?"

"I just want to be alone."

"I've never seen you spend this much time in your room," she said, blinking back at me. "In fact, I don't think I've ever seen you stay still this long."

"This is the new me," I told myself, laying in my bed and staring out the window at the livestock in the pasture beyond the hospital. *"I will be content living life like this. Staring out the window, by myself. No more adventures, no more risks, and no more heartache. I'm locking that part of me away for good."*

Chito came to my door again that next evening. They'd left me alone, like I'd asked, and I was grateful for that. I didn't want to talk to anyone.

"I have a note for you, from Cap," Chito said, from the doorway. "He wanted to come see you himself, but he's fuming. I guess he's a fall risk right now, because he's dizzy. The nurses won't let him walk, and they refused to put him in a wheelchair because they thought it might tear open his leg wound."

I sat up as Chito handed me the folded note. It only had four sentences on it, printed in Cap's tidy handwriting:

"Andi, I'm sorry. The team needs you. I need you. Don't give up on us."

I crumpled it up in my hand and tossed it on the floor. "Thanks for bringing it to me," I said woodenly. I couldn't let anyone know my secret struggle, not even dear Chito. I just prayed that my behavior was enough to convince Cap to give up on the expedition.

"What did it say?" Chito asked.

"Chito, please. I know you read it on the way over."

"Fine, I did," he admitted. "But it's true. We need you. So does Cap. What's going on with you two?"

I sighed and laid back down, pushing my long legs past him on the bed. I didn't answer, but stared glumly out the window again.

Chito stared out the window with me, sitting on the foot of my bed. For a long while, we watched as the sun dipped below the horizon, its last rays lighting up the fine particles of sand blowing endlessly across the desert.

"I know about Arnau," Chito finally said, as we continued to stare out at the bucolic scene outside.

"How?"

"Paz told me. We were worried about you."

"Did you tell Cap about it?"

Chito shook his head. "I figured that's your business to share."

"Good. I wish Paz would've kept his mouth shut and not told you."

"He's feeling guilty, Andi. He's not himself. He feels like he's worthless, that he can't continue with us. He's leaving and joining the Chinook Voyageurs."

"I know. He told me."

Chito sighed. "Paz said he was there, right after you found out about Arnau getting married. That you were despondent."

I didn't answer.

The red sky melted into darkness. Lights twinkled on the horizon. We said nothing for a long time, but sat together on my bed as the room darkened around us. It was in the darkness that Chito finally leaned forward, speaking in a low tone.

"After my wife and baby girl died, I felt like I died, too," Chito said quietly. "I was lost. I vowed that I'd never love anyone, or anything, ever again. I was angry. I wanted to lash out at everything around me. How could they die, when I loved them both so much? I would've given anything to see them live—even given my own life. It wasn't fair."

He sighed deeply. "Life is seldom fair to us, Andi. It never gets easier, and it's never clear cut and predictable. We can never know what's around the next corner, as hard as we try to control it. We can make our best plans, but the unexpected will always knock us off course. Our paths are all twisted, jumbled. Chaotic, sometimes."

He paused, looking out in the darkness. I looked at his face. I could see the lights reflecting in his eyes as he stared.

"I wanted to die, Andi," he confessed. "I thought it would be easier. I was desperate. I took a gun in my hands one night, after drinking myself silly, and loaded it. I wanted to pull the trigger. I wanted to end it all."

His voice cracked and he stopped. For a moment, he simply stared at his hands. Then, softly, he spoke again.

"I needed someone to save me, to pull me out of this hole I'd fallen into," Chito said. "But as I sat there, feeling the weight of the gun, I realized I had to do it *myself*. I had to pull myself out of this pit, this fog that trapped me. I threw the gun down and wept like a baby."

He choked up.

"Molly found me," he said, emotion thick in his voice. "She clung to me as I cried. If it hadn't been for little Molly, staring up at me with those big brown eyes, scared out of her mind and looking to me for help, I don't know what I would've done. I knew I had to keep going, for her sake. Poor Molly was terrified, seeing me that way. She had nightmares for weeks. In the end, I had to go away. She was afraid to be around me. My sister was, too. I couldn't see a way forward, out of the dark. I felt like I was drowning, choking to death on something I couldn't understand."

I thought back to the sensation I had as I drowned, my lungs filling with water. I did feel like I was choking on some emotion that simultaneously filled me and oppressed me.

We sat together in the dark. For several long minutes, neither one of us spoke.

"We make the choice to keep going," Chito finally said, his deep voice husky. "Even when we're cornered. Even when we're lost in the dark. You make the decision to get up every day and keep living."

He turned and sought my eyes.

"Heartache and pain are a part of each of our stories," he said slowly. "But so is joy and laughter and friendship. And love. You make the choice if you're going to let your disappointments and failures and the hurts lead the rest of your life, or if you're going to fight to live a good story, despite the pain you face."

I stared back at him. "I don't know what to do," I whispered.

"Yes you do," he whispered back. "You're going to fight. You're going to fight to save Andiamo Gallivanter."

CHAPTER 60

PAZ LEFT EARLY THE next morning, without saying goodbye to anyone.

Chito carried a breakfast tray into my room to tell me.

"They're already running the story in the newspapers," he said, bringing me a folded article under his arm. "Bernard found it this morning. He must've told a reporter without us knowing. They have quotes from him and everything."

I looked at the paper as he handed it to me.

"Hero Crew from Gallivanter Expedition Switches Sides to Work for Rival Team," boasted the oversized print. A stock picture of Paz in front of one of our cars, blown up from one of our older photographs, showed him grinning proudly at the camera.

So he'd gone through with it after all.

Maybe things would've been different if I would've fought harder with him, persuaded him to stay. I hadn't even talked to him at all in the last several days, and it had been so easy for the two of us to talk freely.

Was this my fault, too?

Chito invited me to explore the town with him and Bernard, but I declined. I still hadn't told them that I was leaving the team, and what was the point of bonding together now? It would only make it harder to tell them the bad news.

I brushed my hair, staring at myself in a tiny mirror over the sink. I couldn't believe what a mess I'd made of my own life.

"Andi?"

I turned to see Cap wobble into my room, using his hand to brace himself against the wall.

"Cap!" I exclaimed. "What are you doing out of bed?"

"Don't you even start with that," he warned playfully, using the foot of my bed to help him limp across the room on his right leg. "The nurses have been driving me insane. How long do they think I can possibly lay in a hospital bed?"

He lowered himself into a chair as I looked at him suspiciously. We hadn't talked in a few days now. He had to know I'd been avoiding him. "Why are you in my room?"

"We need to talk. Things aren't right between us, clearly."

I turned my back on him and continued brushing my hair. It was grown out now, well past my shoulders. I brushed to control my emotions. I wanted nothing more than to hug Cap and confess my love, and beg him to stop this trip before it ended in tragedy.

"I don't want to talk to you," I told him as I studied my reflection. I watched myself say the phrase I knew would hurt him most. "I don't want to be around you anymore. I don't want to be on this team."

"You keep saying that. Didn't you get my note the other day? The one Chito brought?"

"I did."

"And?"

"And you don't need me."

"I do," he said, then corrected himself. "We all do."

"I've already made up my mind, Cap. I'm leaving."

"Andi, what happened between us? This is more than just the Rosie situation, obviously. Why aren't we close anymore?"

"What part of this don't you understand?" I cried, exasperated. "I'm going home. I'm done with the team."

"Home, huh? Or back to Arnau?" Cap challenged, his face suddenly tinged with anger.

I winced as I heard him say the name out loud. Chito had kept his word, and Cap didn't know about Arnau's marriage. Did he assume that I was in love with Arnau? That we were actually engaged? I'd stupidly led him to believe that.

I felt a twinge of remorse, but remembered this was for the best. Cap's life was too precious to waste on this expedition. I couldn't live with myself if I saw him get hurt again and knew that I could've prevented it by putting an end to this madness. If Paz and I both left, maybe Cap would rethink this whole trip.

If the price I had to pay for keeping Cap alive was putting up with his anger, I'd gladly pay it.

"That's my business."

"Actually, it's mine. Take a look, sweetheart."

He pulled a folder from his jacket and tossed it to me. I caught it and opened it. Inside was a single sheaf of carbon copy paper. I read out loud.

"*I, Edith Warren, agree to provide my services in the form of professional representative for the Gallivanter Expedition. The campaign will commence on the date of Captain Grant Gallivanter's choosing, in 1923, and continue through exclusive decisions of Captain Grant Gallivanter or until mutual agreement dictates otherwise. I pledge myself exclusively and fully as a member of the Gallivanter Expedition, representative of the United States of America and her allies.*

By this signature, I render my services in full for the entirety of the expedition. In witness of their agreement to the terms above, the parties or authorized agents hereby affix their signatures, as witnessed by a registered notary."

Below, I saw Cap's signature on top of my own. The signature of a notary and a small stamp were affixed to the bottom corner.

"Where did you get this?" I sputtered. "I don't remember signing this."

"I had my lawyer mail me a copy, from New York. You signed it. You just don't remember. There was a lot going on while we were preparing in France."

I thought back to the whirlwind preparations. I'd signed a lot of documents, in between driving lessons and maintenance tutorials and fittings for my uniform. I must've forgotten about this one.

"What are you trying to tell me, Cap?"

"I'm sorry, Andi. I've tried to reason with you. But you're not listening," Cap replied. "You can't leave the team. Legally, you're bound to continue your services until the expedition ends."

"You let Paz leave!" I said, throwing the folder down. "You didn't stop him!"

"I couldn't. I tried. His contract was different, because we hired him on as a temporary guide in Spain. We kept him on with a gentleman's agreement, a simple handshake. In the eyes of the law, I had nothing to keep him with us," Cap shook his head. "I never imagined he'd walk away like this."

"Is there even an expedition anymore?" I frowned. "Look at you. Look at both of us. Three of us are still recovering from our wounds. Paz is gone. Chito is the only healthy one."

"We'll bring in more people to join our crew," Cap replied, his tone desperate. "We can finally afford to do it right. We'll fix up the damaged Ford, and maybe even add another one to the caravan. We've barely started our trip around the world."

"Yeah, and going through a mere four countries nearly killed half of us."

"But it didn't. Haven't we had some good times, too? Even some great times? Would Andi Gallivanter really want to give that up?"

I stared at him, flashing back to his bloody face and pale skin. Unwillingly, I saw the blood gushing from his temple, his body slack. I remembered the hot blood that bubbled up under my fingers as I pressed on his thigh. The desperation of watching him—the man I loved—dying, right in front of me. I felt my heart racing.

I shook my head. He couldn't possibly understand. I couldn't bear to see him like that again.

"What if we're not so lucky next time?" I shot back. "What if Chito gets killed? Or Bernard? Can you live with that on your conscience? This is just a trip, Cap. What do you want out of it? A trophy? That million dollars that goes to the winning crew? Bragging rights?"

"I don't care about any of that," he said, rising to his feet unsteadily. "How many times do I have to say this? This expedition has been my life's work. It's been my dream. But dreams...they grow."

Abruptly, he stopped himself. We faced each other, chests heaving.

"This can't be the path forward," a small voice inside told me. *"You don't want to leave him. You love this team. Despite its challenges, you love this life. You don't want to be anywhere else. Not France, not America. Here."*

"Listen to me," Cap's voice was low. "This expedition has been my passion, yes. But there's only one thing I care about more than this trip. You know I'd make the choice, if I had to. But don't make me choose, Andi."

I struggled to contain my emotions. *"This expedition means everything to him. How can you deny him his dream?"* I thought. *"It's not just his dream, either. It's yours now, too."*

We stood frozen in the moment. As usual, my mouth got in the way.

"Well, that's convenient," I blurted. "You say all of this now, after you've just hunted down a legal document that tethers me to your side, whether I want to be there or not? Like I said the last time we talked, you'll say anything to try to keep me on the team."

"I showed you that document to remind you where you belong, to stop you from throwing it all away," Cap cried, throwing up his hands. "Face it, Andi. You belong next to me, sitting in those cars, standing on that stage, camping around the fire under the stars."

"I don't belong to you," I retorted. "I'm not a piece of property."

"I never said you belong *to* me. I said you belong *next to* me," he replied. "You've always been an equal, in my eyes. A partner. *My* partner."

We faced each other like boxers in a ring.

My feelings threatened to burst out like the water cascading out of a dam. *"You're not Paz,"* my brain whispered. *"You're not going to do it. You won't leave them."*

Cap's leg suddenly buckled, and I rushed forward, catching him.

"You know you should be back in bed. You're not strong enough for this yet," I chided him, but inwardly I softened.

How could I fight with him like this after I'd nearly lost him? I knew the source of our fight was my desire to protect him from himself, but—what if there was another way forward?

"You'll find a way forward, somehow," my brain whispered to me. *"This is your home—this team, this life—this is where you belong. You'll figure it out together. You don't have to go it alone anymore."*

Something in me swelled hopefully, realizing I'd be staying on the Gallivanter team after all.

I stared at Cap, whose blue eyes searched my face intently. *"Surely you can protect him better if you're by his side,"* I thought, meeting his gaze. *"He's right. He needs you. He's been right on that, all along."*

"Please, Andi," Cap begged softly. "You can't leave us. I want you to understand that. We have a lot more of the world to see together. The adventure has barely begun."

I struggled to hide my smile. I wouldn't fight it anymore. I'd stay right here, on the team, where I belonged. I couldn't leave. I didn't *want* to leave.

I took a step forward. Cap flinched, his face tight. "What?"

I said nothing, but extended my hand to shake his. His face brightened.

"I won't go back on my contract," I replied. "I made a promise to be a part of this team. To be by your side. But Cap, we have to be more careful. I can't handle any more danger."

"Me neither," Cap replied slowly, grinning at me for the first time in weeks. "It's going to be fine, Andi. I just know it. I swear, I won't get crushed by a landslide next time. Nothing else bad could possibly happen to us."

"You're the boss, Captain Gallivanter," I smiled back at him, my heart light for the first time in ages. "Whatever you say."

CHAPTER 61

DESPITE THE BLOW OF losing Paz, the Gallivanter crew doubled down on continuing the expedition.

We were battle-scarred now, but stronger than ever.

Together, we arranged with locals to have the damaged Ford hauled back to town on a flatbed wagon. Bernard took over fixing it as it sat in the road outside the hospital, mangled and lonely. For weeks, he obsessively rebuilt the wood frame of the body, pounding the metal back into shape and reattaching it. Several parts inside the engine had been bent or damaged, and Bernard patiently fixed everything from the choke lever to the coils. He ordered and installed new plate glass panels for the windshield after he shaped the frame back into place.

I went out to check on him one afternoon, the sun bright in my eyes, and found him scrubbing the interior with a soapy bucket of suds.

"What are you doing?" I asked, leaning against the Ford. It felt like ages since I'd been behind the wheel.

"Cleaning up the blood stains," he replied. "Half of it's mine, I figured it's my duty."

By the time the doctor finally took the cast off my arm, my cuts had healed. Only the raised scars indicated where I'd bled as I crunched through the broken glass to pull Bernard and Cap to safety.

Cap's spirits had risen noticeably, and his health improved just as rapidly. Soon, he was allowed to get out of his hospital bed and join us for meals in the dining hall. We played card games together and sat in the commons, reading newspapers and sipping tea. Sometimes Dr. Mathieu joined us in between his rounds, laughing at our stories and sharing his own quirky adventures.

Chito and Bernard and I explored the city together while Cap endured painful physical therapy, the result of having laid in bed for so many weeks.

"My muscles atrophied," he said, gritting his teeth as we walked up and down the halls with him, to keep him company. "They said it's going to take some time to build up the muscle mass again."

After nearly eight weeks at the hospital, Cap secured permission from his doctor to discharge.

"He told me not to push myself too hard, but that we can get back on the trail," he said, holding up a stack of travel notes. "I already know where we're going next. French Sudan. We're going to connect with the Senegal River and follow it across."

"That's perfect timing," Bernard said. "The Ford is back and running in tip-top shape. She's a real beauty, you know. A strong old girl."

"I'll restock the supplies we need," Chito grinned. "Can we make a deal that we'll try our best to avoid sandstorms and rock slides and flash floods this time?"

"Only if we also promise to avoid scheming American ambassadors, too," I joked.

"And Spaniards," Bernard added.

We thanked the hospital staff who had tended to us for so long at St. Jude's mission. Dr. Mathieu hugged me goodbye.

"Thank you, doctor," I smiled. "When you read about us now, you'll be able to boast that you saved the lives of half the crew of the famous Gallivanter Expedition."

"I'll definitely brag about that," Dr. Mathieu grinned. "It's been a pleasure playing a small part in this grand adventure of yours."

Getting back in the Model T after so long out of it felt strange. A crowd of journalists hooted and cheered as we paraded out.

Despite putting the expedition on hold with our extended stay at the hospital, our fame had only seemed to grow.

Cap grinned and waved as he rolled out in the lead automobile, Chito next to him. I pulled out behind him, and Bernard trailed behind me.

Bernard had insisted on driving the Ford that he'd worked so hard to repair. His work was meticulous, and the car showed no trace of the massive damage it had endured. He'd even managed to touch up the paint in our Gallivanter logo on the side of the car, which had been scarred and flaked.

As soon as we traveled out of sight of the towns and into the desert again, Cap signaled us to pull over. We rolled to a stop in front of a large herd of sheep wandering through sparse weeds.

"I'm sorry, I have to trade drivers," Cap said, swinging his left leg out of the passenger door. "Chito, my leg is killing me. Can you drive for a while?"

"What would you do without me?" Chito grinned. "I guess I'll make the sacrifice."

"Mind if I hop in with you?" Cap limped over to my door. "I need a break."

I patted the passenger seat. "It's all yours."

"Thanks," Cap said, wincing as he climbed in. "When the doctor told me I had nerve damage and that it'd take longer than I wanted for this leg to heal, I confess that I had a few choice words for them."

"Uh oh. Remember, that kind of language isn't allowed at the hospital."

"Too late."

I laughed. "Are you going to walk with a limp forever? Should we get you a cane and a top hat, make you look like a distinguished old gentleman?"

"No, but maybe a parrot and a peg leg. I'd prefer to be a pirate, not an old man."

I smiled, glancing at him as we drove. I'd been so close to giving this up. What had I been thinking?

We set up camp that night in the desert, listening to the high-pitched whines of a pack of jackals hunting in the distance. The fire crackled merrily as Cap filled us in on French Sudan and what we could expect.

"It's a huge country, one of the biggest in Africa. It used to be known as the Mali Empire, but it's now a French colony, just like Mauritania," he explained. "Their biggest exports here are gold and salt. We'll need to keep our eyes open to make sure we steer clear of any shady characters lurking out in the wilderness. Men get dangerously irrational about gold."

"Got it," Chito said, sprinkling spices into the stew that bubbled over our campfire. "No gold."

"Interestingly, one of the richest rulers in the history of the world operated in French Sudan, hundreds of years ago," Cap continued. "His name was Mansa Musa."

Chito and I exchanged amused glances. It was good to have our captain back.

"Yeah, we don't care about that," Bernard groaned. "What are the driving conditions going to be like?"

"Northern French Sudan is arid. It'll be like this, mostly deserts and grasslands. As we get closer to the Senegal River, we'll encounter trees and vegetation. We'll follow the river through—it flows east to southwest, across the country—and drive into Bamako, the capital city, to restock supplies."

We laughed and teased each other as we ate dinner around the campfire, the warm glow flickering across our faces. The sunset melted into purple shadows, the stars emerging like old friends. I breathed deep, listening to the hum of insects and night-dwelling animals deep in the darkness.

This was the life I wanted. The life I was choosing.

As we laid in our bed rolls, the fire crackling between our feet, I stared up at the stars. It had been so long since we'd slept outside of a bed. The familiar smell of the hospital had been replaced by the sweet smell of the tall grass that bordered our campsite.

Next to me, Cap shifted in his bed roll. I glanced over and saw him looking at me.

"I told you so," he grinned, the blankets pulled up to his chin. "You belong out here, next to the campfire, under the stars."

I grinned back. "If the next words out of your mouth are 'I was right and you were wrong', I swear to you that I'm going to steal your keys and leave you here."

He laughed and turned his face back to the sky. I rolled over, adjusting my bed roll. As the quiet sounds of sleep stole over our group, I snuck another look at Cap.

He was still wide awake, smiling up at the stars.

CHAPTER 62

OUR JOURNEY CONTINUED on, the landscape ever changing as we rolled by rocks and hills, oceans of high grass, and distant forests.

Noticing several strange formations towering out in the middle of the plains, we detoured off the rough road and into the tall grass, the blades falling softly and springing back together, unbent, as I maneuvered the car through the field.

Cautiously, we drove closer to inspect the mounds.

"What are they?" Chito called, unwilling to get out of his Ford.

"They're made of dirt," Bernard frowned. "It looks like something you'd see at the beach."

Indeed, it looked as if someone had climbed up on a tall ladder and dribbled wet sand down to make huge, organic sandcastle spires.

"What are these?" Cap wondered, poking at them with a stick. "It's rock hard."

"They must be ten or twelve feet tall," I speculated. "I'm pretty sure they're termite mounds."

"How could you possibly know that?" Bernard scoffed.

"I read it in a book," I said, remembering the passage from Arnau's geography book.

"Since when do you read?" Bernard said. "I've only ever seen you hauling around that one book. You know, the one from that Frenchie who dumped you."

"Dumped you?" Cap exclaimed, shooting me a look. "Who dumped you?"

I bit my lip. With our truce still fresh, I didn't want to dredge up old arguments so I'd never bothered to tell him the story about Arnau getting married. But Chito knew. And somehow, Bernard knew...and had now spilled the beans.

"I was just talking about bugs," I replied lightly. I wouldn't be drawn into a fight. "Isn't it amazing how creatures always find a way to survive, even in a hostile environment?"

"It sure is." Cap's eyes stayed on me for a beat longer than necessary. "We should get back on the road."

We bumped back through the tall grass and I guided us onto the rock-strewn road. Behind me, Chito and Bernard rumbled out of the field and joined me, completing our little caravan.

Cap turned in his seat, checking on the other Fords. From the driver's seat, both of the men gave him a thumbs up. Settling into his seat, he pulled out a map and carefully marked our position, then folded it up and slid it into his jacket.

"So," he drew out the word. "Tell me what else you know about termites."

"Oh, stop it."

"What?" Cap exclaimed. "I'm making conversation!"

I shot him a look. "Yes, Arnau dumped me. Okay? It's over. It never really started, actually."

Cap stared out the window and said nothing. I slugged him on the arm.

"What?" he groaned. "I'm trying to respect your boundaries. It's your personal life."

Even as he said it, he could barely keep from smiling. I rolled my eyes.

"You know I have no personal life here," I replied. "I couldn't keep a secret from this ridiculous team if I tried. Bunch of blabbermouths."

"How are you doing with it?"

"How am I doing?" I repeated, glancing at Cap. "I'm fine, I guess."

"Good," he said, staring out the window. We sat in silence for a few moments, before he spoke again. "Why am I the last to know about this?"

"Cap, things have been crazy. Did you forget that you and Bernard almost died? That we had to rebuild the Ford? That Rosie and Paz left? When did we have the time to have this conversation?"

"We should've made time for it."

I exhaled. "Well, we've got plenty of time now."

"Then let's talk about it," Cap replied, his neck pink. "It was a pretty big surprise for me to hear you tell Rosie that you were engaged to this fellow. I thought I knew you, Andi. It hurt to know that you kept such a huge part of your life from me. Why wouldn't you tell me that you were engaged?"

"Because I wasn't, okay? At least, it wasn't clear," I sighed as I gripped the steering wheel. "I thought Arnau wanted to marry me. I thought—I don't know, after we finished all this—somehow, maybe, we'd end up together. He's the only man I've ever known that wasn't afraid of me. But while I was writing to him all these months, he'd apparently been busy falling in love with another girl. They're married now. I didn't find out until I received a letter from him while we stayed in one place long enough for the mail to finally catch up with us."

"I'm sorry, Andi," Cap's tone was understanding. "How did it all go wrong between you?"

I shrugged. "I went away. With you."

"That's hardly fair. You can't blame me."

"I'm not. It's the truth, if I boil it all down. He was happy living in his little village, working in the stables. He was content living in the same small town for the rest of his life. I wanted more."

"He worked in the stables? You told us he owned horses."

"No," I replied. "He was a stablehand at my boarding school. His family was poor. He worked there, after school, to contribute to his home."

"That's admirable, then. When exactly did he propose?"

"I got expelled, for hitting another girl. I was forced to leave the school and go to another school, in France. He proposed the day before I left for Nice, as we said goodbye."

"And you accepted, when he proposed?"

"No."

"You didn't?" he sounded surprised. "Why did you think you'd end up together then?"

I thought for a moment, watching the fields of grass sway in the breeze. "He understood me. He saw who I really was, and didn't tell me to be someone else. He accepted me for who I was."

"Ah," Cap said, his voice soft.

"All my life, it's seemed like the whole world didn't care for me much. No one wanted to get to know me, the *real* me," I added. "They were too busy judging me for being too tall, or too manly, or not being interested in gossip or embroidery or dresses. I've been alone, misunderstood, for most of my life. He was the only one who seemed to understand it."

"I can relate to that," Cap said, staring at the fields in front of us. "I've felt that way all my life, too. Alone. Misunderstood."

From the road on this savanna, we could see rugged hills and patches of green forests in front of us.

"Look at us," Cap said, smiling ruefully. "Two failed engagements and two near death experiences between the two of us. Quite a collection we have going."

I laughed. "If we keep playing those odds, I guess we'll end up with either marriage or death."

Cap reached for the map in his jacket, smoothing it open. Above us, the sun was starting its dance with dusk. He studied the map as we drove, silent save for the wind whistling in our ears.

I reflected on Cap's words, as he confessed how much it hurt him that I kept a huge part of my life from him. I glanced at his face.

"You know, I never really wanted to leave the expedition," I said quietly. "I only wanted to save you. We nearly lost you, Cap. I thought somehow that if I left—I don't know. That maybe you'd slow down, and rethink things. Be more cautious."

Cap looked at me, the sun glinting off his goggles. "But—"

I interrupted him. "I know. I need to be here. *You* need me here."

"I do," he said softly, smiling at the road ahead of us.

The sun dipped into the low clouds on the horizon, the last rays illuminating the sky in a brilliant display of color. Cap tucked the map inside his jacket with one hand, then glanced at me.

"You know, it's the people who never leave our side—even when things are difficult—who really matter in our lives," he said, his voice thoughtful. "We encounter a lot of people in a lifetime. It's the ones who cheer for us when we're succeeding, and cry with us when we're hurting, who are the ones to pay attention to. They're the ones who really love us."

"You're getting poetic in your old age," I teased. "Maybe we do need to get you that cane."

As we made our small camp that night, unpacking the Fords in the dusk of twilight, we noticed campfires and smoke curling in the distance.

"Nomadic tribes," Cap said, squinting at them. "They've been in this region for centuries, I've read."

"Are they safe?" Bernard asked, peering into the dark.

"Probably," Cap lowered himself to the ground with a grunt. "These nomadic tribes keep to themselves, mostly, but they're a private group. They've had quite a lot of hostilities with the government. As long as they aren't a band of mercenaries looking to rob us, we should be fine."

I laid in my bed roll that night, unable to get Cap's words out of my head. "You know, it's the people who never leave our side—even when things are difficult—who really matter in our lives," he had said. "They're the ones who really love us."

"I know," I agreed silently. *"And they're the ones we really love, too."*

CHAPTER 63

"GIRAFFES!" CHITO SHOUTED, pointing out the window.

From my passenger seat, Bernard scrambled to pull the Kinamo camera out of its case. "This darn thing!" he cried, fumbling with the lens.

"There will be more," I replied, craning my neck to look through his window as we drove. "Do you think we'll see another herd of elephants at some point, too?"

The savanna we traveled through was peppered with groves of trees that slowly turned into thick swaths of jungle, the darkness of the dense trees and vegetation a welcome contrast from the stark emptiness of the desert we'd spent so much of our time battling on this expedition.

As we trundled through French Sudan, we passed tiny towns and jumbled collections of tents and shacks, open fires dotting the clearings where dogs ran out, chasing our Fords and growling. Each time we saw people, we slowed to wave and smile, curious if we could stop and talk with them, but their body language warned us that we weren't welcome.

"Why doesn't anyone look like they want us to stop?" Chito frowned.

"People here have a complicated history with white men," Cap replied, rubbing his jaw. "I can't blame them. I'm not sure I would welcome us in, either."

"Yeah, but some of them seem downright hostile," Bernard said. "Did you see that fellow with the spears, at that last village we passed before stopping for lunch?"

"It'd be nice to get some photographs with at least a few people here," Cap said, looking down at his notebook. "We're going to need something to share with the newspapers when we roll into town."

The jungle began pressing into us from all sides, the sounds of our rattling Fords now muffled in the thick undergrowth. Beneath our cars, the ground became slick with dew and fallen leaves. Above our heads, the thick canopy of trees blotted out most of the sunlight. Birds fluttered in the treetops as we drove, startled by our presence.

"It's a huge forest down here," Cap craned his neck out the window. "I read that they can have hundreds of different types of birds in one jungle."

"Anything edible?"

"I'm sure Chito's asking the same question," Cap grinned.

As we rounded a corner, we spotted a small village in the clearing ahead. Cultivated fields surrounded somewhere around fifty huts with thatched roofs. Dozens of horses grazed in the fields where tethered camels rested.

"This is perfect," Cap exclaimed. "Imagine the shots of this place playing in the theaters, when we make it back to Europe. Let's pull in here and see if we can talk with some villagers. Where's the camera?"

"Maybe we should ask them about navigating through these woods, too," I said, peering into the darkness beyond the village. "It looks pretty thick in there."

We slipped our goggles off as villagers slowly emerged from their huts, staring at us. A few men, draped in turbans and large scarves that hid their features, stepped toward our Fords.

"Careful, Cap," I murmured. "I'm not sure they're friendly."

I studied the nomads in front of me, noticing the colorful tribal pattern of their robes and the intricate necklaces and earrings they wore. The women's heads were concealed by fabric, and I wondered if I should keep my helmet on.

The men of the village clustered together, talking amongst themselves. A large man stepped forward from the middle, holding up his hand. The group stopped their excited babble and hushed.

"Must be the chief," Cap muttered to me. He leaned his head out of the window. "Hello! Bonjour!"

The man's eyebrows raised. He lifted his chin, as if to challenge us, and replied rapidly in French.

"What the—" Cap breathed, as I put my hand on his arm to stop him.

"He's speaking French. He asked why we're here in his village."

I motioned for Cap to slide out of the car, and followed behind him. Standing next to Cap, I politely nodded my head to the chief and smiled.

"Hello, friends. We are the Gallivanter Expedition, a team of Americans traveling all over the world in our automobiles," I called out in French, making sure the entire crowd could hear me.

We wanted no misinterpretation of our intentions. The crew had each memorized this greeting, crafting the short phrase for these exact situations.

"We are pleased to meet you," I continued. "We extend a warm offer of friendship as we seek to learn more about your culture."

In response, the chief spat into the dirt. I blinked.

"How dare you allow this woman to speak in the presence of men?" he thundered, glaring at Cap. "Why is this woman permitted to drive, and why is she commanding an army of men? And why is her head uncovered, like a common whore?"

Cap looked at me, helpless, unable to understand his words. "What's he saying?"

I ignored him. This was unraveling quickly.

"Sir, I am an American citizen," I called out calmly, responding in French. "In our country, women are allowed to speak to men. We do not wear the same clothing. I mean no disrespect."

"And we are certainly no army," I added, seeing the crowd start to shift uneasily. "We're a small group of friends traveling through the world, wanting to share our experiences with others. It is merely educational, in nature."

"Do not speak to me," he threatened, his face angry. "You have no right."

"Andi," Cap hissed. "What is he saying?"

I thought quickly. The crowd was getting restless.

"Sir, I am the only member of my party who speaks French," I said. "And though we are small in number, I assure you that we are quite famous. Very famous, actually. People know our names and faces all over the world."

"Famous?" he replied, squinting.

"Very famous," I responded. "We have many newspapers tracking us. They know we were headed right here, to this very village. They expect us to take many photographs, to share your way of life with others. We already have a large group of people waiting for us in the next village."

The chief stepped back to the group of men clustered together, speaking quietly to them. Glancing up, he addressed Cap instead of me.

"Very well," he said. "We will allow your visit, though the whore will wear a veil while she is here. She shows disrespect with her uncovered head."

"I'm sorry," I apologized in French, though I wasn't.

The man turned to the crowd, lifting his hands above his head. "The Americans are welcome here, and we will serve them a banquet tonight, at sunset. We will celebrate together, as friends.

This American woman will remain covered, and no man may speak to her. She is a temptress, a viper in our peaceful pasture."

"Andi, what's going on?" Cap exclaimed, alarmed as the crowds surged toward our cars.

"He welcomed us in for a banquet, but only because I told him we're famous," I spoke quickly. "I was afraid they were going to kill us and eat us if they didn't think we had people waiting for us in the next town."

"I don't think there are cannibals in this region."

I glared at him. "You really want to have this conversation now?"

"No, sorry. What else did he say?"

"I'll tell you later," I said, as a group of women approached and began wrapping fabric around my head. "They're making me wear this," I added, as the women pulled me away from my crew.

The women pulled me inside a large hut, excited to show me the soft fabrics and jewelry they made. I made polite conversation in French, concerned about how the rest of the crew was communicating without me.

"Can I go outside and check on my friends?" I asked.

The women giggled and surrounded me in a friendly mass, pulling me outside into the center of the village where several fires already crackled. Old women squatted over them, stirring and sprinkling spices. Little kids assisted them, darting around and laughing in the excitement of having visitors.

Through the crowd that swarmed around me, I caught only a quick glimpse of Chito's broad shoulders across the clearing. He was standing in a circle of men, showing them one of our rifles.

Women scurried around me, whisking handmade clay bowls in and out of the fires with practiced skill. It seemed like every face I encountered asked me to try a bite of food or asked me how many children I had.

"I have no children," I kept replying, shaking my head. "I'm not married."

They inched away from me.

Dinner was a long affair, as the women first served the men at a massive wooden table. Bernard and Cap caught my eyes, sympathetic, as I helped the nomadic women serve the men.

They ate communally, dipping their hands into large bowls as soon as we dropped them on the table. After setting a final bowl down, I started to sit in the empty seat next to Chito.

"No," an older woman stopped me, grabbing my wrist and pulling me back to the fires. "The men get seats. The women sit together, on the ground."

The children and women ate separately, gathered in small clusters around bowls. I ate with them in silence, listening to laughter coming from the men's table. I hoped that the scant French phrases that Cap had taught himself were enough to avoid any cultural faux pas that might make our short stay even more unpleasant.

After dinner, dozens of the young men and women stood up to dance for us. The men jogged to the pasture to retrieve the camels, pulling them up to their feet.

"How do I ask them if I can film this?" Cap whispered, appearing at my side. I told him the words and he darted away.

Cap cranked the camera as he filmed the nomads whirling around and dancing for us.

"This is the tam tam, a very special dance," the girl next to me told me as we watched the men slide onto the camels, riding them rhythmically around the women who chanted, clapped, and beat their drums.

Gradually, the older men pushed their way into the large circle, taking turns dancing, while the rest of the group clapped.

They danced and chanted until the moon rose high in the sky, the hum of the jungle filling our ears. As I yawned, the women led me to a large structure where dozens of other women were taking off their veils and jewelry and unbraiding their hair. "You can sleep here," they told me.

Too tired to protest, I shrugged and unrolled my bed roll. I stared up at the thatched roof and listened to the nighttime jungle drone, missing the familiar sound of the snoring Gallivanter crew to lull me to sleep.

CHAPTER 64

OUT OF HABIT, I AWOKE as dawn's first light warmed the sky. I tiptoed over the sleeping women in my hut and made my way out to the campfires that smoldered from last night's late celebration.

Cap and Bernard hunched together over one, talking quietly. A few villagers moved around the clearing, beginning their morning chores.

"Hey," I joined them. "I hate it here."

They both laughed, keeping their voices soft.

"They haven't seemed to speak kindly about you," Cap admitted. "My French isn't nearly as good as yours, but did I hear them call you a whore?"

"Yes, among other things. Tell me we're leaving as soon as we can."

"We are," Cap said. "I already asked the chief about getting through the jungle. The bad news is that we can't. It's far too thick here—no roads inside. He said locals don't even go in it themselves. It's too dangerous, especially at dusk. Apparently all sorts of wild animals come down to the river as a watering hole. Rhinos, lions, elephants, cheetahs, leopards, crocodiles...you know, everything that could kill us."

"So what does he suggest?"

Bernard pointed to the other side of the fields that surrounded the village. "He told us to aim toward those cliffs, and go all the way around. He told us there's no way we could even walk through the jungle, let alone drive it. But we've got the general idea. It shouldn't set us back too much."

"Great," I stood, dusting off my pants. "Let's get going. They won't miss me, I guarantee you that."

"Hold on," Cap held up his hand, as Chito lumbered out to join us. "He insisted that we see the horses before we go. They're horse breeders, I guess. I'm pretty sure they want to sell us a few."

"You're not going to buy a horse, right?" Chito grumbled, rubbing his eyes. "I can't possibly feed that thing *and* us."

Cap laughed. "They've fed us and let us stay here overnight. We have to be polite. What harm could it possibly do to check out some horses before we head out?"

The women fed us again, a breakfast of spiced rice and yams. Cap asked me to tell the chief that we needed to depart very soon, but we wanted to see his horses before we left. I translated to French and the chief nodded.

"I will show you right now," he said, motioning for the men to follow him into the field. They took off without me.

I brushed past the women and headed out with the group, catching up to Chito. He looked at me and winked. "Glad you could join us," he whispered. "Maybe you can offend the horses with your presence, too, before we split."

I grinned as we walked between the horses who chewed grass, slowly, blinking up at us. A horse nickered as I walked by and I stopped to rub its nose.

"We have the finest horses in the land," the chief boasted. "We have bred them carefully for centuries. They are very important to us, very special animals. Would any of you like the honor of a ride?"

"I'm too big," Chito shook his head, slapping his belly. The villagers laughed, understanding his actions without understanding his words.

Bernard also shook his head. "I don't like horses." I wondered if he had resisted the urge to add, *"I don't like people either."*

Cap patted his lame leg apologetically. "I'm sorry, I was injured in a bad accident a few weeks ago. My leg is still recovering."

The chief pursed his lips, staring back at him.

"Andi, help me out," Cap said, turning to me. Obediently, I translated.

The chief shrugged. "That's too bad," he replied. "These horses are some of the finest in the world. It'd be the ride of a lifetime for you."

Impulsively, I spoke up. "I'll do it."

"What?"

"I'll do it. I'll ride one."

The chief sneered at me. "You're a woman," he growled. "Your job is to cook my meals and raise my children and give me your body when I want it. You don't belong on a horse like this."

His words goaded me. I flushed.

"Let me show you what a woman can do," I said, tossing my head back and spitting my reply at him in rapid French. "I grew up riding horses every day. I tended the stables all through my childhood. I know my way around a horse. Give me your hardest stallion, and I will ride him."

"You could never handle him. Only a man can handle a strong horse like that."

"I'll show you," I retorted. "Show me which one is the most difficult to tame."

The chief laughed sharply and stormed across the paddock, motioning. Cap grabbed my elbow as I strode across the field behind him.

"What are you two saying to each other?" Cap whispered. "Something about you riding a horse?"

"Yes," I replied, angry, studying the black stallion that the chief was leading me toward.

We were still several yards away from him, and already the horse was alert and straining at his rope, watching us approach. He yanked his head, whipping the rope against the post that held him down.

"Look, I know you can ride well," Cap said, tugging at my arm. "But that horse looks awfully wild."

"I asked for the wildest one." My eyes narrowed as I studied it. "I need to show him I can ride."

"Andi, stop," Cap urged, his long strides matching mine. "We're heading out any minute. You don't need to prove yourself to this man, or anyone else here. The people who matter already know your worth."

The horse reared back and thrashed as we neared it.

"Shhh, it's okay," I said, reaching out to touch his side. He bucked wildly, and Cap and I ducked out of the way.

The chief laughed. "I told you, you can't handle him," he said gleefully. "He's never been ridden by any man here. He's never even had a saddle on his back."

I reached out again, trying to calm the horse. He bolted away from me, pulling up short as the rope snapped against the post.

"Come on, Andi," Cap backed up. "Let's go."

"I told you, woman. You could never do it," the chief crossed his arms. "You're all the same. Only good for one thing."

I felt my cheeks burn and turned to Cap. "Hoist me up," I demanded, pulling him toward the horse.

"No!" he replied, his voice filled with anger. "What are you trying to do here?"

I whirled around to the chief. "Help me up," I said to him in French.

He smirked and stepped to the side of the horse. He interlaced his fingers, and without a second of hesitation, I stepped up with my left foot and swung my long right leg neatly over the horse's rear.

The horse bucked again, screaming, and yanked at the rope. I wrapped my arms around his neck and dug my knees into his sides as hard as I could.

Too late, I realized the stallion was about to buck me off. I just had to hold on long enough for him to calm down.

"Andi!" Bernard and Chito screamed, as Cap lurched toward me.

It was like everything was suddenly happening in slow motion.

The big stallion shot forward, breaking the rope that tethered him to the post. He took off across the field, galloping hard, with me holding on for dear life.

We raced straight for the jungle.

CHAPTER 65

"WHOA! WHOA!" I YELLED at the horse, trying to get his attention. I pushed against him hard, trying in vain to slow him.

The stallion streaked through the field, gliding over potholes without breaking stride.

"Why, he's faster than my car," I marveled, even as I clung to him in terror. I knew that falling off now could get me trampled, or worse yet—killed.

My veil had flown off and my hair streamed behind me. As if in a dream, I remembered the thousands of times I'd galloped with Arnau through the fields and forests in France.

The wind blew against my face and the horse's flanks heaved underneath me. They were sensations I'd felt every time I'd ever ridden. To me, they represented freedom, an escape from my boring life.

But this time, I was experiencing a new sensation: fear.

The stallion galloped furiously toward the jungle. Quickly, I tried to remember how I'd ridden the tame stable horses through the thick brush of the woods behind my boarding school.

"Keep your head down, and your body tight to the horse," I told myself. *"Shield your eyes, press them into his mane. Hold onto him, he's sure to veer away from the dense brush."*

We crashed headlong into the jungle without slowing, tree branches and vines slapping painfully against my body. I cried out involuntarily, my mouth muffled against the stallion's mane.

I couldn't understand why he hadn't slowed down or skirted away once he encountered the dense vegetation. Where was he going?

In a flash of horror, I thought back to what Cap told me this morning. His words echoed through my head. "Apparently all sorts of wild animals come down to the river as a watering hole. Rhinos, lions, elephants, cheetahs, leopards, crocodiles...you know, everything that could kill us."

This stallion was wild. He was instinctively heading to the river.

I knew my arms and legs were getting sliced to ribbons as we sprinted through the jungle. My hair tangled against branches, painfully yanking strands out as we tore through vines. I could hear nothing but the wild panting of the horse and the crash of foliage as we careened, out of control, through the jungle.

"Hold on," I urged myself, thankful for my long arms and legs. I'd always been a good rider, and my height worked in my favor now, giving me extra leverage to grasp around the stallion's big body.

If I could just balance on his back until he finally slowed his panicked pace, I could calm him down and lead him back to the village.

We continued to crash through the brush, the horse wildly sprinting through narrow openings in the thick trees. Fearful to lift my face and risk blinding myself with an errant branch, I peeked through his mane and tried in vain to keep track of what direction we were heading.

The jungle was dark, the canopy blotting out the sun overhead. Movement flickered all around us, but I couldn't see anything but green as we blurred through.

"How much farther is this river?" I thought desperately, the length of the ride a growing source of dread. A big horse like this could easily cover a few miles, even in these conditions. I considered rolling off his back, but knew my chances of survival out here, without the aid of the stallion to carry me back to the village, would be slim.

As I held on to the horse, my frightened mind raced. All those years of riding with Arnau had made me an excellent horsewoman, but to what end? For me to stupidly jump on a strange horse's back, halfway around the globe?

What if the horse bucked me off out here? One wrong toss could break my neck.

I didn't want to die. For the first time in my life, I had too much to live for.

"No," I cried aloud, suddenly panicked, pulling the stallion's mane to try to slow him.

Without warning, the horse skidded to a halt, the rapid change in course flinging me over his head. I didn't even have time to scream as I thudded painfully onto the ground.

I landed awkwardly on my neck as I flung out my arms to try to slow my stop. I lay facedown on the ground, the horse sprinting madly away from me.

"Come back!" I tried to scream, but he had already disappeared through the gloom. The sound of his thundering hooves was swallowed by the hum of the jungle.

"Thank God I'm still alive," I thought, as I tried to get up. It was a miracle.

Only, I couldn't get up.

"My body's just in shock," I told myself, forcing my hands to push me up off my stomach.

But I couldn't move.

I was paralyzed.

CHAPTER 66

I LAID ON THE GROUND, trying to make sense of what was happening to me. Fear swept through me as I tried, over and over again, to move.

"Calm down," I thought frantically, trying to slow my rapid breathing. *"You're in shock. You're fine. You just need to calm down."*

Cold logic seeped through my mind. *"You felt those branches slicing into your skin as you sprinted through the forest,"* it told me. *"You landed hard on your neck. You're paralyzed. That's why you can't feel your cuts right now. You can't feel the blood that must be trickling. You've broken your neck, Andi."*

I closed my eyes. "Count to ten," I whispered. "When you finish, you'll be able to stand up."

I counted.

One...two...three...

"My team will never be able to find me out here."

Four...five...

"I'm bleeding. I'll be easy for a wild animal to track and kill."

Six...

"I'll never see my mother and sister again. They'll never know what really happened to me. They won't even be able to find my body."

Seven...

"Arnau will live the rest of his life with guilt, knowing my arrogant attitude about horses got me killed, and he was to blame for teaching me to ride."

Eight...

"You're Chito's little girl, dying, all over again. How can you put him through this pain?"

Nine...

"Cap will never be the same. You've ruined his life."

Ten...

"Stand up, Andi."

I couldn't.

I lay with my face in the dirt, not feeling the ground against my cheek. I stared at the base of the trees surrounding me, ferns peeking out between thick branches.

These would be the last things I ever saw.

I was strangely calm. Everything was crystal clear, now that I lay here dying.

I saw my father and mother embracing, smiling at their love. I realized how his death had torn a hole in my heart, pushing me to step up as the man of the family. I understood how my mother let me be me, shielding me from criticism or reproof. She saw my hunger for adventure, and let me sail across the ocean, to boarding school, in search of it. I watched my little sister Evelyn grow into a proper young lady, and knew she'd live a conventional life, and be happy with it—one that I never could.

I saw myself through my school days, lanky and awkward. I spent time alone because the girls didn't know what to do with me and I didn't know how to open up to them. I'd wrapped myself in independence and loneliness in France, only letting Clara and Arnau get close to me. I'd pushed everyone away, except them, thinking no one could ever love me if they actually knew me. I shut out the entire world, by the time I got to my school in Nice.

I watched the friendship blossom between my crew and me. Chito taking me in as his surrogate daughter, Paz needing a real friend in his world of shallowness. Bernard valued the kindness I showed him, never treating him like the outsider he always felt he was.

And Cap.

Cap was the love of my life.

But I'd never be able to tell him that now.

I understood in this moment, finally, that Arnau's love was simple, like him. I could never be content with him, but I had built him up as my ideal man as I tried to understand, in my loneliness, who could ever love me. The despondence I'd felt as I learned about his marriage was out of embarrassment. It was an ache of losing an old friendship that bothered me, not heartache.

Cap had come along, and loved me from the start. He loved me just as I was, impulsive and stubborn and different from everyone else. He loved my courage, my intelligence, and my bluntness. He loved *me*.

Cap was swept away with the force of his feelings with me, and struggled to control himself for the sake of our team—for the sake of me. He knew I needed to stand on my own two feet and finish the expedition, as an equal to any man there. He knew that by confessing his love to me, I'd question if he'd brought me onto the Gallivanter team just because he was attracted to me.

He had hidden his heartbreak over my refusal to listen to him as he repeatedly tried to tell me how he felt without actually *telling* me he was in love with me.

He was hopelessly devoted to me, even as I lied about being engaged to Arnau and made plans to go home.

He'd held me to my word, forcing me not to give up on the team and go home. He held me to the dreams I was ready to walk away from. No matter how much I pushed him away, he fought to stay by my side.

It's the small actions, every day, that show where our hearts truly are, I realized. I had missed a thousand tiny declarations of his love, buried in the mundane. I'd been blind, looking for a single moment to pinpoint, a single instance to define it, when he'd already been living it out in every moment. He'd brought out the best in me. He'd brought out the *real* me.

And I loved him for all of this.

I loved *him*.

And I'd never be able to tell him.

I lay in the dirt, my body unresponsive. *"You dodged death once, when you drowned,"* I told myself. *"You can't escape it twice."*

"Try again," I argued with myself, praying that this time would be different.

I tried each of my arms, and both of my legs. I tried to move my head. I couldn't move. My eyes snapped shut in defeat. I was going to die out here.

With my eyes closed, I wondered how long it would take. Would an animal find me first, or would I slowly die of thirst? Would it be painful?

A single tear welled out of my eye, and slid down my nose. It tickled.

I stared at a beetle crawling on the ground underneath the bush.

Only this sole beetle would ever know what had happened to me here. Perhaps he would be the only witness as a pack of lions tore into me, violently ripping into my arteries and flesh while I lay here, helpless. *"At least I wouldn't be able to feel the pain,"* I thought desperately.

Another tear slid down my cheek, tickling on the way down.

Wait. It tickled.

I could *feel* it.

Was I imagining this? I forced myself to cry. It wasn't hard.

I could feel the tears cascading down, one after another.

Euphoric with relief, I struggled again with my face. Sure enough, I could feel the packed dirt beneath me. I tried over and over again to wriggle my fingers and toes. Slowly, the feeling was coming back and they were moving.

I still couldn't move my body, but my extremities were tingling. I lay on my stomach, pushing myself to keep working my muscles.

Elated by my progress, I was completely focused on myself until I noticed a slight movement across the clearing.

A large snake slithered silently, slowly, down the trunk of a tree across from me. It was brown and spotted, with a triangular head. Its tongue flicked out, smelling me.

I swiftly recalled a memory of my father showing me the body of a dead snake we found in the woods. He'd held my hand as I crept up to the snake on my little legs, teaching me to spot the difference from venomous snakes and harmless snakes.

"The easiest way to tell is to look at the head," he explained, turning the dead snake over with his shovel. "This here is a massasauga rattler. See how the head is shaped like a triangle? Their fangs lay flat in their mouths, but the venom sacks make their cheeks puff out like that. If you ever see a snake like that, don't mess with it. It's deadly."

I was bleeding. Were snakes attracted to blood? I had no idea.

Oh, the irony of this moment. I'd made fun of Rosie for sleeping in the Ford because she was afraid of snakes. I remembered Chito telling her that we'd never seen a single snake as we traveled. Now, I was about to be killed by one.

I watched it approach, its belly scraping dead leaves on the forest floor. It was heading right toward me.

Desperately, I wriggled my toes and hands. Maybe sudden movement would scare it away.

My efforts were too feeble. My hands twitched helplessly in the dirt, like a dying mouse.

I forced myself to remember Cap's face. His grin and the look he gave me through his goggles as we bounced along on the road. If

I was going to die now, I wanted him to be the last earthly thought I had.

I thought back to the romantic stories I'd read as a child. How unrealistic. The hero always swept in on his horse to save the damsel in distress from the brink of danger. I had no such hero. No one was coming to save me.

Words suddenly rang through my brain, as if someone was calling out to me. I remembered back to Chito sitting heavily on the foot of my bed in the hospital, speaking to me in the darkness.

"I don't know what to do," I had whispered to him.

"Yes you do," he whispered back to me. "You're going to fight. You're going to fight to save Andiamo Gallivanter."

I knew now. He was right. I was going to fight.

Andiamo Gallivanter was going to survive.

With herculean strength, I willed myself to move. My chest and head lurched up, and fell, hard, back to the ground. Again I lurched, this time crying out. "No!"

The snake flicked its tongue out and froze. For an endless moment, we stared at each other.

It flicked its tongue again, inching toward me. It was so close now that I could see the tiny scales on its pointy snout and its nostrils. It wove side-to-side, studying me with beady eyes.

I shoved myself up again, attempting to fire every muscle in my weak body. With a jolt, my legs spasmed as my torso lifted up off the ground and thudded back down, scattering dead leaves below me.

Scared by the sudden movement of the leaves and my body, the snake rapidly changed course and darted away from me, into the undergrowth.

Pushing again, I lifted off the ground enough to flop my left hand under me, pinning it down. Grunting, I used the leverage to roll myself over, sprawling out flat on my back.

I stared at the green canopy above me. The branches interwove with each other, creating a living mat of life high above me. Birds fluttered through the treetops, hopping from limb to limb, calling out their cheerful songs.

My legs and arms now prickled like I was being stung by millions of bees. I relished the sensation, knowing it meant that feeling was returning to my body. I wiggled my legs and arms spastically, urging myself to move.

I struggled to my side, pushing myself up so my torso leaned off the ground. My hand sunk into the damp, mossy soil underneath the weight of my body.

"This is not how my story ends," I told myself firmly. *"I'm going to make it."*

I thought of all the children in the world following my stories in the newspapers. I had to survive. If I didn't, I'd go from an inspiration to a cautionary tale. They'd never be allowed to live out their adventures.

I pictured the little girl who'd sent me her photograph, wearing her tiny boots and goggles. "I want to be just like you when I grow up," she'd written to me.

I pushed myself forward into a kneeling position, working slowly to drag my legs underneath me. Unsteady, I pushed myself up.

I stared around me as I stood still, flexing my legs. My neck ached, but I could finally move. I must have stunned my nerves, as I hit the ground after falling off of the stallion. I remembered the times in grade school when I'd had the wind knocked out of me and my body temporarily froze. Maybe this was something similar.

Either way, I didn't have time to dwell on it. I had to get moving.

My team would be searching for me.

CHAPTER 67

I SUCKED IN MY BREATH and turned, taking in the jungle. How would I possibly be able to get out of here? I had no idea where to start.

"Think, Andi," I said aloud. "You've spent most of your life reading and rereading adventure stories. What have you learned?"

Animals would naturally flock to the river, where I assumed the horse might be headed, but that would be dangerous for me. As Cap had pointed out, all sorts of animals used it as a watering hole, which meant I could encounter a deadly creature that wouldn't hesitate to attack me.

On top of that, the water could be full of crocodiles. Assuming I made it safely to the river bank and had to wade out into the water to avoid something that tried to attack me there, I might not see a crocodile hiding under the water until it was too late.

But without making my way to the river, I wouldn't know which direction to head back out of the woods.

I wracked my brain, trying to remember what Cap had told our crew as we sat around the campfire. I regretted all the times we'd listened only closely enough to tease him and interrupt with jokes. He had always prepared so diligently for each leg of the trip, but many of the facts he shared went in one ear and out the other. I had naively assumed that he would always be there with us, telling us where to go and what to do.

Now my life hung in the balance, and I couldn't remember which direction Cap had said the Senegal River flowed across French Sudan.

Was it east to west, or west to east? Or was it east to southeast?

I tried to think what my team would do. They'd follow me straight in, where the horse crashed into the jungle. But once the horse had entered the woods, he'd darted all over, panicked and dodging trees and stumps. He hadn't gone in a straight line.

Would they push through in a straight line, right for the river? Or would they spread out and look for me along the edge of the jungle?

Should I just stay here and wait?

Recalling the snake, I decided not to sit in one place too long. I'd mark that I'd been here, somehow, so if the team made it out this far—I doubted they could—they'd know they were on the right track.

Pulling my belt out slowly from my uniform, I held the large metal buckle in my right hand. I roamed slowly, looking for a large tree that would stand out. My eyes landed on a giant tree in the middle of a small clearing, ferns clustered around the base.

I grabbed a handful of sticks and tossed them hard into the clump of ferns, seeing if anything would slither out. I wrestled a larger stick off a nearby tree and poked around in the dense shrubbery, making sure I hadn't missed something. I didn't want to risk stepping on something poisonous.

Satisfied, I stepped into the green tendrils.

"Thank God that Cap made us all wear boots," I thought, as my foot sank into the ferns. They came up to my waist.

Using the corner of my belt buckle, I chopped at the thick wood until I caught an edge. Slowly, I pried off a large hunk of bark. Bugs and larvae scurried away under the surface as I pulled. I used my fingertips to clear smaller strips away, working until I had a two-foot wide bare spot, revealing the soft inner trunk.

I considered what to carve that would identify me. Slowly, I scratched out my initials at eye level. "A.G."

A small dart of fear stabbed me. *"Maybe you've just marked your own grave,"* it said.

I pushed it away. I had to keep moving. But which direction should I go?

I thought back to our campfire the last night, recalling which direction the sun set. It had set in the west. I'd purposely sat with my back to it to avoid the shafts of sunlight blinding me.

The next morning, we'd driven our cars west. We'd come upon the village, which backed up to the jungle. That meant that to get out of the jungle, I'd need to head due east, in a straight line.

The shade from the tall trees made it impossible to tell where the sun was shining. Without seeing the sunset, I couldn't decipher which way to go. I hung my head, defeated. I'd be walking blindly.

Staring at my feet, I saw that I stood on spongy moss.

"Can't I eat moss?" I thought. I tried to remember if I'd ever heard that before. I knelt down and pulled up wads of it, stuffing it in my jacket pockets until they were bulging. Even if I couldn't eat it, I could dry it out and use it for fire kindling later.

But there was something else about moss, wasn't there? It grew thicker on one side of the tree. The side that got more light.

I couldn't quite remember if it was the north or south side of a tree—it was different in the northern and southern hemispheres, I knew—but I realized at least I'd be able to head in the same direction consistently.

I heard rustling above me, and glimpsed monkeys hopping through the treetops. A mother monkey soaring across an open space, her tiny infant clinging tightly to her chest as they landed on a springy branch and dipped down.

Seeing the troop of monkeys frolicking together underscored the solitude I felt.

"You need to keep moving right now," I thought. *"Don't stop and drown in your emotions."*

To stop fighting out here would mean certain death. I had to press on, alone, through this jungle.

CHAPTER 68

I TRUDGED THROUGH THE thick jungle, pushing my damp hair out of my eyes and using a stick to press vines and leaves out of my way.

It was stiflingly hot. Sweat trickled down my back. I stopped and removed my thick jacket, tying the ends around my waist.

When I came to a fallen log, I carefully tapped the log first, then stepped on top of it and paused, making sure that the next tread down didn't land me on a hidden snake curled up in the shadows.

It was slow going as my eyes darted everywhere, looking for wildlife. Every hundred yards or so, I picked a dead branch off the ground and snapped it over my knee, shoving both ends into the ground right next to each other so they stuck up as a crude signpost. If I got turned around somehow, at least I'd know that I had already walked this path.

I hoped that the team would notice the branches sticking out of the ground, but I stopped to peel off the bark and carve my initials into a few other trees along the way, just in case.

"Hello?" I called out in English as I walked, and then switched to French. "Bonjour?"

I continued pressing forward, winding my way through the jungle. I walked without stopping, my body flushed and dripping sweat. I had to get out.

After a few hours, my mouth was so dry that it hurt. It felt like cotton had been wedged inside, soaking up all the liquid in my body. I had been looking for water, but hadn't come across any streams or rivers the entire time I'd been walking.

"I need to find water," I told myself, knowing I'd die without it. My body couldn't go on much longer, especially in this heat.

I leaned up against a tree, panting.

I knew I could either dig into the ground to try to find water, or I could try to find a plant to slice open and suck on. Unfortunately, it was a toss up. Should I dig, wasting my energy and not knowing how far I'd have to go to find water, or should I risk consuming a toxic plant and poisoning myself?

A memory floated down out of nowhere. I flashed back to a cold winter morning, sitting in the kitchen with my parents. My father sat at the table, his jacket thrown over the chair behind him, sipping coffee and reading the newspaper.

"Listen to this," he told us, and he read aloud an article about former President Teddy Roosevelt's account of his wild travels in Brazil, down the River of Doubt. Fevered and starving, Teddy and his crew of scientists and hunters survived only by catching fish and consuming hearts of palm.

"Why's it called the River of Doubt?" I asked in childish wonder.

"Because you doubt that you'll make it out alive, sweetie," he responded. "By Jove, I don't always agree with the man's politics, but there's no doubting that Teddy is quite the character."

I had no fish near me, but I could try to find some palms.

Leaning against a tree for support, I studied the area around me. The jungle was a sea of unfamiliar trees and plants. I wryly considered the irony that I'd ended up stranded in the woods, when we'd been traveling for so many months through barren desert.

I stepped forward, looking carefully at the vegetation. Ahead of me, I spotted a slender palm. I reached it, looking up as its leaves extended far above my head. I looked in vain for a smaller palm, but I couldn't see one.

My mouth was so dry that it hurt to suck in breath. My tongue had swollen. I needed water badly.

I crouched to the ground, and took a running leap at the tree, slamming against it hard with my shoulder. The tree didn't budge, but my shoulder ached. I backed up, and tried again, aiming for the top to try to bow it over and break the stalk.

I managed to pull a few leaves off, but the palm merely swayed back into place.

Again, I crashed into the tree with no success before sliding to the ground.

"Maybe I can use my belt for this," I thought. I held the heavy buckle in my hand and attacked the smooth trunk. I stabbed and shredded, but couldn't easily mash through the hard surface.

After several minutes of effort, the only headway I'd made was a fist-sized depression into the shaft of the tree. The interior was fibrous and pulpy. I put my mouth up to it, in desperation. It was faintly moist but not enough to wet my tongue.

I collapsed back from the tree, onto the ground. My head was swimming, and small insects buzzed around my face.

"And this is why no one lives out here in the jungle," I thought. At least I hadn't lost my sense of humor.

I knelt in the thick moss, panting. I looked down and remembered that I'd stuffed my pockets with moss to use as fire kindling. I wouldn't be needing to make a fire after all, as I doubted I could make it much longer without collapsing. The skin across my fingers was wrinkled, and my arms and legs were starting to cramp.

Comprehension slowly dawned on me as I looked at the moss.

I unwrapped the jacket from around my waist and tossed it on the ground. Carefully, I unbuttoned the cotton shirt I was wearing—now streaked with sweat and blood—and pulled it off.

I lay the shirt flat in the moss and pressed down on it with both hands. I leaned against it, hard, and waited. When I pulled it back up, I smiled.

It was damp.

I lay it back down on the moss, and leaned down so my elbows and arms balanced across the shirt. I pressed my entire body weight into the fabric, pushing deeper and deeper as I used my feet to shove me into the ground.

Exhausted, I flopped over on my back. I reached for the shirt and held it over my face.

It was soaked.

I twisted the fabric between my hands. As I squeezed it, the water dribbled into my mouth. It tasted faintly salty, from all the sweat, but it was the sweetest liquid I'd ever held on my tongue.

I wrung the fabric a second time, letting the droplets land on my tongue. Closing my mouth, I swished the water around. It didn't do much, but it was better than nothing.

I repeated the action of pushing my shirt down and soaking up liquid from the moss several times, wringing the droplets into my mouth, but it still wasn't enough water to hydrate my tired body.

I'd been sweating far more than normal, which meant I'd need more water to keep my brain sharp. I needed to stay alert out here.

I'd have to think of something else. Wearily, I pushed myself to my feet and dutifully carved my initials into the palm I'd mangled before moving forward.

In front of me lay a vast, thick carpet of ferns. They glistened with wetness. In the dark gloom of the canopies, the sunlight couldn't penetrate to dry out the droplets resting lightly on the curled tendrils. But how to collect it? I didn't have a cup.

I glanced around, looking at the plants around me. Could I fashion a drinking vessel out of a large leaf? As soon as I had the thought, I paused. What if I picked the wrong type of leaf, and accidentally poisoned myself? I knew nothing about the foliage out here.

"Well, let's try it again," I thought, kneeling to take off my damp shirt. *"It worked the first time."* Carefully, I tore the left sleeve, and then the right sleeve, from the cotton fabric. I put the armless shirt back on, and tied the jacket around my waist once more.

I stuck my leg out and wrapped the fabric of the left sleeve carefully above my boots, right below my knee. I did the same with my right sleeve, putting it on the opposite leg. I stood up and prayed that maybe I'd be able to collect more water this way.

Carefully, I tossed several sticks into the fern grove and waited to see if it would flush any snakes out. I watched and waited for a few moments, then waded in.

I marched through the ferns, wandering in circles. I could feel my pants start to get wet, then soaked, as I walked back and forth through the tall greenery.

After a few minutes, I stepped out. I peeled the wet sleeves off my shins, then stripped down out of my pants. Taking my time, I carefully squeezed the water from each sleeve, then my pant legs, into my mouth.

It wasn't pretty. Specks of dirt and bits of frond fluttered down onto my face. But it was life-giving liquid.

I put my wet pants back on and continued through the jungle.

CHAPTER 69

AS I WALKED THROUGH the jungle, I analyzed my wild ride on the stallion.

We'd crashed into the tree line, and though it felt like we went miles in the darkness, it was likely that we'd actually gone a much shorter distance. I was reasonably sure I was walking in a straight line, in the same direction. I'd been keeping track of the moss and putting the stick markers along the path behind me.

Sooner or later, I'd either come out of the jungle, into the edge of the fields, or arrive at the banks of the Senegal River. It all depended on which direction I'd originally headed.

Now that I'd been inside the woods for several hours, I was starting to walk wisely. I no longer startled at every rustle in the trees above me, and I was learning where to look for snakes. I'd seen several, draped lazily on low tree branches. It must have been sheer bad luck that the horse dumped me right at the base of a tree where a snake had undoubtedly been peacefully resting, until I rudely interrupted it.

My voice rang out through the trees, becoming more cracked as exhaustion caught up with me. "Bonjour? Hello? Is anyone out there? Help me!"

I fought against the urge to give up. My legs ached and cramped, my dehydrated body swollen with bug bites. Mosquitoes swarmed my field of vision.

"Just lay down," my brain kept whispering. *"You're never getting out of here. You know you're helplessly lost."*

I sat for a long time, watching the ants. I'd given up fighting the mosquitoes, and they landed indiscriminately all over my head and neck. I felt the itchy welts spring up on my exposed skin.

After I carved my name into the trunk of a tree, I stared up at the letters.

Inexplicably, I'd felt the urge to carve my entire name, as if I was responsible for making my own headstone.

Andiamo Gallivanter, 1923.

1923.

The year my dreams finally began to unfold, and the year I would die.

"Fight, Andi," I told myself.

How could I ever make it out of here? I was all alone. I had nothing. No supplies, no direction, no hope.

"Stop it. You will."

Even if I did make it out, by some miracle, what about the rest of my crew? They'd surely gone in themselves to rescue me. What if they all died? The blame would be mine.

"You need to fight. It won't be easy. It will never be easy. But you need to save yourself, Andi."

I stood, sheer determination forcing me to my feet. I wasn't sure how long my moment of despair had stretched, but I noticed that the noises around me in the forest had changed.

Nightfall was upon us. Birds had ceased their movements, and soft hoots and insect calls were becoming bolder and more desperate as the wildlife sang their symphony around me.

Now I faced a challenging choice. I could try to sleep out here in the jungle, or continue pushing through the night to try to find my way out.

I was keenly aware that my strength was depleted from the hard work of the day. I had sweated profusely as I pushed through the jungle slowly and carved my name into trees and searched for water.

If I became overly tired, my brain could start to make poor judgment calls. I had to rest, at least for a short time.

"Where, Andi?" I asked myself, glancing around. The day had revealed a whole host of alarming bugs, snakes, and spiders that could easily get to me if I lay on the ground, zonked out.

Could I build a hammock of some sort? I pondered the question, looking around for vines and considering what I had on me. I cursed myself for the umpteenth time for hopping on the stallion without wearing my goggles or aviator cap. At least my face could have been protected overnight.

"Oh, to have access to the Fords, where we had matches and rope and supplies," I thought.

How much time would it take to try to build a hammock? And where could I suspend it? I'd have to gather all the vines and teach myself to weave, and then try to find a safe place to hang it. It could take hours.

I didn't have that much time.

I'd noticed snakes draped on tree branches as I'd walked through the woods. Some of the snakes were alarmingly large, too. I couldn't imagine how I could safely sleep up a tree. Did snakes hunt at night? I knew scorpions did. I wasn't sure, and I didn't want to find out the hard way.

What else could I do? I wracked my brain.

"I needed to stay off the ground. I couldn't climb a tree and I couldn't make a hammock," I thought. *"But what if I was somehow suspended between trees, off the ground?"*

Turning, I searched for trees that were clumped together in bunches. I noticed a gathering of young trees with low branches, only two feet or so off the ground, and spaced close enough together that I could balance some longer branches against them.

I carefully studied the trees to make sure they were free of snakes. Thankfully, they were.

I untied one of my sleeves from the top of my boot, where I'd left it on to occasionally squeeze water out onto my parched tongue, and tied the sleeve to the grove of trees to mark it.

Next, I went on the hunt for several long, straight branches that would be thick enough to support my body weight. Frowning, I realized the branches would need to be extra long to support my lanky frame.

"Hurry, Andi," my brain urged. I was losing what little light I had in the gloomy jungle as twilight fell.

Small noises scuttled in the brush as I searched quickly for what I needed. I didn't manage to find the ideal branches, but I grabbed what was good enough and scurried back quickly to the spot I'd marked in the grove of trees.

Working rapidly, I laid four branches across the low limbs in the trees—two vertically, and two horizontally—making crosspieces for a crude bed frame. I considered trying to lash them to the tree with torn pieces of my uniform, to give me some extra stabilization, but I realized that I'd need to keep my uniform on as I slept, and cover my face with my jacket to protect me from bugs overnight. I couldn't tear my jacket or pants to pieces.

Carefully, I placed the next four branches across the bed frame I'd just made in the short trees. I spaced the four branches equally apart, hoping that would be enough to evenly distribute my weight as I climbed into it.

I tested it, laying my hands on top and pressing down.

The branches wobbled but held firm. But how would I possibly climb into this now? If I jumped up, the branches would likely slip and I'd end up sprawled on the ground.

Looking around, I had a sudden stroke of genius. If I could find some sort of fallen tree or log, I'd be able to drag it over and climb on top of that, then carefully lower myself onto the bed.

I searched the forest floor, discovering a long-dead trunk that I could use. Kicking it, I watched bugs stream out from underneath.

I kicked again, and a large centipede scurried across the top. Impatiently, I kicked hard and watched the whole thing lurch over like a dead animal. The underside was soft and mushy, and beetles raced in and out of the bark as I kicked violently, slowly rolling the log over to the grove of trees where I'd made my bed.

The log thudded softly into place under one side of my crude stick bed. *"Just in the nick of time,"* I told myself, looking up at the sky. The sun had already set, and the forest was dark. I could hear the sound of bats swooping through the trees and chirping in their weird, garbled low tones.

Without hesitation, I climbed onto the log and braced myself against the tree bark. Gently, I lowered myself down onto the bed like I was sitting down in a chair. It held steady until I attempted to lay back.

I crashed onto the ground, hard, as the sticks gave away. I swore out loud.

"Of course I need more sticks," I told myself bitterly. *"We wouldn't want anything to be easy, right?"*

I rebuilt the rudimentary bed frame again, quickly, then searched for more sticks to balance across like bed slats. I needed to distribute the weight of my body more evenly, across more surface. Within a few minutes, I had seven more straight sticks, and I hurried back to my campsite.

This time, I laid all eleven sticks across. I pressed both hands down to test the sturdiness. It was better. It should work.

I swatted at the mosquitoes bombarding me, and remembered what I'd read in the school library once, as I was researching on a rainy day when I couldn't go down to the barn. I'd been flipping through a book on Africa, and I stopped at an amusing illustration of a rhinoceros rolling in a patch of mud, like a troublesome dog rolling in animal dung.

The caption explained how the rhinos rolled in mud to protect their hides from sunburn and parasites.

"Rhinos roll in mud to protect themselves from bugs," I mused. Maybe that could help me, too. I stooped down and dug into the ground a few inches. Ants scurried over my hand as I scooped up a handful of the dark dirt. I rubbed it over my exposed arms and neck and hands, packing it on as thickly as I could.

I wriggled out of my jacket, and draped it over my head like a monk's hood. Climbing up again onto the log, I braced myself and gently sat down in the center of the bed.

It held.

I felt like screaming my joy, but I was too tired. I eased my body down against the hard branches, feeling them dig into my shoulders and hips. Once I was completely prone, I pulled my jacket down and tucked it around my head, pulling it as tight as I could. The interior lining was sweaty and stifled me with its heat, but I didn't want bugs crawling on my face while I slept.

I was so thirsty.

"You should've made a fire, though," my brain whispered as exhaustion took possession of my weary body. *"Fire is the only thing that will protect you from wild animals overnight."*

It was too late.

I was already asleep.

CHAPTER 70

I SLEPT FITFULLY, JOLTING awake more times than I could count.

Each time, my eyes peered into the darkness, trying to discern what had woken me up. My heart raced as I lay still, straining to listen. The sticks under me dug into my exhausted body, but I didn't care.

I heard rustling in the trees around me and above me, the sounds of small creatures scurrying through bushes and dead leaves, but I didn't hear the tread of anything large.

When the first light of dawn started peeking through the trees overhead, I was already awake. I'd never felt more full of wonder than I had in that moment.

I'd survived a night in the jungle. Alone. With no supplies.

The simple joy of living was an overwhelming emotion.

I slid out of my homemade bed, the branches tumbling to the forest floor. I considered carrying them with me, in case I needed to build another bed tonight, but they were too heavy to carry without using up what little energy I already had, from lack of food and water.

"I better make it out today," I said aloud to the cawing birds in the trees above my head.

My stomach felt hollow as I trekked through the forest. Yesterday, I'd felt pangs of hunger as I went all day without eating. But today it didn't hurt, it just felt empty.

I passed the time by remembering the meals I'd enjoyed. My mother's apple pie, spiced to perfection. The savory dishes they served at boarding school, piled high with steaming cheeses and decadent sauces. Salty paella. Crusty bread.

Walking slowly, I thought about rice and beans. Even Chito's simple campfire staple sounded intoxicating to me right now. In desperation, I tried to remember what coffee smelled like and how it tasted on my tongue.

Suddenly, through the trees, I saw sand.

I froze and blinked. Was I imagining this? Did I have an infected bug bite that was making me hallucinate?

I stepped forward, hesitating. And then I ran. I scrambled through the edge of the forest into the open desert. I blinked in the bright sunlight, a shock after so many hours under the dark canopy of the trees. I could see mountains in the distance.

My heart swelled with hope. I could make it. I was going to live.

Scanning the horizon slowly, I saw no signs of life. No dwellings, no people, no sheep or horses. But surely my team would be driving the edge of the woods, looking for me.

"Hello?" I cried, cupping my hands around my mouth. "Bonjour? Hello?"

I looked down. Tire treads were visible in the sand, scissored one direction and then the other. My team had indeed been here, driving back and forth along the edge, looking for me.

I knelt and checked the direction of the tire tread. It appeared that they'd driven first to the right of me, and then crossed back over their original treads to head back to the left. If I had to guess, they'd started driving farther up the road. They had cruised down along the edge, looking for me, then turned around after a few miles.

I started walking to the left of where I'd come out of the jungle. The wind across the open plain whipped through my hair, lifting it from where it stuck against my neck. I tried to stay in the shadow of the trees, at the very edge of the woods, to protect myself from the harsh glare of the sun.

I was already weakened from lack of food and water. I didn't want to pass out now that I was this close to finding my crew.

The walk was much longer than I thought. Somehow, I'd tricked myself into thinking that Cap and Chito and Bernard would be sitting in their Fords, just around the corner, and I'd gleefully run into their arms and tell them the whole story, after I first drank a gallon of water.

My steps melted into an endless refrain. Left foot, right foot. Left foot, right foot. I was tired in my very soul.

Still, I pressed on. "Hello?" I yelled, my voice cracking. "Bonjour?"

Rounding the corner, I saw a stunning vista in front of me. Mountains lifted softly out of the dunes, miles in the distance. The morning sun lit the vast swath of desert in front of me to an almost blinding white. I held my hand to my forehead and peered across the view, slowly.

Almost as if in a dream, I saw the outline of huts and animals in the distance. It was so far away that I could barely make it out, but it was there.

It was the village.

I nearly dropped to my knees in shock. My parched mouth wheezed out a prayer of gratitude. I'd made it back.

Studying the tree line, I counted how many dips the forest took, obscuring sight of the village, before leading me to its edge. It appeared that there were about a dozen blind spots between me and the buildings, which meant my team could be standing on the hood of their automobiles, peering through binoculars, and they could still miss seeing me as I walked in a low spot, hidden along the edge of this winding jungle.

"You're almost to them," I told myself, gritting my teeth. *"A few more steps. You're nearly there."*

I counted aloud as I hiked through the blind spots. The fifth spot was particularly deep, and as I came to the far edge I pulled up short, stunned.

Cap's empty car was parked at the edge.

I stumbled through the sand, scrambling down the small rise, and threw myself against the hood. I hugged the engine like I was embracing a soldier who'd come home from war.

It was cold. The engine had been off for quite some time.

Running my hands along the metal, I went straight to the back of the trunk. I never loved Chito more than I did in that moment, as I cracked open the crate that held extra water. It was warm from sitting out in the sun, but I didn't care.

I tipped open a container of water and greedily guzzled. I knew there was some sort of guideline about drinking water slowly when you were dehydrated, but I couldn't control myself. Water rained down my face, wetting my neck and shirt.

Suddenly, my stomach constricted and I gagged. Clutching the side of the car, I vomited into the back seat.

"Well, I knew there was some rule," I thought, wiping my face with the back of my hand and taking another sip of water to swish out my mouth. *"Apparently that's why."*

I set the container of water in the front seat, and went back to the trunk again to search for food. Chito had pounds of dry rice and beans and seasoning neatly organized in one crate. I pried off the top of another crate. Inside, next to the canisters of tea, I found a few tins of canned meat that Chito rotated into our rice and beans, giving our meals variety.

I opened the can, not bothering to dig out the silverware. I carried the can to the door of the Ford and slid in. Hungrily, I used my fingers to spoon out chunks of the canned meat. I devoured a few bites, but once more my stomach lurched. Frowning, I set the can aside and tried not to throw up again.

"I could make it two for two," I thought, waiting for the nausea to pass as I clutched my empty stomach. *"I could ruin both the front and back seats."*

As I sat there, queasy, I looked around the car. Cap had left the keys in it.

Should I drive to the village and tell them that I had made it out, and then drive back to pick up Cap?

No, I decided. Cap might come out at any moment and then he'd be stranded out here, too. Even worse, he might think he'd come out at the wrong spot and turn around to go back into the jungle.

"Cap?" I called out, hoping he was near. I heard nothing except the sounds of the jungle in front of me. I rose to my knees on the driver's seat, and cupped my hands around my mouth.

"Cap! I'm here! Cap! Hello!"

I listened for a response, but heard nothing.

Still kneeling, I leaned into the horn. It blared loudly, startling a colorful bird at the edge of the clearing.

I honked repeatedly, using morse code. I beeped a pattern of distress, hoping someone in the distance might notice it and listen. As I took a break from honking, I stood up and yelled.

Still, I heard nothing. I remembered how muffled it had been in the forest, the buzzing insects and foliage blocking all outside sounds. *"He may not be able to hear me even if he's fairly close,"* I realized.

I alternated between taking small sips of water and nibbles of canned meat. My strength was returning, and my mind felt sharper. I knew I'd need to make a fire—not only to signal to people for miles that I was here, but to keep animals away at night.

Our trunk was loaded with wooden crates and boxes. Knowing Chito, he'd squirreled a supply of matches away in here somewhere. I opened several boxes before finding a box of matches. I tossed the matches out into the sand, and proceeded to tear apart the crates to use as firewood. I had no desire to go back into the woods to look for sticks, which were sure to be damp anyway. I carried the wood over several feet away from the car, and swiftly laid the wood out.

"Kids who grew up in cold places can build a fire faster than anyone else in the world," I thought to myself, grinning. I retrieved the dried moss from my jacket pockets and stuffed it in between the wood, watching it curl up and burn.

Once I'd made the fire and the smoke was lazily drifting up in a large column, I plopped back in the driver's seat. I honked again, hoping to hear Cap's voice in return.

I didn't.

Now I regretted my choice to stay and wait here. I could tell by where the sun moved in the sky that it had been several hours since I'd found the empty Ford. As we approached evening, I was worrying that Cap might get stranded in the jungle overnight.

I should've gone for help already.

Where were Bernard and Chito? Why hadn't they come to find us? Did they go into the jungle, too?

The sun was low in the sky now. I was getting antsy.

Biting my lip, I made the decision.

I was going in after Cap.

CHAPTER 71

I POPPED OUT OF THE car and ran back to the supplies, thinking fast.

If I was going back into the jungle to search for Cap, I needed to utilize whatever I could find to try to save us both.

"It's getting dark," I thought, frowning. *"Can I make a torch?"*

Quickly, I pulled out the heavy bags of rice and upended them in the trunk. Rice cascaded down, pooling at my feet. I dumped it all out, and then shook the cloth bags.

I tore the bags into smaller strips and tied them all together, making one long continuous strip of fabric that was several feet long.

I looked for a wooden slat in the firewood pile, and chose a long piece. Laying it in the sand, I carried the fabric strip over and tied it tightly to one end of the slat. I grabbed the slat and fabric and darted to the front of the Ford.

Lifting the bench seat and unscrewing the top of the gas tank, I slowly dipped the fabric in to saturate it with gasoline.

While the fabric soaked, I jogged to the edge of the woods, looking for a young sapling. I searched until I found a young tree, about my height. I grasped the thickest branch with both hands, twisting until it came off. The interior was green and moist.

I smiled. "Perfect," I said.

I carried the branch back to the front of the Ford, and removed the wet fabric from the gas tank. Carefully, I wrapped the wet fabric around the branch, making a thick bundle. My hands were slick with gas, but I wiped them off with satisfaction as I lit my crude torch in the fire. It blazed to life.

I stuffed my pockets with matches, a can of meat, and a canister of water. They weighed me down, but after the time I'd spent in the jungle, I didn't want to risk getting stranded again without them.

As I turned to head into the jungle, I stopped to select a wooden slat that had nails sticking out of one end. *"This will do as a weapon,"* I thought.

The sun threw its last rays over me as I pushed through the dark curtain and back into the jungle.

"Cap!" I yelled as I held the burning torch in front of me, hoping he'd see it. "Hello! Are you in there?"

I didn't want to be in here again.

But Cap was in here, somewhere, still looking for me. He hadn't given up on me yet. I wouldn't give up on him.

"Cap!" I screamed, walking forward, the torch making me bolder than I had been when I walked through by myself.

Every few yards, I slowed and purposely used my torch to singe tree trunks as I walked. I had to be able to find my way out again.

The gloom of the forest darkened around me. I continued walking. I watched the shift of the light above the canopy of trees closely, calculating that I'd been walking for over an hour. I pressed on, sure that eventually Cap would hear my voice and respond. How far could he have gone? Could he possibly have gone so far that he couldn't hear me yelling?

Vines dangled across my path as I trudged. The torch was still burning, but its light cast weird shadows across the clearing.

I pushed through the gloom, yelling.

"Please, Cap!" I screamed, feeling fear prickling uneasily at me. I babbled out loud, trying to overcome the uncomfortable emotion. "Tell me you're here! I know you went out into this jungle to look for me! I'm here, Cap! Please, come find me! Where are you?"

The hairs on the back of my neck rose inexplicably. There was danger here.

"After all this," I yelled aloud in the darkness. "After all that I've faced out here, you will not get the best of me! You won't beat me!"

I whirled around, holding my torch up. I was angry, even in my fear.

I thought back to the moment Cap and I first talked, as he'd slipped out from the back of the theater. I was elated when he chose me to be a member of the team. It was if he'd suddenly pulled me out of a drab black and white photograph into a vibrant life, one teeming with excitement.

We'd only just begun our expedition around the world.

This wasn't fair.

Cap had spent years preparing for this journey. I'd thrown my heart and soul into it, too. How could we not get to complete it?

Rage broke over me unexpectedly, and I gave in. I'd worked hard to control my emotions for the last two days, struggling to survive, and I was at my breaking point.

Giving in to my fury, I screamed my frustration nonsensically at the forest.

"Let me go on! We're going to make it! It's not fair! We aren't done yet!"

Without warning, I swung the wooden weapon in my hand against a tree and roared. I was angrier than I'd ever been. How could this be happening? How had we ended up here?

All of a sudden, everything was happening at once.

I heard a crash coming from the bushes near me as a voice screamed out, startling me.

"Andi! Run!"

Something massive thundered away from me, sprinting deeper into the woods. I froze, shocked, as Cap tumbled down from a tree and screamed at me.

"Leopard!" he screamed. "Look out! Leopard!"

Cap collapsed onto the ground, and sprinted toward me, his eyes wild. "There's a leopard!" he screamed, throwing himself painfully against me. The force of his body colliding into mine nearly knocked me off my feet. My wooden weapon went flying into the brush.

Frantically, he clutched me close. Our bodies scrabbled together, a tangle of limbs and legs, as we righted ourselves, my back against his.

"He's out there, where is he?" he screamed, brandishing his knife. Panicked, we spun in the clearing, our backs pressed against each other, our chests heaving with adrenaline.

"Shoot it!" I screamed, brandishing the torch in front of me, desperately trying to see the big cat out in the gloom.

"I can't!" Cap yelled behind me, pushing against me with his broad shoulders.

"What's going on?" I cried, my eyes searching the darkness for a glimmer of animal eyes.

"A leopard had me cornered," Cap shouted. I could feel every muscle of his back against mine, tense and alert. "He had me up a tree!"

I whipped the torch around as we continued to spin, our backs against each other. The sweat from his back soaked into my own shirt.

"I heard him rush by me, into those bushes," I swung the torch. "I think he ran off. Or would he be waiting to attack us both?"

"I don't know!" Cap cried, gripping his knife. "How would I possibly know what he's going to do? He's a wild animal!"

"Was it just one?"

"*Just* one?"

"Where's your gun?" I shouted frantically. "Do they travel in packs?"

"How the hell do I know?" Cap yelled, frustration evident in his voice. "I'm not an expert in everything!"

We continued to circle, standing back to back, straining to see in the darkness. My nerves had never felt so electrified.

"Do you hear him? Do you hear anything moving?" Cap cried, pressed against me so hard that I could feel the vibrations from his shouts. We listened. I could barely hear past the rushing sound in my own head and Cap's ragged breathing behind me.

"I don't hear anything," I said, lowering my torch cautiously. "Do you?"

I felt Cap's back flex, and he abruptly dropped his shoulders and stepped away from me. I spun around.

"What?"

Cap stared at me, his eyes big. "I—I have to," he blurted.

Out of nowhere, he pulled me to his chest and kissed me passionately.

CHAPTER 72

WE HUNGRILY INTERLOCKED our lips. For a brief moment, there was only us.

As we kissed, I knew that this was the moment that changed both of our lives forever. We'd crossed the line now, sweeping aside all of our professionalism. All our excuses. Our past.

We were two independent people who had never needed anybody else before—and now, as we embraced each other, we admitted that we *did* need someone: each other.

We'd both known it and fought it for months. And now, our bodies enfolded, we admitted it to each other.

The reality we were still in danger crashed over us like a wave, and we simultaneously pushed apart.

"Not right now!" I yelled, clutching his shoulder as we both stood alert, staring out into the dark jungle.

Cap groaned. "I swear, the timing is never right for us!"

We again stood back to back, listening to the jungle around us.

"This is us," I thought to myself, my back tight against his. *"Two fighters, evenly matched, ready to battle our way through anything in front of us. Weapons drawn against the world. This is the man I've needed my whole life. A man addicted to adventure, like me. A man who will fight—for me, against me, and next to me. A man who will let me join the fight, trusting the strength I know I have. A man who never asked me to prove myself to him, because he already knows my capabilities."*

After a few moments of hearing nothing but the hooting sounds of night creatures stirring in the darkness, we saw nothing. I let out a breath I hadn't realized I'd been holding.

"Do you think it's still there, watching us and waiting?" I cried, adrenaline still coursing through my veins. "They wait and hunt by stalking, don't they?"

"Leopards are notoriously elusive," Cap responded cautiously, still alert to the small noises we heard around us. "They're territorial, but they're lone hunters. This one was stalking me. By myself, with a lame leg, I was easy prey. But I have a feeling that you showing up suddenly tipped the balance."

"The torch," I said, staring at the burning rags.

"Well, the torch and the woman holding it, who just crashed in out of nowhere and screamed like a maniac. I think he's probably long gone by now, but we shouldn't let our guard down."

"Where's your rifle?"

Cap rolled his eyes and swore. "The chief took it. He said he wouldn't go into the jungle to help us unless he had one, too. Bernard had the other one, so I tossed him mine and took off. I didn't have time to argue. We had to find you."

"No rifle? We're sitting ducks, here," I pointed out. "Let's get out of here."

"Don't you think that's what I've been trying to do already?"

For the first time in days, I smiled.

"I know the way out," I replied. "I marked it as I came back in here to find you. Come on. You can tell me what happened while we walk."

"Oh, me first? Sure, I'll tell you the whole story," he said, limping next to me as we pushed through the trees. "You went crashing into the woods, and you sucked the life out of me right then and there. I doubt you noticed, but I'd gone running after you and that damn horse. I followed you in, but I couldn't keep up. That thing carried you off, changing directions as it ran. I've never seen anything like it from a horse—I swear it was possessed."

He glanced at me, and interrupted his own story. "Are you hurt? Your clothing is all torn up. He must've crashed you through the brush pretty painfully."

"No, not really," I responded. "Cuts and bruises, but I'll live. Are you?"

"No," he shook his head. "Anyway, I ran after you, but it was like you fell off the face of the earth. I yelled and yelled, but I didn't know if you were a mile away or five miles away, with how fast that horse was going. I ended up running back out, to the village. Chito and Bernard already had the cars pulled up. They were screaming for you, too."

He laughed ruefully.

"Bernard apparently put a rifle up to that chief's head and demanded that they organize a search party. The chief resisted, and said that to go into the jungle was against their spiritual beliefs," Cap grinned. "I guess Bernard didn't take that too well, because he cocked the trigger and coolly told him he'd be happy to blow his head off, and that he had plenty more bullets for the rest of the group."

I smiled. Good for Bernard.

"Well, that right there convinced the chief to rethink his position. He agreed to help, but on one condition—he got my rifle," Cap continued. "I suppose he wanted to be able to keep Bernard at bay. I was so desperate I could barely think straight, so I just handed it to him and took off. The men organized themselves and headed in after you. We looked all day, but none of us knew where you were."

He stopped suddenly and grabbed for my hand.

"You're alive, Andi," he said, squeezing my fingers. "You're *alive*. I can't believe it! You're here!"

I laughed. "I am. And I'm not going anywhere."

"I thought you were dead," his voice cracked. "For the second time," he added.

"You know what they say about the third time."

We continued pushing through the darkness together, following the singed trees that I'd marked on the way in. Cap resumed his story.

"The men all looked, but we had split opinions on where we thought you'd go," he said. "Chito and the villagers thought you'd go to the river, and wait for us there. Bernard and I thought you'd fight your way through the jungle, to try to get back to us."

"Half the group went down to the river, Chito with them. Apparently those liars do go into the jungle, because there's a game path they follow to get there when they need to fish. They carried boats down. We agreed to search until nightfall tonight—Bernard and me looking in the jungle, aided by our Fords, and Chito and the men paddling the river."

"I never went toward the river," I said. "It's—"

"Too dangerous," he finished for me. "Yeah, I know."

"But really, isn't that a toss up at this point?" I said, looking around us. "You saw a leopard?"

"Right, let me get to that. So Bernard and I were looking for you, together, but this morning we decided to split up to cover more ground. He went north, I went south. We planned to meet back at the village at nightfall. I gave him my compass, but that meant I was wandering around out here, directionless. I got lost."

Cap absently fished for my hand and held it. I smiled into the darkness, feeling his fingers clutch mine.

"As it got later in the day, around dusk, I started to get an odd feeling. Somehow, I felt that something was watching me. Like I was being stalked. I was moving quickly, looking for you and calling out, but I'd suddenly get a feeling something was there, just beyond the shadows, waiting for the right moment."

I interlaced my fingers between his, silently prodding him to go on. We trudged through the jungle, the sounds of insects filling our ears.

"I couldn't shake the feeling of being watched," he said. "I intentionally doubled back at one point, as I crossed an area of dirt, and there I saw it: a large paw print. A leopard."

I inhaled, biting my lip.

"I knew I couldn't outrun an animal, with my bad leg. I decided my best course of action was to climb a tree and wait. I'd be able to see him coming, and I could drop down and skewer him. I only had my knife, remember? I climbed up a tree and waited, looking out into the woods. Sure enough, as I stared into the gloom, I could see the faint reflection of eyes staring back at me. We both stared at each other, watching."

I shuddered. His hand squeezed mine again.

"Eventually, I could hear you yelling in the distance, but I didn't want to spook the animal by responding. I was petrified, too, that if I called out you'd run right toward me—right into the path of the leopard. I listened with dread as your shouting got closer and closer. I felt like fate was drawing you toward me."

"I scared him away, didn't I?" I said, realizing what had happened. "All my screaming. The torch."

"Yeah, that and the fact that you crashed through the forest like a herd of wildebeests," he said, smiling at me. "It sounded like an army coming through. Sometimes I forget how lucky we are that you dive impulsively into things. But, here we are now. You're all caught up."

"Who gets the credit for this one, huh?" I asked.

"What?"

"You've saved me, and I've saved you. Who gets the credit for this one?"

"Does it really matter who saved who?" Cap laughed. "We saved each other this time."

I smiled. "We'll call it even, then."

Abruptly, Cap stopped and stared at me. "I need to say this, Andi. I can't keep it in anymore. You have no idea how many times I've regretted not telling you."

He took a deep breath. "That day I saw you go under the water? When we pulled you in and you lay there lifeless, not breathing—it was like I had just died, too. I already knew I loved you, but seeing you there on the ground in front of me? It broke me."

"I know," I replied, smiling at him. "You kissed me right after. You held me. You wouldn't let me go. At first, I thought you'd just been swept up with emotion. But now I see that it was more."

"Oh, I couldn't contain myself," he blurted out. "I knew I should keep it together, that you probably had a boyfriend, that we hadn't known each other long enough, that it was the very beginning of a *very* long trip if you said no to me. None of it mattered. I would have proposed right then and there, if it hadn't been for Chito glaring at me. He's protective of you, you know."

"Hold on," I froze, staring at him. "Proposed?"

He stared back, caught by his blunder. His eyes widened as he inhaled sharply through his nose. For a long moment, we gazed at each other. Then slowly, a smile tugged at his mouth. "Yes."

We looked at each other silently for a long moment. Cap squirmed. "Andi, I—sorry, no. Edi. Let me do this right. Edi—Edith—"

I interrupted him, holding up my hand. "Wait."

"What?"

"Why are you calling me Edith now, all of a sudden? You always call me Andi."

"It's your name. Your real name. And this is an important moment."

"Do you want me to start calling you Walenty?"

"Well...fine. Cap and Andi it is, then."

He paused and looked at me, his eyes reflecting the torch light that was slowly sputtering.

"Andi, I love you. I have always loved you, from the first moment. You may think that Arnau knew you better than anyone on earth, but that's not true. I do. I've spent every waking hour with you these last few months, at your side. I've seen you stretch and grow. I've seen the light in your eyes when you discover something new, when you see something that enchants you. I've heard your laugh, a thousand times, and tried to understand just what it is that brings it to your lips. I've been there with you, at your side, through the highs and lows. When you've let your guard down."

His face was tender as he looked at me. "Together, we're never alone. No one else can ever share the bond that we've had. It's not just a bond of companionship or childhood affection. No. Together, we've fought—and we've won."

He smiled so wide that his eyes crinkled. "I have always known it would be you. Always, from the very beginning. Will you—"

"Yes."

His mouth was on mine, kissing me. We came up for air, and he pretended to pout as he cradled my face in his hands.

"You didn't even let me finish my question," he exclaimed. "Did you even know whether I was asking you to marry me, or asking you to finish the expedition with me?"

"It doesn't matter," I replied, smiling up at him. "Yes to both."

CHAPTER 73

FOR A FEW PRECIOUS minutes, the world around us didn't matter. Cap and I embraced each other, the joy of our love, finally spoken aloud, mingled with the raw elation of surviving a terrible danger.

We'd survived. *We*, Cap and Andi, had survived. The moment was electric.

But we were explorers, first and foremost. We had a job to do.

Reluctantly, we pulled apart to discuss our options. We knew we'd have to keep fighting to make it out of the forest and back to the Ford. Our chances of survival out here in the darkness were better now that there were two of us and we both had supplies, but neither one of us wanted to camp out here overnight.

We continued to push our way through the forest, following my trail, moving slowly.

I told Cap about the fire I'd made, which should still be burning—or at least smoldering—and how it should be a beacon to us with its glow as we moved through the black night.

"How'd you stay hydrated out here?" I asked, looking at Cap. I still had my container of water and can of meat, but he didn't seem to have anything on him. Though it was nighttime, it was still hot. Sweat rolled down both of our faces.

He laughed and fished a flask from his jacket pocket. He rattled it, and I heard the liquid sloshing inside.

"It's full of water," he said. "I took small sips as I walked."

"How long have you had that?" I asked. Cap rarely drank alcohol.

"Rosie gave it to me. She brought it with her, in one of her suitcases."

"Oh, jeepers. She was gunning for you hard, Cap. I'm sure you were the ideal man, in her eyes. Young, handsome, intelligent..."

"I never had any interest in her, you know."

"No way," I thought of Rosie's beauty and shook my head. "She's probably the most gorgeous girl I've ever seen."

"So?"

"So? No guy can resist that. You'd have to be blind not to see it. Paz certainly saw it."

Cap shoved the flask back into his jacket pocket and grinned at me.

"That's not what I want in a woman, you know. Give me a woman who's smart, driven, and not afraid to be herself. That's the most beautiful thing about any girl. I've always wanted someone who'll be there for me, but who'll also be willing to stand back-to-back and fight with me. And that's you, Andi. It's always been you and me, in my mind. No question."

He paused, and glanced over at me, smiling. "Do you remember what I told you when we first met? After our very first press conference? I told the reporters that you were the lady of every man's dreams, and you argued with me afterwards. Remember what I told you?"

I thought back, absently pushing a long trailing vine out from in front of me. "You told me it didn't matter if I was the woman of every man's dreams. That it mattered instead that I live my own dreams."

"Right," Cap said as we climbed over a large fallen tree, our boots thudding through the leaves carpeting the forest floor. "Well, you're the woman of *my* dreams. I knew it, even then."

I laughed as he added, "Besides, Rosie took three suitcases with her. Three! Who needs that much luggage?"

The sounds of the jungle at night seemed friendlier tonight, as we walked through it hand-in-hand. Monkeys howled in the treetops, and a symphony of bugs sang their rhythms as we listened. The trees swayed, their leaves rubbing together.

We pushed through another thick curtain of vines, and I glimpsed a tiny shimmer of orange through the foliage. I pointed, and my heart swelled with joy.

"There," I said. "The fire."

We pushed forward through the vines, the fire a welcome beacon in the darkness. Soon, I could see the faint openness of the desert beyond the darkness of the trees. We heard the crackle of the wood being licked by the flames.

Shoving our way through the last of the jungle gloom, we stepped out into sand.

We'd made it.

Simultaneously, we fell to our knees, overcome. We clutched each other wordlessly and embraced for an endless, perfect, moment.

Someone coughed.

"Well, it's about time," Bernard grunted.

We rose, Cap's arms still around me.

"Bernard!" I cried, darting out of Cap's arms and running to him. He sat in his Ford, which he'd parked on the other side of the fire. He must've tended the fire while we were gone, because it was even bigger than it had been when I left it.

He slid out of the car and hugged me hard. Even without words, I felt the affection in his fierce grip.

"Bernard! I'm so glad you're here!"

He grinned at me, patting me awkwardly on the head. He had to reach up to do it, because I was taller than him.

"I'm glad you're here, too, Andi. We were real worried about you."

Cap joined us, slipping his arm around my waist. "Bernard, thanks for everything," he said, using his free hand to clutch his shoulder meaningfully. "You're a good man. No, a great man."

Bernard stared at Cap's arm around my waist. I could tell he hadn't heard anything Cap had just said. I beamed.

"What is this?" Bernard said accusingly, staring pointedly at Cap's arm.

Cap and I looked at each other, smiling. His ears were pink.

"Oh, it's no big deal," I said lightly, my cheeks hurting from the wide grin I couldn't help but displaying. "We're just engaged now."

Bernard grunted. "Yep," he drawled slowly, pursing his lips.

"What?" Cap asked.

"Yep, yep," Bernard nodded. "I figured that would happen, at some point. It's about time."

Cap squeezed my waist conspiratorially as we laughed. "That's his way of saying congratulations, I think."

"What will your last name be?" Bernard said, a small smile appearing on his weathered face. "You already both go by Gallivanter."

We laughed. "I guess I'm already used to it, then," I replied.

Bernard smiled wryly. "That's good." His tone suddenly became businesslike, and severe.

"Listen, you two," he said grimly, "We've got bigger issues here."

"What?" Cap said, alarmed.

"Who exactly threw up in the back of the Ford?"

CHAPTER 74

BERNARD AND CAP AND I drove back to the village together, the familiar rumble of the Fords and the feeling of Cap's arm around me, as we drove, filling me with deep contentment.

I had fought hard to be right here—back exactly where I belonged.

When we pulled in amidst their small huts and I stepped out of the Ford, the village women screamed in shock and rushed to embrace me. I was like a ghost that had come back to life, in their eyes.

"The men are all still down at the river looking for you!" said one young woman to me, in French.

I laughed. "You better send someone to call them back, then."

I sensed a newfound sense of admiration from the village women, as they pulled me into their huts and undressed me. My uniform was torn, stained with sweat, and streaked with blood. They carefully pulled it off and scurried away to wash it.

I smiled at them as they clucked over the state of my clothes. "Thank you. I appreciate it."

Carefully, they carried in a large tub of water and a soft robe for me to change into, proudly presenting me with both. I had a feeling that I was getting a special honor from them.

"You're very dirty!" they exclaimed to each other, staring at my arms and face as I stripped off my undergarments. They watched me, curious, until I asked for some privacy to bathe.

"Yes, of course," they said, giggling and exiting the tent. I took my time scrubbing and rinsing with the cold water. I'd never felt

425

happier or more alive. I was just changing into the robe when I heard Chito's voice outside my tent.

"Andi?" he yelled frantically, his voice cracking. "Where is she? She's really here?"

"She's fine, I promise," I heard Cap say, calming him. "She's cleaning up."

I hurriedly pulled on the robe and ran out in my bare feet, throwing myself into Chito's arms.

"Andi!" Chito yelled, clutching me tightly and lifting me off my feet. I could feel his big chest heaving and I knew he was crying. "I thought we'd lost you!"

"You're stuck with me," I responded, hugging him.

"I'm so sorry," Chito sobbed, still clinging to me. "I thought you'd go down to the river. I thought we'd find you there. I'm sorry I didn't go to the jungle like Cap and Bernard."

I pulled away and placed my hands on either side of Chito's face. His brown eyes swam with tears as he stared down at me, his hair and beard wild. He looked as exhausted as I felt.

"Look at me, Chito," I said firmly. "You *did* save me. Your supplies, in Cap's car? They saved my life. And they gave me the strength to make it back into the jungle to find Cap."

"Really?" he said, staring at me through his tears.

"Really," I responded, looking him in the eyes. "And Chito, your advice—the words you told me that day in the hospital—you remember what you told me?"

He gazed back at me and nodded, his brown eyes swimming.

"That saved me, too," I smiled. "I fought. I fought *hard*. And I won. I saved Andiamo Gallivanter."

Chito hugged me again, his big arms wrapping around me. I felt his ragged breathing as he struggled to contain his emotion.

Finally, we pulled apart and Cap abruptly swooped in, pulling me into his arms.

"My turn," he said, kissing me fiercely.

Over Cap's shoulder, I saw Chito raise both eyebrows at Bernard. Bernard rolled his eyes and shook his head, grinning, in response.

<hr>

THE VILLAGERS TREATED us to a celebratory banquet that evening, at the request of the chief. I knew he wouldn't apologize to me, but I sensed a newfound respect from him as I told my story of survival to the enraptured men and women.

Though the men again ate at the big wooden table, Cap refused to leave my side. "We eat together," he said firmly, motioning for me to translate his words to the chief.

Eyes narrowed, the chief shook his head.

Bernard joined us, his thin shoulders close to mine. "Then we'll all take our meal over there," he growled, pointing to the Fords. "It won't be the first time I've used that hood as a dining table."

Behind me, Chito spoke up. "I'll get the silverware."

The chief glared as we took our food over to our automobiles, sitting together on the ground and sharing our bowls with each other, laughing and joking as we ate.

As we scraped the last of our stew, Bernard leaned over and spoke into my ear. "You know I don't know French, but has that guy finally stopped calling you a whore?"

"Yes," I grinned at him.

"Good. I'll take care of it if he starts up again. Let me know."

I laughed and made a mental note to keep the rifle safely out of Bernard's hands from now on.

The next morning, I dressed in my cleaned uniform and climbed back into the Fords with my crew. We thanked the villagers for their hospitality and help, and headed back onto the open road.

Like lightning, our dramatic story of survival flew through the nomad groups and little settlements ahead of us. Everywhere we stopped, they'd already heard our story. We were mobbed before we even pulled the Fords to a stop. In the eyes of the local people, we were walking miracles—a bunch of Americans who had managed to survive the harsh African wilderness by the skin of their teeth.

The press already was waiting for us as we drove into Bamako. As we approached from a distance, a huge cheer went up. Men and women lined the streets, clapping and chanting rhythmically as our Fords rumbled in.

"Listen to that. It's a celebratory cheer, I think," Chito said as he sat next to me, waving at the crowd.

"It's beautiful," I said, listening to the keening wails. It gave me goosebumps.

We slowly pulled through the massive crowd, beeping our horns to join in the joyful celebration. We rolled to a stop in the center of the plaza, guiding the cars expertly to the curb.

"I finally feel like a real celebrity," Chito remarked as we climbed out together. "I hope they serve extra dessert to famous people."

I laughed. "I don't know. But I'm taking seconds on it, too."

Cap pulled his helmet off. His hair was mashed down, but he was elated. He held out his hands to the crowd and took a deep bow. They hooted and clapped in admiration. Cameras flashed and popped like fireworks.

"Thank you, ladies and gentlemen. Your kindness and hospitality is so very appreciated, after the journey we've taken to get here," Cap shouted.

The crowd roared its approval, getting even louder. Laughing, Cap cupped his hands over his mouth and hollered, "We'll be holding a short press conference at our hotel, after dinner tonight.

Please join us there, and we'll be happy to take any questions you may have for us then. For now, please allow us to rest and refresh after the difficult few days we've endured."

He bowed again, and the crowd cheered uproariously.

"A bed will never feel so good," I groaned as we walked into the lobby. Friendly men from the crowd had rushed to help us move the boxes and bags inside, volunteering to bring them up to our rooms for us.

As we wove through the lobby, the hotel manager stopped us, pressing glasses of cold champagne into each of our hands.

"To the Gallivanters!" he shouted, toasting, as the entire staff clapped for us.

Cap caught my eye across the crowded room and raised his bubbling drink to me, a meaningful smile on his face.

He was toasting our engagement with the double meaning from the manager's words, I knew.

I grinned wide, and toasted him back.

CHAPTER 75

FOR THE FIRST TIME in a long time, our little crew had the chance to relax. We agreed to take dinner in our own rooms, to give everyone time to clean up and get a nap in.

I entered my room and found my bags already sitting inside, at the foot of my bed. Pulling out a pile of fresh clothes, I carried them to the tiny bathroom. I drew a bath, making the water as hot as possible.

Sitting on the edge of the tub, I yanked off my dirty boots. A cascade of grit sprayed all over the clean tile.

Thinking back, I remembered how it had first felt to pull on this uniform. It was stiff and foreign. I wasn't sure if it would ever be comfortable. I recalled the dark days in the hospital in Kiffa, where I thought I'd hang up these boots forever and leave the Gallivanter Expedition for good.

Now, I couldn't imagine life outside of my uniform. In fact, this uniform had saved my life out there in the jungle. I recalled how I tore the sleeves off and wrapped them around my boots to collect water from the ferns, how my belt buckle had carved my name into the trees.

I removed my ragged uniform slowly, folding each garment and setting it on the sink. This outfit had certainly served me well. Its fabric sported the scars of the months of weary travel.

My body did, too.

I stared at my knee, seeing the healed scar and remembering how I'd nearly drowned. I flexed my wrist, reliving the painful moment it slammed against the steering column and fractured.

Twisting my arms around, I examined the bloody gashes still healing on my arms. I knew chunks of my hair had been ripped out, as well, as the horse rushed me through the jungle.

I'd been bruised and battered. But I'd fought back. Nothing had managed to keep me down for long.

I savored the warm water, laying in it and feeling my muscles relax. I closed my eyes, and felt peace—real peace—for perhaps the first time in my life.

I'd spent so much of my life feeling like I never belonged anywhere. I had been afraid to be myself, worried that no one would love me, the oddball who didn't fit in. I had fretted over being too tall, too unwomanly, too impulsive, and too discontent.

It didn't matter.

I felt as if I'd been on an endless journey to find where I fit into the world. But somehow, I belonged here.

I wasn't quite sure how. But I knew it to be true. I belonged here, in Bamako.

And in Kiffa. And Marrakesh and Tarragona.

I belonged anywhere, and everywhere, I wanted to belong. Because this was my life. I belonged to the unknowable possibilities of adventure.

Who could guess where it would take me? I didn't know. But I was willing to trade safety and predictability to find out.

"Let the others stay home and read stories," I thought to myself. *"I'll be out here making them."*

After my bath, I napped. Dinner arrived in my room, and I ate and then changed into clean clothes for the press conference. Tucking my shirt into my brown pants, I rummaged through my bag in search of a pair of socks. While I searched, my fingers closed around the small metal tube of red lipstick.

Smiling, I pulled it out and tossed it in the trash.

I walked downstairs to the lobby for our press conference. Cap was waiting there and grinned at me as I descended the stairs, his eyes shining. Bernard stood fidgeting with his sleeves, clearly wanting to be anywhere else but here in the crowded room.

Chito caught my gaze and patted his stomach, holding up two fingers. "Double desserts," he mouthed as I laughed.

"Ladies and gentleman, we thank you for coming tonight, and we thank you for your patience in letting our team rest today, after our long journey," Cap said, his voice clear. "We're feeling quite refreshed, and pleased to share all about our expedition with you all. Let's get started. We'll take any questions you'd like to ask, so please take turns raising your hands and we'll make sure to get to everyone."

The cameras whirred and their flashes blinded us. The reporters buzzed, scribbling answers down on notepads as they peppered us with questions. I noticed that a half dozen different languages were being whispered in the room.

Apparently, even foreign reporters and agents had come here to see us.

Chito, Cap, Bernard, and I each took questions, sharing our stories as the crowd listened in wonder. I saw more than one reporter shudder as I recounted the moment I laid in the dirt, paralyzed, and watched the snake head toward me.

As we continued to talk, it dawned on me that the Gallivanters were unquestionably famous now. We already had more money than we needed, and more funds were sure to come in now. Every household in the world probably knew us by name.

There would be nothing standing in the way of us blazing through a hundred more countries. Why, we could travel around the globe for a decade and still have money to spare.

After nearly two hours of answering questions, a bald man near the back of the group stood up and raised his hand.

"Captain Gallivanter, sir," he said, holding his notebook. "You've been through four countries now and sure had a real doozy of a time in each of them. Where are you off to next?"

Cap looked at me and grinned. "Andiamo?"

I smiled back. "Let's go everywhere."

AUTHOR'S NOTE

ANDIAMO FOUGHT TO SURVIVE, and so did this book.

Though this story poured out of my head as fast as I could type it, I finished it and walked away from it for four years. I walked away from my dream to publish an adventure story...for a while. But it refused to die.

This story is fiction, brought to life with my imagination, but it was inspired by real-life adventurers. Aloha Wanderwell Baker was the first woman to drive herself around the world, starting and ending her journey in Nice, France, from 1922-1927. She was my muse for this fictional series, my inspiration for Andiamo Gallivanter.

Aloha, who spoke 11 languages, became the face of a crew at age 16 and shared her travel adventures with people all over the world. Walter Wanderwell, her partner and eventual husband, was from Poland and had indeed been jailed on suspicion of being a spy during World War I. The "Million Dollar Wager," two teams racing against each other, was a real competition. Though this is not her story, I peppered a few details into my manuscript in tribute to this fearless woman. This was a story for the ages, and deserved to be told.

Despite the fact that all these characters were created by me, I attempted to stay as historically accurate to the period as possible, albeit I wrote with a progressive tone in the way that women and varying races and ethnicities were actually treated and talked about at the time. Reality was not so kind.

I owe tremendous thanks to many people who helped me bring this book to fruition.

To Tyler, my husband—the love of my life and the partner at my side as we face every adventure together—you deserve the biggest thanks. You never let me walk away from this dream and you never let me give up on myself. We landed on the moon.

To my family and in-laws, thanks for inspiring me to live my own adventures. Mom, your feedback and enthusiasm for this was priceless. When I was a kid, you punished me by making me write essays about my bad behavior—I suppose you get some credit for me becoming a writer. Dad, your example of working hard but never losing your sense of humor has made me who I am today.

Beckham, Bentley, Arya, Kensley, Ingrid, Henry—I hope you know that Auntie Cassie is ready to travel anywhere in the world with you, as you grow up to chase your own adventures.

To the dear friends who have become like family to me—Cory, Joanna, Ash, Carsten, Chip, Chelsea, Jena, Jami, Vincent, Kerry, and Jeremy—thank you for your endless encouragement and support as I pushed through these last few years and crossed the finish line with this manuscript. Your friendship shaped the way I wrote about the Gallivanter crew.

Pete, you gave me the experience of a lifetime as I lived out the exact scene I'd written in my book, with Bernard showing Andi how to operate and drive a Model T Ford. Thanks for the hours you spent teaching me about the car, and for convincing the staff at the Western Antique Aeroplane and Automobile Museum in Hood River, Oregon, to roll one out of the museum display so you could drive me around in it. I still haven't stopped smiling.

Chip, Jared, and Kevin, thanks for sharing your medical expertise for the injuries my characters endured. You pointed out that I accidentally killed Cap and Bernard, forcing several rewrites. Chip, you even tested my jungle torch scene for accuracy, much to my delight.

Mark, thanks for sharing your knowledge about rescue diving to help me with Andi's drowning scene. Brian and Ariana, thanks for the insight about living in harsh desert conditions and what life in Africa is like. Jacob, thank you for checking my historical accuracy. Chloe, Harry, and Ludka, thanks for checking my foreign language accuracy.

Thanks to my early proofreaders, especially Eric, Sarah, and my high school girls' group, who encouraged me to keep going with this story. Marenda, Bella, Olivia, Jaden, Julia, and Emma—your squeals of joy over Cap and Andi's romance is a treasured memory.

To my dog, Quigley, thank you for being a badly-behaved puppy. Because you couldn't stop waking me up early, I started writing this series to have something to do in those empty dawn hours. You're a good dog...now.

Soli Deo gloria.

OTHER BOOKS IN *THE GALLIVANTER SAGA*

The thrilling adventures of a ragtag team of world travelers, navigating danger and discovery in the Roaring Twenties.

Saving Andiamo
Book One, *The Gallivanter Saga*

A New Wild
Book Two, *The Gallivanter Saga*

Savage World
Book Three, *The Gallivanter Saga*

Uncharted Within
Book Four, *The Gallivanter Saga*

Audacia Always
Book Five, *The Gallivanter Saga*

A Dream Uninvited
Book Six, *The Gallivanter Saga*

About the Author

Cassie A. H. Moore is an author, speaker, educator, and consultant with over 15 years of experience working with young people.

She earned her master's degree in organizational leadership from the Townsend Institute at Concordia University in Irvine, California, has published non-fiction books, curriculum, and articles, and has taught and spoken to thousands of students and leaders all over North America.

As a lifelong student of culture, Moore weaves her interests in humanity, history, travel, and new experiences into her writing and speaking.

A travel enthusiast, Moore has enjoyed her own adventures traveling to 50 states, 21 countries, 10 islands, 6 Canadian provinces, and one erupting volcano. She and her husband live in Hood River, Oregon, with their two dogs, where they hike or kayak every chance they can get.

Learn more at cassieahmoore.com.